IN DOCTOR'S HANDS

Vivienne Laker had put herself in the hands of two very different doctors.

One was the legendary Dr. Benjamin Talmidge, whose clients were the world's most wealthy, powerful, and beautiful people, and whose private hospital in Spain was the Holy Grail for those seeking the ultimate in healing.

The other was Dr. Eric Rose, a young physician on Dr. Talmidge's staff who claimed to be investigating horrifying hints of what was really going on behind locked doors . . . even as he was tempting Vivienne to be unfaithful to the man she was to marry.

Could Vivienne trust one doctor with her life? Could Vivienne trust the other with her love? And could she survive the terror of the truth in a hospital from which there was no escape . . . !

VITAL
PARTS

VITAL PARTS

Nancy Fisher

A SIGNET BOOK

SIGNET
Published by the Penguin Group
Penguin Books USA Inc., 375 Hudson Street,
New York, New York 10014, U.S.A.
Penguin Books Ltd, 27 Wrights Lane,
London W8 5TZ, England
Penguin Books Australia Ltd, Ringwood,
Victoria, Australia
Penguin Books Canada Ltd, 10 Alcorn Avenue,
Toronto, Ontario, Canada M4V 3B2
Penguin Books (N.Z.) Ltd, 182-190 Wairau Road,
Auckland 10, New Zealand

Penguin Books Ltd, Registered Offices:
Harmondsworth, Middlesex, England

First published by Signet, an imprint of New American Library,
a division of Penguin Books USA Inc.

First Printing, February, 1993
10 9 8 7 6 5 4 3 2 1

PUBLISHER'S NOTE
This is a work of fiction. Names, characters, places, and incidents either are
the product of the author's imagination or are used fictitiously, and any resem-
blance to actual persons, living or dead, events, or locales is entirely coinci-
dental.

For my mother, Tema, whose constant support, counsel, and love has made this book, and so much else, possible.

And for my daughter, Sarah, who fills my life with joy.

ACKNOWLEDGMENTS

I would like to express my gratitude to my brother, Dr. Robert Fisher of Minneapolis, and to Dr. Barry Zide of New York for sharing their knowledge and enthusiasm. Any factual errors in this text are mine, not theirs.

I'm also grateful for the invaluable advice and support of my agent, Robert Diforio, and for his confidence in me.

My thanks go also to my editor, Hilary Ross, and her team at Penguin/NAL for their guidance and suggestions.

And Sarah, thanks for letting me use your computer!

PROLOGUE

She emerges slowly, as from a dream, and looks around her wonderingly. Her tunic is simple, her dark hair falls in a straight clean line to her shoulders. The room is warm and very bright, and she blinks as she walks to the chair.

A man stands near the chair. Two other men stand against the wall. They all study her, but only one speaks.

"Anna," says the man at the chair. His round freckled face looks kind.

"I am Anna," she says tentatively.

"Welcome, Anna," the man tells her. "Sit here."

"Where am I?" she asks.

"You are home, Anna," he says.

She sits in the chair and looks around. It all seems familiar somehow.

"I am home," she says softly.

The man asks her questions: "Are you hungry? Are you thirsty?" He shows her objects on a table: "What is this? And this? Very good!"

Then he smiles. "Come and meet the others," he says. He takes her hand and attempts to lead her from the room.

She follows him to the silver door, then stops. She seems confused. Again the man speaks gently, kindly, but still she resists.

"What is wrong?" he asks her. "Don't be afraid."

The woman shakes her head and attempts to pull away, but the man is holding her strongly.

"I won't!" she says, not sure why she feels this need to refuse. With a sudden movement she yanks her hand free and whirls around in retreat. The men against the wall move forward but the freckle-faced man waves them back.

Slowly he approaches her again, a gentle smile on his lips. "Anna," he says, "don't disappoint me. You belong here. We need you."

He stretches his arms out toward her and advances slowly. He is so kind. She walks a few steps toward him, then stops as a wash of fear floods through her. Why am I afraid? she wonders.

He puts his arms on her shoulders, grasping them gently but firmly, and draws her toward him. He moves one arm around her waist and guides her toward the door. She pretends to acquiesce, then suddenly rakes his face with her nails. Why did I do that? she wonders, but it pleases her to see the blood run.

With an oath he draws back, waving at the other men, who rush in to grapple with her. They are not gentle. Shouting and struggling, she is at last immobilized, pinned between the two large men. She is bruised. She feels pain. Her head swings from side to side as she screams.

The first man sighs as he fills a syringe. Her screams rise as he approaches her, and the other men hold her tighter. She watches in horror as the needle punctures her skin. She tries to bite the man's hand, but he stays carefully out of range.

All at once her head nods and her limbs relax. She slumps down onto the floor, her tunic bunched and wrinkled, her hair in wild tendrils around her face.

Still holding the syringe, the freckle-faced man shoves the door open. "Bring her," he tells the others.

They lift the lifeless form from the floor and follow him out of the room.

I

1

A spoonful of coffee . . . hot water . . . so far, so good. Now some milk, and half a spoonful of sugar . . .

It had been a long night and he was tired, but that wasn't unusual. He stretched his long limbs, ran his fingers through his dark curling hair, then massaged his temples. Wake up! he told himself.

The coffee would help. He reached for a plastic spoon and was stirring with vigor when the intercom spoke his name. "Dr. Rose . . . Dr. Eric Rose, emergency room! Stat!"

"Damn!"

He gulped at the coffee, then set it back down on the makeshift counter in the residents' lounge. Just once, he thought, I'd like to finish a cup of coffee while it's still hot.

Female heads turned and he hurried across the corridor into the ER. Eric Rose was considered a catch: tall, slim, and good-looking, a skilled surgeon, and best of all, single. As the senior surgical resident in one of the country's most prestigious hospitals, he sensed he was well-placed for a bit of dalliance. But he was smart enough to realize the kind of trouble on-the-job romance could quickly produce. This catch was determined to remain uncaught.

He entered the emergency room at a dash, his experienced eye taking in the usual carnage, and headed for the small busy group swarming around an unseen figure on a transport stretcher.

"What have we got?" he called across the room. A tall red-haired woman in a white smock smeared with blood turned toward him in relief. People usually felt relieved when Eric appeared. Though just past his twenty-eighth birthday, he had an innate ability both as a diagnostician and as a surgeon, without the over-blown ego which all too often accompanies such gifts.

"Car crash," the woman told him. "Some guy hit him and he jumped the divider. They had to cut him out." She turned her attention again to the figure being transferred onto the ER gurney.

"You heading up the FDR Drive, you better bring something to read," offered the ambulance driver. He and his partner rolled the bloody transport stretcher out the back door toward their vehicle as Eric began to examine the stricken man.

"Name's Abbott," the redhead told him, checking the information on a clipboard someone had hung off the end of the gurney. "James Thomas Abbott. Fifty-two years old. His wife's on her way over."

"Didn't they give him anything for pain?" Eric asked, studying the man's tortured features, his blue eyes soft with concern.

But James Abbott's face was contorted not with pain, but in pure fury. He considered himself an exemplary driver. He hadn't had a ticket for years. Well, parking tickets, sure, but they didn't count. And now, because of some speed-hungry young asshole who thought fifty was too slow for the fast lane of a forty-mile-per-hour highway, he was bleeding all over the emergency room of New York General Hospital. Thank God he was covered.

A young doctor, too young, leaned over him, touched him, spoke to people he couldn't focus on.

"Hey, listen," he tried to tell the doctor, "I don't want anyone operating on me."

"You're badly hurt, Mr. Abbott," Eric said. "But you're gonna be OK. We've called your wife. Now we're going to make you sleep."

"Wait . . . remind my wife . . ." The older man

was forcing the words out in desperation. "It's OK, only tell her . . . remind her I'm covered!"

Eric had to smile. A time like this and the poor bastard was worried about paying.

"No problem," he said. "We take checks, credit cards, your kids . . ."

"No . . . no," Abbott protested. "You don't understand. I'm covered!"

Half an hour later, having diagnosed and then sedated his patient, ordered the necessary tests, and reserved the OR for emergency surgery to remove what he was certain was a ruptured kidney, Eric, his eyes smudged with weariness, made his way to the visitors' lounge. A woman sat quietly twisting a handkerchief between her fingers. She looked up anxiously as he entered.

"Are you Dr. Rose?" she asked. He nodded, seating himself across from the chair on which she tentatively perched.

"I'm Mrs. Abbott," she said softly. "They called me from emergency.'

They should hire special people to talk to relatives, Eric thought to himself. I'm no good at it. He forced himself to look at the tall well-dressed woman in front of him.

"I'm the senior surgical resident. Your husband . . . well, he has some internal injuries."

"Will he . . . is he . . . ?" Michelle Abbott was controlling herself well, but the strain and fear showed clearly in her pretty face, and made her soft Belgian accent more pronounced.

"The X rays and test results should be up in a little while, and then we'll have a better idea of what we're dealing with."

Mrs. Abbott had started to cry softly.

Eric fumbled with the charts on the table. God, how he hated this part of the job.

"Mrs. Abbott," he said, "I'm pretty sure there's been serious injury to the left kidney. I understand your husband lost his right kidney to a cancerous tumor . . . uh, five years ago?''

Michelle Abbott nodded.

''Well, I'm going to need you to sign this consent paper so I can remove the left one too.'' Mrs. Abbott's sobs grew audible, and Eric found his own eyes brimming too. Other doctors had told him he identified too much with his patients—''Learn some detachment!'' they urged. But although it made his job more stressful, he just didn't know any other way.

''Look, Mrs. Abbott,'' he said, ''if a man has two kidneys and he loses one, he can live on the other. But both . . . well, unless he wants to spend the rest of his life on and off a dialysis machine, he's going to need a transplant, and fast. And even then, transplants fail. They often fail.''

There. He'd said it.

He glanced back at the woman; had she fainted? How he hated this part of doctoring. To his amazement, she was smiling. Dear God, smiling! Was the woman mad? Had she misheard him?

''A kidney transplant? And then he'll be better? That's easy! Let me make a call.''

Easy. Right.

''Uh, Mrs. Abbott, transplants, this kind of transplant, it has to come from someone whose tissue is genetically compatible with your husband's. Someone like a brother, a sister. Even a cousin might be too far away physiologically.''

''I know all that,'' said Mrs. Abbott, now brisk and efficient. ''Jim has a brother and I know he'll want to give Jim a kidney. I'll call him now.''

Eric stared at her. Incredible. In his experience, few people would donate an organ even after they were *dead*.

''That's wonderful!'' said Eric, putting as much enthusiasm into his voice as he could. ''But please, be prepared for disappointment. Many people offer organs when everyone's healthy, but when they actually have to go through with it . . . And of course the chemistry, even with a brother, might be off. He might be sick, or . . ."

"No, Dr. Rose, he won't be sick. And he won't refuse. That's what we have the coverage for."

"I'm not talking about money, Mrs. Abbott."

"Neither am I. Please show me a phone I can use."

Dr. John Harris strolled down Park Avenue toward his private office—hours Wednesday and Friday by appointment. Here and there along the Park Avenue divider, skinny sticks of grass were sticking their heads up out of the mush of the spring thaw, looking around at the grime, and wondering if it was worth the effort.

At East Seventy-second Street Harris paused, admiring the pattern the clouds made against the sky; a surgeon didn't get much chance to enjoy the changing of the seasons. Sometimes, coming out of the hospital into the sun or the rain, he found himself staring around him like a tourist at a world he'd completely forgotten existed.

He pushed through the heavy oak door to his office. He knew everything within would be quiet, well-organized. It was. Mrs. Riley was on the case.

Mrs. Riley ran a tight waiting room. You signed in, took a magazine, sat down, and waited. No chitchat with the other nurses. No sneaking in ahead of anyone else. Mrs. Riley gave the lie to the popular misconception that only men enjoy war. Mrs. Riley had been an army nurse for twenty-two years. Give her a good war anytime.

Mrs. Riley had been Dr. Harris's private nurse/receptionist for twelve years now, and she worshiped him. He was smart, he was disorganized, and he needed her.

"Good morning, Doctor. Here is the list of your appointments today. Mr. Ginsberg is here, Mrs. Bateman is going to be late. And a Dr. Benjamin Talmidge called. He said he had good news."

"Great! Get him for me first, would you, Mrs. Riley?"

Harris went straight to his inner office and pulled a pencil and pad from his desk drawer. Good news! That had to mean a kidney. Just in time too; Abbott was doing very poorly on that dialysis machine. Mrs. Riley followed him inside.

"From Barcelona," she said.

"Excuse me?"

"Dr. Talmidge called from Barcelona."

Well, thought Harris, there's a Paris, Texas, and a Rome, New York. "Let's call him back anyway," he said with a twitch of a smile.

A beep, then Mrs. Riley's voice came through the phone intercom. "Dr. Harris, Dr. Talmidge is on the line."

"Hello, Dr. Talmidge."

"Dr. Harris. Good news. The brother's offered to donate a kidney."

"Health?"

"Excellent."

"Age?"

"Eleven years younger than your patient."

"Wonderful! How soon can he be here?"

"Uh, that's the snag." Dr. Talmidge paused. "The brother will only donate if the operation takes place here."

"Here? Where is 'here,' Doctor?"

"My hospital, just outside Barcelona."

"Barcelona as in Spain?"

"*Sí, señor,*" said Dr. Talmidge.

Oh, great, thought Harris. A comedian.

"You can't be serious," he said. "Surely you've explained the risks involved in moving a man as sick as Abbott. Three thousand miles across an ocean will probably kill him. Doesn't the brother understand?"

"Oh, I don't think the risks are that great, not with medical attendants. Besides, he insists, and frankly, I wouldn't risk losing the kidney by trying to convince him otherwise."

"Of course that's a factor, but surely—"

"I assure you, Dr. Harris, my hospital is small but extremely well-equipped. We have performed a large number of transplants in our time."

Have you indeed? thought Harris. I'll look into that.

"Of course we'll coordinate the aftercare with you," Talmidge offered. Did Harris only imagine the patronizing tone?

"Yes, we'll need to monitor him for rejection," Harris agreed. "You'll be using cyclosporine?"

"Oh, I don't believe an antirejection drug is called for in this case," said Talmidge.

"Not called for?"

"Well, the man's recently recovered from cancer."

"Not so recently. Five years ago. Antirejection drugs won't be a problem for him now."

"Possibly. In any event, we've developed our own technique for this sort of thing. There's no need for immune suppression. We do things differently here."

"Sounds like you do things dangerously there."

"Doctor." Talmidge's voice was quite hard. "Let me assure you of one thing. This operation happens at my hospital, my way, or not at all. Do you understand?"

Dr. Harris was silent. He could understand Abbott's brother insisting that a particular doctor do the surgery; presumably Abbott's brother knew Dr. Talmidge. But that didn't seem to be the issue, somehow. And he resented the implication that New York General wasn't up to an operation of this sort. By God, New York General had a good transplant record too. He was also deeply troubled by Talmidge's decision not to use an immuno-suppressant. Surely the man knew it was perfectly safe, so many years after the cancerous kidney had been removed. Without such drugs, the chances of rejection were practically guaranteed, whatever Talmidge's new technique might be.

"Don't threaten me, Doctor," Harris said at last. "I will advise my patient of our discussion, and tell him that he is in no condition to undertake such a journey. I will ask him to call his brother, to talk to him. There is no reason why the kidney cannot be implanted here. *With* immune suppression."

Dr. Talmidge laughed. "You talk to him, yes. It's his decision, after all. I think you'll find he agrees with his brother."

"Dr. Talmidge, I don't know what your interest is in this matter . . . money, glory, or just pure cussedness, but a wrong decision here could cost a man his life."

"Yes, that's it exactly, Dr. Harris. So glad you understand. Spread the happy news!"

A click. Talmidge had disconnected.

Slowly Dr. Harris lowered the phone. He was angry. But he was also puzzled. Something had been tickling in the back of his mind for some days, and now it came forward.

He hit the intercom. "Mrs. Riley, would you bring me Mr. Abbott's records please?"

It's not possible, he thought as he waited. I must be wrong.

He took the buff-colored folder from Mrs. Riley almost reluctantly, and held it for a moment before opening it and sliding out the medical-history sheet.

Name. Address. Phone Number. Wife's Name. Allergies. Previous Operations. Parents: living. Children: two. Sisters: none. Brothers: none.

2

The waiter removed the two plates wordlessly. In a lesser establishment he might have commented on the amount of food still left on one of them: "Mademoiselle did not care for the scalloped potatoes? But they are a specialty of the chef!" Le Chanticleer, however, catered primarily to an older, monied crowd, which liked their women slim. Besides, he thought he remembered that face from a recent magazine ad. Models never ate potatoes. Or much else, in his experience.

Vivienne tried not to think of the scalloped potatoes. By now she was pretty good at steeling herself against food. But those potatoes had looked really delicious. Never mind, she thought. When I'm forty and worth twenty billion trillion dollars, I'll eat all the potatoes I want and it won't matter. But she knew it would always matter, somehow.

Vivienne Laker was twenty-four years old and the envy of every woman in every room she entered. She was beautiful, of course, but it was the kind of beauty which owed as much to the character of its owner as it did to the wide-set green eyes, straight tip-tilted nose, and honey blond hair. It was the kind of beauty that, well-managed, could produce a mid-six-figure income.

"Charles, it's nearly eleven. We really should go." Vivienne smiled up at him a little tentatively. He hated when her work interfered with his social life, but she'd already warned him about her eight-A.M. photo session the next day. Vivienne took pride in arriving at the studio rested and on time. She felt it was the least she could do, for all that money.

Charles Spencer-Moore, fair-haired descendant of minor robber barons and chairman of the Spencer-Moore Investment Corporation, gazed at her with affection marred by the very slightest edge of irritation. He got to New York only twice a week; why couldn't she arrange her schedule so she could stay out and party?

"Already? I thought we might have a drink at the Rainbow Room, dance a little, live dangerously." He smiled and she smiled back.

"No can do," she said. "You know I'm a working girl." With a dainty manicured fingertip she traced the line of his nose, ending at his upper lip, then traveled across to the corner of his mouth on the side that sort of tilted up so he looked like he was always smiling. He play-bit at it, and she whipped it away and they both laughed.

The waiter approached with dessert menus. Don't know why I bother, thought the waiter. But of course he did know: as much as thirty percent on a good night.

Vivienne waved the little cards away while the waiter was still several steps from the table. "Don't tempt me any more!" she laughed. "You've already cost me about a thousand extra sit-ups tomorrow!"

"Some raspberries, perhaps?" asked the waiter smoothly. "Very light!"

"That's what I love about New York," said Vivienne. "Raspberries all year round!"

"But not always very good ones," said Charles, still regretting the Rainbow Room.

"They probably make them in a lab, like lettuce," said Vivienne. "What do they call it? Hydro-something?"

"Ponic," said Charles.

"Lettuce oui, raspberries no," said the waiter.

"These come from Morocco, land of eternal sunshine."

"I did a photo assignment in Morocco once," said Vivienne. "Rained for days. The photographer won some artsy award and we all had colds for weeks."

"No raspberries, thank you," said Charles.

"Would you care for some coffee?"

"A double espresso," said Charles.

"Charles, you shouldn't," said Viv.

"I know," said Charles. "But I'm going to anyway." He turned back to the waiter. "And a cappuccino for the lady. And the bill."

Charles and Vivienne had been seeing each other for over a year now, but only recently had the relationship turned serious. She'd met him at a pivotal time in her life, when she'd just begun making really big money and was still working at feeling comfortable about it.

She'd grown up in a small town just outside Charlotte, North Carolina, in a caring, supportive family of modest means. Becoming a cheerleader and going steady with the football captain was the height of glamorous living. (She'd done both). Charles was part of an excitingly different world, and although Vivienne prided herself on her levelheadedness, she would have been the first to admit that he had dazzled her.

It had always been assumed that after high school she'd attend the local college, then marry some nice young man and settle down. But halfway through her senior year, encouraged by several successful local modeling assignments, she'd had a long talk with her father. She wanted to try for the big time. Would he stake her to six months in New York? If she didn't make it by then, she'd come home and matriculate.

He wasn't happy. "You've got a good mind, honey," he'd told her. "I hate to see you waste it."

"Modeling careers are short," she'd assured him. "I'll go to college later on, I promise!"

It took nearly half a year and excellent college-board

scores to convince him, but two days after graduation,
Vivienne was on a plane to New York.

Three months later, she booked her first job, and
she never looked back. Her face and her figure made
it all so easy. She liked to think her winning person-
ality and inherent intelligence had something to do
with it too, but she knew better. She'd since met too
many stupid, nasty, wildly successful women. Still,
though she was grateful for her looks, she was determined not to live by that alone.

She looked at Charles, solemnly drinking his forbidden brew, and her heart swelled with love . . . or
something like it. Of course she was right to marry
him, despite the difference in their ages. Of course
she'd made the right decision.

She stirred her cappuccino, mixing the cinnamon
into the hot coffee the way Charles was always telling
her not to, and thought about the fund-raiser where
they'd first met. Marcella, owner of the model agency
through which Vivienne worked, liked her "girls" to
be seen around town. She'd arranged for invitations
for Vivienne and another model Vivienne barely knew,
borrowed what Vivienne thought were horrendously
expensive designer gowns, and sent them off to the
black-tie affair at the Pierre much as Cinderella's god-
mother had done. And just like Cinderella, Vivienne
had met her prince.

He'd been seated on the dais, a golden boy among
the graybeards. After dinner, when people began to
move around the silver-and-white ballroom, he'd come
up and introduced himself, and she'd realized he was
older than she'd thought; nearly forty.

Everything about him seemed to glitter: his pale
golden hair, his expensive yet understated jewelry, his
eyes. She'd felt so out-of-place there, but he was obviously relaxed and comfortable. And in his company,
suddenly she was too.

After that night he'd pursued her relentlessly, and
yes, he'd dazzled her. But it wasn't just the gifts and
the expensive dinners; she could buy such things for

herself. Rather, it was the world to which he introduced her, a world of Palm Beach estates and ocean-going yachts and people you read about in the newspapers. It was exciting. And Charles's attentions were so flattering.

"You're very quiet suddenly," said Charles, breaking in on her thoughts. She started slightly and grinned at him.

"I'm thinking about you."

"Good," he said with a smile, and turned away to deal with the bill.

The first time they'd made love, Vivienne thought she would faint. Aside from the usual high school gropings, her only sexual experiences had been with her football-captain "steady": illicit, frightening moments in his car, and once in the team locker room. Charles was a revelation. Now, nearly a year and a half later, the excitement of their lovemaking was undimmed.

Undimmed despite the doubts that now and then arose. Was she really comfortable with Charles's rather conventional tastes and ideas? Did she really like being the "junior member," always being advised and taught—and judged? Did he love the person she was, or only the person he was turning her into?

Overthink, she told herself, stealing a look at his perfect profile as he reached for the small white espresso cup. Everyone has doubts before marriage; it's only natural. She'd been right to ignore hers and say yes when he'd proposed to her that rainy night in Southampton. Living with Charles would be bliss, wouldn't it? And he'd said he didn't mind her continuing to model; in fact he was proud of her career. He was proud of her. He loved her. Didn't he?

Charles put down his cup and reached into his pocket.

"Viv, I'd like you to see my doctor." He handed her a small white card. Engraved, of course. The lettering was small and elegant. Dr. Brian Arnold. An address in the East Sixties. A telephone number.

"Your doctor? What on earth for?"

"For a blood test. You know, marriage license, blood test. 'I do, I do . . .' "

Charles chuckled. I hate that chuckle, Vivienne thought. It's so self-satisfied.

"Okay," she said, putting the card in her purse.

"Call him tomorrow and make an appointment," he said.

"Charles, the wedding's not for five months."

"Call him tomorrow."

She looked up, caught by the tone of his voice. Harsh. Determined. A little scary. His eyes, the set of his face, matched this new voice. Who is this man? she thought.

Suddenly his face softened and he smiled. "Sorry, darling, didn't mean to get heavy about it. It's just . . . well, do it for me, will you?"

Vivienne smiled too. Who is this man indeed! "If it means that much to you, I'll call as soon as I get to the studio," she said.

"Good girl. And now I've got a little surprise for you."

From his jacket pocket he took a small slim package wrapped in dark gold paper and tied with a thin red velvet ribbon. "I was going to save it for after you'd seen the good doctor, but now that you've promised . . ."

For a moment Vivienne was aware of a vague disquiet, but distracted by the gift, she brushed it aside and pulled off the wrapping.

Charles laughed at her enthusiasm. "I love unwrapping presents," she said, "I love the sound the paper makes."

Then her eyes grew big as she drew from the box a long, thin, beautifully made chain of gold on which hung a diamond of two blue-bright carats. "My God," she said.

"Put it on," said Charles.

Slowly she unclasped the chain and put it around her neck. The diamond hung in the deep décolletage of her black designer evening dress. Charles, eyes hot, leaned over and pressed his lips to the diamond, and then to the flesh on each side of it.

Flushing with embarrassment, Vivienne tried to draw back, but Charles's arms went around her, holding her still.

"Charles, please," she said, torn between her embarrassment and rising desire.

What must people think of me? she thought. A model and an older man and a diamond and a kiss like this?

At last Charles lifted his head. "You're mine," he said. "You belong to me." He looked around the room challengingly, and several people turned away.

"I've always known I'd marry a woman like you. You're perfect. And you'll be perfect for me." He looked into her eyes with ruthless determination. "You're mine," he repeated. "And everyone else can go to hell."

Like all doctors, Harris grieved to lose a patient. It happened, sure. Even in his custom-made suit and imported shoes, a doctor is not God. But some losses cut more deeply than others, losses which, on reflection, one feels might have been prevented. If only . . . if only . . .

This case, Harris felt, was a case in point. There was stupidity here . . . greed . . . and something else, something Harris did not understand. And did not like one little bit.

He studied the two people in front of him, the woman in the cheap straight-backed hospital chair, the sick man in the bed. Harris had learned a lot about James Abbott in the last week, and what he'd learned confused him. Abbott just didn't seem the type to make a stupid decision. CEO of a well-known electronics corporation which under his leadership had grown into a profitable multinational giant, Abbott had a reputation for both brilliance and caution. So why would a savvy, wealthy, non-risk-taker decide to tear himself off the machine that was keeping him alive and drag himself across the world to an unknown hospital in Spain?

"I wish you'd change your mind, Jim," Harris told him, not for the first time.

Abbott gave him a weak smile. "Trust me," he said. "It'll be okay." He turned his head away and closed his eyes, effectively ending the conversation.

Harris sighed and turned to Michelle Abbott. "May I speak with you outside?"

She nodded and followed him out of the flower-filled private room and down the corridor to the patients' lounge. It was empty; Michelle seated herself in a chair facing the picture window and Harris closed the door behind them, determined to have it out at last.

He sat down across from her and studied the tall, intelligent-looking Belgian woman. Surely she knew the risks she and her husband were taking. It made no sense. Nothing made any sense.

"Mrs. Abbott," he said gently, "your husband is dying."

"I know that," she said with a touch of asperity. "That's why we're doing this."

"Don't you understand? He's dying right now! His nitrogen urea is going up all the time. If you move him . . ."

Mrs. Abbott was silent.

"We'll get a kidney here," Harris told her. "Just hang on a little longer and I'm sure we'll get a match."

"From whom?" Mrs. Abbott challenged. "How soon? And what about hepatitis? AIDS? Rejection?"

"Even a brother might give you rejection problems."

"Not this brother."

Harris rubbed his temples. He was tired. Saving a man's life was hard enough; doing it against the man's will was exhausting.

"I won't even mention the cost of transporting your husband to this private hospital in Spain," he said at last. "I assume you know the cost and can live with it. Anyway, that's not my concern. What I find totally bewildering is how you and your husband, people smart enough to understand the risks involved, can take the enormous chance of pulling a dying man off dialysis and moving him anywhere, let alone out of the country.''

"It's the only place the surgery can be done," she replied. Her eyes refused to meet his. "Jim's brother says so, his doctor says so . . .''

"His doctor," said Harris evenly, "has an ego problem. And your husband has no brother."

He'd taken Abbott's patient file from the office just for this meeting. Now he pushed the buff folder toward Mrs. Abbott. "Dr. Fox, your internist, forwarded Jim's medical records to me. Records that go back to 1975, when he first became Fox's patient. He never mentioned a brother."

Mrs. Abbott colored slightly, but didn't take the folder. "They've . . . they've been estranged, I guess you could say, for a long time. They've only recently renewed . . . contact."

"So estranged he doesn't even list him on a medical form?"

"Maybe the nurse forgot to write it in. Oh, what does it matter?" The words were delivered softly, yet with force. "That's the only place and he's the only doctor, so there's no choice."

Harris watched her carefully. "Why?" he asked. "Why is there no choice?"

But Mrs. Abbott was silent, studying the veneer of the coffee table.

Dr. Harris sighed. He'd never spoken against another doctor, not even to other doctors, and Lord knew he'd seen enough, one time or another. He was about to ruin his perfect record, and he hated doing it.

"Talmidge's hospital, Mrs. Abbott. How much do you really know about it?" He paused. "I've been doing a little research. It's a small, wealthy hospital, yes. A well-equipped one, presumably. Supposedly they have done this sort of thing before, though they're known primarily for their cosmetic face lifts, things like that."

For a moment he hesitated, gazing at her clear, smooth face; it occurred to him fleetingly that she looked a good deal younger than Abbott. Yet her manner was mature, controlled. Perhaps she had had first-hand experience of Talmidge's skill. Well, that sort of thing was different.

"They are by no means a major hospital with major resources," he continued. "And transplants require major resources, believe me. The staff is unknown. It's in a foreign country."

Michelle Abbott's eyes laughed sardonically at him, and he suddenly felt slightly ridiculous. She was a European and no doubt thought him insular. But he truly believed that American medicine was second to none. And there was the issue of Talmidge himself . . .

"It's been over five years since your husband lost a kidney to cancer," said Harris. "Yet Dr. Talmidge tells me he doesn't intend to use antirejection drugs. In fact, he says that's part of his reason for insisting that the procedure take place at his hospital."

Harris put down the papers he'd forgotten he was holding, and looked at her steadily. "Do you know the seriousness of that decision?" he asked.

"You can't use those drugs after cancer."

Who told her to say that? Harris wondered. "No, you can't," he agreed aloud. "Not for a year or so. But it's been five years. There's no problem with using them now."

"But there's no need for them," Mrs. Abbott said.

"There's always a need for them, except in those rare cases in which the donor is—"

"Jim doesn't need them," Mrs. Abbott repeated, interrupting him. "Dr. Talmidge has discovered a new way of doing things."

"Too bad he hasn't shared it with the rest of the world," Harris said sarcastically, then immediately regretted it. "Look, I know you want the best for Jim," he told her. "So do I. And frankly, there have been some serious questions about Dr. Talmidge in the past. There are good reasons he's never served on the staff of any hospital but his own. Whatever he's prom-

ised to do, whatever miracles he claims to perform
. . . please, Mrs. Abbott, I urge you to reconsider.''

Mrs. Abbott gathered up her handbag and gloves.
She regarded the doctor with a peculiar expression of
sympathy.

''I'm sorry, Doctor. I've arranged to fly him to Spain
tonight. It really is the only way. And Dr. Talmidge is
the only one who can do . . . what has to be done. In
his way, he's a genius. But you Americans, you could
never accept what he does. You are innocent, morally
naive. It doesn't surprise me that he had to leave
America to do his work. To help people like my husband and myself. Yes, me also, Doctor.''

Michelle Abbott stood up. The sunlight, filtering
through the curtain-covered windows behind the desk,
played softly across her lovely face. ''I am fifty-seven
years old,'' she said. ''Five years older than my husband.''

Startled, Dr. Harris started to rise too. But she was
gone.

Eric maneuvered himself and his tray through the
lunchtime crush in the hospital cafeteria, one eye on
the big clock that always reminded him of his high
school gym back in Brooklyn, site of his many basketball victories. One such victory had been bought at
the cost of a broken nose. His mother had cried, but
Eric had always thought his conventionally handsome
features boring; he'd been secretly pleased at the Belmondo look, a sort of vulnerable masculinity, which
had resulted.

Not the tallest on the team at just under six feet, Eric
had had instead the advantage of speed. Now, as he dodged
around a slow-moving nurse, neatly sidestepped a mis-
placed chair, and swiveled to avoid a jostling elbow, he
could hear the crowd cheering: Go, Rose!

From a Brooklyn gym to a Manhattan hospital is not
far geographically, but for Eric it had been a long,
hard journey.

Cheated of his own dream of medical school by unyielding financial pressures, his father had felt fortunate to have managed to complete a pharmacology degree at night school. Financing his son's medical career was beyond him. But Eric's mother, an intelligent woman who regretted her own lack of educational opportunities, encouraged Eric's early interest in science; it was she who'd first raised the subject of medical school.

Eric worked hard for the scholarships that had taken him through eight years of schooling, realizing that high grades were the only way to finance his studies. He'd regretted not being tall enough for a college basketball scholarship; giving up the physical competition of his high school years had been tough.

For most doctors, the demands of the three or four years of required hospital residency are highly stressful. But for Eric, finally free of the part-time jobs that had plagued him from his teens right through medical school, concentrating his energies on medicine had been a big improvement.

Twelve minutes to two, he noted, tilting his tray to pivot sharply around a clump of interns. Just time to gulp down a sandwich and cup of—

"Dr. Rose! Over here! Do you suppose you could spare me a moment?"

Was that really Dr. John Harris, chief of the transplant unit, signaling to him from a nearby table? Surely Harris's question was rhetorical; to refuse a medical word with Harris was not only unthinkable politically, it was like refusing to discuss religion with the pope. Eric executed a neat forty-five-degree lunge around the condiment counter and jogged down the court toward the table at which Harris sat in splendid isolation.

He'd often scrubbed in with Harris as part of his training, and he enjoyed it. Though Harris was demanding and rather formidable, he was smart as hell; Eric had learned a lot from him. Still, he had no illusions that it was his brilliant medical opinions Harris wanted. What have I done now? he wondered.

He slid into the proffered chair, carefully removing his commercially pickled pickle from his commercially custardized custard pie.

"You were in the ER the night they brought in the guy with the kidney, weren't you? The corned beef is fatty."

"The guy *without* the kidney, you mean? Yeah, that was me."

The corned beef *was* fatty.

"Did he seem like a nut case to you, Rose? Suicidal? Eager to make his wife a rich widow? The pie is lousy."

"Actually, Dr. Harris, he was rather under the weather at the time, as I recall. He kept reassuring me that he could pay for his treatment. His wife, now, she was something else. So sure she could get a kidney from his brother. I hear she did, too. Probably removed it herself."

The pie *was* lousy.

"He's checked out."

Eric lowered his fork. "He was your patient, wasn't he?" he said. "I'm sorry."

Harris sighed. "No, Rose. He checked out of the hospital. His brother lives in Spain, of all places, and wouldn't come back here for the operation. Very strange. The man was practically dead, yet his wife pulled him off dialysis and flew him there last night. Well, maybe I'd do the same for a kidney if I didn't have one, but it's unconscionably risky."

"It does seem strange," Eric agreed. "Someone who cares enough about you to donate a kidney but makes you travel to Spain for it."

Harris looked at Eric meditatively. "Ever hear the name Benjamin Talmidge? No? Well, you're too young. It seems this Spanish Talmidge is the same Talmidge I went to medical school with, years ago. A nasty piece of work then. And now . . . I just don't know what to think. Or rather, I do, and it scares me silly."

Eric stared, fascinated. Harris had never spoken to

him like this before. Harris had never spoken like this to anyone at the hospital before.

"You're interested in cell regeneration, aren't you?" Harris continued. "Did some independent research on it at one point, I recall."

"Recall," my left eyebrow, thought Eric in some surprise. The old man's been checking me out.

Eric's interest in cell regeneration went way back to his undergraduate years. He'd found the implications of even the early research very exciting. These days there seemed to be a constant flow of discoveries involving the applications of DNA research to the detection and treatment of disease. He often wished he had time to keep up with them all.

"I'd like you to look up the stuff Ben Talmidge published in the *Lancet,*" Harris told him. "Early seventies, it would have been. See what you think."

"I'm afraid . . . I don't exactly understand, Dr. Harris."

"Of course you don't," Harris replied impatiently. "That's why I'd like to know how it strikes you. Is it really possible, do you think? I'd like the opinion of a young mind. Oh yes, and bear in mind that Talmidge doesn't plan to use antirejection drugs."

"With the kidney, you mean? But that's impossible!"

"Apparently not. At least . . . Well, you tell me." Harris studied the interior of his cup as though searching for clues, then took a small experimental sip. "The coffee is—"

"Please," said Eric. "Leave me something!"

"No, no," Harris smiled. "It's good. The coffee's terrific! Of course the rest of your lunch is a nutritional disaster."

Eric grinned, prying up the plastic top.

"Two o'clock," Harris announced, stretching and rising. "I'm due in the OR."

Eric's smile froze. He was due on A Ward at two o'clock for rounds. He put the top back on his coffee for later. Damn.

3

The first thing Vivienne thought of on Monday morning as she came awake in a pale pink sea of Laura Ashley flowers was roller-skating. She hadn't had a good long skate for a week or more, thanks to the unseasonably wet May weather, and even before she opened her eyes she knew the sun was shining at last. Her second thought was of fresh orange juice.

She stretched luxuriously, her eyes still closed, as Charles emerged from the dressing-room-cum-bathroom. He was wrapped in the dramatic black terry robe she'd bought him to keep in her apartment, but she wore nothing. How beautiful she is, he thought as he approached the bed.

The diamond necklace he'd given her the previous week gleamed in a molten heap on the bedside table. It aroused him to see it glitter against her bare skin when they made love, but she'd insisted on taking it off for sleeping, afraid the chain would break.

Then his eye was caught by a photo in a silver frame on the night table, and he frowned. Runny-nosed brat, he thought. The photo was a new one; the kid had grown.

She looked over toward him questioningly, sensing his mood shift, then realized its source.

"Come on, Charles," she said soothingly. "You can't be jealous of a Peruvian orphan!"

But Charles only shrugged. She reached for his hand

and pulled him toward her, but he sat on the edge of the bed and turned his face away in a pout.

"It's important to me," she said.

"How can you care so much about a kid you've never even met?" he said peevishly.

Vivienne sighed. They'd been through this so many times. At first she'd tried to explain how she felt, to put into words her feelings of social responsibility, but he'd laughed at her fondly. Bad stuff happens, he'd said. Some people are luckier than others.

But we actually met at a charity fund-raiser, she'd chided him. You can't really be so cynical.

That was business, he'd told her. This is personal. Anyway, you can't save the world.

But in her own small way she couldn't help trying. Even as a teenager she'd sent part of her allowance to the Children's Fund. These days, in addition to sponsoring little Pilar, she served on the charity's advisory board.

Charles was staring sourly at the photo. Better not tell him I've taken on Pilar's brothers, too, she thought.

She reached over and mussed his damp blond hair. "What an old grouch you are this morning!"

She's right, he thought. He turned to her with a dazzling smile, and pounced on her, tickling her until she was breathless with laughter.

Still laughing, they began to make love, and he thought, as he often did, how perfect she was; how much he would hate it when she began to change, to age. Still, that was taken care of now.

Afterward they had breakfast at a small white wicker table on the terrace outside her bedroom. The apartment was so high, it was not overlooked; Vivienne often sunbathed nude. The view was one of the best in New York, east and south toward the East River, over a landscape most people saw only in films or from airplanes. Vivienne had squeezed fresh orange juice, set out warm, buttery croissants, and brewed some of her special stock of Blue Mountain coffee, brought back from a shoot in Jamaica. Sometimes she felt a little self-conscious, a cheerleader from Carolina, living this life, but then she reminded herself that this was her life now. She'd earned it, and by golly she'd enjoy it.

She tried to follow Charles as he described the real estate development deal he was putting together, but he lost her in the maze of financing details. He didn't really expect her to understand. Talking her through his business deals was his way of thinking them through himself; it helped him to put his ideas into words, and to run the words around for a while. At first Vivienne had asked questions about things she didn't understand, but now she knew it only distracted him, and she was silent. She let her thoughts wander, watched a sailboat make its way along the river against the current, nibbled the point of a croissant. She felt calm. She had always thought of love as exciting, something that made you feel jumpy and high. But aside from the sex, which was incredible, being with Charles wasn't like that at all. The life he led, and the people she met through him, were exciting, but Charles himself, out of bed, didn't make her tingle. She desired him, but did she love him? Sometimes she wasn't sure.

After Charles left, she pulled on her hot-pink leggings and red sweatshirt. A New York skater needs all the visibility she can get. No makeup. Why bother? She pulled her tawny hair back in a ponytail, capturing it in a large black-and-red clip, and began to lace up her skates.

Vivienne's usual route was up Park Avenue to the corner of Seventy-fifth, then west to Madison and uptown to Eighty-sixth, checking out the stores and the people. She was a bold, confident skater, dodging buses, taxis, and bicycles with aplomb. It was great exercise, but more than that, it was fun.

At Eighty-sixth Street, she pulled off her skates in the lobby of her health club and climbed the stairs to the pool and locker rooms in her socks. She tried to swim at least four times a week, fifty laps a session. She considered it part of her job.

Back when she was growing up, she wore the wheels off her skates regularly, and hers was the rope that she and the other kids tied to a tree by the side of the creek to see who could swing out the farthest before dropping into the water. She usually won. Living in New York City was great, but she was glad she hadn't had to grow up here.

Having paid appropriate homage to the Stay Fit Goddess, she headed downtown again to the East Sixties to keep her promise to Charles. Although she'd called Dr. Arnold's office last week, today was the earliest he'd been able to see her.

The entrance to the doctor's office was just off the lobby of a small but showy apartment building; a stately doorman waved her in the direction of a cream-colored door with ornate moldings. She rang the small gold bell and was buzzed inside, only then realizing the door was actually made of thick painted steel.

The waiting room was done in charming patterns of chintz and plaid, a decorating combination both risky and successful. Someone was spending money here, she thought, recalling the more straightforward waiting rooms that the doctors she consulted considered sufficient. Well, Charles wouldn't go to just anyone.

A friendly and attractive woman wearing a nurse's uniform looked up at her from a French Provincial desk at the end of the room, next to a corridor which presumably led back to the treatment rooms. Beside the desk stood a small service table with urns of coffee and hot water. How civilized, thought Vivienne.

She smiled as she approached the nurse. "I'm Vivienne—"

"Laker," said the nurse. "Or course! And you skated all the way here? How brave! I'm Berta, Dr. Arnold's nurse. I'll go and tell Dr. Arnold you've arrived. He won't be a minute. Coffee? No? We also have diet soda." She indicated a small fridge below the table. "Just help yourself!" She smiled at Vivienne again and disappeared down the corridor.

Popping the top of a cold can of Sprite, Vivienne sat down across from the only other person in the room, a short baby-faced man she recognized but couldn't place. He seemed to feel her stare, for he looked up petulantly. Embarrassed, she reached for a magazine and began to page through it idly.

"The famous Vivienne Laker!" A tall, slim, elegantly tailored man of about fifty stood before her, his pale brown hair moussed straight back from his forehead, his hand stretched out in greeting, his thin lips pulled back in a feral smile. "I'm Dr. Arnold," he told her. "But you can call me Brian. Please come in. Bring your soda with you if you like." His accent was faintly British.

Slowly she stood and grasped his hand in greeting. It seemed to her he held it slightly longer than necessary as his eyes, radiating some fierce energy, bore into hers. Then, noting her discomfort with satisfaction, he dropped her hand and turned away, and she followed him past the nurse's desk, unoccupied now, and down the corridor.

The examining room into which he showed her was more like a small den, complete with potted plants and carpeting. The examining table was upholstered in a smooth pale green leatherlike material over which the nurse now drew a soft white fabric cover. "I hate those paper things, don't you?" she said to Vivienne with a smile. Then she turned to the doctor. "Everything's all laid out on the tray," she told him. "Shall I stay?"

"No need," he said. "Vivienne—may I call you that?—and I will be fine on our own."

Vivienne was not so sure. Despite the plush decor and all those smiles, she was feeling a little uneasy. There was an edge to Brian Arnold's charm which felt—well, dangerous. An odd feeling to have about a doctor, she reflected.

"Stretch out for me, please," he told her. Puzzled,

she got up on the examining table as he positioned a small opaque screen on rollers against the side of the table. A narrow hole had been cut through it, and a padded armrest was fastened along one side.

"Just put your arm through here, that's it . . . and rest it here. Comfy?"

"Yes, but I really don't understand the need for all this," Vivienne protested. "I've had blood tests before, and—"

"Don't want anyone fainting at the sight of their own blood," Arnold told her, swabbing her inner elbow with something cold. Alcohol?

"Well, *I* won't faint!" said Vivienne, annoyed.

"Humor me, okay?"

Charles, baby, you really owe me for this one, she thought with a smile. Then she remembered the diamond necklace Charles had given her when she'd agreed to see Dr. Arnold, and felt very guilty. Of course he doesn't owe me. I'm doing this because I love him. And in truth, Charles's money was the smallest part of his appeal for her.

The test seemed to take an awfully long while, longer than she remembered such tests taking. She wondered what time it was—she was due to meet her friend Angie for lunch at noon—but her watch was on the other side of the screen, along with her left arm.

"Nearly done," Arnold told her at last. She felt him applying gauze and tape. "You okay?"

"Of course!" she said. Good Lord, why wouldn't I be?

As he helped her down from the table, she sneaked a look toward the work area along the opposite side of the room, but it was masked by the screen. All she could see through the armhole were some tubes of blood. There was a large gauze bandage on the inside of her elbow.

The waiting room was empty when Arnold walked her out; presumably the nurse was with Mr. Babyface in one of the other examining rooms along the corridor. Arnold smiled at her and kissed her hand as he ushered her out the door. "An exemplary patient!" he proclaimed. "Come and see us again."

What on earth for? she thought, but she smiled back as she hurriedly retrieved her hand and skated away. It was already eleven-fifty-five and she had twenty blocks to go.

The cab veered across three lanes of traffic and stopped with a skid, its passenger door directly across a small body of water left over from yesterday's rainshowers. Charles managed to get the door open and himself inside with only minor water damage to his Churchill brogues. "Fifty-second and Fifth," he said.

"Is in Manhattan?"

Charles sighed. "Fifty-second Street," he repeated slowly. "Five. Two." He held up some fingers.

At last the light dawned. "Ohhhh, I think you say something . . . I don't know the word." The driver shrugged his shoulders apologetically. "So now I go. Yes, okay!" The taxi jerked forward throwing Charles back against the torn seat. He straightened his jacket and wondered if he'd arrive in a fit state to eat the excellent lunch he was about to be bought.

God, how I hate New York! he thought. Well, not all of New York. Just the bad bits. Unfortunately, the bad bits were beginning to outnumber the good bits.

O. Henry had called it "Baghdad on the Hudson." Well, it was getting more like Baghdad every day, he reflected, not for the first time. You needed a Berlitz course in Middle East languages to get around town in a cab. If you could find a cab.

Still, Vivienne seemed to thrive here. To her it was the Big Apple, the city she'd idolized back in North Carolina, and she seemed able to forgive it anything.

Elizabeth, on the other hand, would have found it all unforgivably vulgar. Especially the taxis. So crude, she'd have said. So unsanitary. Why put up with it, Charles? Call those nice Fugazy people and tell them to come and get you.

Elizabeth. So few experiences, Charles reflected,

had ever come up to his mother's high standards. And when a less-than-desirable individual had managed to slip through her formidable defenses—an impolite gardener, an alcoholic dinner guest, a son—she'd been adept at firing, banishing, and . . . training. As soon as Charles could talk, she'd made it quite clear that he was never to call her Mother. Peasants do that, her tone implied. We patricians know nothing of the messy process of childbirth. Our children are found beneath the rosebushes.

She'd created him in her image. Taught him how to dress, to order a meal, to behave in society. She'd taught him everything about perfection, and nothing about fun.

He'd worshiped her: her beauty, her confidence, her "rightness." But no matter how hard he'd tried all those years to make up for having put her through the embarrassment of motherhood, her approval was always conditional.

Even Charles's father, wealthy and well-bred, did not wholly meet with her approval. He was, after all, a man. And men had loud voices and smoked cigars, and were importunate about sex. Perhaps that was why his father found so many projects which took him away from home. Later, when Charles moved out on his own, he got to know his father well, and that relationship, begun relatively late in life, became deep and important to them both, developing to some extent Charles's latent appetite for living. Yet the damage done by Elizabeth remained palpable.

Since her death the year before, Charles often found himself wondering what his mother had really felt for him. Had she loved him at all? Sometimes he thought he hated her for making it impossible for him to simply enjoy life, warts and all. To wear pink shirts, and eat pizza with his hands. Yet now that he no longer had to measure everything he did by her standards, he found he knew no other way.

He shifted uncomfortably on the spavined seat, already regretting his reaction to Pilar's photo. *I should* be proud of Viv, he thought. She could just coast along on her beauty, but she doesn't; she works hard and thinks about other people.

And yet, when he thought about the volunteer work she did at that hospital across town, his skin crawled. He hated her being tainted by the messy realities of life. And God, wouldn't Elizabeth have absolutely hated the idea of a Spencer-Moore wife carrying bed-pans or whatever it was that Vivienne did at Park Hill. . . .

"Excuse, mister. You want this side of street here or next side?"

Charles started, and looked around. Thinking about Elizabeth, he'd lost track of their progress.

"But this is Fifty-seventh Street," he protested.

The driver beamed. "Fifty-seven," he agreed. "Hey, mister, I learn good the English, yes?"

Charles threw some bills at the driver and wrenched the door open in disgust. "I'll walk," he said angrily, and set off down the street to the Union Club. His host, a major player at a large brokerage firm, was waiting for him just beyond the impressive entrance hall.

"Mind if I use a phone?" Charles asked as soon as they had greeted each other. "Just take a moment. I'll meet you in the dining room. Yes, I know where it is."

Once inside the wood-paneled telephone booth, Charles dialed quickly from memory. The phone rang twice. Pick up the damn phone, Charles fumed silently.

"Dr. Arnold's office," obliged an efficient female voice.

"Berta, it's Charles Spencer-Moore. Put me through to him, would you?"

"Of course. Just hold a moment." And indeed it was only a moment before Brian Arnold's cold, measured voice said, "Hello, Charles. What's up?"

"How did it go?"

"Go?" Arnold's voice sounded puzzled.

"With Vivienne," said Charles impatiently. "Any problems?"

"No, of course not," Arnold told him. "I put up the screen, of course."

"And you have the, uh, what you need?"

"Yes, of course. Why are you so jumpy?" Brian Arnold had just left one of the world's most famous rock singers alone in an examining room in order to answer Charles's call. He hoped the conversation wouldn't take long; rockers were all crazy.

"This one's important to me, Brian. Really important."

"They're all important to me, Charles. Don't worry. It's over and done with."

"Good, good," Charles felt the tension lift from his shoulders. "Just wanted to make sure."

"I understand. Good-bye, Charles."

Charles left the phone booth and headed for the dining room with a light step.

Brian Arnold went back to his rock star who was, mercifully, not ripping the plants from their pots or tossing chairs out the window. Quickly he wrote out the prescription and handed it to the leather-clad figure, who casually thrust it up his sleeve and tossed a handful of crumpled bills in Arnold's direction. As the idol of millions sauntered out, swaying slightly, Arnold buzzed Berta on the intercom.

"Yes, Doctor?"

"Berta, did you pack the Laker material in ice?"

"Of course, Doctor."

"Good. And you called Medi-Ship?"

Berta allowed herself a small exasperated sigh. She'd worked for Brian Arnold for nearly five years. Surely he could trust her to know the drill by now. "I called Medi-Ship ten minutes ago," she told him. "They'll pick up by four o'clock. It'll be in Barcelona by tomorrow morning."

"Good." Brian Arnold bent down and began picking up the hundred-dollar bills.

4

"Mexican cheeseburger with everything, side of onion rings, and a strawberry shake."

"It always amazes me, the way the other half lives," said Vivienne, smiling fondly at Angela, her oldest and best friend in New York.

Angela Tredanari was a booker at Lens, the modeling agency which represented Vivienne, and she didn't believe in counting calories. Vivacious and bright, she was at least forty pounds overweight. Her lustrous black hair, deep dark eyes, and creamy complexion made people who had just met her remark that "she'd be so pretty if only she'd drop a few pounds!" It didn't seem likely. Over her office desk was a framed blow-up of an article from a trendy health-and-fitness magazine, sporting the headline "Carbohydrates Make You Happy."

"A chef's salad," said Vivienne. "Dressing on the side. And an iced tea with lemon, please."

"You are what you eat," said the waiter, and wandered off.

"Now, there's a depressing thought," said Angela.

"Did you ever think about how much of our lives revolves around food?" Vivienne asked.

"Uneaten food, in your case," said Angela.

"True. Sad but true."

"I guess that's why you glamour pusses are always getting blood tests, huh? To make sure you still have some."

"What? Oh, yes, this," said Vivienne, glancing at the rather large bandage on the inside of her left elbow. "I had a test this morning for the marriage license."

"I didn't know they still did that," said Angela. "Anyhow, the wedding's months away."

"I know, but Charles insisted."

"And what Charles says . . ." Angela left the sentence unfinished. She understood Charles's attraction but didn't trust him somehow. Not fair, she knew. "May-Ann had a bandage just like that last week. Looked kinda big for a blood test, I thought. Still, they're making all kinds of advances in medical science these days."

Angela's tone was scathing. May-Ann was the agency's famous Hungarian discovery. Only eighteen years old, May-Ann had been earning in the seven figures for two years, and rumor had it that there was nothing illegal she hadn't tried. If you booked her these days, you stood a fifty-fifty chance she'd actually show up.

"It was a little strange," Vivienne admitted. "Charles insisted I go to his doctor, who's nice enough really . . . he even insisted I call him Brian, but . . ."

She paused as their food was placed on the small marble-topped table in front of them.

Angela took a long swallow of milkshake. "Go on," she said.

"Well," Vivienne continued, "Dr. Arnold, uh, Brian that is, put up this sort of screen that my arm stuck through so I couldn't see what he was doing."

Angela paused in mid-bite. "He what?"

"Yes, I thought it was funny too. He said he didn't want his patients fainting at the sight of their blood. I tried to tell him I wasn't like that, but he was quite firm."

"And then what?" asked Angela.

"Well, I guess he drew the blood. I mean, it felt like he sort of deadened the feeling in my arm first, so I couldn't really tell. It felt kind of like scraping, and then I felt the needle go in, I think. Oh, I don't know. I'm probably making a big thing out of nothing."

"Does it hurt?"

Vivienne pressed experimentally with a forefinger. It did. She didn't remember blood tests hurting like that.

"Well, eat up your lettuce and cucumber and replace some of that nice green blood the doctor took!"

"Green?" Vivienne smiled.

"You don't think your body can make red blood with what you eat, do you? Now tell me about all the glamorous things you did this week and make me jealous!"

"Angie, you don't have a jealous bone in your body."

"That's true," mused Angela. "I don't. I wonder why."

After lunch, Vivienne skated home to change her clothes and replace her skates with sensible shoes. Stuffing her identity badge into the pocket of her jean jacket, she headed for the elevator again, both worried and excited. It had been several weeks since she'd had time for the Park Hill Hospital, and today she had a surprise planned—if only the others showed up as promised.

Much to her relief, they were waiting for her in the second-floor locker room, laughing and complaining.

"Do we really have to wear these?"

"I feel about ten years old!"

"Jeez, wouldn't *Vogue* like a shot of us!"

Vivienne grinned. Four of the country's highest-paid models were reluctantly buttoning themselves into the clunky pink-and-white "candy-striper" pinafores every hospital volunteer hates and most hospitals had by now discarded. *Vogue* would indeed love a shot of this, she thought. On them, the uniforms actually looked good.

"Pink isn't my color. Does it come in mauve?"

"Hey, is this a bloodstain?"

"Only one little spot? They must have bought new uniforms. We volunteers usually get drenched in the stuff," Vivienne answered. Then, seeing the fluffy blond turn pale, Vivienne laughed. "Coffee, Sharon," she said. "Just coffee, I promise!"

Dawn Brown, Park Hill's coordinator of volunteers, had loved the idea when Vivienne had suggested surprising the medical and nursing staff with famous-faced candy-stripers for one day. "But you mustn't tell anyone," Vivienne had made her promise. "I want to see their expressions when we descend upon them in all our glory!" Now, as she handed out their temporary ID badges, Dawn was glad she'd kept quiet about it. How long would it take the busy staff to notice?

"What do we do, exactly?" asked Maura, a tall brunette who was known across the country as the Chanel Woman.

"First I'll take you all on a little tour," said Dawn. "So you know where things are, sort of. Then each of you will be assigned to a different area. We always need volunteers to read to the children in Pediatrics, and play with them. And someone has to ferry charts and papers to different departments. Most of our elderly patients appreciate it when a volunteer takes time to chat with them, maybe join them for a walk to the solarium. Viv's real good at that," she added.

"Somehow they all remind me of my grandparents," said Viv, flushing at the compliment.

Dawn glanced down at the checklist on her clipboard. "The lab has asked if we have anyone who can help with their paperwork. And . . . oh yes, anyone want to assist in the autopsy room? Never mind, just kidding."

"Don't scare them away now," Vivienne pleaded. "It took me weeks to persuade them to show up at all!"

Heads turned as the group made its way along the corridor. Even a young man strapped onto a gurney did a double-take as they crowded into the elevator beside him. "I may be sick," he said, "but I ain't *dead*!"

Starting on the fourth floor of the small private hospital, Dawn walked them through pertinent areas of the building, avoiding the infectious wards (which were off-limits to candy-stripers), and hurrying them past the intensive-care units. Everywhere, men and women glanced up and nodded, then looked again and grinned. Even the formidable chief of medicine, surprised on his way to a conference, smiled and chatted for a moment. But the most fun was watching a young intern pretend he wasn't at all impressed by their arrival, no, not at all. He was far too busy for such frivolity, his expression said, as he stepped smartly into a wastebasket.

One by one, Vivienne's friends were dropped off at their assigned work stations, Maura, in the children's ward, the dark exotic Tara in the lab, Sharon in the communications center, and Chelsea, a pale English rose, at the nurses' station in Pulmonary.

"Everyone's really enjoying this," Dawn told Vivienne. "It was sweet of you to organize it."

"Well, I did have to twist a few arms," Vivienne admitted. "But I think they're all really glad they're here today. Of course, you'll probably never see them here again—let's be realistic—but today they're having fun."

"Well, so are we. You wanted to work here in Cardiac Care again, right?"

Vivienne nodded.

"Kathy, Bianca, you remember Vivienne?" Dawn asked the two RN's at the nurses' station.

"How're you doing?" Bianca asked, then turned to answer a shrilling phone.

"You're in good hands," said Dawn. "I'll go check on the others, make sure we don't lose any more interns!"

"See you later," Vivienne called as Dawn headed rapidly toward the staff stairway.

"Hear you brought an entourage," said Kathy. "We

going to be in the movies or something?'' A light on
the callboard lit up and a buzzer sounded.

Vivienne laughed. ''No, I just thought I'd shake
things up a little around here. It's such a dull, quiet
place!''

''Right!'' said Kathy. ''Excuse me, gotta go.'' She
flipped up a switch and the buzzer stopped. ''Make
yourself at home,'' she called out as she headed down
the corridor. ''Oh, Mr. Kaplan's been asking for you.''

''Five-oh-one,'' said Bianca, holding a hand over
the receiver.

Mr. Kaplan was one of Vivienne's favorites. Talking
to him, she often forgot that he was nearly ninety. His
mind was young and alert, his spirit unquenchable.
The trouble was, Mr. Kaplan's heart was simply wearing out. He'd been in and out of the hospital three
times during the past year, suffering from chronic fib-
rillation. The pacemaker they'd installed several
months ago had probably saved his life during the on-
set of his recent heart attack. Now he was recovering,
weak, angry at his body, yet determined to leave the
hospital on his feet.

Vivienne knocked softly in case he was sleeping,
but Mr. Kaplan's voice, quiet yet firm, called, ''Come
on in!'' so she did. Room 501 was small but cheerful,
thanks to the constant influx of flowers from his large
family. It smelled wonderful.

''Lilacs,'' said Vivienne, spying the large branches
set prominently in front of the window. ''My favorite!''

''Take them, take them,'' Mr. Kaplan said. ''I got
flowers I could open a flower store with them! Take!''
He made a sweeping gesture toward the window, swip-
ing his lunch tray with his sleeve.

Vivienne shook her head, smiling. ''I can't take your
flowers, Mr. Kaplan. What if the person who sent them
came to visit and didn't see them?'' *He looks pale,*
she thought.

''So, I'll say I gave them to a beautiful woman.

Good for my image!'' He squeezed her hand. ''How you doing?''

''Fine, Mr. Kaplan. I'm doing just great. How about you?'' She glanced at the lunch tray. ''You didn't eat much.''

''Pahhh! This stuff!'' He waved at the tray disdainfully. ''I told them, 'Bring me a pastrami on rye, you'll see me eat!' ''

''You know you're not allowed—''

''I know, I know! So sit already, tell me about your glamorous life. My daughter, she saw your picture in some magazine last week, she got so excited!''

Vivienne smiled. ''Nice to be appreciated,'' she said. ''Actually it's not that glamorous while you're doing it. The lights are hot, the makeup clogs your pores, and the money's only *fabulous*!'' Kaplan chortled appreciatively.

Viv reached for the newspaper that an earlier visitor had abandoned on one of the guest chairs.

''Want me to read you the news? I used to read the paper to my grammy when I was little. I'd slip in silly parts I'd make up, and see how long it took her to catch on.'' Viv smiled at the memory. ''She'd say, 'Girl, you sure you readin' that right?' ''

''The paper I can live without,'' said Mr. Kaplan. ''Troubles, nothing but troubles. At my age, I want to hear good news.''

''At any age, Mr. Kaplan.''

''Yeah, but it's different when you're young. You have time on your side. You read something, and first you say, 'How terrible!' But then you say, 'Hey, I have an idea how to fix it, make it work better.' ''

''Sometimes I think nobody can do anything anymore,'' Vivienne said. ''We've been disenfranchised. No one has the power to make a difference.''

''Little ways,'' Mr. Kaplan said. ''Little things. You change a little here, a little there, soon you've changed a lot.'' He grinned at her. ''Anyhow, you're a big shot, and people listen to big shots.''

"They do? Then how about some more lunch? A little here, a little there . . ."

"Very funny," said Mr. Kaplan. "No."

"A walk?"

Kaplan shook his head. "Truth is," he confided, "I'm a little tired. I wouldn't want you should think it's the company, but I feel like a nap."

Vivienne pushed away the bed table holding the lunch tray and straightened the white cotton blanket. "Sweet dreams," she said, and kissed him lightly on the forehead.

"Sweet dreams," he repeated, grinning wickedly. "At my age, what else?"

It isn't fair, she thought as she closed the door gently behind her. Only one part of him is failing; why does the rest have to go too?

Through the closing door she heard his voice, already slurred with sleep. "You forgot the lilacs," he called softly. "Believe me, I got flowers I could open a flower store. . . ."

Back at the nurses' station, the renowned cardiologist and bridge player Dr. Alfred Mitchell, chart in hand, was deep in discussion with Kathy. His round face, framed by tufts of unruly white hair, radiated the calm intelligence which patients and colleagues alike found so reassuring. He was one of the few doctors Vivienne had met who treated her as an equal, not a servant.

Vivienne hovered in the corridor until they were finished. Kathy noticed her first, and beckoned her over.

"How's Mr. K?" she asked Vivienne.

"Quite perky at first. Then he got tired. He's asleep now."

Dr. Mitchell finished his notations and handed the chart to Kathy. "My favorite striper," he said to Vivienne. "You're looking very glamorous today."

"Who wouldn't, in these uniforms? Listen, how's Mr. Kaplan doing? Really?"

"The man is ninety years old. How should he be doing?"

"It doesn't seem fair," Vivienne told him.

"You think that's not fair? I have a forty-four-year-old man, keeps in shape, eats right, doesn't smoke, all of a sudden he keels over in his office. Right now he's in worse shape than Mr. Kaplan. Fibrillating all over the place, lots of damage to the heart muscle. Has two young kids too. Shit happens."

"What will you do for him?"

"What we can. And that's a lot more than it was twenty years ago. But it isn't always enough." He checked his wristwatch against the large wall clock, then reached across the desk and chose another chart. "You know, for forty years I've been bringing my patients' troubles home with me," he told Vivienne. "Finally my wife made me a sampler to hang in my office. It says—"

" 'Shit Happens'?"

"In the office of a man who charges three hundred dollars a visit?" said Mitchell in mock horror. "No, it says 'Life Isn't Fair.' "

"And does it make your patients feel better?"

Mitchell smiled wryly. "It's not for them," he said. "It's for me."

Later, back at her apartment, Vivienne served the women white wine spritzers and green pasta salad as they talked about their afternoon.

"It was fun," Maura decided, spearing a shard of carrot. "It was kind of sad, all those sick kids, but a lot of them are getting better. . . . Anyhow, doing it made me feel good."

" 'As the actress said to the bishop,' " said Chelsea in her clipped British accent.

"Some of the doctors were cute," offered Sharon. "Doesn't Charles get jealous?"

"Not of the doctors," said Vivienne darkly. "Maybe of Mr. Kaplan."

"Who's he?" asked Tara.

"A cute fella of about ninety," said Vivienne. Then, seeing their confusion, she added, "I mean, Charles doesn't like the whole idea. It's too . . . real, or something."

"Real it is," said Sharon, her blue eyes big and round. "I was terrified somebody was going to start bleeding or something right in front of me. Doesn't that terrify you, Viv?"

"Not really," Vivienne replied. "I've had more skinned knees than you've had hot dinners, as they say. Blood doesn't scare me." She thought a minute. "Actually," she said, "I kind of like the realness of it. We, all of us here, lead very rarefied lives, don't you think? When was the last time any of you were on the subway?"

"I took the subway to a booking a few weeks ago—couldn't find a cab," said Chelsea. "Believe me, I do not recommend the experience!"

"Neither do I," Vivienne agreed. "But my point is, we're the lucky ones. And it's so easy to forget about the rest of the world. Doing volunteer work now and then makes me feel less . . . I don't know, not guilty exactly, but . . ."

"It's a way of giving something back, is that what you mean?" Maura asked.

"Yes," said Vivienne gratefully. "I think it is."

"Bullshit," said Chelsea.

"Well," offered Tara, "it was an experience, I'll grant you that. But you'll never get me back in there again!"

"Nor me," Chelsea agreed.

"Fair enough," Vivienne told them. "Once was all you signed on for."

"It wasn't really so bad," said Sharon. "And some of the patients were cute!"

"Anyway, I'm glad we did it," Maura said. "I might even do it again sometime—"

"Really? That would be great!"

"—in about twenty years!"

* * *

After the women left, Vivienne checked her answering machine and felt faintly guilty to discover that the message light was blinking. Reaching for a pencil, she hit the playback button.

"You, yes you, have won an all-expense-paid trip to New Mexico!" Angela's high-energy voice boomed out at her. "Not much money, but these editorial spreads never are. However, there is a cover in it! To claim your prize, call Angela. Uh, as soon as possible, Viv, okay?"

Mmmm, nice, thought Vivienne.

The rest of the messages weren't nearly as interesting, but she noted them down before she reset the machine, then called the agency.

"*Vogue,*" Angela told her. "Four days starting the twelfth. It's insane here today. The money sucks—what else is new?—but Hervé is shooting. You want it?"

In the background Vivienne could hear about a thousand phones ringing and people shouting back and forth. Just another normal day at Lens.

"Sure I want it," she said. "Tell 'em yes and call me with details when you can."

"You got it!" said Angela, and disconnected.

Vivienne went into the oversize kitchen and refilled her glass from the seltzer bottle in the Sub Zero refrigerator. On second thought, she decided to take the bottle with her.

The apartment, a classic seven-room prewar layout with high ceilings and a central hallway, had been completely restored, rewired, and replumbed by the previous owner just before his Wall Street firm had gone belly-up. There was a Jacuzzi in the master bedroom, a walk-in closet in place of the maid's room, and a gourmet kitchen from which you could cater a dinner for 150 of your closest friends. These days it primarily dispensed salads, grilled fish, and vegetable juice.

Carrying the glass and bottle, she went down the central hallway to the large light living room and slid the glass doors open to the second terrace, a large square space fringed with plants and trees and paved with terra-cotta tile. She stood for a moment looking out. Behind her, a warm breeze ruffled the pages of the magazines on the marble coffee table inside.

Turning back, she set the bottle on the table and curled up on the sleek silk-covered sofa, glass in hand, enjoying the room. It was part decorator, part her, and although the decorator did not agree, she liked the clash of ideas. It would be too "white bread," she thought, without that funny temperance banner I picked up in London, or that touristy brass elephant table.

Only the pale sofa she now sat on felt out-of-place to her. Expensive, fragile, easily stained, it made her faintly nervous, like a child visiting a rich aunt. Feeling slightly silly, she resettled herself in a homey Victorian wicker rocker, spray-painted a soft blue-green and filled with flowered chintz cushions. She smiled, remembering the look of horror on the decorator's face when she'd refused to relegate this old favorite to the spare bedroom.

Late sun streamed in through the filmy curtains, striping her with warmth as it fell across her legs. The evening stretched before her, full of interesting possibilities.

5

Eric hadn't visited the stacks since his student days. He remembered fondly an all-too-brief escapade with an ardent female medical student one spring; yes, stacks were a worthy institution. Today, though, he'd approached with exhausted resignation the idea of researching what he'd come to call (to himself, of course) Harris's Folly. Never enough sleep, or time to eat a decent meal, or even wash out your socks. But Harris seemed to think he had time to dig into old issues of the *Lancet,* digest the information, and then offer an insightful analysis of the possibility of . . . What? He didn't even know what Harris was after. But actually he was quite flattered.

And now, barely an hour after disappearing into the dusty depths, Eric was stunned.

According to the twenty-year-old *Lancet* article, Talmidge had gone further during his very earliest years than anyone working in the field of cell regeneration and DNA research today. Why hadn't he known about Talmidge? Why wasn't the world applauding and building on the man's incredible achievement?

And then the answer was revealed, and Eric's excitement died. For soon after the first article was published, another proclaimed Talmidge's work to be a fraud, and then Talmidge himself repudiated his results, crowing at the deceit he had practiced on the medical community.

It was pouring again. The drumming of the rain,

such a cozy sound in the stacks, had flooded every street crossing by the time Eric emerged from the medical library, hungry, dusty and puzzled. He'd have liked nothing better than to head for home and a takeout pizza, but instead he hiked over to Madison Avenue and caught an uptown bus. His curiosity was piqued. He needed more information.

The imposing limestone building which housed the New York Academy of Medicine dominated the corner of East 103rd Street and Fifth Avenue. The receptionist looked slightly askance as Eric pushed through the large wrought-iron-and-glass doors, deposited his umbrella in the thoughtfully provided bin, and squelched wetly through the ornate lobby toward her desk. But his hospital identification card seemed to reassure her, and his dark good looks didn't hurt either. She noticed he wore no wedding ring, and wondered whether she dared suggest he call her unmarried niece.

"You'll need to speak to someone in the Membership Office," she told him pleasantly when he'd explained the purpose of his visit. "Please have a seat." Maybe she could mention Cindy to him on his way out . . .

She spoke quietly into the phone, and soon a short bearded man of about forty materialized, extending a hand in greeting.

"Dr. Rose? I'm Simon MacKenzie. How can I help?"

"I'm doing research on the history of transplants," Eric extemporized. "Dr. Harris, uh, John Harris of New York General, suggested I check out Dr. Benjamin Talmidge. I thought you might have some information on him."

Simon looked impressed at the mention of John Harris; most people did.

"Benjamin Talmidge?" he asked. "He's a current member?"

"I don't know. He left the country back in the seventies."

"Before my time here, I'm afraid," Simon said with

a smile. "Come back to my office and let's see if we can bring him up on the computer."

Simon's office was small and cramped. "Pull up a chair," he told Eric as he slid behind his desk. "Seventies, you said?" He rifled among an assortment of computer disks. "You're lucky. We've just recently finished transferring our membership files to these things." He drew out a disk and fitted it into the computer drive.

He typed away on the keyboard and soon was scrolling through a lengthy membership list. Next to each name was a series of letters. "Each letter is a sort of code," Simon explained. "See, A means current member, D means dues paid up-to-date, F means non-resident member—sometimes people move out of state but still retain their membership here . . . Ah, here we are . . . Talbot . . . Talman . . . Uh-oh!" Next to Benjamin Talmidge's name was a large X. "You sure you've got the right name?"

"Yes," said Eric. "Why? What's the X mean?"

"Kicked out," Simon replied. "Expelled. Your Dr. Talmidge must have been a very naughty boy."

"Would you still have any records on him?"

Simon looked doubtful. "We'd have his CV on file; that's sort of standard, even when someone's asked to resign. I suppose there might be some information in the file itself."

"Could I see it?" asked Eric hopefully.

Simon studied him for a moment. "It's rather irregular," he said. "Mind if I check you out with Dr. Harris?"

"Go ahead."

Simon looked at his watch; just after five. The academy closed at five-thirty. "Why don't you leave me your phone number?" he suggested. "I'll get back to you later in the week."

Eric put on his most charming smile. "Please," he said. "I'm doing this research in my spare time, and if you know medicine, you know I don't *have* any spare time. All I want is to see the file, make some notes.

The guy isn't even a member anymore. I mean, if you kicked him out, you don't owe him anything, right?''

Simon hesitated. "Well . . . okay," he said at last. "Only you'll have to wade through some cartons to find what you need. Everything's in a jumble since we started computerizing."

He led Eric out of his office and down the hall to a tiny room crowded with file boxes. Part of a desk was visible. "It's somewhere in here. I think stuff's more or less in alphabetical order. You need a pad, a pencil?"

"Nope, I'm all set," Eric said. "And thanks. A lot!"

"Don't mention it," Simon told him. "I mean really, don't mention it to anyone! Oh, and you've only got about twenty minutes before we close." He looked around at the stacked boxes doubtfully. "Good luck!" He gave a little wave and disappeared, and Eric began tackling the files.

It took him nearly half of the allotted time to find Talmidge's file. Opening it on the section of desk uncluttered by file boxes, he was disappointed to find it was rather thin. Checking his watch, he hurriedly began to read and write. There was little time to reflect; he knew that would come later. Now he just concentrated on recording whatever he thought might help him figure out the puzzle Harris had set him.

He jotted down the salient facts of Talmidge's curriculum vitae, current to 1973, the date he'd been expelled from the academy. He noted the date—1972—when Talmidge had announced his incredible discovery, and then rescinded it. The reason for expulsion was spelled out in a copy of the letter the academy had sent to Talmidge at the time: scientific fraud. That jibed with the *Lancet* articles Eric had read earlier in the day. The file also contained a letter of recommendation Talmidge had written on behalf of a female colleague who was applying for membership. Someone had scrawled "membership denied" across it. The

letter was dated October 1972. Presumably a referral
by Talmidge was by then the kiss of death.

When Simon came by at five-thirty, Eric was packing up his papers.

"Got what you needed?" Simon asked.

"I got what there was," Eric said with a small
shrug.

"Not much, huh? We usually keep reprints of articles about our members, copies of papers they write,
addresses they deliver to the membership. Wasn't any
of that stuff useful?"

"There wasn't anything like that in the file," Eric
told him truthfully.

"I guess I'm not really surprised," said Simon. "I
went up to the library just now and asked one of our
older members if he remembered Talmidge being expelled—doesn't happen often here. He said it was quite
a scandal. Your friend Talmidge had made a presentation to the academy prior to publication and was quite
lionized because of it. After the smoke cleared, a lot
of people were very embarrassed." He lowered his
voice slightly. "The director probably cleaned up the
file afterward."

"Why wouldn't he discard it altogether?" Eric
mused.

Simon shrugged. "Beats me," he said.

They walked toward the street door together. The
receptionist had left; Cindy would be single a little
longer. Outside, the rain was still sheeting down.

"Maybe Talmidge did it himself," Eric suggested.

"Talmidge? Seems unlikely," said Simon.

"Yeah . . . you're probably right." But a dim idea
was forming somewhere in the back of his brain. He
groped for it, but it slid away.

"Well, thanks again for your help," Eric said, re-
trieving his umbrella.

"Don't mention it," Simon told him. "I mean, really, don't—"

"—mention it to anyone. I know!" Eric laughed

and went out into the drenched evening in search of transportation.

The downtown bus stopped several blocks from the two-room walk-up he called home, and he slopped through the wet streets, stopping along the way for pizza and a carton of milk.

Stripped of his soaked clothing and wrapped in an old terry-cloth bathrobe, Eric chewed his dinner thoughtfully as he reviewed the facts, hoping to recapture the vague idea he'd had, and lost, as he was leaving the academy.

Talmidge had perpetrated an elaborate scientific fraud and gotten himself kicked out of the academy. Having been discredited within the medical community, he'd gone off to practice in Spain. He was certainly an unsavory character. No wonder Harris was indignant and concerned that such a man was performing a kidney transplant on one of his own patients.

An unpleasant situation but a straightforward one. Or was he missing something?

He glanced down at his notes again, laid out in front of him on the coffee table. Why had Harris thought it worthwhile sending him on this paper chase? There must be a connection, but what was it? What did a kidney transplant have to do with faking evidence of cloning a mouse?

"She's got *what*?"

Vivienne held the phone away from her ear; when Charles was mad, she reflected, you could hear him halfway across the East River.

"Chickenpox," Vivienne repeated. "She caught it from a kid she did a commercial with last week. Occupational hazard."

"The hell it is!" Charles stormed. "Well, I hope you've got someone else lined up."

"Er, yes," said Vivienne, but . . ."

"But?"

"Well, it was very short notice. Everyone was busy or not interested or . . . I got Angie."

"Angie? The fat one who works in the office? Are you out of your mind?"

"Angie can look very nice when she tries," said Vivienne, hoping that for once Angie would try. "And she's a lot of fun. Anyway, it's Angie or nobody."

"Nobody would be preferable," Charles said sourly. "I promised O'Connell a good time with a pretty lady." O'Connell was a political hack from Boston, whose influence Charles was courting.

"Hey, O'Connell's no beauty himself," Vivienne countered. "He's sixty if he's a day, he spits when he talks, and he calls me 'honey.' Which, by the way, I hate a lot. Okay, Angie's no Miss America, but she's a lot better than he could do on his own."

"He does all right in Boston," Charles said sulkily.

"Yeah, in spite of his wife and kiddies. Look, I'll go over to Angie's, do her makeup, make her wear a dress . . . you can pick us up there."

Charles took down the address with bad grace and disconnected, and Vivienne began to pull together an assortment of scarves, jewelry, and makeup to try out on Angie. If Angie would let her.

An hour later, Vivienne was leaning across a rickety kitchen table in Angela's apartment, making her beautiful.

"Stop squirming!" she told Angela for the forty-seventh time.

"I hate that stuff, Viv!"

The makeup base which Vivienne had with much persuasion managed Angie to accept, had heightened the effect of her already porcelain skin. Now Viv was working on the eyes, making them glow larger and deeper. Angie's deep black hair had already been put up in a graceful twist, and her cheeks had been modeled and gently blushed. She looked faintly exotic, Vivienne reflected.

Next she went through Angela's closet, augmenting the clothes she found there with her own scarf, belt, earrings. Only when she was finished did she allow

Angela to look at herself in the warped mirror inse-
curely attached to the bathroom door.

"Who the hell is that?" said Angela nervously.

"You'll get used to being beautiful." Viv smiled at
her.

In fact, Angela looked very nice. There wasn't much
Vivienne could do about the weight, but she'd professionally de-emphasized it with tricks learned from a
hundred photo sessions. And her expert make-over led
the eye away from the body and up to the face and
hair.

By the time they passed the lobby doorman on the
way to Charles's car, Angela was feeling more confident. The doorman's double-take helped too.

Even Charles seemed surprised by the transformation, although he still hadn't forgiven Vivienne for his
not being able to offer O'Connell a date with a professional model. I don't ask much of her, he thought
bitterly. You'd think she could do this one thing for me
without screwing it up.

But the evening went surprisingly well. O'Connell
seemed to enjoy Angie's dry humor and exotic
madonna-like looks. They'd had similar ethnically ori-
ented inner-city childhoods, albeit years apart, and that
made for a certain bond. Angela's initial self-conscious
stiffness he took for an aloofness which piqued his
interest, and he found her directness and lack of pre-
tension refreshing.

Unfazed by the myriad of French-speaking waiters
at the ultra-expensive restaurant Charles had chosen,
Angela calmly ordered her dinner in English. "Duck
with cherry sauce" may not sound as elegant as *"ca-
nard à la cerise,"* but the food on the plate is the
same.

Momentarily puzzled by the vast array of forks at
each place, Ray O'Connell turned to Angie: "Is this
supposed to be for the salad?"

"Who cares!" She grinned at him, and choosing a
fork at random, dug in.

She's absolutely right, Ray said to himself, and did the same, chuckling like a naughty boy.

Who would have guessed? thought Charles. Old Angie and Ray. No accounting for tastes.

In the rest room outside the Bemelman Bar, where they'd gone for drinks and music after dinner, Vivienne repaired their faces while Angie glowed.

"Thanks so much for tonight. I'm having just the best time!"

Then a thought hit her. "What if he wants to come home with me?"

"Do you want him to?"

"Are you kidding?"

"Then say no."

"Won't Charles be mad? I know he probably wasn't too keen on my coming in the first place . . ."

Vivienne lowered her lipstick and stared at Angela in amazement.

"It's dinner, Angie. That's all you signed on for. A night on the town. Anything else is up to you. And frankly, if you want my opinion, I think you should say good-bye in the lobby. Even if you were interested, which I find impossible to believe, the man has a wife and kids in Boston."

She looked closely at Angela, who seemed genuinely troubled. "Don't let any of this impress you, sweetie," she said. "It's only money. Jeez, I invited you because I thought it would be fun for you, that's all. You can tell Ray to go to hell if you want to. Slap his face, I don't care. I was never too crazy about the guy anyway."

Angela looked very young all of a sudden, and very relieved.

"Just checking," she said. "Now who do you have to screw to get a brandy alexander around here?"

The next morning, Vivienne received two phone calls. The first was from Angela, telling her a messenger had just delivered a dozen long-stemmed red roses from Ray, whom she'd left standing in the lobby the night before. The second was from Charles, now back in Boston, admitting that the evening had gone well but asking her not to pull that kind of switch on him again.

She countered the second call with the first, and a mollified Charles promised to bring her a special surprise when they met at the New York Yacht Club the following evening. He can be so sweet sometimes, she reflected as she cradled the receiver. And he can be such a bastard.

For once, she didn't simply push away the doubts that assailed her. Was a real, whole, life with Charles truly possible, or, indeed, desirable? Lately there seemed to be more and more things, seemingly small yet somehow significant, that divided them. They were great in bed, but were they really compatible in other ways? Was it truly she herself that he loved, or was he dazzled by her beauty, by the glamour of her profession, the way his world still dazzled her? Was there enough between them to build a life on?

He can be such fun, she reflected. But sometimes he's so stuffy, so . . . proper. So afraid to put a foot wrong. Yet, especially with his money and social connections, he shouldn't be afraid to make a mistake or to live by his own rules. That bitch really did a job on him!

Elizabeth had died shortly before she and Charles had met, but Vivienne had heard enough about Charles's mother to feel both morbid curiosity and hearty dislike. She couldn't help but compare Elizabeth to her own parents: supportive, kind, unselfconscious about who they were and what they valued: honesty, hard work, caring about others. No doubt Elizabeth would have thought them rather infra dig, but Vivienne wouldn't have swapped parents with Charles for all the money in the world.

Poor Charles. Poor little rich boy. A wave of sympathy and longing swept over her, and at that moment Vivienne believed she truly loved him, loved him despite their disagreements and differences, as if there were another, better Charles deep inside.

How will she take it? Charles wondered, sipping his vodka gimlet and rating the attractiveness of his fellow members' guests. It pleased him that none were in Vivienne's league. Too bad she wasn't here with him now, so he could show her off. Absentmindedly he raised his cuff an extra half-inch to reveal more of his gold Rolex.

One of the most selective private clubs in New York, the New York Yacht Club boasted (no, it was far too well-bred to boast) one of the most magnificent clubhouses in the city. Hidden away behind a massive stone frontage designed to resemble a galleon, the interior accurately echoed the nautical theme. Appropriately named, the Model Room itself was filled with hundreds of intricately detailed scale models of sailing ships and hulls dating back to the last century. Many were famous racers, and all had been custom-built for club members. The massive fireplace, nearly twenty feet high, dominated one wall. Above, the stained-glass ceiling made the huge room seem higher still. Yet the banquette seats and tables tucked under the galleon windows at one end were curiously cozy. It was here that Charles sat, nursing his drink and idly watching the passing well-dressed throng.

The Model Room was unusually full, since many members would be attending a Library Committee dinner and lecture that evening. Occasionally a man or a couple approached him, and they had the sort of bland, well-mannered social conversation Charles was so good at and Vivienne hated. Charles knew only a few members well, and a rehash of last year's America's Cup Race complete with slides was apparently not of sufficient interest to lure them in from Connecticut this steamy June evening.

A flurry of activity drew Charles's attention to the wide stairs leading up into the room. A tanned white-haired gentleman of about sixty was heading into the

Model Room on the arm of a lean, weathered, yet handsome woman. The crowd which had gathered to greet him on his arrival thinned slightly as he tacked to port, and Charles was startled to recognize the well-known industrialist Hiram Stone. A long-time member of the club, Stone was a keen ocean racer and an avid supporter of the sport. It was natural that his appearance in the club would create a certain amount of excitement. But it wasn't simply because of Stone's celebrity value. It was because Stone was dead.

Every newspaper and magazine in the country had carried the story of his massive stroke two weeks before. His valet, who had found the body, had been interviewed at length, describing again and again how he had come into Stone's room with early-morning tea. "Stone-cold dead in his bed!" had become a comedy catchphrase, thanks to the man's media hunger and the *David Letterman Show*. Stone's children by his first marriage had been widely quoted too, especially after they declared their intention to challenge Stone's will, which left nearly eighty percent of his personal estate as well as the controlling interest in his mammoth interlocking corporations to his current wife, Claire. Stone's second in command had immediately taken over Stone's business responsibilities—apparently such an emergency measure had been arranged between the two men years ago—but refused to comment. Claire, too, had been silent. In fact, she'd disappeared. So, quietly, had the body.

And now here she was. And somehow, here was Hiram too. Intensely curious, Charles rose and made his way toward the knot of people surrounding the great man. Stone was smiling in a vague yet friendly way, like a candidate at a fund-raiser. Claire was doing most of the talking.

". . . a miracle, really . . . hard to believe, but it's true . . ."

Charles slowed his pace and listened.

". . . he'd had these attacks before, but we always kept it quiet . . . called him and he flew in at once

. . . revolutionary technique, of course I don't understand it . . .''

"Excuse me, Mr. Spencer-Moore."

One of the front desk clerks had moved discreetly
to Charles's side. "Miss Laker, sir. She's arrived."

Club rules required that members escort their guests
beyond the marble entrance hall. Thanking the man,
Charles began to make his way upstream through the
group of people still clustered around the Stones. Mrs.
Stone had turned her attention to a thin, earnest-
looking younger man wearing a club tie.

"Quite right," she was saying. "All that publicity
was very ugly. Unnecessary too, as it turned out."

She smiled radiantly at her husband.

"This is Hiram's first outing since . . . it happened," she continued, turning back to the young
man. "Here, among friends."

Now Charles was past them, descending the red-
carpeted stairs toward Vivienne, who was chatting
amiably with the desk staff. She was decorously
dressed in black linen slacks and a white silk blouse,
set off by a patterned scarf tied loosely around her
neck. Her hair was pulled up and back, revealing the
graceful curve of her neck. A softly patterned black-
and-rust blazer, worn casually unbuttoned, completed
her outfit. Charles smiled approvingly. The first time
she'd met him here, she'd worn acid-green striped leggings and an oversize black sweater tunic. He'd turned
her right around and marched her back out onto the
street.

During the two days since her double date with Angela, Vivienne had found she'd missed Charles rather
a lot. Once more she'd banished her doubts about the
viability of a future together and instead had concentrated her energies on the positive parts of their relationship.

Now she grinned as she saw him, and went forward
to meet him partway up the stairs. They kissed and he
began to compliment her on her choice of costume,
but she interrupted excitedly.

"They said at the desk that Stone is here!"

Slightly miffed, Charles stopped in mid-sentence, then gave in to the inevitable.

"He's here, all right," he said. "Let's get you a drink and then you can have a look at him."

They continued down and around the staircase, past the little room which had for many years been home to the America's Cup trophy, and down a few steps to the large dark lounge. Most of the tables were empty, but members crowded along the bar which ran the length of the room. Drinks were no longer served in the Model Room except during special parties; instead, you got your drink at the bar downstairs and then carried it up.

Here too the talk was of Stone's resurrection, but no one seemed to know any more than Charles had already heard.

"Let's go up," said Vivienne as soon as her drink was served. "I wonder if he'll remember me."

Charles looked at her in surprise. "You know him?"

"No, of course not!" Vivienne laughed. "I was introduced to him once at a party about a year ago. He tried to put his hand on my ass, but I moved too fast."

Charles looked disgusted.

"There were only about three hundred people there," she continued. "I don't really think he'll remember. I mean, it's not as though he actually made contact or anything . . . Oh, lighten up, Charles!"

"It's not funny," he said.

"Sure it is," Vivienne told him. "Happens all the time. I'm getting pretty good at taking evasive action."

"It's cheap," said Charles.

"Well, don't tell me. Tell him." And she headed for the door.

Upstairs, the crowd around the Stones had dispersed and the couple had seated themselves with several friends at the banquette Charles had relinquished when he'd gone to claim Vivienne. There were only four banquetted windows, and they were in high demand.

"Shall we dispossess them?" Charles asked with a smile.

"Evict a captain of industry? Heavens, no!" Vivienne answered. "Hey, he looks pretty good for a dead person."

"I'll just reclaim my drink," said Charles, and they made their way toward the windows looking out onto Forty-fourth Street. Stone still wasn't talking much, but he seemed to be enjoying himself, looking around at the room and the people as though to say, "By God, I'm still here!"

He studied them curiously as they approached, and smiled politely as Charles identified his drink among the bottles and glasses on the table.

"He didn't recognize me," said Vivienne mock-sadly as they retreated to a pair of club chairs across the room. "I guess ass-grabbing is nothing special to him."

Charles was not amused.

"Or maybe he's trying to leave his old life . . . uh, behind, if you'll excuse the expression," said Vivienne. "The time I met him, he was reeking, and I mean reeking, of booze. And now I see he's on Perrier. Even the blue veins in his nose are gone. Just goes to show what a near-death experience can do for a person."

Charles smiled, but only just.

"You're unusually dour this evening, sweetie," Vivienne told him, patting his hand in a way he genuinely detested. "Is my slip showing or something?"

"Just thinking," said Charles. "Nothing to do with you."

"You can't imagine how much better that makes me feel," Vivienne teased. But in fact she did feel relieved.

Suddenly Charles seemed to come to a decision. He put his hand on top of hers to prevent any more of those odious little pats, and with his free hand reached into his inside jacket pocket and brought out a small flat package wrapped in shiny pink paper. He put it in her lap, then looked steadily into her lovely, questioning eyes and spoke softly.

"Not a bracelet. Not earrings. Something far more precious than that. Open it."

Her hands fumbled blindly with the wrapping paper, her eyes riveted on his, as he continued.

"To my love, my wife-to-be. May you always be as lovely as you are today. And now you will be!"

She looked down at the torn paper and the flat box beneath it. Slowly she removed the cover and pushed aside the tissue paper. She stared in confusion, then raised her eyes again to his.

"It's empty," she whispered.

"It only looks empty," said Charles. "You see, my darling, I've given you . . . a secret. The most wonderful secret in the world!"

6

"Interesting possibilities?" said Harris with some force. "Is that all?"

Eric sighed and took a defensive forkful of baklava. He was still puzzled about what Harris actually wanted from him, but his mind was buzzing with the implications of the Talmidge research.

He'd wondered how to play this meeting. Showing excitement over spurious research could cost him the spot he was hoping for next year, an invitation to join the staff at New York General. Conservative, he'd decided. That was the way. He'd even worn a tie. But it seemed "conservative" wasn't what Harris wanted.

Harris too had debated in his mind how to approach Eric, how to draw him out without overwhelming him. Harris was aware that even his contemporaries considered him rather formidable. And many of the residents who rotated onto his service were so terrified, he often had trouble eliciting simple answers and diagnoses from them.

For this reason, though he was well-known at several excellent restaurants near the hospital, he had decided against inviting Eric to dinner, choosing instead the Greek coffee shop in which they now sat, as being less intimidating for him. But still Eric was nervous.

He studied the young man across the Formica table, his face haggard from lack of sleep, yet his eyes bright and intelligent. His black hair was slightly tousled, and his face pale in the harsh fluorescents. Good-looking, he thought, but not overly conscious of it. A lot of natural charm. A bright, maybe brilliant mind, but too self-deprecating. Well, he was young. He would grow into his looks, his mind, his life.

What he liked about Eric, Harris thought to himself, was not just that he'd graduated at the top of his class from Columbia P&S. Or that he was a diligent and caring doctor and an extremely talented surgeon. What really intrigued John Harris was the way Eric was able to take intellectual chances, to leap in oblique, untraditional directions, not just plod down the respectable by-the-book mental pathways. It was just such a leap that he sought now.

Eric sipped his coffee, which was hot and fragrant, and wondered what to say next. The silence was deadly. Eric decided to try again.

"Dr. Harris," he began.

"John," said Harris. "Call me John."

John?

"Well, uh, John," said Eric, feeling a thrill that was part elation, part panic, "the second article kind of negates the first, doesn't it? Of course, if it didn't . . . but it does, although . . ." He trailed off into silence again.

"Look, Rose," Harris said finally, "If we're going to work together on this thing, you're going to have to be brave enough to tell me what you really think. I promise you I'm not grading you, and you've already been assured a surgical position working with me in the transplant unit next year. That's confidential, of course. So why don't you tell me what the hell you're thinking."

Eric stared at Harris across his cup, then slowly lowered it, slopping coffee into the saucer. He smiled. It was a very nice smile.

"Well, uh, John . . . I've gotta tell you it's going to be hard to call you John, but I'll try . . . I'm in for next year, huh?" The smile had become a large grin. The fatigue was less noticeable.

"Yes," said Harris. "You're in. So talk."

"Okay." Eric took a deep breath, then plunged.

"The first article was very, very exciting. I mean, if he really did what he claimed to do, the possibilities are endless. I'd be jumping up and down if I hadn't read the second article, where he said he didn't do it after all. And yet . . ."

"Go on," Harris said.

"Well, I was intrigued. I mean, something about it just bothered me. So I went to the New York Academy of Medicine yesterday. They tossed him out in 1973, but they still had his file, at least part of it. And that was funny too."

"In what way?" Harris said.

"Well, someone weeded out all the scientific papers and articles Talmidge had written, even the copy of the lecture he delivered to the academy membership about his research before he went public with it. Now, why would someone do that? I mean, why not dump the whole file?"

"You tell me."

"I don't think someone from the academy did it. I think Talmidge did."

"Why?"

"So that no one would be able to review it all, years later. No one would have any second thoughts."

I was right about the boy, Harris thought. "Go on," he said.

"Well, I've thought about it all a lot," Eric told him. "At first I didn't see the connection. And then when I did, it seemed so . . . unlikely. But once you accept it as possible, it's incredibly exciting. If the man could actually reproduce a mouse, with the identical genetic structure, maybe he could figure out how to reproduce a specific organ using cells from a donor. It would match perfectly, so he wouldn't need to use antirejection drugs. Maybe that's what he's doing with Abbott."

"But he said he didn't do it," said Harris softly. "He renounced all his data, admitted that the research results he had published were fraudulent."

"That's what he *said,* yes."

Harris studied him. "You don't believe him," he said.

"Why would he lie?" said Eric. "That's what's been bothering me. I mean, if we assume he didn't clone the mouse, then he perpetrated a scientific fraud and destroyed his career just for a laugh. But look at it the other way. Let's say he did clone that mouse. Why did he withdraw his research, repudiate his results, call it fraud? Because the connection with the Abbott thing is so strong, it fits so well . . ."

Harris's eyes gleamed. "Let me tell you a little about Ben Talmidge," he said. "Maybe it'll help you, us, decide what he may or may not have done."

He sipped his coffee, marshaling his thoughts, his memories.

"Talmidge was always a rebel, not that that's bad. But he seemed to enjoy antagonizing people. He'd go out of his way to get them mad at him, even if they agreed with him. He'd create animosity for its own sake, then bask in it.

"He was a genius, no question. But he hated the establishment, just because it was there, even when it supported him, nurtured him. In fact, the more it lauded him, the more he resented it. It was actually pathological. And he was selfish too. Not about sharing credit, that never came up. He rarely worked with anyone except his 'menials'—his word, not mine—undergraduate students who did his scut work. No, he was selfish with his results. It wasn't just a matter of not wanting to help a colleague, it went deeper."

Harris paused. "Does any of this help?"

Outside, the late spring rain had begun painting streaks on the blue evening air. People were hurrying along the sidewalk, holding newspapers over their heads. Unlike yesterday's, this rain had not been forecast.

"I think he did it," said Eric quietly. "I think he got so excited, he announced it and then was sorry. Or maybe he did it once and then couldn't repeat it.

But I think he's been working on it all these years. And I'll bet you he can repeat it now.''

"And he's cloning organs,'' said Harris.

"Seems likely,'' said Eric.

"But how does he do it?'' Harris asked, more to himself than to Eric. "How does he control the cellular determination, turn a cell into a kidney or a liver or . . . And what about the growth rate? I'd love to know. I'd love us all to know.''

"Uh, of course there is another possibility,'' said Eric diffidently.

"Yes?'' said Harris. "Tell me.''

Eric told him.

The lights are bright, so bright. They spin dizzyingly above his head, yellow-white, then sway, then settle. He doesn't remember opening his eyes, but they are open, watching the lights. He doesn't want to look at the lights, so he closes his eyes and watches the echo-image dance on his retinas. Slowly, experimentally, he opens his eyes again, and turns his head to the side. The wall is softly green. A cabinet with medicine hangs on the wall. A nurse walks to the cabinet, unlocks it, takes something out, relocks it. Suddenly he remembers where he is, and a rush of pure elation tingles in his chest. He's in the hospital. Now he feels the beginnings of the pain. But he expected pain, he can deal with pain. He knows his back will be bandaged. It is the source of his pain and his joy. The pain will pass. And then everything will be better, much better.

A voice speaks and he turns a little to refocus on the man who now stands next to the hospital trolley on which he lies. He recognizes the doctor. Such a kind man.

"How do you feel, Jim?'' the doctor asks.

"Good!'' he says. "Better than when I came here.''

The doctor nods, smiles. "You will have pain,'' the doctor tells him. "But then the pain will stop.''

"I know that,'' he says.

"You will eat differently," says the doctor. "For a while, anyway. You must be careful at first. I will write down what you should not eat."

The doctor smiles down at him. "Well done!"

Jim smiles too. "I have been waiting for this day," he says.

7

The sloop swung gently at anchor, its decks wet and gleaming white in the morning sun. On board, a young man hoisted a large sailbag up through the forehatch and climbed out after it.

"I'll bring her alongside," Charles told Vivienne as he stepped smartly into the motor launch that would take him out to the *Elizabeth*. "You wait on the fuel dock with the bags."

"Yes, sir, Captain, sir!" answered Vivienne jauntily, and was rewarded with a smile and a wink. Charles was always more relaxed on the water.

She headed toward the fuel pumps with a light heart. For days the secret had been floating just under the surface of her mind, popping up from time to time and filling her with joy. What exciting news! How lucky she was! How Charles must love her!

Across the water, Charles clambered up onto the yacht and with a nod to the young man who was now hanking on the foresail, he started the engine. Vivienne could hear the whine of the electronic starter and then the deep steady "chunka-chunka-chunka" as the diesel engine thrummed to life. The young man leaned out over the bow to let go the mooring wand, which was attached by a heavy line to the deep-water mooring. "Clear!" he called, and Charles spun the wheel, turning the bow toward the dock.

Vivienne looked around at the other boats tied up along the other side of the dock. Several of them were very beautiful. Do you share my secret? she wondered, this secret that will help me and protect me in ways most people couldn't possibly imagine? She felt a sudden brief twinge of guilt as she pictured Mr. Kaplan in his hospital bed. Well, Charles was right: it would obviously be impossible for them to do it for everyone. Too expensive. Too experimental. Too . . . exclusive. Maybe someday that would change, he'd told her, but for now it had to be restricted to a group of insiders. And now she was one of them.

She turned back to the sloop, then scanned the enclosed bay. A little knot of trepidation formed in her stomach as she began to regret not having used the Scopolamine ear patches Charles had ordered for her seasickness. It looked pretty calm out there, but you could never tell.

As Charles brought the trim boat neatly alongside, Vivienne managed to catch the line he threw and sighed with relief. It was so embarrassing when she missed it. The docking line was promptly taken from her by one of several dock boys who'd come running up as the *Elizabeth* approached, and soon the boat was secured to pylons along the dock, a fuel hose hooked up to the diesel intake. Only then did Charles introduce her to the young man in white Levi's and faded denim shirt who was now coiling line on the stern.

"Chris, this is my fiancée Vivienne Laker. Chris is one of our juniors in Mergers and Acquisitions. Gonna give us a hand today."

Chris grinned and held out a slightly grimy hand. "It's a pleasure to meet you, Miss Laker," he said politely.

"Please," she said, "call me Vivienne."

Chris looked at Charles for approval. "Yes, of course," said Charles grandly. "All friends here. Get these bags aboard, would you, Chris?"

Chris had been up since five that morning, cleaning the galley and scrubbing the decks and stowing the provisions Charles had ordered him to purchase. If this was the way to get ahead in the grand old firm of

Spencer-Moore, Chris anticipated a rapid rise. An avid sailor, he'd been crewing on his family's and friends' families' boats since he was fourteen. His father's sloop was in fact ten feet longer than the *Elizabeth*, though he'd never dream of mentioning it.

"Here, let me help," Vivienne offered. She'd never sailed before she'd met Charles, and still felt rather helpless on board. "I'm not much of a sailor," she explained, "but I'm an ace at stowing gear and pouring coffee!"

"No need," said Chris pleasantly as he lifted the duffels over the lifelines. "I can handle it."

Vivienne climbed aboard while Charles signed the fuel chit, and soon they were motoring toward the breakwater. Beyond it, the horizon looked uneven against the sky.

"A little chop out there today," Chris commented. "Should be some good wind."

Oh, great, thought Vivienne, wondering if Charles had any Dramamine on board. It was hopeless to think about the patches now; she should have put them on the night before, but she hated the dizziness they produced.

Now they were past the first channel markers and Charles headed the boat into the wind while Chris raised the sails. Charles killed the engine, and the sudden silence, broken only by the flap of the sails luffing in the freshening breeze, was dramatic.

"I thought we'd head over to Cuddy Island, maybe dock at Oscar's for a late lunch. Tide's against us but it's diminishing, and it'll be well in our favor coming back."

"Sounds good," said Chris. He studied the wind vane on top of the mainmast. "We've got a nice reaching wind."

Sounds bumpy, thought Vivienne nervously, as the boat, heeled well over, headed into the chop on port tack.

"Why don't you take her?" Charles offered generously. Chris agreed with alacrity. Casually yet carefully the two men changed places in the sloping cockpit, Chris settling himself happily behind the large highly varnished wooden wheel. Charles joined Vivienne, who was perched on the high side of the cockpit, holding to the end of the winched mainsheet. Her hair blew around her face in a flurry of honey-colored strands as she turned to smile at him.

"God, I love this!" Charles sighed happily, settling beside her and leaning back against the lifelines. The water rushed along the hull with a hiss, and sunlight sparkled off the stainless-steel fittings.

"It's wonderful!" Vivienne agreed, mustering her enthusiasm. The chop had worsened, and although she felt all right so far, she knew it was nearly a three-hour sail to Cuddy Island. If only she'd used those patches! She was determined to enjoy sailing, for Charles's sake. But her tender stomach always made it a nervous business. And after the first half-hour, if she wasn't sick, she was bored.

The two men fell silent, enjoying the feel of the boat moving through the water, the sound of the wind in the sails, the damply pungent smell of the sea. Vivienne focused on the horizon. You're fine, she told herself. You'll be just fine.

She tried to distract herself by concentrating on the secret gift. She wished she could tell someone, Angie perhaps. But Charles had insisted that she tell no one. Still, it was exciting to know that she shared a secret with an ex-president, a world-famous opera singer, and many other notables as yet unknown to her. People like May-Ann? she thought, but pushed the thought away. May-Ann was not the sort of person with whom one would want to have anything in common.

"We're gonna have to tack around Green Ledge Light in a minute," Chris called.

"Right!" Charles shifted back aft of the large genoa winch and checked that the winch handle was ready in its pocket. "You call it," he told Chris. "Viv, you wanna tail?"

"Sure," she said. Charles extended his hand and

she slid down from her perch and stood leaning against the slope of cockpit. Slowly she moved past him and positioned herself to take the slack from the winch.

"Ready about!" said Chris. Holding the boat on course with a sneakered foot, he leaned across to the downwind genoa winch, and holding the sheet firmly against the winch with a flattened palm, undid the figure-eight knot which secured the sheet to the cleat. Then he took the weighted sheet firmly into his left hand; his bicep bulged as he pulled against the weight of the straining genoa foresail. Centering his body behind the wheel again, he began to turn the bow up through the wind.

"Lee-o!"

As the bow swung over into the wind, he let go the genoa sheet. It whipped off the winch and released the foresail, which crashed and flapped its way across the turning bow until Charles, pulling rapidly hand over hand, hauled it in; the boat was now heeled over on the starboard tack.

Charles took two turns around the starboard winch and inserted the winch handle.

"Ready, Viv?"

Vivienne gulped and nodded. Moving around the boat had not been a great idea, she reflected. Charles began to grind in the sheet and she dutifully pulled on the slack as it came off the winch.

Chris leaned out around the main and inspected the lie of the sail. "Looks good," he said.

Charles unlocked the winch handle and put it back in its sleeve. "Finish it off," he told Vivienne with a smile. "You remember that figure eight we practiced last time?"

Vivienne nodded and pulled her eyes off the undulating horizon. "Hold your hand flat against the winch," he directed. "You don't want to lose one of those lovely fingers . . . That's it, nice and firm so it doesn't run away from you."

She held the weighted, coiled sheet against the winch and began to lead the slack end to the cleat on the deck. She took a turn around the cleat—no, that wasn't right, where was the eight? She unwound it and tried again. The chop was worse, and she could feel the boat moving around in the swells beneath her. Concentrate, she thought.

She looked up at the horizon just for moment to clear her head, and unconsciously loosened her hand against the winch. The sheet whizzed around, burning her palm, and she jumped back and dropped the sheet. In seconds the sheet had whipped off the winch and the large foresail went flying forward off the bow, flailing and snapping, and dropped into the water.

"Shit!" Charles lunged across the cockpit and grabbed and cleated the lazy sheet.

"Take her!" Chris shouted, and pushing past a stricken Vivienne, he charged up forward as Charles jumped for the wheel and headed the boat into the wind to slacken the strain on the flailing sail.

"I'm sorry—" Vivienne began, but Charles, concentrating on the boat's heading, simply waved at her to sit down somewhere. Chris, leaning out over the bow, was frantically pulling in the wet genoa and securing it with sail ties. When the large sail was safely on board, he re-led the escaped genoa sheet aft, wound it round the winch, and handed it to Charles. Then he went forward again to release the sail ties, and came aft yet again to winch the sail into position. It seemed like hours until Charles turned back on course, but in fact it was only six or seven minutes. Chris's clothing was wet clear through.

"There are sweaters in the aft locker," Charles told him. "Don't be macho; go put one on."

Chris grinned gratefully and disappeared below.

Vivienne started to apologize again, then thought better of it. The bobbing of the boat in the swell during the sail capture had made her feel slightly light-headed.

Chris reappeared wearing a thick white woolen sweater, and balancing against the heel of the boat, he seated himself on the upwind side of the cockpit and leaned back to peer around the foresail. "Lobster pot at twelve o'clock," he announced, and Charles adjusted their course to skirt it. Vivienne watched Chris enviously. He looks very much at home, she thought. Lucky him.

They sliced through the chop for several minutes, passing an impressive Victorian lighthouse painted green and white. Fishermen in small boats with outboard motors bobbed up and down near the rocks around its base. Just watching them made Vivienne feel sick.

"Ready about," said Charles. "This tack should get us around Green Ledge and put us on course for Cuddy."

"Right," said Chris. Together they brought the boat onto its new tack; Charles did his own tailing this time, for which Vivienne was grateful.

"I could use some coffee," Charles said. "Anyone else?"

"Coffee sounds great," said Chris. He rose and started forward.

"I'll do it," Vivienne heard herself say. Shakily she stood up and walked the few steps to the cabin hatchway, determined to make some positive contribution to the day's sailing. Pushing back the sliding hatch cover, she began to climb down into the galley. She got about halfway. The swaying of the boat was far worse in the airless cabin, and a deep wave of nausea flooded over her. Her hands began to tingle. She couldn't go on and she couldn't go back. She held the handrails tightly as she swayed and gulped.

"I stowed the coffee in the sliding cupboard behind the sink," Chris called. "Find it?"

When Vivienne didn't answer, Chris went forward. "It's on the right, next to the sugar . . ." Then he saw her and turned to Charles. "I think Vivienne's ill," he told Charles. "Want me to take the wheel?"

"She's just seasick," Charles said. "She'll be all right."

Chris looked at him in amazement. He'd heard the man was cold, but to his own fiancée?

Charles must have caught the censure in Chris's expression, because at once he relinquished the wheel. "You'll feel better up here, Viv," he called impatiently as he headed for the hatchway.

"I think you'll have to help her," said Chris at his elbow, his kind brown eyes radiating concern and sympathy. He set down a yellow bucket with a rope tied to it, and went back to the wheel.

Viv turned to Charles, her face pale and sweaty. Suddenly she put a hand to her mouth. Charles grabbed for the bucket and held her steady on the steps as she retched. "I'm sorry," she moaned. "I should have put on the damn patches . . ."

Suddenly Charles's irritation turned to pity. Poor kid, he thought. She's not cut out for this. He helped her up the steps and into the cockpit. Vivienne held tightly to the bucket as he got her settled. She began to shiver and he put his arms around her.

"It's OK," he told her. "We'll go back."

Viv looked up in alarm. "No!" she said quickly. "I'll be OK in a minute."

Charles wiped her face with a handkerchief, but she pushed his hand away and leaned into the bucket again. She'll hate herself if we turn back, he thought. Chris looked at him questioningly.

"You sure, Viv?" Charles asked softly. "I really don't mind. I've been to Cuddy a hundred times."

She shook her head vehemently.

"Hold your course," he told Chris.

He held her in his arms all the way to Cuddy Island, feeling love and guilt and regret all mixed together. In the lee of the bluffs which formed Cuddy Bay, the water smoothed out and Vivienne began to recover, but Charles left her only briefly, to help Chris thread the narrow channel to Oscar's. Will she ever make a sailor? he wondered sadly. Will she be able to share with me what I love so much? Then he thought: Why should I feel guilty about all this? Is it my fault Scopolamine makes her dizzy?

Oscar's was a popular destination with the sailing

crowd, and the atmosphere was casual and convivial. Charles waved to several acquaintances, and both he and Chris ate heartily. At their urging, Vivienne managed to swallow a little salad and some bread, but the clams, a house specialty, were beyond her.

Chris gave her an encouraging smile. "Don't feel bad," he said. "You're not the first to use the bucket. And it really was rough out there."

"Better take some Dramamine," Charles told her over coffee. "Take it now. We'll walk around a little, give it a chance to work before we head back."

Vivienne downed the two little pills without argument; a repeat of the morning was unthinkable.

The island was only lightly inhabited, with public "nature paths" through large undeveloped areas. They chose the popular Cliff Walk, which took them through rising terrain of grass and thicket up to and along Cuddy Bluffs. The view was glorious.

At one point the dirt road forked and a steep narrow path descended to the beach below. Charles took Vivienne's arm to help her down, but Chris held back.

"You go ahead," he told them tactfully. "I'm going to walk out to the old Coast Guard station. See you back on board."

It was much warmer down on the beach, and Vivienne pulled off her jacket as Charles seated himself beside her on the sand.

Vivienne had been uncharacteristically quiet all afternoon. She too had been feeling guilty and sad. She was also, despite the Dramamine, worried about the return trip. As they gazed out at the sea in silence, she began to cry softly.

"What's wrong now?" Charles asked irritably. His earlier feelings of guilt had turned to resentment. Most people he knew considered it a privilege to sail with him. Look at Chris. Why couldn't Vivienne just sit back and enjoy the ride? Elizabeth had been a superb sailor.

As if reading his thoughts, Vivienne looked up sharply through her tears. "I hate sailing," she said forcefully. "I will always hate sailing. I hate all that crap about the romance of the sea and I hate having to use the damn patches or take pills all the time, and throwing up in a bucket if I don't, and I hate all those boring hours it takes to get anywhere and all those boring hours it takes to get back!" She took a deep breath. "And I hate your boat being named after your goddamn mother!" She began to sob again, her body racked with despair.

Charles was stunned and hurt. If she really hated sailing that much, she should have said so. And why bring his mother into it?

"I named the boat after Mother because she loved to sail," he told her. "She was very fond of this boat."

"You mean it wasn't too small for her? The hull wasn't too blue? The sails weren't too white? Did she make you wear a yachting blazer and a cap?"

"You've always hated my mother," he said accusingly.

"Yes," Vivienne agreed. "Haven't you?"

Suddenly horrified at what she'd said, Vivienne put her arms around him and hugged him, and he could feel her tears through his shirt.

"Oh, I'm sorry, I'm so sorry," she sobbed. "It's not your fault, or your mother's. It's just, I tried so hard to like it, for your sake, but I really do hate it all, and having her name on the boat was like the last straw or something . . ."

Charles stroked her hair as he gazed at the boats bobbing gently in the bay. "It's all right," he told her. "I understand. Not everyone likes to sail. It's all right. Really."

But they both knew it wasn't all right, really.

He thought her volunteer work trivial; she found his business deals dull. They both felt his mother's baleful influence, even from the grave. And now there was one more thing that divided them.

8

"Pressure one hundred over sixty-five and holding."

"Breathing regulated and steady."

"Can we begin? Okay, let's go in. Rose, follow me through . . . scalpel, please . . ."

Just like the movies, Eric thought to himself for about the ten-thousandth time. It never failed to thrill him, the drama of the operating theater, the dialogue, the costumes, the action. Most of all, the action.

As the senior surgical resident, Eric got his share of the action. In many hospitals that action would consist mainly of appendixes and knife wounds. But here, doctors were often generous. That generosity, coupled with Eric's superb skill with a scalpel, had provided him with a fairly adventurous year.

"Pressure's falling."

"Albumin's on the way . . . okay, that ought to hold him till the blood's ready . . ."

Today Harris had asked him to assist in a complicated renal-blockage resection, an unusual procedure Eric had read about but never seen. Eric liked operating with Harris. He still found him daunting at times, but always brilliant and surprisingly patient. Throughout the year he'd been very generous with both OR time and practical advice.

"Shit!" A stream of blood shot out, soaking Harris's surgical greens. "Tie off the fucking bleeder!" But Eric was already in there, clamping, while Millie, the scrub nurse, was sponging rapidly.

Three hours later, the operation was declared a success, and Eric was closing, tired, bloody and relieved.

Usually the attending was out of the OR the minute the resident started to close, but Harris seemed in no hurry to leave. Instead, he seemed eager to chat.

"Firmed up your summer plans yet, Rose?" he asked.

Of course Eric had firmed up his summer plans. It was early June. Hospital Summer began in four weeks. Rose was planning to sleep for three solid days, and then to spend five weeks at St. Thomas's, a new genetics-research facility recently affiliated with New York General. Surely Harris knew that. Harris knew everything.

"I hear you're going to spend some time at St. Thomas'," said Harris. "Probably sleep for a few days first, right? That suture's a little large."

The suture *was* a little large.

Eric began to correct it.

"Goddammit, Rose!" exclaimed Harris. "You're not a first-year resident! Here, let me close!"

Eric stepped back, stunned.

Harris walked forward and began to close. Everyone in the OR looked embarrassed, or as embarrassed as you could look with a surgical mask over your face.

Eric turned to leave, but Harris's voice boomed out at him: "Where in hell do you think you're going? You stay here and learn something!"

Flushing red under his mask, Eric turned back toward the patient.

"And another thing." Harris spoke in a deceptively soft voice, as though his words were intended only for Eric, yet they were clearly audible to everyone present.

"I heard what you said about Talmidge and that organ clinic of his. I think your attitude is more than deplorable. I think it's unprofessional, unethical. Any doctor who can admire something as immoral as what Talmidge is doing in Spain is not a doctor who would be happy here at New York General. And New York General will not be happy with him."

Eric stood frozen.

He'd scrubbed with Harris a number of times since their coffee shop meeting over a month ago, and neither he nor Harris had reopened the subject that now seemed to be the source of Harris's amazing outburst. Without more information, which seemed impossible to obtain, Eric had felt he had nothing more to contribute. Nor had he discussed the subject with anyone else. What in hell was going on?

Later, stripping off his scrubs in the locker room, Eric thought back over the coffee-shop conversation. He'd been excited, sure. But he was positive that at no point had he ever ventured an opinion as to the moral and ethical implications of Talmidge's work. More to the point, he and Harris had parted friends. His promised appointment for the following year had indeed materialized, been accepted and confirmed. And he and Harris had remained on pleasant if not intimate terms.

By evening the hospital grapevine had efficiently delivered the information to anyone who cared to listen that Dr. Eric Rose and Dr. John Harris had had a royal run-in in the OR and that there just might be a new staff opening for next year. Eric was mortified. He was mystified. And he was mad as hell.

That evening there were two envelopes in his message cubicle on C-119. The first was from the board of directors of the hospital, officially withdrawing their offer of a staff position in the autumn. The other was a handwritten scrawl proposing a meeting at an uptown bar at eleven that evening. It recommended secrecy. It was unsigned. It was extremely hard to read. It could only have been written by a doctor.

The Riverside Bar had seen better days. The paint was fresh and glossy, the seats unripped, the fittings shiny. Even the sawdust on the floor seemed more like a design element than a practical necessity. The whole place was neat, clean, and totally sterile. Chalk up another victory for gentrification.

Harris was seated in a rear booth, trying to look unobtrusive. He wore khaki slacks, a new blue work-shirt, and sneakers. He sipped at a beer and kept his head down. Eric spotted him at once.

Nestled in the shadow of Columbia University, the Riverside was nearly three miles from the hospital, and Rose had walked. He'd needed the air, as well as the time to think. It all seemed unreal to him. As he walked, the knot of anger that burned in his chest seemed to dissipate, which surprised him until he realized that instinctively he'd known that what had happened in the OR hadn't been real. It couldn't have been.

Eric slid into the booth across from Harris. "Okay, cowboy," he said, "let's have it."

Harris gave him a weak, embarrassed smile. "I was afraid you wouldn't come," he said.

"Of course I came," said Eric. "I came to shove your teeth down your throat."

Startled, Harris started to rise.

"Sit down," said Eric tiredly.

A girl in jeans and a Riverside T-shirt approached with a tray, and Eric ordered a beer.

"I haven't been here in years," said Harris. "Not since I was an undergraduate at Columbia. It was better then."

"It was better six months ago," said Eric. "Before they got the decorators in. Everyone goes to Lonigan's now."

The beer arrived and Eric drained half of it before looking over at Harris, who had placed a manila envelope on the damp table between them.

"I think you'd better tell me what you think you're doing," Eric said. "And then you can tell me how you plan to get my job back for next year."

"Look," Harris said, "I couldn't have told you ahead of time. Your reactions wouldn't have been right."

"How the hell do you know what my reactions would have been?" Eric answered angrily. "I might be one hell of an actor."

"I'm sorry," said Harris. "I couldn't take the chance."

"You couldn't . . . Hey, it's my life we're talking

about here!'' Eric exclaimed. ''Who gave you the right to screw it up?''

Harris pushed the envelope over toward Eric.

''It's okay, Eric. You'll have your job in September, I promise. I, uh, I know I owe you an apology. But I had to make sure everyone knew, so when Talmidge checks—and he will—''

Eric turned the envelope over, undid the clasp, and dumped the contents out onto the table. There was a packet with a rubber band around it.

''Open it,'' said Harris.

Eric pulled off the rubber band. A typewritten paper was wrapped around a sealed letter envelope, an airline ticket, a credit card, and two thousand dollars in pesetas.

''Give the envelope to a friend to keep for you. There's a letter in it to protect you in case I get hit by a truck or something. It says your being fired wasn't real and that this whole thing was my idea.''

''What whole thing?'' Eric asked. But he had a feeling he already knew.

''Get yourself a passport,'' said Harris. ''You're going to Spain.''

''Imagine my surprise,'' said Eric dryly.

Tinkle. Splash. Woosh. The Abbotts were celebrating.

Five couples were gathered in the elegant Greenwich, Connecticut, living room cantilevered out over the swimming pool, enjoying the conversation and Michelle's delicious canapés.

Jim, surrounded by well-wishers, was nursing a weak Scotch and water—against doctor's orders, but he was feeling so much better these days, he couldn't believe it would do any harm.

''Lookin' good, Jim!'' Bob Milhauser refreshed his drink at the bar behind the sofa where Jim was holding court. ''Another for you?''

''I wish!'' Jim replied. ''But Michelle'd kill me. We're on for Saturday?''

''Sure, if you're up to it,'' Bob replied. The two men had been partners on and off the course for years, and both were eager to resume their regular weekend golf game.

"I played five holes yesterday afternoon, right, Pat?" Pat Corey was the golf pro at the country club, and a longtime friend of the Abbotts'.

"Sure did," said Pat. "I won't comment on your form, though."

"I guess I kind of favor my right side a little," Jim admitted. "But I can still whip your tail, Bob!"

Michelle looked over at the men and smiled. Jim's accident suddenly seemed a long time ago. God bless Dr. Talmidge, she thought.

"So how's your brother doing, Abbott?" Pat asked.

"My brother? Oh, uh, Steven's doing just fine. Just fine."

"It must be tough for you, his being so far away," said Janet Milhauser, who had joined them. "Being such a close family and all."

"Close?"

"Well, giving you part of his own body like that. You must be very close."

"Yes, we . . . we are, in a way."

"Funny," Bob said reflectively, "I've known you . . . what? . . . ten, twelve years, and I never knew you had a brother. . . . He's never come home in all those years, not even to visit?"

"Is he back on the course yet?" Pat asked. "I mean, I naturally assume that anyone who's related to you has got to be a golf nut!"

"My brother's not interested in stuff like that . . . golf, traveling . . . The fact is," said Jim, warming to his subject, "he doesn't get out much."

"A recluse? Sounds mysterious!"

"Not at all," Jim laughed. "He just has sort of limited interests, I guess you could say. All he really likes is music."

9

The sweet sharp smell of lemon oil filled the bathroom as Angela lathered the large golden bar between her palms and spread the bubbles along her arms and shoulders. I must get that wallpaper replaced, she thought idly, noticing how the steam had curled and lifted its edges. Maybe I'll redo the whole room. Change the color scheme. Peach, maybe. And green.

She ran the lather over her upper body, luxuriating in the heat of the water and the scent of the soap. Then suddenly she froze. Slowly she brought her hand to her left breast again, pressing gently. What the hell was that?

Beneath her probing fingers was a small hard mass.

She didn't remember feeling it before. But it couldn't have grown there overnight, could it? Don't panic, she told herself. It could be anything. A cyst, maybe . . . they're not anything to worry about, are they?

Quickly she rinsed off now, all enjoyment of the shower gone. It's probably nothing, she thought with rising panic, I'm sure it's nothing. But what if it isn't? God, what'll I do?

Still wrapped in a towel, she dug out her address book and paged through it as she went to the phone. She didn't expect her gynecologist to be in his office on a Saturday morning, but she felt better doing something, anything. The answering service put her on hold for what seemed like hours, and she was too nervous to wait; she hung up and called back, but after eleven rings she gave up again. She'd try him Monday. Two days wouldn't make any difference. Besides, it was probably nothing. Nothing at all.

She probed again with her fingers. Nothing. Yeah. Sure.

The weekend went by; it was not a good weekend. First thing Monday, she called the doctor again.

David Posner was used to women panicking over breast lumps, and he welcomed it. Years ago, when women were far less aware of their own ability to detect changes in their breasts, doctors often didn't get to see problems until too late. Nowadays many women checked their breasts regularly, and although most of what they found were normal irregularities, if it took a hundred false alarms to uncover a real problem early, Dr. Posner was all for it. He didn't begrudge the time these panic exams took. He wanted his patients to live.

The woman lying on the examining table before him had sounded terrified when she'd called this morning, so he'd squeezed her into his schedule. Now he was very, very glad he had.

"I want you to have a mammogram," he said. "I'll call Dr. Zucker and set it up for today. Don't worry," he added, seeing the fright in her eyes, "not all tumors are malignant. Many—most, in fact—are benign. And I might be wrong, it could still be a cyst."

He smiled encouragingly. "Let's not jump to conclusions," he said kindly. "But remember, there's a lot we can do these days, if we have to. Get dressed, Angela, and come into my office."

Tears welled up in her eyes, but she tried to smile back.

"Give me a minute," she said. "I'll be OK."

He patted her hand reassuringly. "We don't know anything for sure yet," he said. "I just want to be cautious."

He left the examining room and stopped at his nurse's desk. "Call Zucker right now, and get a time

for Ms. Tredanari today. I don't care how busy they
are.''

The nurse looked at him inquiringly.

''Not good,'' he said. ''Tell Zucker 'today,' and
don't take no for an answer.''

A week went by. It was not a good week. She saw
Zucker. She saw Posner again. She saw Cole, the on-
cologist. Everyone was encouraging, reassuring. We
can do so much these days, they said. We caught it
early, they said. Lenox Hill Hospital, they said. A biopsy. As soon as possible.

''Tomorrow is Friday. I can do it tomorrow,'' said
Betsy Cole.

''Monday would be better,'' Angela said. ''Can I
wait till Monday?''

Cole hemmed and hawed. ''The sooner the better,''
she said. ''Still, two days more or less . . . OK, get
to the hospital by nine in the morning on Monday, but
let's get the blood work done today.''

I won't tell anyone, Angela thought. I can call in
sick Monday morning, say I have a cold or something.
Nobody has to know.

''How long will I have to stay there?'' she asked.

''I don't know,'' Cole told her. ''It depends on what
we find when we get in there. We'll send the biopsy
sample to the lab while you're still in the operating
room. If it's malignant, we'll want to go in and get it
out then and there. If it's extensive, we'll have to remove part of that breast and the lymph nodes in the
armpit.''

Angela went white; she felt dizzy. This is not happening, she thought fiercely.

''It may be premature to talk about reconstruction
at this point,'' Dr. Cole continued, ''but it might be
better to think about it now, ahead of time. If you want
me to, I can get you an emergency consult with a plastic surgeon in the next day or so. Whoever you choose
will have to be available when we do the biopsy. Also,
I'll need to make time in the operating room.''

"How long . . . will it take?"

"That's hard to say. It depends on the procedure. It could take half a hour, three hours . . . even longer. That's why it might be good to talk to somebody soon, so we can coordinate our schedules."

I don't want to talk about it, Angela thought. I don't want to think about it.

"It doesn't seem real," she said. "It's happening so fast."

Cole nodded sympathetically. "I know," she said. "But believe me, faster is better. Get another opinion if you like. But whatever you decide, don't wait. Do it fast."

"OK," said Angela. "Monday. And, uh, you better give me those names."

Dr. Cole got up and walked around the desk. She put her arm around Angela's shoulders. "We can do so much more these days than we ever could before," she said. "As long as we get it early."

"Is this 'early'?"

Dr. Cole looked serious. "That's what we have to find out," she said.

Eric couldn't decide which was worse, the forced pleasantries of fellow residents pretending they didn't know he'd been booted out, or the embarrassment and pain of being cut dead by those doctors who were into self-protection.

Eric himself suffered much from conflicting emotions during those last weeks at the hospital. Sometimes he was elated, thinking of the adventure he was about to begin, the incredible potential of the information he hoped to uncover. Often he was fearful; would Talmidge accept him, believe him? And if he didn't, what then? How far Rose was prepared to go, he didn't know himself. And always there was an undercurrent of loneliness.

Along with the cash and credit card, Harris had provided him with an open draft on a bank in Barcelona. Money was not an immediate problem. But come autumn, what then? Even if he returned with the information Harris was so eager for, would Harris really have the clout to reinstate his appointment? And if Eric failed, would Harris even try? On those frequent nights when Eric lay awake at three in the morning, unable to sleep, his doubts and fears assailed him unmercifully.

Then he woke to the hectic pulse of hospital life, a reaffirmation of his skill and enthusiasm, and felt positive and vital again. As he cut and sutured, palpated and diagnosed, made endless rounds and filled in interminable reports, he felt again as he had when Harris had first laid out his plan: he was Michael Douglas, he was Tom Cruise. He was Harrison Ford.

He bought a Spanish phrasebook and carried on halting conversations with Pete Rojas, one of the orderlies, who wrote a list of medical translations for him. No one wondered at this; they all knew he was going abroad and would try to scare up some work there for the summer; possibly, it was rumored, longer.

Now he sat on the sofa bed in his apartment, eating an apple—the only thing in the fridge if you didn't count the mold—and waited for the resident from Wichita—Wayne? Dwayne?—who was subletting the place for the summer. He'd skipped the party in the residents' lounge the evening before, which made him sad. Sure he'd bitched and moaned with the best of them, but suddenly he missed it all. For the first time in years, he had two full weeks ahead that belonged only to him. And the first few days had been curiously empty.

He checked his watch. Wayne-or-Dwayne wasn't due for another half-hour. Idly he looked around; the apartment wasn't too bad, all things considered. He'd packed away his books and extra clothing in cartons and shoved them behind the sofa. He'd cleaned the kitchenette and put fresh sheets on the bed. He'd even left a bottle of cheap Spanish wine on the coffee table as a welcoming present.

His suitcases stood by the door. Eric had arranged
to spend his weeks of freedom with two buddies from
medical school who'd gotten married last year, his old
roommate and his old dissecting partner. He hoped
his old dissecting partner was driving.

The weather had turned very warm, and Eric was
looking forward to a little R&R on Long Island Sound.
He didn't think he could live out there, as Dave and
Faye did, but at the moment it was just what the doctor
ordered.

He'd finished the apple and shot the core straight
into the wastebasket from half a room away, a small
but satisfying victory, when the intercom buzzed, and
shortly thereafter, voices and footsteps and banging on
the door announced that Frick and Frack had arrived.
He opened the door and they tumbled into the room.

Plump, cute, and freckle-faced, Dave and Faye Co-
hen resembled nothing so much as two Cavalier King
Charles spaniels. Two extremely brilliant spaniels,
Rose reflected, remembering Faye in gross anatomy,
giggling and googly-eyed and unerringly dissecting and
identifying every organ, muscle, and blood vessel.
He'd nearly fallen in love with her himself.

Faye planted a damp kiss on his cheek while Dave
pumped his hand energetically. They both talked nonstop.

". . . weatherman says sunny and warm all week
. . . no hypodermics have washed up on the beach
lately, so we might chance a swim . . . did you eat
yet? . . . sandwiches in the car . . . three-hour drive,
so let's boogie . . . Jeez, you got rocks in this bag?"

"Hey, slow down!" Eric laughed. Dave had a suitcase in each hand and Faye had taken hold of his arm
and was pulling him toward the door with grim determination. "I'm waiting for the guy who's subletting.
He should be—"

"Who? What's his name? Wayne? Dwayne? . . .
must be from out of town, nobody in New York would
name a kid Dwayne . . . wait in the car with the sandwiches. . . . Well, leave the key with a neighbor!"

Fortunately for all concerned, Wayne-not-Dwayne soon materialized, and having shown him over the apartment ("Just make a three-hundred-and-sixty-degree turn. That's it.") and handed him the key, Eric found himself comfortably ensconced in the back seat of the Cohenmobile, a five-year-old Toyota bought on time.

Heading out along the Long Island Expressway, Eric thought not for the first time how much he liked these two, and how much he valued their support. They'd be the perfect friends to hang on to Harris's letter for him, with no questions asked. When they'd heard from others about his difficulties, they'd immediately assumed Harris and the entire administration of New York General were in the wrong, and invited Eric to stay with them until things cooled off. Best of all, they hadn't grilled him about what had happened, which was a great relief. It would have been impossible to lie to them. And equally impossible to tell them the truth.

10

"Merde!"

He examined the woman with growing displeasure. Another botch job, he thought. We're going to lose her.

He specified medicines, schedules; he ordered the incisions checked and the bandages changed every two hours. The woman was delirious, the infection spreading throughout her body.

No excuse for this, he thought angrily. Years of hard work down the drain. And how do I tell the countess?

I won't, he decided.

"Bring me a culture kit!" he barked to the hovering nurse. "And send Dr. Haddad to my office! Now!"

Haddad was waiting for him when he finished. Smarmy and self-confident, he lounged in the heavy oak visitor's chair, one leg looped over its upholstered arm.

"I've just seen Nadia," he told Haddad harshly. "And sit up when I talk to you."

Dr. Haddad continued to lounge. He stared back arrogantly. "A little mistake," he said. "They happen."

"They happen too damn often!"

Talmidge rubbed his eyes with his hands; he was tired, so tired. Now he had to get rid of Haddad, which meant a double shift until Haddad could be replaced. Look at the bastard, Talmidge thought. Calls himself a doctor. No, he corrected himself, I called him a doctor. He called himself a medical student when I first met him.

"I will try to improve," said Dr. Haddad languidly. He uncoiled himself and turned toward the door, but Talmidge's voice stopped him.

"I don't want you here any longer," he said. "You will leave now."

Haddad turned around in surprise. "But you need me."

"I'll manage," said Talmidge.

"But I don't want to leave," Haddad said. "It would be wrong to make me leave."

"I'll have your things packed up and sent to you," Talmidge told him. "I want you off the grounds now."

"It would be wrong," Haddad repeated. "I would feel angry. I might say things you would not like."

Talmidge sighed tiredly. "That would be very unwise, Haddad," he said.

"An angry man is often unwise," Haddad said sorrowfully. "And his lack of wisdom can hurt many people."

It always comes down to this, thought Talmidge. Such a pity. So unnecessary. With what Haddad has learned—or should have learned—from me, he can practice medicine in some backwater, false diplomas on his walls, no problem. But he won't let go. Just like the others. So stupid.

"OK, Haddad," he said. "You can stay. But no more mistakes like the one I saw today. You understand?"

Of course I can stay, you old bastard, Haddad thought to himself. You can't risk my talking about what I've seen here. And you can't afford to lose my pair of hands, even if they're not as clever or as clean as yours.

He smiled wolfishly, and his gold molar glowed malevolently. "I understand," he said. "But I think a little bonus would help me to improve my work."

Stupid, so stupid, Talmidge thought. "Of course,"

he said, and unlocked the lower drawer in which he kept the checkbook for the account at the local bank.

Haddad's greedy eyes tried to read the upside-down figures as Talmidge wrote the check. Lots of zeros, he thought. Good.

When Haddad had gone, Talmidge dialed a three-digit number and spoke briefly. Replacing the receiver, he rubbed his eyes again. He considered for the thousandth time his unique staffing problems; he'd recruited Haddad eight months ago in a Madrid bar frequented by medical students. Five assistants in as many years; it was no good. Vassily—now, he'd been great, the best. But like the others, he'd gotten too curious, and then too greedy.

He wasn't looking forward to double shifts again, but Haddad had given him no choice. Well, it would certainly cut the mortality rate. And he could always use the parts.

"Viv, I'm so scared!"

It was Sunday morning. The two women sat around the scrubbed oak breakfast table in Vivienne's kitchen, drinking tea. An old-fashioned blue-and-white serving plate held the three carrot muffins Angela had brought in self-defense; Vivienne never had anything in the house worth eating. Now she crumbled one between her fingers, unable to swallow.

"You said that on the phone," said Vivienne. "You said that when you got here. You said that when you set the table. What you haven't said yet is why. By the way, if you'll excuse an old friend saying so, you look lousy."

Angela picked at her muffin nervously. She hadn't slept since her meeting with Dr. Cole. We have some options, Cole had said. None of the options sounded good.

"I have to tell someone," she said softly. "I wasn't going to, but I have to. I can't handle it alone." Her eyes began to fill.

"Now I'm scared. What is it?"

"They keep saying they can't be sure," Angela said, "but they know, all right." She paused. "Viv, I think I have breast cancer."

"Christ!"

Neither of them said anything for a moment; then Vivienne reached across the table and took her friend's hands in hers. She held them firmly.

Finally she spoke. "I'm so sorry, so very sorry," she said. Then, "What's going to happen?"

"I go for a biopsy tomorrow," said Angela. "Lenox Hill. Depending on what they find, they'll . . . cut."

Vivienne winced. "I'll go with you," she said.

"No, no!"

"Yes, of course I will. No, don't even talk about it. Have you told Marcella yet?" Marcella Strong was president of the Lens Model Agency.

"No, and don't you tell her either," Angela begged. "I don't want anyone to know."

"It's nothing to be ashamed of," Vivienne said.

"It's not that. Well, it is that, but it's more than that too. I don't want any of that pity stuff, where everybody looks at you like you're dying and says how sorry they feel for you and meanwhile they're figuring out how they can steal your accounts. I can't handle all that right now."

"You'll have to put in for medical reimbursement. Accounting will see your claim form . . . God, why are we talking about medical forms? Listen, Angie, the cure rate is high, it's very high these days. You're gonna be fine!"

"That's what they all keep telling me. But what I'm afraid of, what I'm really afraid of is . . . what I'll look like, after. I mean, what if they have to . . . ? I don't want to lose my breast!"

Tears were running down her cheeks; she dabbed at her face with a paper napkin. "I know I never cared much about how I looked. I never cared that I was fat—"

"You're not fat, Angie!"

"I am, I'm fat, but I never cared. So it's kind of

funny, isn't it, that the thing that scares me most is being . . . disfigured.''

''But you won't be! They do wonderful reconstructive surgery these days.''

''They told me. With implants and things. But it's still not the same. It isn't. And then there's the chemotherapy afterward. Your hair falls out and you throw up . . . I'll have to wear a wig as well as falsies!''

Angela was crying in great gasping gulps. Vivienne went and put her arms around her and rocked her; she too was crying.

Suddenly Angela felt her friend stiffen.

''Angie, it's gonna be OK,'' she said. ''No, really OK. You remember when I had that weird blood test? When they put that big bandage on my arm?''

Angela looked up, bleary-eyed, and nodded.

''Well, Charles made me promise not to tell, but it'll solve everything!''

Vivienne pulled a chair around so she could sit next to her friend; Angela looked up at her hopefully.

''He said a lot of people already know about it,'' she said excitedly. ''Rich, powerful people, people who can afford it. But it's a secret. See, Charles says that if you have one, it's in your own best interest not to talk about it. I mean, if the lab got closed down, you'd lose it. Then, if you needed a liver or something, they couldn't grow one for you.''

''What? Slow down, Viv!''

Vivienne took a deep breath and began again.

''Charles gave me a gift, a secret gift. It's a kind of genetic blueprint, he said. That's what they needed the sample for. They keep it in some lab in Spain because they're not allowed to do it here, he says.''

''Why not?''

''Who cares? It doesn't matter. The point is, with the genetic blueprint, they can sort of grow parts of you if you need them, you see? If your liver packs up, they can grow you a new one to replace it. Because they use your own genetics or something, it's just like your old one. So that's our answer!''

"You're saying that if I had a genetic blueprint they could grow me a new breast?"

"Exactly! What time is it? Damn, he's still in the air. But he's going to that political thing at the Ritz Carlton straight from the airport. Trying to make points for some corporate merger he's working on. I'll call him there!"

"I don't think that's a very good idea," said Angela cautiously.

"They're operating tomorrow, right? We don't have much time."

"Viv, I don't think I can afford all this. I mean, can you see me putting in for it on my medical insurance?" Angela was laughing through her tears.

"I can afford it," said Vivienne. "How much can it cost? They just take a tissue sample and probably do some kind of computer analysis. Charles said his father was an early investor in this thing, a big one, too. He can probably get me a discount!"

"I can't let you pay—"

"Shut up," said Vivienne firmly. "Eat your muffin. We'll get you covered!"

"Covered?"

"That's what they call it, having a blueprint. If anything happens to you, you're covered."

"You really think it will work?"

"Piece of cake!" said Vivienne excitedly.

Angela snuffled and smiled and reached for a muffin.

"Do you have any butter?" she asked.

In the hour it took to get from La Guardia to Logan, Vivienne's mood went from worry to worse. By the time the taxi reached the Ritz Carlton, she was nervous and upset. Charles had been furious she'd had him pulled off the dais to take her call. And when he'd heard why she'd phoned, he'd nearly hung up on her.

His voice had been tight and angry.

"Grab the next shuttle to Boston," he'd said. "Meet me in the hotel bar at three and we'll talk. And if you get here early, for God's sake don't come up to the ballroom, just go to the bar and wait. Got that? And Vivienne, if you ever pull me off a dais that way again . . . !'' Bang went the receiver on Charles's end, the unspoken threat reverberating in her head.

Now she sat hunched in a wing chair in a corner of the elegant wood-paneled hotel bar, dressed in the same blue slacks, pink striped shirt, and white Top-Siders she'd worn at breakfast. A club soda with a twist of lemon stood alongside a dish of mixed nuts on the small zinc-topped table in front of her. She'd been waiting half an hour, and her mood had not improved.

At last Charles appeared, looking substantial and confident in a dark blue three-piece custom-made suit and a subtly striped Harvey and Hudson shirt. A New York Yacht Club tie completed his power outfit. In her current mood, even Charles's clothes seemed slightly threatening.

But when he saw her looking up at him like a forlorn and repentant child, his face softened and his eyes smiled. Going to her, he kissed her forehead in forgiveness.

"I'm so sorry, Charles," said Vivienne. "I know I shouldn't have called you the way I did, but . . ."

"Actually, you did me a favor." Charles smiled. "They were just about to ask for donations."

Pulling his chair close to hers, he ordered a brandy and soda from the hovering waiter, then turned back to Vivienne. "Start from the beginning," he said.

But as she told him about the events of the morning, and how she planned to help Angela, his face darkened.

"It's not that easy," he said.

"But, darling, why not? You told me it was a blueprint. Well, why can't we get one for Angela? If it's money, I'll pay for it—"

"Of course it's not the money, Viv. It's . . . well, it takes time to, uh . . ."

"To what?"

"Well, to activate the blueprint."

"How much time?"

"Well, er . . . years. Two years."

"Two years?" Vivienne was astounded. "But you told me . . ."

"I said what I was allowed to say."

"Allowed? Charles, what is all this?"

"I told you it was a secret. Well, it is. And it's important that it remain a secret. You told Angela—yes, I know, for a good reason—but still, if she talks, it could hurt us all. Listen to me."

He marshaled his thoughts as he took a long pull at his drink.

"My father was one of the investors in the lab, the Reproduction Institute it's called. I told you that already. It could have saved his life if they'd been up and running sooner. But by the time they were ready to start . . . activation, he'd already had his heart attack. And the, uh, activation time was nearly three years then.

"We can take a culture on Angela, start her blueprint, but it'll be two years before she can use any parts. Still, if you want to—"

"Wait a sec," Vivienne interrupted. "What parts?"

Charles looked away. He studied the drapes, the upholstery.

"Charles?"

"It's not just a blueprint, exactly," he said finally. "It's . . . cells. They cultivate your cells."

"If it's cells, why did you say 'parts'?"

"The cells . . . they're biologically organized."

"Tell me what that means."

"It means that they're alive."

Vivienne stared at him. "Alive?"

"It starts with a few cells. It grows. As long as I keep paying the maintenance fees, they'll keep it for you."

"And if you don't?"

"Don't worry about that . . ."

"I want to know!"

"Ownership reverts to the Institute."

"And?"

"They'd probably destroy it. Or sell the parts. It's just some cells, after all. But," he reassured her, "that almost never happens, darling. And I've set up a trust fund, irrevocable. The fees will always be paid. Don't even think about it."

"It seems so . . . so creepy!"

"Someday it might save your life, Viv. It would have saved my father's. Every day, people go on living who would have been dead without it. Think of it that way."

"Yes," Vivienne said. "Yes, I see . . . The thing is, it's a little more . . . substantial than I realized. But if it's not actually . . . I mean, if it's just a bunch of cells . . ."

Slowly Charles unbunched the muscles in his shoulders; it was going to be all right.

"How about an early dinner before you go back? Or can you stay over?"

"I'll stay. I'd really like to. I don't have anything urgent to do tomorrow . . ." Then it hit her. Angela.

"My God, I forgot. I actually forgot about her! I have to go back to Angela. Jesus, I have to call her. What'll I tell her? Damn! She was so happy when I left her, when I promised she could grow a new breast . . . but she still can, can't she, Charles? It'll take a while, but if she has the reconstruction now, she can wait . . ."

Vivienne was excited again. "It's not a complete no, is it?" She looked at Charles beseechingly. "I can give her hope."

"Yes, you can give her that. You can also tell her to keep her mouth shut."

"Okay, but why? I mean, all cells are alive, aren't they? Who would care what I do with a few of mine?"

"I would, darling." He leaned over to kiss the tip of her nose. Then the hardness came back into his face, and he looked at her steadily for a very long second. "Tell her," he said firmly. "And that goes for you too."

Then, putting some bills on the table, he stood up.
"Come on," he said. "I'll drive you to the airport."

She called Angela as soon as she got home, worried
sick over how she would take this new disappointment. But as it turned out, Angie had talked again
with the plastic surgeon and decided on immediate reconstruction.

"They'll put in this sort of little balloon thing," she
explained. "It's called a tissue expander. It'll sort of
puff me up there, you know?"

Vivienne said nothing. She also was suffering from
too much reality.

"The other choice is an implant," Angela continued, "but there are some real problems with those.
Anyhow, it won't be like a real breast, but at least I
won't be lopsided." She attempted a laugh, unsuc-
cessfully.

"Well, I have good news too," Vivienne told her.
"I think I can convince Charles to culture you for a
blueprint as soon as you're out of the hospital. For
futures."

"That's great, Viv. But, well, let's see how I feel
about it . . . afterward."

Vivienne looked surprised. This was quite an attitude change.

"Dr. Cole called me today," said Angela. "We
talked a lot, and I feel much better about everything.
She thinks it's contained, and they'll probably be able
to get all of it. Don't get me wrong—it's still scary as
hell, but . . . all that stuff of Charles's about living
cells and don't tell anybody, that's kind of scary too."

"You think so?"

"Yeah, I do. But that's just my mood at the moment. Don't mind me."

Early the next morning Vivienne picked up Angela
at her apartment, and they taxied to Lenox Hill Hospital. No one should do this alone, she thought.

The morning was hurts-your-eyes-sunny, and still cool. It was one of those mornings when for about fifteen minutes the city looks fresh and clean.

"I love this city," said Angela.

They passed a young woman who was encouraging a large black dog to defecate at the base of a newly planted tree. Nearby, a janitor poked ineffectually at a smelly pile of debris spilling from several ripped black plastic garbage bags.

"I hate this city," said the taxi driver.

At a red light, a well-dressed man approached the cab. Looking inside, he yelled, "Fuck Bloomingdale's!"

"I live in Queens," the cabdriver said. "I wouldn't live here if you paid me."

"Actually, I agree with him," said Angela.

"You said it!" said the cabdriver.

"Not you. Him." Angela indicated the man with the grudge against Bloomingdale's, who was now delivering his message to no one in particular.

The light began to change, and the driver stamped hard on the accelerator. Swinging across several traffic lanes, he beat out a fast-moving bus by six inches.

"The whole city is nuts," said the driver. "You gotta be crazy to live here."

After Angela had registered, they went up to the small, neat semiprivate hospital room. Its other patient, an older woman who spoke only Spanish, was post-op and due for release later in the day.

They talked about small, unimportant things until Dr. Cole came in for a pre-op check. Viv liked Dr. Cole right away. She was concerned and caring, and obviously highly respected by the hospital staff.

When Vivienne kissed her friend good-bye, there were tears in her eyes, but Angela's were dry and determined. I never knew she was so strong, thought Vivienne. God, I hope everything goes OK for her.

* * *

Exhaustion hit her when she got home, and kicking off her shoes, she lay down on the unmade bed. I'll just rest a moment, she thought, and closed her eyes.

She imagined Angela on a hospital gurney, being wheeled into the operating room. The anesthesiologist spoke to her and started an IV in her left arm. Suddenly it was Vivienne's arm, and they weren't putting things in, they were taking things out.

A voice behind a screen said, "We need more cells!" and she felt something leave her body in a great stream.

Then she was lying on a flat iron bed in a darkish room, looking up at a murky gray blob which floated in the air above her. It rolled like a storm cloud, and like a cloud, its shape was changing.

It came lower, and she could make out eyes, hot red eyes glowing like fires. The thing came closer as the face took shape: a nose, a forehead . . . strands of cloudlike material began to stream off the head like hair. It was almost upon her now, and the face resolved itself into a recognizable visage. My God, she thought, it's me!

Without warning, arms shot out from the body of the apparition and reached for her and grabbed her and held her, and she screamed and woke up, tangled in the bedsheets and covered with sweat.

11

"Jesus, that sonofabitch behind us is using his high beams. I can hardly see!"

"He's signaling you, Dave. He's trying to tell you to get over. He'd like to go faster than fifteen miles an hour."

Faye was on call at the hospital, which put Dave at the wheel of the Cohenmobile, and Eric was not at all sanguine about his ability to survive, much less catch, Iberia's evening nonstop to Barcelona.

"Traffic in our lane is doing at least thirty, Dave. He wants you to speed up or move over."

Vroom. Honk! Screech.

"Are we still alive?" said Eric.

"Stop complaining," said Dave. "All I need is practice."

" 'As the surgical resident said to the next of kin.' I wonder what time it is."

Swerve. Honk! Screech.

"Jesus, Dave, I have a watch! Keep your eyes on the road!"

The sluggish traffic bottlenecked at the feeder into the Van Wyck Expressway, then speeded up slightly once the merge was completed.

"You lucky duck," sighed Dave. "Romance. Adventure. Foreign intrigue."

Eric smiled to himself. You should only know, he thought.

"I don't think it'll be very exciting," he said aloud.

"It just seemed like a good idea to put some space between me and General until Harris cools down."

"Not being on call for two whole months!" Dave swung jauntily across two lanes of traffic toward where he imagined the airport exit would be. It wasn't.

"Stay where you are," Eric begged as Dave began swinging back through the two middle lanes. Drivers in the other cars were stomping on their brakes and swearing. "This lane'll take you right into the airport. Trust me. Just look for the Iberia sign . . . No! I'll look for it. You drive."

Now safely belted into a window seat, a glass of red wine and a tray with brown food of no known origin in front of him, Eric felt fine. Never mind that terrorists hijacked Americans out of the skies every day, thunderstorms were forecast halfway across the Atlantic, and both pilots had just ordered fish. He was out of the Cohenmobile.

The flight attendants came through the cabin with headsets for the movie, and he rented one. He'd missed their announcement of the title, but it didn't matter. With the kind of hours he'd been putting in this year, chances were excellent he hadn't seen it.

He'd have another drink, he thought. Eat some plastic dinner. Watch the film. Doze. Test his glucose tolerance with an airplane breakfast. Assuming he survived all that, he'd stagger off the plane into a brand-new morning and try to figure out what the hell to do next.

"Welcome to the Scottsdale Inn, Dr. Harris. If you'd just fill out this registration card . . ."

Harris liked medical conventions. New information, old faces. A good combination.

"Here's your key, sir. Room 1615. We'll have your luggage sent right up. If there is anything we can do to make your stay more pleasurable, please let us know."

Pleasant, Harris thought automatically, not pleasurable. Unless room service includes loose women.

"John!"

A voice he recognized stopped him a few steps from the elevator, and he turned to see Sam Robertson, an amiable balding cosmetic surgeon from Utah. The two men had met at a convention on microsurgery several years back, and their paths had crossed once or twice since then. Although they didn't keep in touch between these chance meetings, it was always good to see each other again.

"Just checked in?"

"Yes. You?"

"Got here this morning. Had a swim, lunch by the pool."

"A swim sounds good," said Harris. "Where's the nearest pool?" The convention center was large and sprawling.

"Where are you . . . 1615 . . . that's the East Tower. I'm West. There's a pool in between. Take the elevator to LL, that's lower level, and hang a left. You can't miss it, it's the size of Lake Superior. I'll meet you there. Twenty minutes do it for you?"

"Fine," said Harris, and followed his luggage onto the elevator.

The room was large, and well decorated in muted tones of blue and beige. A large round table and four chairs were placed in front of sliding glass doors opening onto the small terrace. A mock-Regency tallboy hid the television set. The bed was king-size, and a small dressing room led into the bathroom. Best of all, the red message light on the phone wasn't blinking and the phone itself was silent.

Tipping the bellboy, he stripped off his clothes and dug his bathing suit out of the suitcase. He checked himself out in the long mirror on the dressing-room door. Not bad for fifty-four, he thought. Not great, but not bad.

Sam was waiting for him when he got down to the pool. He's put on some weight, Harris thought. Sam had been busy; two large yellow hotel towels graced the chaises facing the sun, and on the low table nearby stood two rum punches garnished with pineapple.

"I'm always warning my patients about solar exposure," Sam said, rubbing a white lotion onto his balding scalp, "but at times like this I can appreciate why they don't always listen. Want some?" He tossed Harris a tube of sunscreen with the words "Sample—Not For Resale" prominently stamped on it.

"Thanks," said Harris, "but I think I'll have a swim first."

The water was cool and invigorating, the air hot and dry. As Harris stroked methodically through the water, he felt the tension of the past weeks wash away. It had been hard on Rose, he knew, but hard on him too. Often he'd had doubts about his plan. What if they were wrong about what Talmidge was doing? And if they were right, would Eric be in danger? That was why it had been so important for him to keep up the appearance of anger. For Eric's sake. God knew he'd come close to blowing it any number of times. When Eric did that superb colon resection last Tuesday, he'd wanted to clap him on the back and buy him a drink instead of scowl and stalk away. And was he really sure he could get Eric's appointment back for him in the fall? Well, they'd passed the point of no return.

He rolled onto his back and floated, looking up at the cloudless sky, and felt the tightness drain from his shoulders, his neck . . .

Later he and Sam sipped their drinks, crunching the pineapple and discarding the preserved cherries (". . . pure poison, John, oughta be outlawed!"), and traded shop talk. The pool area began to fill with afternoon arrivals.

Mimi Young, a pretty black doctor from Detroit, joined them briefly. One of the organizers of the meeting, she was eager to make sure everyone was pleased with the hotel, the accommodations, the service. She'd received much favorable national newspaper coverage recently for her work in the field of public medicine; rumor had it she was ripe for political appointment.

Harris watched her move away to another group, admiring her firm high bottom and large breasts.

Noticing, Sam smiled in amusement. "Very nice. Still, it's hard to know what's real and what isn't, these days!"

Harris looked at him in surprise. It had never occurred to him to wonder, or care.

"Don't mind me," said Sam. "Occupational hazard. I've done those procedures so often, I automatically think the worst."

"Worst? Since when does a plastic surgeon cast aspersions on his art?"

"Sorry. Bad choice of words. No, when I see something that good, I just can't help looking for the scars."

"Bet you don't often find them, though. Not with the quality of work being done these days."

"Oh, I don't know. You have to know where to look."

"Well, I've seen Mimi around these conventions for at least, oh, five years now," said Harris defensively. "She's always looked good."

Sam laughed. "Go get her, tiger!" he said. Harris gave him a look. "Come on, John. It was just a joke."

An uncomfortable silence fell. Christ, Sam thought, I'd forgotten how stiff John can be about some things. He searched for some way to change the subject.

"Talking about lifts," he said, "I saw a most interesting case a couple of months ago. Patient of mine I'd done several lifts on over the years, started when she was only forty-one. Anyhow, about two years ago she asked me to do another lift, and I told her frankly that her skin wouldn't stand up to it. It was so stretched out, another lift was just impossible. She was nearly sixty at that point, looked late forties, but that wasn't good enough."

Harris idly watched Mimi approach a third group, chat and laugh with them, move on. He felt sorry he'd barked at Sam; the man hadn't meant any harm, it was just his way. Yes, and barking is mine, Harris thought sadly.

"She was angry, of course, and upset, as though it was my fault. I said no reputable surgeon would operate on her. She said she'd see about that. We, uh, we didn't part friends, you might say."

Harris had stopped listening. The sun felt good on his chest and arms, and the warm breeze ruffled his hair. He spent so little time out-of-doors. His mind drifted. . . .

". . . Barcelona, and I had to admit she . . ."

"What did you say?" Harris was suddenly alert, the tension in his neck blooming.

"Barcelona," Sam repeated. "She'd had it done just outside Barcelona. Quite incredible. I mean, I could see the faint scarring around the hairline, but on the face itself . . . well, the skin was fresh, young. Not stretched at all."

"How did they do it?" Harris asked.

"Damned if I know," replied Sam. "And that's what puzzles me. Frankly, it's a medical impossibility. I tried prying information out of the woman, but she claimed she knew nothing about their techniques. Nonsense, of course; any reputable surgeon would have explained the procedure beforehand."

Sam paused, scowling. His professional pride had been injured, certainly; the woman had fully enjoyed scoring off him. But that wasn't all that bothered him.

Harris was silent.

"It's just so hard to believe that someone could develop a technique with results as dramatic as that, and we wouldn't know about it in the States," Sam said. "It's . . . it's odd."

Then he brightened. "Enough of mysteries," he said. "What's new in your neck of the woods?"

I had a transplant patient whose brother offered to donate a kidney on condition the operation take place in Barcelona, thought Harris. I pretended to fire my star resident on the chance the head of that hospital would take him in and show him what's going on. I may have ruined his career. Or we may be on the trail of one of the most revolutionary discoveries in modern medicine. And now you've given me another part of the puzzle.

"Not much," said Harris. "Pass the sunscreen, will you?"

12

Vivienne slept most of the way to Boston. She'd had to be on location at six that morning for a bathing-suit feature, and although it was only two in the afternoon now, she felt drained and exhausted.

Well, Charles was feeling even worse, she thought.

"Maybe," a recovering Angela had told her from her hospital bed. "And maybe not."

"Oh, Angie, he sounded so pathetic and lonely," Vivienne had protested, tossing things in an overnight bag while gripping the cellular phone between ear and shoulder. "Summer colds can make you feel so rotten."

"I take it Charles does not suffer flus gladly."

"That was awful!" Vivienne moaned. "You must be getting better! But actually you're right, he's miserable when he's sick. And this is the least I can do, after the way he took care of me on the boat."

"Ah, the dreaded *Elizabeth*!"

" 'Dreaded' is right!"

Now the dark blue Lincoln slowed, and Vivienne, her sleeping mind registering the change, came slowly awake. The tires crunched over the decorative loose white gravel of the circular driveway as the car pulled up in front of the rambling old colonial home Charles had shared with his mother until her death.

Still slightly muzzy, Vivienne signed the driver's receipt and stepped out of the car onto the driveway, promptly turning her ankle on the loose stones. What ever happened to good old asphalt paving? she wondered.

The driver placed her overnight bag on the porch and drove off as Vivienne looked around her. She'd seen photos of the mini-estate, but had never visited it. The house was a perfect example of its type, right down to the antique wicker porch furniture set at careful angles on the wide veranda. The grounds had that ultra-manicured look that implied money and time and only the gardener's footsteps. It all felt rather like a movie set.

Alerted to her arrival by the sound of the car, Silverton opened the door within seconds of her ring and welcomed her inside. Silverton was the epitome of Elizabeth's idea of an English butler: slim, tall, and pale, well past middle age, with slightly bulging watery blue eyes and an air of quiet desperation. She'd imported him from London many years before and installed him in the small apartment over the four-car garage. In Elizabeth's mind, butlers had no personal lives, and so Silverton was kept in virtual isolation, a remunerative but lonely existence. He'd been pathetically grateful when Charles had decided to keep him on after Elizabeth's death, and during the intervening year had managed to acquire a dog, a mistress, and a sports jacket.

"Happy to meet you, Miss Vivienne," Silverton told her with a smile. "Mr. Charles is napping, but I expect he'll wake soon. Meanwhile, perhaps you'd care for a tour of the house or a drink? I've just made some lemonade."

"Lemonade?" said Vivienne, amused.

"Mrs. Spencer-Moore always said there was nothing better for a cold than hot lemonade. You, of course, may prefer it iced."

Vivienne's smile faded at the reference to Elizabeth. Now don't start that again, she told herself firmly. "Iced lemonade would be wonderful," she said aloud. "And I'd love a tour."

Setting her carryall to one side, Silverton led her

along the large paneled entrance hall to the magnificent drawing room with its Adams mantel. Above it, an impressive portrait of Elizabeth dominated the room. Beyond was a formal dining room done in dusty blue. Across the hall were a morning room in shades of dove gray and ivory, and a cozy masculine study filled with open file boxes. The hall ended at the door to the large contemporary kitchen, warm with stripped pine and butcher block. A pitcher of lemonade and glasses stood ready on a bright red tray.

"Shall I bring it to the drawing room?" asked Silverton, lifting the tray.

"I'd just as soon stay here," said Vivienne, thinking of Elizabeth gazing chillingly down from her frame. "Would that be all right?"

"Of course." Silverton poured her a glassful of lemonade as she seated herself in the country-pine chair. "If you need me, I'll be in there." He indicated a small door leading to a butler's pantry lined with cabinets.

"Why don't you join me?" Vivienne said. "I'd like to hear about Charles. Did the doctor say anything to you about his condition?"

Silverton looked surprised but pleased. "I, er, don't know whether, uh . . ." His eyes flickered upward in the direction of Charles's bedroom.

"Charles is sleeping," Vivienne said with a smile. "And I'll never tell. Please sit down. How is he?"

Silverton seated himself across from her. "May I?" he asked, indicating the pitcher. When Vivienne nodded and smiled, he filled a second glass and took a delicate sip. "Mr. Charles has got the flu," he told her. "But then, you know that."

"Is he very uncomfortable?"

"Well, a summer cold *can* be very uncomfortable, of course," said Silverton. "But it is, after all, only a summer cold."

"In other words, he's being a pain in the . . . er, difficult."

Silverton smiled. "I've known Mr. Charles for a

very long time," he said. "And he has many wonderful qualities, as you know. But—"

"But not when he's sick."

"Oh, I expect you'll brighten him up a bit. He's been looking forward to your visit."

From somewhere nearby came a loud buzzing noise. Silverton rose. "He's awake." He opened a panel set flush into the wall and flicked one of a number of switches; the buzzing stopped.

"That would drive me crazy," Vivienne said.

"You get used to it." Silverton shrugged. "Shall we go up?"

They mounted the magnificent central staircase with its gracefully curving banister. At the top, a wide landing gave onto a long hallway which ran from one end of the house to the other. Doors—bedrooms and bathrooms—opened onto the hallway. There seemed to be a lot of them.

"I've put you in the Ivory Room," Silverton told her, indicating a partially open door through which Vivienne glimpsed the edge of a white marble fireplace and a pale silk-lined wall flooded with sunlight. "I'll bring your things up straightaway. Mr. Charles is down here."

He led her along the opposite corridor and knocked at a nearly closed door. "You've got a visitor, Mr. Charles," he announced.

From behind the door came a prolonged rustling sound followed by a brief silence. "Come in," a voice croaked weakly.

Silverton winked at Vivienne and swung the door wide. Charles lay in state in a huge four-poster bed, propped against a sea of pillows. Red damask draperies had been pulled across the high windows, leaving the room in semidarkness. As Vivienne approached him across the intricate Chinese silk carpet, she smiled as she spotted the newspaper he'd hurriedly discarded upon her arrival. No doubt the bulb in the now-dark bedside lamp was still hot.

The discreet Silverton disappeared as Vivienne
hugged Charles, then leaned back to study him.

"Poor baby," she said. "You look awful."

"I feel awful," he told her. "I'm glad you're here."

Again she hugged him, but he pushed her away a
little. "Don't catch this thing," he warned. "It's
deadly!"

"I don't care," she said.

"Well, in that case . . ." He grabbed her and wrestled her onto the bed on top of him, kissing her face,
her neck, her breasts.

"Damn blankets!" she exclaimed, kissing him back
and laughing.

"Damn clothes!" he retorted, slipping his hands
under her blouse.

"But surely you're too sick to make love," Vivienne
teased him.

"On the contrary," replied Charles. "They say it's
the only thing that'll save me!"

Later Vivienne brought Charles downstairs for tea.
They gave Silverton the evening off, and Vivienne
hunted up a canister of Darjeeling and a box of ginger
wafers. To Charles's surprise, she set out the cups and
saucers on the kitchen table.

"Are you sure you want it in here?" he asked. "I
could carry everything into the drawing room."

"Oh, let's stay in the kitchen," said Vivienne. "It's
. . . homier."

"It *is* cozy," Charles agreed, looking around him.
He couldn't remember ever having had a meal in the
kitchen. It was kind of nice, he thought.

"Did Silverton give you the tour?"

"Yes, he did. Oh, Charles, it's such a wonderful
house! Everything in it is so beautiful."

Charles looked pleased. "Actually, it's been kind of
a mess ever since Elizabeth died," he said. Vivienne
winced; she'd never get used to Charles referring to
his mother by her first name. It sounded so . . . so

removed. Precisely what Elizabeth had intended, she decided.

"It's taken me so long to sort through her things," Charles continued as Vivienne poured the tea. "Her bedroom and sitting room are still full of stuff. And there are cartons of papers in my study. I was just starting to go through them when this flu thing hit me."

They chatted companionably for a while, but Charles soon grew weary and she helped him back upstairs and tucked him in. She sat beside him as he dozed, reading the newspaper he'd discarded. She must have dozed off too, because they were both suddenly awakened by the shrilling of a phone on the small antique table that served as a nightstand.

Vivienne reached for it and listened for a moment, then turned to Charles, who was making impatient noises. "It's your office," she told him. "They need some papers or something."

Charles sighed and took the phone from her. "Yes, hello," he said impatiently. "What is it?" His voice was thick with sleep and sickness.

"I'll get you some water," Vivienne mouthed silently, and went in search of his bathroom. When she returned, tooth glass in hand, Charles had finished his conversation and was again collapsed against the pillows. He looked tired and pale.

Vivienne extended the water, but he waved her away. "Damn," he said. "Sorry, not you. I had a bunch of files sent over when I got sick. Now they need some information in one of them."

"Where is it?" Vivienne asked, looking around the room. "Can I get it for you?"

"It's not here, it's downstairs. In the study."

"Okay."

"Ingersoll Bank. Merging it with Continental. Major coup, if we can pull it off. Working on it for months. Everything came over in a file box. Look under I."

Vivienne put the glass of water on the nightstand. "Ingersoll Bank," she repeated. "I'll be right back."

She descended the stairs and entered the hall. Which way to the study? Oh, yes, back here. She passed the morning room and had her hand on the knob of the study door when Charles's voice rang out from above.

"Stop!" he shouted down to her.

Startled, she hesitated, then went back to the foot of the stairs. Charles loomed above her, grasping the banister rail. "Are you all right?" she asked, concerned. He looked so strange.

"Don't go into the study!" he said forcefully.

"But the file—"

Slowly Charles came down the stairs, his eyes feverish. "I'll find it," he told her. "Go wait upstairs."

"You're not well," she protested. "Let me—"

"No. Upstairs. Wait." He brushed past her, then turned back when he reached the study. "Upstairs," he repeated, then added softly, "Please."

Somewhat shaken, Vivienne climbed the stairs again. Why should Charles want to keep her out of the study? Silverton had shown her the room when she'd arrived; it had looked perfectly harmless. A desk. Cabinets. File boxes. Stuff from the office.

He's not feeling well, she told herself. People get testy when they're not feeling well. To hide her annoyance, she picked up the newspaper and began to scan it again. Eventually an exhausted Charles returned with a fat beige file and climbed into bed. Vivienne looked at him severely.

"You'll give yourself pneumonia, running around like that," she told him. "If you didn't think I could find it, you could have waited for Silverton."

"Silverton won't be back till late," Charles said. "Anyway, nobody knows my filing system." He sneezed four times, and looked at Vivienne penitently. She extended the tissue box in silence.

Charles blew his nose mightily. "I'm sorry," he told her. "I just feel lousy."

"I know," she told him. "I forgive you." She

kissed him gently on the forehead. "Do you really have to call the office back today? It's nearly six. Can't it wait till tomorrow morning?"

Charles sneezed again. "Sure," he said. "It'll wait." He reached for her hand and squeezed it. "I think I just might sleep some more. Would you mind?"

"Of course not," she said. "Sleep as long as you can. I know where my room is. I'll make myself comfortable, maybe read for a while. I could use an early night too."

Charles smiled at her. "It's for your own sake," he murmured, turning his cheek against the pillow. His eyes closed.

"What's that? What's for my own sake?"

But Charles was asleep.

Vivienne's overnight bag had been unpacked and her clothes neatly distributed between closet and dresser. Assorted light reading filled the built-in bookshelves to one side of the fireplace, and a chaise was strategically placed to catch both the last rays of the sun and the light from a brass reading lamp. A large bowl of dried hydrangeas, blue and white, dominated the round table in front of the high windows.

Vivienne looked out over the rolling lawn to the woods beyond. It was very peaceful. The sun was nearly down and she drew the soft silk draperies and turned on the reading lamp. Then, turning her attention to the bookshelf, she selected a novel and settled herself in the chaise.

She read for a while, but couldn't concentrate. Why didn't Charles want her in the study? From somewhere a clock struck eight; had she really been reading for two hours? Perhaps she'd dozed off.

Hungry, she decided to see what secrets the refrigerator might reveal. Charles's door was closed and no light seeped from beneath it. Good, she thought. He needs to rest.

The house was darker now that the sun had set; the

ceilings seemed higher, the shadows longer. Silverton had left several lights burning in the rooms downstairs, but the hallway to the kitchen was dark.

Quietly, so as not to wake Charles, Vivienne made her way to the kitchen and eventually found the light switch. A cold roast chicken and a salad had been left ready for them in the fridge, and Vivienne set out her small feast on the kitchen table, propping her book against a knife rest. When she finished, she carefully cleaned up after herself and made a cup of tea. Then she thought of her cheerful bedroom with its flowers and its chaise, and decided to take the tea upstairs.

She moved slowly and carefully through the darkened hallway so as not to spill her tea on the pale carpeting. The door to the study was firmly closed now, and again she wondered about Charles's sudden aversion to her entering the room. She passed the morning room and then the drawing room. Glancing in, she was struck by the formidable strength of the face that looked back at her from above the mantel. Elizabeth would never have approved of carrying one's own tea, she thought with amusement. Face it: Elizabeth would never have approved of her.

Thinking idly about Elizabeth, she began to mount the stairs to her room. She was nearly at the top when it hit her: what was that Charles had said? Something about Elizabeth's papers . . .

He had just started going through her papers when he'd gotten sick . . . the house was kind of a mess . . . all those file cartons in his study . . . cartons of Elizabeth's papers.

Was that why he didn't want her inside? Yet why should Elizabeth's papers be of any concern to her?

It's for your own good, he'd said as he'd fallen asleep. What was for her own good? Not going into the study? Not reading Elizabeth's papers? But she'd never intended to.

Slowly she turned around and descended the stairs again. This is silly, she told herself. He was just feeling rotten. It's a coincidence. Yet she continued to make her way along the hall to the study door.

She thought it might be locked, but it wasn't. Cautiously she pushed the door open; the wooden shutters were closed and the room was dark. Her searching hand found a switch and suddenly the room was flooded with soft light. She stood for a moment, surveying the open file boxes which crowded the room. I shouldn't be doing this, she thought.

She walked around the room, staring at the boxes. Where to start? Most of the boxes seemed filled with miscellaneous paper: letters, receipts, printed notices of various kinds. But in several boxes on the desk, file folders had been set up and labeled in a strong masculine hand: Charles's work. The folders had been arranged in alphabetical order. She flicked through the folders in the first box: Bantry Financial . . . Dexter-Hoving . . . these must be the files he'd had sent over from the office, she decided. This is where I would have found the Ingersoll file. So what's the big deal?

She turned her attention to the file box next to the office box. It too had alphabetically arranged file folders: Balenciaga . . . Correspondence, Social . . . Flowers by Renny . . .

Vivienne was puzzled. This stuff was so trivial. Hairdresser . . . Income Tax Returns . . . Institute . . .

Had Elizabeth been institutionalized at one time? Charles certainly might want to keep that hidden, she thought. Not that it would matter to her.

She pulled out the thin file and opened it. Nice to have something against the perfect Elizabeth, she thought, if only for my own peace of mind.

But the letterhead on the top sheet of paper was not that of a mental hospital. Vivienne stared at it: The Reproduction Institute. Slowly she began to read.

"Thank you so much for the generous funding you and your wife have given toward our important work. It is still 'early days,' as they say, but I would indeed welcome a visit from you at your convenience . . ."

Not a surprising letter, Vivienne thought. Charles

had said that his family had been involved with the institute from the beginning.

"I would caution you to prepare yourself, however," the letter continued. "Reality is so much stronger than theory."

Vivienne shivered. Why should one need to prepare oneself for the reality of a genetic blueprint? The remainder of the short letter was bland and pleasant, and Vivienne put it aside. Yet it revived the half-fears she'd felt when Charles had said the cells were . . . how had he put it? Biologically organized.

Her shoulders ached, and she wriggled them to release the tension. She looked again at the salutation and realized it was addressed not to Elizabeth but to Charles's father, Daniel. Well, if Elizabeth had kept the letter, surely there was nothing incriminating or weird about any of this stuff.

She turned to the next item in the file, a canceled check, and gasped at the amount. She hadn't realized the blueprint process was so expensive.

The last paper in the folder was a handwritten letter of several pages, addressed to Elizabeth. She turned to the last page; it was signed "Daniel." An envelope stapled to the back of the last page bore a Barcelona postmark.

Better not read it, she thought instinctively. Reality is so much stronger than theory. From somewhere in the house a clock chimed the hour: nine. She breathed deeply and began to read.

From the first enthusiastic paragraph, she knew why Charles hadn't wanted her in the study; the letter had been written by Daniel immediately following his first visit to what would become the Institute, all those years ago.

Vivienne read half of the first page, then lifted her eyes from the paper and breathed deeply, her mind racing. Daniel had not been at all specific, but the implications of the first few paragraphs were horrifying. Or was it just her imagination working overtime? She found herself hesitant to read further.

As she stood there troubled and undecided, she heard Charles's voice call to her. She jumped, then realized he must still be upstairs. She jammed the letter back in the file and the file back in the carton, then rushed to the study door and listened. The jiggle of a doorknob came faintly to her from above. Instinctively she hit the light switch and the room went dark. He wouldn't expect me to hear him from the kitchen, she thought, and grabbing her cup of stone-cold tea, left the study, closing the door quietly behind her.

When Charles came downstairs, robe flapping, he found her at the kitchen table, asleep over a cold cup of tea. Head on her arm and heart beating rapidly, she allowed him to wake her and even managed a sleepy smile as he led her up to bed.

All night she lay awake in the Ivory Room, confused and frightened. For a time she decided that she was glad she'd been forced to stop reading Daniel's letter; she really was better off not being sure. Then she'd think, I don't need to read any more; how could it be anything else?

You're imagining things, she told herself. If you'd read the whole letter, you'd have found out it wasn't . . . so bad. Maybe.

The next morning she told Charles she thought she'd caught his flu. He was sweet and contrite, and fussed over her like a mother hen.

"I never should have let you come up here," he sighed, tucking the covers around her. "I hope you'll be better for the dinner party next week."

He studied her face, sallow with worry and lack of sleep, and instructed Silverton to make her some hot lemonade. While she was drinking it, Lens called with a booking for that afternoon and could she come back right away? Yes? Wonderful.

While she was on the phone, Charles went downstairs and locked the study door.

II

13

Barcelona is an elegant city. Situated as it is on the coast of the Mediterranean, the warmth of its summer sun is cooled by breezes off the sea. Once, before the sea was killed by pollution and effluent, you could sit outside at a restaurant table overlooking the harbor, and a waiter would bring you grilled langostino and shrimp cooked with saffron and a carafe of the local wine. The restaurant, the sun, the wine are still there. But inflation has quadrupled the bill. And the fish had better not be local.

North of the city stretch the bright beaches of the Costa Brava, dotted with the ruins of medieval castles and littered with high-rise hotels and tourists from England and Germany.

Eric had never been abroad before, and he loved it. He rented a car and drove. It was something he enjoyed, and it helped him think. Winding along the coast road, clambering over ancient ruins, or exploring narrow streets and open-air markets, he felt light-years away from everything he had ever known. It cleared his head. People smiled and nodded as he tried his halting Spanish, and sometimes they even understood him.

For the first time in years he exercised every morning, feeling somehow, suddenly, a need to be fit. He ate well, enjoying the pervasive flavor of olive oil, enjoying the tender squid and the tough escalopes, enjoying it all.

He felt detached, floating; alone but not lonely. It was good, and his soul soaked up the solitude as his body soaked up the sun and the food. He experienced again that same sense of unreality he had felt during the last few weeks of hospital work. Occasionally he wondered what the hell he was doing here, and why he had allowed his life to be turned around. But he recognized that after the many years of study and work, he loved this dramatic change, the freedom, the excitement, the hint of danger. Of course he was highly intrigued by the idea of what he might find at Talmidge's hospital, but he was honest enough with himself to recognize that he also craved the idea of change for its own sake. Playing such a dramatic role in the unfolding events had its appeal, too. I'm Clark Kent, he thought, about to step into a phone booth. I wonder who'll step out?

After five days he headed back to town, parking but not relinquishing his car. He sat at a table at a bar along Las Ramblas, where all the world went between seven and ten in the evening for a drink or two before dinner. He ordered a copita, a small sherry, and drank it and watched the people around him. He felt centered. He was ready to think about Talmidge.

He'd bought a Spanish road map, and now he opened and refolded it so that he could concentrate on the area between Barcelona and the Pyrenees. It shaded from green at the coast to purple up in the high mountains. The tiny town of San Lorenzo de Calvera lay in a brown section some seventy miles northwest of Barcelona, in the lower mountains south of Andorra. It appeared to be set partway up a raised mesa some six thousand feet high.

He unfolded Harris's information sheet and checked the directions against the map. The Reproduction Institute was several miles north of the town, along a small snake of a road. Talmidge, Eric decided, would not be overly troubled by neighbors.

Tomorrow, he thought. He put away the maps and ordered another sherry. Decision time. What story would he tell Talmidge? This problem had nibbled at him intermittently during the past week. Now he examined his options.

Talmidge must get staff from somewhere. I could hang around wherever he picks up his people, and see if he picks me. If I knew where that was. Which I don't.

I could tell him I'd read about his work, heard about him from a patient, and I'm fascinated by him and want to sit at his feet and . . . Sure.

I could say I was doing some hiking in the mountains and got lost and by the way I could use a summer job and since the villagers said the doctor in the castle on the hill was making monsters again . . . Very funny.

He finished his drink and reached into his pocket for some bills. Then, shouldering his carryall, he stood up and joined the throng strolling back and forth beneath the venerable trees. It was on the fourth circuit that it came to him. The perfect cover story. It was logical. It was simple. It was persuasive. It would stand up to investigation. It hit the right note. It was, in all its essentials, elegant.

It was the truth.

Harris directed me to an old article about Talmidge's work when a situation with a patient made him suspect what might be going on at the laboratory outside Barcelona. True.

Harris was appalled at what he took to be my moral turpitude when I expressed enthusiasm for what Talmidge might be doing. He put pressure on the board to withdraw its offer of a job next year. I have nothing to go back for and I'm mad as hell. True as far as everyone knows, save Harris and me.

I have decided to volunteer to work for Talmidge, thereby learning for myself the truth about the fascinating possibilities I suspect Talmidge has turned into realities. True, and no one need know that Harris is paying the freight.

Eric turned the story around in his mind, viewing it from various angles. If it seemed a little too pat, a little too easy, the loss of his job was real enough and could be checked. And perhaps both professionally and psychologically, Talmidge had sufficient need of a worshipful young American surgeon to ignore Eric's overly fortuitous arrival.

OK. He'd go with it.

He returned to his room at the small hotel on the Avenida del Mar and packed his things. Then he returned to the streets in search of dinner. It was still only about half-past eight, but he found a small friendly place prepared to honor his strange request for a meal at that early hour. He had the restaurant nearly to himself as he feasted, and he struck up a conversation with one of the waiters. The mountains were very beautiful, the man told him, but rugged. He hoped Rose had a car of strength. He should bring some food and some petrol, in case he got stuck somewhere. No, he knew of no hospital up in the hills. Did the señor desire any dessert? He could recommend the flan.

Afterward Eric walked a little, and took a café negro and a brandy at a bar near the wharf, and thought about women. That wasn't very productive, so he headed back to the hotel.

Undressing, he glanced at himself in the mirrored door of the tall wooden wardrobe, and decided his time off had done him a lot of good. The workouts had made his body harder, his stomach flatter despite all that good Spanish food. The face that looked back at him was no longer tense and tired, and the dark circles under his eyes were gone. He appeared calm and confident and ready for anything. Just shows how wrong appearances can be, he thought wryly.

Vivienne buttoned herself into the candy-striper pinafore with nervous hands. It had been some time since she'd managed to get over to Park Hill Hospital, and today she had an ulterior motive. Today she was going to lay to rest the worries engendered by Daniel's letter to Elizabeth.

The caterer and the florist were busy at work on the dinner she was giving for Charles and some of his New York business associates that evening in aid of the Ingersoll Bank acquisition he'd been finessing. He'd expect her to spend the day hovering over them, but they'd given far more parties than she had; they'd be fine. And with no bookings for the next few days, it was the perfect opportunity to do a little investigating and set her mind at ease.

She'd decided that the best place to find the reassurance she needed was right here at Park Hill. After all, did what she had imagined from those few sketchy paragraphs really have any basis in fact? Most likely she had misunderstood what she'd read. Or dramatized some simple scientific process that any schooled medical person would recognize as standard procedure. And the secrecy the Institute insisted on was no doubt due to professional jealousy.

Of course, she couldn't go right up to a Park Hill doctor and ask about it; she'd sound like a jerk. No, she'd have to find a way to slip it into a conversation, bring it up casually. She smiled at herself in the small changing-room mirror. Piece of cake.

She was still smiling when she stepped off the elevator at Cardiac Care and headed for the nurses' station. When Bianca looked up from her charts, Vivienne grinned and waved gaily, but there was no answering smile.

Instead, Bianca came around in front of the desk and put a hand on her shoulder.

"What's happened?" Vivienne asked, her smile fading.

"I'm sorry, Viv," Bianca said gently. "It's . . . Mr. Kaplan died last week." She paused. "Er, Kathy thought we should call you at home, but I said you'd soon be in again and I wanted to tell you in person."

Vivienne felt tears sting her eyes. Bianca patted her awkwardly. "It's hard," she said. "We all liked him."

"I'll be okay," Vivienne said at last. "Just give me something to do."

As she filed the charts and papers Bianca and Kathy stacked up for her, Vivienne kept picturing Mr. Kaplan propped up in his bed, surrounded by flowers.

At the end of their shift, Bianca and Kathy took Vivienne down to the staff cafeteria for some coffee. Dr. Mitchell greeted them as they carried their trays from the self-service counter, and waved them over to his table.

"How're you doing?" he asked Vivienne kindly.

"Okay," she said softly. "It's just . . ."

"Life isn't fair," he said with a quiet smile. "I know."

"All he needed was a heart," she said. "I mean, the rest of him wasn't too bad, was it?"

"No, the rest of him wasn't too bad."

She swallowed her coffee in silence. Then a thought struck her, and she wondered guiltily whether she could turn this into the opening she needed. She took a deep breath and plunged. "Speaking of hearts, I heard about something interesting the other day," she said, trying to sound casual. "From a very, uh, rich friend of mine. It's a special sort of, uh, coverage. For organs."

"Medical coverage, you mean?" asked Kathy.

"Not exactly. Well, I'm not sure. They take a sample of your blood, and then they can use it to replace one of your organs. Like Mr. Kaplan's heart. I mean, if you need it," she finished lamely.

Dr. Mitchell looked at her, puzzled. "You mean you can order an organ?"

"Yes, something like that."

The doctor stared at her sternly. "Let me tell you a story," he said. "The man who told it to me swears it's true. Seems some guy at a convention meets this beautiful woman who invites him to spend the night with her. Somewhere around midnight, his friends get a phone call from him. He sounds kind of strange. They ask him if he's OK, and he manages to tell them where he is, in some hotel room. They get to the room and he's lying on the floor, covered in blood, all alone.

Seems two other people were waiting in the hotel room when the woman got him up there. They drugged him and removed one of his kidneys.''

"Jesus!" Bianca breathed.

"There's big money in supplying black-market organs for transplant,'' Mitchell said gravely. ''And it probably happens more often than we realize. In this case the guy was lucky. He lived, although I can't imagine how. That's why I'm not sure I believe the story.''

He studied Vivienne as he sipped his tea. ''Maybe your friend's 'coverage' is a setup for receiving stolen organs. The blood sample would help them match the donor.''

"I, uh, don't think so," Vivienne said slowly. "They told my friend that they'd use the sample to make a sort of genetic blueprint.''

"Well, that would fit.''

"I'm not explaining this right.'' Vivienne paused. The others were staring at her with open curiosity. ''They told my friend that they would culture the cells, make them alive.''

"All cells are alive.''

"Yes, but this, er, process would make them . . . biologically organized.''

"You mean, make them into kidneys and things?'' We really should improve the way we teach the basic sciences, Mitchell thought.

"Not exactly. It's more like . . . something with parts you can use. Is that possible?''

Now Mitchell was smiling. The gullibility of the undereducated was really very amusing. ''Quite *im*-possible, I assure you.''

"But Charles says . . .''

"I think Charles is trying to scare you.'' Mitchell chuckled. ''Don't you let him! It's completely outside the realm of modern medicine.''

He looked at her kindly. Poor kid, she really does look frightened.

"Of course it could be some kind of scam," he added. "You say he's rich . . . ?"

But Vivienne just shook her head.

"Well, if you do find out that somebody's using your friend's cells to make spare parts or something, let me and the ethics committee know!"

He picked up his empty tray and started for the door, then stopped and looked back at her. A nice kid, he thought, not dumb, but probably flunked high-school biology and never took another science course in her life. No wonder she believes in ghost stories.

With a warning finger on his lips for the two nurses, he leaned down behind her. "Booga booga!" he whispered hoarsely. Vivienne jumped, the nurses yelped with good-natured laughter, and Mitchell chuckled all the way to the tray racks.

Vivienne laughed self-deprecatingly, but her mind was icy. If only Mitchell had said that doctors did it every day. If only he'd told her where at Park Hill she could go and see exactly what she'd described. But no, he'd laughed and dismissed the idea, and instead of reassuring her, it worried her.

She was quite sure the process implied in Daniel's letter was real. And if it wasn't a common, accepted process, if an experienced doctor like Mitchell didn't believe it was even possible, then suddenly it seemed to her that anything was possible.

Back home, Vivienne slumped against the pillows of her beloved wicker chair as the predinner activity swirled around her. So it wasn't her imagination: something unusual was going on at the institute. Still, she couldn't really be certain what it was; she could only speculate.

She ran her fingers through her hair; I should shower, she thought. I should do something with myself. But she remained seated. They're my cells, she thought. I want to know what's going on. If Charles won't tell me, I'll find out on my own.

The buzz of the intercom broke through her reverie

and she glanced at her watch. Jeez! Was it really seven-thirty already? She jumped up and ran for her bedroom and the shower, calling to someone, anyone, to let Charles in.

Charles went straight to the kitchen to deposit the carton of champagne he'd brought. He nodded approvingly to the fashionable caterer clucking over his staff, and headed into the living room. A noted party designer was obsessing over the flower arrangements for the highly polished dining table, and an assistant was setting out crystal and silver and candles in stylish profusion. Everything looked just right. But where was Vivienne?

He strode into the bedroom as Vivienne rushed out of the adjoining bathroom, hair wrapped in a towel.

He looked at her in dismay. "You know what time it is?" he demanded impatiently. "How long before you're ready?"

"Hours," Vivienne replied tartly.

"I've told you how important this dinner is," he said hotly. "Ingersoll's an old family firm, very conservative. Personal relationships mean a lot to these guys. I've been working on them for months."

"Why don't you take them to La Grenouille? They do a great dinner!"

Oops, Charles thought, backing off. "Sorry," he told her. "I'm a little edgy too. This deal means a lot to me." He paused. "You look tired."

"I'm just a little edgy," she told him. "And . . . I'm sorry too." She gave him a little apologetic kiss and sat down at the mirrored vanity table to blow-dry her hair.

After a while Charles spoke again. "The place looks terrific," he said placatingly.

Vivienne gave him a grateful smile. "Thanks," she said. "I wanted everything to be perfect." She pinned up her hair and added a black silk rose. Then she began to work on her face.

"Can I fix you something to drink?" Charles asked. "A glass of champagne?" When she didn't respond, he patted her back vaguely and wandered off to the kitchen again, soon returning with a bottle and two crystal flutes. He set the glasses on the edge of the vanity table and filled them.

Vivienne rose and went to the large walk-in closet. She pulled an elegantly simple black-and-white silk dress from under its protective plastic cover and slipped it on. Charles came up behind her and kissed her neck, then handed her a glass of champagne. She accepted it silently and nibbled at the rim. She stood there half-dressed, deep in thought.

"I'll do that," Charles said, and carefully closed the long rear zipper of her dress, wondering if it was cut just a trifle too low for the Ingersoll Bank crowd. "What's wrong, Viv?"

But Vivienne just shook her head.

"Still worrying about Angela?" he asked her. "I thought everything was going okay."

"It is," she said. "The margins were clear, so they got it all. She even started work again this week, did I tell you? I mean, she's nervous about how the chemo will affect her, but . . . no, she's doing fine."

"Then what is it? Have a fight with a photographer? Caterer burn the soup? What?"

Vivienne gestured absently and shrugged. It wasn't just the genetic blueprint itself that was making her edgy; the whole idea of the blueprint seemed to encourage her growing doubts about her relationship with Charles. She downed all her champagne and held out the glass to him.

Oh, great, Charles thought. Just what I need right now. But he refilled it.

"Don't worry," she said. "I'm just . . . a little preoccupied. I'll snap out of it, I promise." And she gave him a ghost of a smile.

By the time the guests began arriving, Vivienne was enjoying an alcoholic lift. And she brightened further as the evening progressed: a seasoned performer, playing to an audience had become second nature to her. Despite her slight air of distraction, she was rea-

sonably attentive to her guests, and contrary to
Charles's fears, the Ingersoll men seemed to appreciate the provocative way her dress moved as she walked.

The food, served on china she'd recently acquired
under Charles's guidance, was delicious, the service
smooth. As the caterer's assistants removed plates that
had until recently contained rounds of warm goat
cheese on a froth of greens, and presented platters of
roast duck prior to carving, Charles was positively
beaming.

Soon after the duck had been served, Vivienne ex-
cused herself to talk to the caterer. For a while her
absence went unremarked, but as the assistants began
clearing the remains of the duck and she still hadn't
returned, conversation lagged, and several guests
glanced uneasily at her empty chair. Charles, making
a joke about her getting lost in the kitchen she never
used, went in search of her.

He found her at the sink in the butler's pantry, sipping a tumblerful of wine and looking off into the middle distance; around her the kitchen staff ebbed and
flowed.

"What the hell . . . ?"

She seemed startled to see him, as if she'd forgotten
she'd left eleven guests in the middle of dinner.
Charles's anger gave way to concern and he put his
arm around her and held her close to him.

"What's going on?" he said softly.

"Nothing," she said vaguely. "It's just . . . something's been bothering me lately, and I can't stop
thinking about it."

"Anything I can help with?"

"Not really. I mean, yes, you can, but you probably
won't want to."

Charles looked puzzled. "Why on earth not?"

"Well, it's . . . it's that thing about the cells. You
said they were alive, and it's been . . . haunting me.
I can't get the idea out of my mind."

Charles pulled back in annoyance. "Cells?" he said.
"You mean that genetic-blueprint thing? We went over

all that, Viv. I thought you were thrilled with the idea. You even wanted one for Angela.''

''Yes, I know, but . . . Charles, if it has a heart and a liver and everything—''

''What makes you think it has 'a heart and a liver and everything'?'' Charles interrupted, a suspicious scowl darkening his face. He thought of Elizabeth's papers and the unlocked study. Christ!

''No reason, really,'' Vivienne said quickly. ''It's just that I keep wondering what it looks like.''

''Looks like? I have no idea—''

''And if it's alive, where do they keep it?''

''In the lab. Look, Viv—''

''Charles, I don't understand. Is it like a real person? Can it move? Does it talk?''

Vivienne's raised voice and nervous mannerisms had attracted attention; Charles saw curiosity on several faces as the kitchen staff moved around nearby.

''For God's sake, lower your voice!'' he hissed. ''Of course it's not a real person. It can't live outside the lab.''

''How do you know? Have you ever been to the lab?''

''No, of course not. Why would I want to see the lab?''

''Then you don't really know. Maybe it's like a . . . a zombie or something!''

Vivienne's hands shook, and wine leapt from the glass she held and stained her skirt. Gently Charles took the glass from her and set it in the sink. Then he held her hands tightly until the shaking stopped.

''Is that what's upsetting you? Zombies? Monsters?'' He smiled at her foolishness. ''People do this every day, Viv, and it doesn't bother any of them.'' He paused. ''I think it's just this coming on top of the Angela thing that's made your imagination go crazy.''

Vivienne shrugged.

''Let's go back to our guests now,'' Charles told her. ''We'll talk about it later.''

''I knew you wouldn't want to talk about it,'' she

told him accusingly. "I should never have mentioned it." But she stayed rooted by the sink.

"Vivienne, ten people are sitting in your dining room right now wondering if you've put your head in the oven or something. We will not talk about this now. We will go out and be charming." The "or else" was implied.

But she looked down at the stains on her dress and said nothing.

Charles's patience was wearing thin. "I've been trying to get close to Ingersoll for nearly a year," he said. "Those people out there can make or break this deal for me. And apparently, so can you!" He banged the heel of his hand on the edge of the sink in frustration. "Christ, if I'd known you were going to be so bloody stupid about this, I'd never have told you!"

Vivienne's head came up, and she looked at him sharply.

"You wouldn't have told me," she repeated. "But you'd have gone ahead and done it anyway? The way you lied to me about what you said was a blood test?"

"You're being silly."

"Really? It's my cells we're talking about here, remember. My blueprint. My zombie!"

"Stop it, Vivienne!" He raised his hand as if to strike her, but perhaps aware of their surroundings, he stopped himself and touched her cheek instead. "Of course I'd have done it anyway," he said gently. "I love you. I'd have done it, I did do it, because I love you. So that if you ever needed it, it would be there for you."

"That's what I thought," said Vivienne softly. "At first. Then I thought about it some more. I don't think you did it for me. I think you did it for you."

"What are you saying?"

"I see how you look at me. How you look at other people looking at me. I'm a possession to you. And you like your possessions to be perfect."

"That's not fair!"

"Isn't it? You use people, Charles. You use me.

Maybe you really do think you love me, but I'm also useful to you. I'm useful because I'm perfect!''

"Not so perfect!" Charles retorted.

"But you're working on me, aren't you, Charles? How I dress, how I eat . . .''

"Vivienne, don't do this. I love you . . .''

"Ah, but would you love me if I weren't so . . . teachable? And if my face weren't on the front of those glossy magazines everybody reads? I'm not so sure, Charles." Her voice rose, clear and shrill. "I've been thinking about us a lot lately. And I wonder . . . if anything happened to me and I wasn't beautiful anymore, could you still love me? I wonder if you could love anyone who didn't measure up to your idea of perfection . . . your mother's idea of perfection!''

People were openly staring now, and Charles was sure their voices could be heard in the dining room.

"You're being irrational, Viv," he said. But was she? He had a sudden terrible thought that she might be right. Was he that damaged? Then he thought, No, of course not! How could she believe such things? "You're irrational," he repeated angrily.

"Am I? Well, what happens when I get old and wrinkled? You may be able to replace an ear or a liver, but there's nothing you can do about old and wrinkled. Will you throw me out? Or do you have some other little trick up your sleeve?''

Charles's face had gone white, and his mouth was tight and hard. His eyes were filled with fury and hurt. He knew he shouldn't speak, but he was beyond caring.

"No new trick," he said in a dangerously quiet voice. "Just the same one. And you wait until you're forty before you tell me you don't want to look twenty-two again. No, you're a model. Make that thirty.''

"What the hell is that supposed to mean?''

"Think about it, Vivienne. Think hard.''

Charles turned on his heel and strode past the kitchen staff, who quickly turned away. Vivienne remained at the sink. Think hard.

At the door to the dining room, Charles composed his face, his manner. Then he entered, smiling and gracious. "A little trouble with the caterer," he said smoothly. "You know these temperamental artistic types."

The male guests, all hardheaded business people, smiled condescendingly at the thought of those artistic types. The females just smiled; they knew who paid their bills.

Think hard.

"It's all given Viv a terrible headache, and she's gone to lie down for a while." She's another of those artistic types, his smile said. "Jason, more wine? Yes?"

Think hard.

Vivienne thought hard. Then she threw up in the sink.

14

The drive up into the hills was glorious. The day was bright and clear, and Eric took his time, entranced by the rugged landscape studded with the ruins of many ages. The road went higher, the temperature dropped, and he stopped to put on a sweater. The view was magnificent: the snow-capped Pyrenees seemed very close.

San Lorenzo turned out to be a small town with a large fortress-like outer wall and a distinct medieval flavor, perched dramatically on the edge of an ancient volcanic rise. Remnants of a ruined Romanesque church and castle guarded the entrance to its narrow streets, so narrow in fact that several times he was forced to labor the car around in a U-turn and retreat. Few people were on the streets, and those who were stared at him without expression. As he rounded the blank side wall of a two-story building, he saw why.

In front of him in the tiny main square he'd inadvertently blundered into were assembled most of the town's two hundred or so inhabitants, surrounded by produce and animals both dead and alive. It was market day. The last piece of civilization before Talmidge's place, thought Eric. Better check it out.

An attempt to leave his car in a pocket of shade against one wall of the square appeared not to be popular with two old women selling vegetables, so he drove several streets away and tucked it under an overhang of foliage and stone and walked back.

To Eric the scene seemed as ageless as the ruins he had so often glimpsed from behind the wheel that morning. Men and women dressed in an assortment of dark-colored garments bargained and socialized at makeshift tables which held comestibles of all sorts. Children chewed chunks of bread and chased each other round the dried-up fountain in front of the small stone church. Two young bloods sporting U2 T-shirts lounged outside what was obviously the in place in town for vino and tapas. A chipped hand-painted sign proclaimed its name to be "El Lobo"—The Wolf.

Hungry, Eric settled himself at one of the rusty tables outside the bar. The young men eyed him with open curiosity but no hostility. He smiled at them. They looked a little embarrassed but smiled back.

"Americano?" the braver one asked.

"Sí," said Eric. Then, *"Es posible comer aquí?"*

Yes, they told him with words and sign language, food was served, but he had to go inside to request it.

Inside, the bar was dark and grimy. A large brown dog of unknown ancestry sprawled across the floor and scratched. Eric stepped over him with some trepidation, but the dog ignored him, so he went up to the bar and ordered a bocadillo of ham and cheese, and a cerveza to wash it down. When it was ready he carried the sandwich and beer outside to his table. The U2 boys had obviously been talking about him, and they looked over at him shyly as he began to eat.

"Good, yes?" one asked him.

"Very good," Eric replied.

"Serrano ham is the best," the youth told him. "You have come to see the castle?"

"The castle is very pretty," Eric told him, "pretty" being a completely inappropriate description of the twelfth-century ruin, but one of the few adjectives he had memorized. "But I have come to visit the hospital."

They nodded sagely. Many made such a visit, they said. The sick ones stayed at the hospital but the others stayed here at the hotel. He did not look sick. Would he then stay at the hotel?

Hotel?

Sí. El Lobo. Upstairs there were rooms.

Eric explained that he was a *médico*, a doctor.

This news was treated with respect. He was to work in the hospital then?

Yes, Eric lied.

This seemed to reassure the two young men, who now rose and introduced themselves, and Eric did the same. "My aunt works in the hospital," Vicente explained. Felipe nodded. "Many people from the village work there," he said.

"Many?"

"Oh, yes. At least twenty."

"Is your aunt a doctor?" Eric asked, interested.

The boys laughed good-naturedly at the idea of a woman being a doctor. "She cooks the food," Vincente said. "She cooks for all the patients."

"That must be a lot of work," Eric offered. "There must be many patients."

"Not so many on this side," said Felipe expansively. "But on the other side . . ."

Then he caught Vicente's eye and stopped abruptly. Vicente rose. Felipe followed. They both smiled, held out their hands politely, and were gone.

Eric sipped his beer, his face expressionless, but inside he was exultant. The other side. Of course. That's how Talmidge would have set it up.

He went into the bar to pay, nearly tripping over the dog, which looked up at him with the patient scorn of the native for the tourist, and returned to the market square, where he bought a dozen oranges and a string bag to carry them in. He moved almost automatically as his mind danced and his heart racketed around in his chest—the other side. Yes. Of course.

It took him twenty minutes to find his way through the tiny streets to the narrow road the Spanish government laughingly called a third-class highway—he kept arriving back at the main square—but at last he was switchbacking his way up the ridge. The landscape around and below him spread out like a living map, beautiful but barren. Then he came around a final curve and there before him, like a mirage, was a low, wide, modern structure with a cleanly white cinder-block exterior and a wide paved turning circle in front. Off to one side was a parking area which held several cars including a sleek black limo. A neat standing sign welcomed him to the Reproduction Institute and directed visitors toward the solid oak double doors set centrally into the facade.

A feeder road led left off the turning circle, and Eric followed it around to the side of the hospital, where it dead-ended in a small cul-de-sac beside an unobtrusive metal door. He drove back to the front of the building and parked next to the limo. He sat in the car and studied the building; detectives in books always deduced a lot from such observations, as he recalled.

Eric observed that the windows were clean and unbarred, but he couldn't see inside. He deduced that there were curtains on the windows. He observed that the only way he could see if the back of the building looked like the front was to walk around behind it. He deduced that by now people were aware of his arrival and that if he walked around to the back instead of going in through the front door, some large person would emerge from the Institute and kick his ass off Talmidge's property.

He opened the car door and got out, then reached back in for the bag of oranges before swinging the door shut. He wasn't quite sure why. Perhaps the altitude was getting to him. Carrying the oranges, he walked back through the parking area and followed the edge of the turning circle to the front door.

He looked for a bell or a knocker, but found none. How do people get inside this place? he wondered. Maybe they sent you one of those computer keys when you registered. Maybe they only opened the doors when they were expecting you.

Eric took a deep breath. It's kinda way-out, kid, he

told himself, but maybe you push on the doors and they open. You know, like in a hospital. He pushed on the doors. They opened.

The walls were a somber grayish brown, unrelieved by lighter accents. The space was cramped and dark: there were no windows. In one corner a large figure loomed threateningly. Frightening and savage, with gaping scarlet jaws and protruding eyes, it was chained by the foot to an iron spike set low in the floor. Next to this apparition was a door, its brass handle ancient and dented. Slowly the handle turned, and slowly the door opened; a shaft of white light flashed out in a widening arc.

"Come in, Charles," said Dr. Brian Arnold.

Making a wide path around the towering figure, Charles Spencer-Moore entered a large cluttered living room.

"What you see in those things I'll never understand," he said.

"He's worth a fortune," Arnold replied. "I stole him from under the nose of the director of the Chicago Museum of Primitive Art."

"He gives me the heebie-jeebies," Charles complained. "This whole place does."

Admittedly, Brian Arnold's apartment was not to everyone's taste. A fanatic collector of African art, he had filled every inch of his living space with museum-quality pieces: statues, furniture, paintings, wall hangings. A late-night thunderstorm experienced in such surroundings would not easily be forgotten.

"What are you drinking?" asked Brian, opening the door of a low cabinet decorated with what he claimed were authentic shrunken human heads smuggled out of Uganda.

"It's a little early for me," Charles replied.

"Nonsense. It's nearly noon."

Charles seated himself in a zebraskin chair facing away from the heads. "All right," he said ungraciously. "Scotch. And do me a favor, will you? Put it in a glass, not one of those things with dead monkey paws around it. I'm nervous enough right now.''

"So she got a little overexcited," said Arnold, pouring Scotch into two tumblers.

"You didn't hear her last night," said Charles. "She went ballistic on me in the middle of a dinner party for the Ingersoll people, said it's been haunting her. She kept asking me if it could walk and talk and think. She calls it a zombie.''

Arnold handed him his drink—Scotch and ice in a plain glass—and Charles examined it suspiciously. It looked normal. He risked a sip, then continued.

"She wanted to know if it could live outside the lab. Then she accused me of not being able to love her if she weren't perfect-looking.''

"You told her it couldn't and you could, of course?''

"Sure, sure," Charles said morosely. "But I don't think she believed me.''

"Well, give her time," said Arnold, settling himself into the cushions of a deep leather sofa, drink in hand.

"I never should have told her about it in the first place.''

"Sounds like you told her too much. Is there any real danger, do you think?''

Charles's reply was forestalled by the shrilling of the telephone at his elbow.

"Pass it over here, will you? . . . Hello, this is Dr. Arnold . . . She what? . . . How long ago? . . . OK, I'm on my way!''

Handing the phone back to Charles, Arnold relaxed into the sofa again and took a long pull at his drink. Charles looked at him in some surprise.

"That beautiful Hungarian idiot," said Arnold testily. "May-Ann, the famous model . . . ever hear of her?'' Charles nodded vaguely. "Well, she came in for a vitamin shot this morning, and never told me she'd already taken half a dozen uppers. From a prescription bottle with my name on it.''

"Vitamin shot?''

"Well, it has vitamins in it too.''

Arnold's vitamin shots were famous among those with a need for such things. His treatments were expensive, but much safer than going out on the street for what they contained. He treated nervous disorders, weight problems, and general angst among the well-heeled, and a large number of celebrities in various fields called him Brian. He enjoyed being on a first-name basis with such people, and it paid for a lot of carvings and artifacts. So far he'd had no real trouble with the AMA's ethics committee. And he didn't want any.

Charles put down his drink. "We can talk about it later," he said. "I'll call you."

"Sit," Arnold ordered. "Let her stew for a while. Teach her a lesson."

He went to the cabinet for more ice.

"A refill, Charles? No? Oh, don't be alarmed. She's safe in a hospital ward . . . she won't like that, I can tell you. When I get there I'll have her put in a private room and give her a little lecture. I do have my reputation to protect."

"Such as it is," said Charles.

"Indeed. Now, what shall we do about Vivienne?"

Charles thought for a moment. "She's suspicious," he said, "but I don't think she's actually dangerous to us. Still . . ."

"Calm her down, Charles. Calm her down and shut her up."

"I'll try."

"Try hard. Otherwise . . ."

"Otherwise what?"

"Otherwise you might suggest she try some vitamin shots."

Charles blanched. "This isn't one of your bimbos," he said fiercely. "This is the woman I'm going to marry."

"Save the histrionics, Charles," said Arnold. "You asked for this meeting. Now I'm telling you the cold hard truth: you've got to keep her quiet, any way you can."

He set his glass down on the coffee table, a slab of glass supported on four ibex horns, and stood up, stretching his long, lean frame.

"I suppose I'd better get down to the hospital. And," he added, sensing a movement from Charles, "taking a swing at me won't change anything. There's just too much at risk: my license, your Ingersoll merger. How's that going, by the way?"

"Fine," said Charles sullenly.

"A very old firm, aren't they, Charles? One of the last of the major family-owned banks, yes? Quite conservative, I believe. Upright and moral and all that. Very particular about whom they do business with."

Charles said nothing.

"So you're close to a deal?" Arnold continued. "Worth quite a bit of money, I'm sure. And prestige. But of course the merest breath of scandal . . ."

He headed for the door, grabbing his coat and briefcase from the chair where he'd tossed them the night before; his enthusiastic date had given him no time for neatness.

Charles followed more slowly. Arnold was right, of course. They both had too much to lose.

The studio was buzzing with rumors. May-Ann had been arrested. Deported. She'd been hit by a bus, a taxi. She was in the hospital. She'd overslept. One thing was certain: she wasn't in the studio.

Vivienne was. Angela had called her frantically at a quarter past ten, when everyone had become reconciled to May-Ann's non-appearance and decided on a substitute instead of a postponement.

"We're not the same type at all," Vivienne had said, surprised.

"Yeah," said Angela. "Like, you show up on time. I know it's not your first cover, but you might act a little pleased."

"I'm sorry, Angie. I didn't sleep much last night. I gave this dinner party for Charles's clients and in the middle of it we had a terrible fight, all my fault, and—" She broke off, feeling guilty. This was Angie's first week back at work and she was feeling the effects of the chemo; she probably wasn't sleeping well either.

"Tell me about it later, toots," said Angie. "The meter's running."

"I look truly awful, Angie."

"That's why God invented makeup artists. Now, grab a cab and get your buns over there."

"Angie, I really don't feel like working today. I feel distracted, and . . ."

There was a brief silence; then, "Excuse me," Angela said, "can I please talk to Vivienne Laker? You sure don't sound like her."

"It's stupid, I know. But Charles . . . and then this lab thing . . . it's all making me a little crazy, Angie. I can't seem to concentrate on anything."

"Look, sweetie," said Angela, "if I can work, you can work. About the lab, well, maybe you're making a big something out of a big nothing. You don't know, you can't know. Meanwhile, you have a life to live here. So get your act together and get down to the studio. And bring an umbrella. It looks like rain."

"Yes, Mother."

And so here she was in the makeup room, becoming a lot more beautiful than she felt.

Out on the studio floor, a giant loft space in the heart of SoHo, the magazine's art director was conferring with the fashion coordinator about background colors while a studio assistant pulled out roll after giant roll of colored cyclorama paper for their approval. Bert Maylor, the photographer, was checking the lighting setup with his camera assistant.

"I still think the crumpled silk is more interesting," he told the magazine people. The assistant began pulling out samples of parachute cloth.

Everyone was eating. Bagels with cream cheese and smoked salmon. (You didn't call it "nova" in the glamour business.) Buttery cinnamon Danish, bursting with raisins. Melon slices and strawberries. And coffee, coffee, coffee, coffee.

"Want some more, Vivienne?" the makeup man asked.

"Thanks, Jeremy, but any more caffeine this morning and they'll have to scrape me off the ceiling."

"Thought you looked tense," he said. "Got a lot on your mind, huh?"

"Not exactly," said Vivienne. "Just some stuff I have to work out."

"Boyfriend problems? Can I help?"

"Would that you could, Jeremy lad," Vivienne told him.

"Try me," he offered.

Oh, sure, she thought to herself. She'd worked with Jeremy before; he was a sweetie, but he dearly loved to gossip. Anything you told him you might just as well put on the ten-o'clock news.

She couldn't help but smile a little as she pictured it: Flash! Bulletin! This Just In! At a dinner party at the elegant home of model Vivienne Laker, her fiancé, the wealthy man-about-town Charles Spencer-Moore, left his bride-to-be throwing up in the kitchen sink while he went back to his pals and proceeded to open bottle after bottle of red wine until the entire company finally floated out to sea around three in the morning. Then Chuckie baby informed the fair Miss L. that she was nutty as a fruitcake, obsessed with something called "The Institute," and that she should forget all about it if she knew what was good for her. Just before he stormed out into the dawn, he suggested they postpone the wedding. Yes, girls, Charles Spencer-Moore just might be back on the market!

Maybe I *am* being a little obsessive about the Institute, thought Vivienne, but I'm no fruitcake. "I don't want to talk about it," she said.

Jeremy shrugged. There was a short pause as he applied more base. Then, "Did you hear why May-Ann didn't make it today?" he asked, now remembering that Vivienne was one of the closemouthed ones.

"I heard a lot of guesses," said Vivienne.

"She OD'd," said Jeremy with relish. "Her doctor left her in a ward—can you imagine?—for over two hours before he had her transferred to a private room. She was furious."

"That's terrible," Vivienne said. "I mean about her overdose. What did she take? Will she be OK?"

"I heard it was a combination of what she took and what she was given," said Jeremy mysteriously. "They say she'll be fine, though. I'm gonna go see her after the session. Want me to say hi for you?"

"Sure. I mean, I don't really know her, not well."

"Who does?" Jeremy shrugged philosophically. Suddenly he looked worried. "I sure hope she doesn't kick up a fuss about Dr. Feelgood and mess it up for the rest of us.

"Dr. Feelgood?"

"Brian Arnold, the vitamin doctor. Don't tell me you've never heard of him, darling. He gives these divine shots. They're magic!"

"Vitamin shots?"

"That's what we call them!" Jeremy gave her a conspiratorial wink, then sighed theatrically. "The man is too gorgeous. But straight, unfortunately. What a waste! But I hear . . ."

Warming to his subject, he chattered away about Brian Arnold's sexual proclivities, but Vivienne was no longer listening. She was wondering why Charles would choose such a man as his doctor. Surely Charles didn't take such shots. Did he?

"Ready, Viv?" One of Maylor's assistants stood at the dressing-room door. Behind him lurked the wardrobe woman and the fashion coordinator.

"One sec more!" Jeremy applied a final coat of lip gloss.

The wardrobe woman chose a red silk suit from the pipe rack of clothes. "This first?" she asked the coordinator.

"Yes. And no blouse underneath the jacket. We're going for sexy."

Viv stood up quickly and turned toward the rack,

knocking over the remains of Jeremy's coffee. The brown liquid ran everywhere.

"*Merde!*" Jeremy jumped back, saving his white linen pants by seconds.

"Oh, God, I'm sorry!" Vivienne exclaimed, grabbing for tissues.

"Leave it, leave it!" he said. "You're making it worse. Never seen you so wired."

Under the lights, the jumpiness and sense of distraction got worse. "Loosen up, kid!" Bert smiled at her. "Jeremy, pat her down. She's getting shiny."

The art director whispered in Bert's ear. He didn't look happy. Viv could see Bert doing his reassuring act. He'd been an art director himself, years ago; he was good with clients.

"Let's take ten minutes," said Bert finally. "Save the lights!"

With the giant lights turned off and the high casement windows opened, the studio began to cool. Bert put his arm around Vivienne and led her aside.

"Babe, you're not getting it across," he told her. "You're looking *at* the lens, not through it . . . there's, like, this wall between you and the camera. You worried about something? You want a Valium?"

"God, no, Bert. I don't use that stuff."

"Well, concentrate, sweetie. You look beautiful, absolutely great, but you're so . . . withdrawn. And your whole face is sort of tight, you know? Are you nervous because this was supposed to be May-Ann's cover? Don't be. When you walked in front of the camera they all started whispering about how lucky they were that she didn't show up. They love you."

"They don't love me."

"They will if you just relax and do what you do so well. Make them love you, babe. You know how to do it."

He gave her a little hug and a reassuring grin. "We're in this together, babe. Come on, make me look good!"

Vivienne gave him a big grateful smile. As though

the great Bert Maylor needed anyone to make him look good. The opposite was true: he made every model look great, if she just gave him a chance.

"I'm really sorry, Bert," she said. "I'm being a jerk. Let's try again. I promise I won't let you down."

"I know you won't, babe." He turned her around toward the shooting area, calling to his assistant, "Okay, Lenny, let's go!"

The rest of the session went well; Vivienne forced herself to turn her attention outward. They wanted sexy, she gave them sexy. Good. Let's change the outfit. They wanted warm, she gave them warm. Good. Now the blue and white with the blouse. They wanted saucy, she gave them saucy. You're a genius, Bert, they said.

But in the dressing room afterward, she again grew preoccupied, absentmindedly pulling the elaborate one-of-a-kind blouse over her head and smearing it with make-up.

Jeremy gasped in horror. "Honey, you're a mess!" he exclaimed. "You got your monthly?"

Vivienne shook her head.

"Well, you almost blew it in there, sweetie, and now you ruin this sample, I don't want to guess what it cost. You need help. You in therapy? I could recommend somebody. No? Hey, why don't you go see Dr. Feelgood? He'll fix you up. I'll write down his number." And Jeremy reached for a pencil.

"I already have it," Vivienne said softly.

A sudden look of understanding came over Jeremy's face. "I see," he said knowingly. "Well, you call him right away and tell him you need another shot, and fast! You can't go on like this, honey."

That's right, thought Vivienne. I can't.

She changed back into her jeans and shirt, apologized profusely for the damaged sample, and called Brian Arnold from Bert's office. At least I can tackle one part of the problem, she thought.

* * *

Berta greeted her warmly as she entered the empty waiting room. "Vivienne, how nice to see you again! Diet Coke? Coffee? No? Well, make yourself comfortable and I'll tell Dr. Brian you're here." But Vivienne was too nervous to sit. What if he won't answer my questions? she thought. What if he will?

She watched the nurse disappear into the corridor which led to the examining rooms. She peeked around the corner in time to see the woman enter one of the rooms, then ducked back as Brian Arnold stepped out into the hall. She was demurely reading a magazine by the time he came into the waiting room looking puzzled but pleasant.

"The lovely Vivienne!" he said, as he had the first time they'd met. She hadn't liked it then; she didn't like it now. She smiled. "Thank you for seeing me on such short notice," she told him.

"You told my nurse it wasn't a medical problem you wanted to discuss. Is that right?"

"Yes. I, er, want to talk about the Institute . . ."

A bell rang somewhere and Berta came hurrying back into the waiting room, reaching for the release buzzer under her desk.

Arnold glanced toward the street door. "Let's go somewhere more private," he suggested. He led her toward the examining rooms, then made a sharp left turn and entered a small office filled with color-coded file folders on open metal shelves. As she followed him into the room, Vivienne heard the front door open and close and the sound of voices. Arnold seated himself behind the small steel desk; next to it stood a dented file cabinet. He offered her the only other chair, steel gray and plastic like his own. She looked around; the floor was covered with linoleum, the windows clean but uncurtained.

"I don't usually bring patients in here," he told her. "Just suspicious young girls."

Vivienne turned back to him, flushing with embarrassment, but he smiled reassuringly. "You're not the first to wonder what all that blood-test hocus-pocus was about," he told her. "Just ask me what you want to know. I'll answer if I can."

"Great," said Vivienne, surprised. "Thank you." She marshaled her thoughts. Where to start? "OK, first question: Why all the mystery about the Institute?"

"Beats me," Arnold told her, his eyes wide and innocent. "Never did understand it myself."

"It must be because of what they're doing."

"You're probably right," Arnold agreed.

"Well, what exactly *are* they doing?"

"Ah, now there you have me," he told her. "Unfortunately, I haven't the remotest idea."

"But that's impossible. I mean, you take the samples . . ."

"Yes, and that's all I do. I take them, I ship them, good-bye." He sighed. "I often wish I *did* know more. I must admit to a strong curiosity."

"Charles says they make genetic blueprints. He says they're alive."

Arnold leaned forward. "Really? Fascinating!"

"You mean you really didn't know?"

"Of course not. What else did he tell you?"

"I can't believe you don't know!"

"Believe what you like," said Arnold, leaning back as though resigned to learning no more than what she had just told him.

"But you said you'd answer my questions!" Vivienne protested.

"Well, I'm trying to," Arnold told her with an air of injured innocence. "Just ask me something I know about."

Right, Vivienne thought. I know something you know about. "Vitamin shots," she said. "What's in them?"

But it was not so easy to discomfit Arnold. "Vitamin shots contain vitamins, of course," he said with a smile.

"Not your shots," she replied. "May-Ann had one just before she OD'd. Vitamins don't do that."

"She also took a lot of pills before she had the shot."

"Did you prescribe them too?"

"I never told her to take them all at once. Look, Vivienne, if you think that insulting me professionally is going to make me spill my guts, you're mistaken. I do what I do. I give vitamin shots. I take samples for the Institute. Both those activities make me lots of money and lots of friends in high places. I don't actually give a rat's ass what they do at the Institute. All I care about is the thousand dollars they pay me for each sample."

"A thousand dollars? Isn't that an incredibly high fee for a blood test? Doesn't that make you suspicious?"

"Only if I think about it," he said evenly. "So I don't. 'Take the money and run,' that's my motto."

Her line of questioning effectively deflected, she looked idly around the room, hoping for new inspiration. "You've got an awful lot of files," she said. "You must send them an awful lot of samples."

"Those are my vitamin patients," he said.

How about that file cabinet? Vivienne thought. More vitamin patients? Or something more interesting? If I could only figure out a way to—

"Well, if that's it," Arnold said, rising from his chair and moving toward the door, "I do have a patient to see . . ."

Vivienne rose too, and stretched out her hand. "I'm awfully sorry if I came on too strong," she said. "It's just, well, it seemed so weird, you know? I didn't realize you weren't in on it." She smiled, pouring on the charm. "Do forgive me."

"Of course," Arnold told her, taking her hand between his. His eyes gazed deep into hers, and he began to stroke her hand suggestively with the tips of his fingers. Vivienne was shocked; he knew she was Charles's fiancée. But she held her smile steady. Let him think you trust him, she thought. You've got to get back in here again. Make him think you like him.

He moved close to her. His gaze was hypnotic. Still
holding her hand in one of his, he reached over and
caressed her breast. She was motionless with shock
and embarrassment; her nipple was hardening under
his touch. He felt it too, and smiled challengingly as
he squeezed it between his fingers. It hurt. He saw the
expression of pain cross her face and pleasure flooded
through him. What beautiful violence they could do to
each other! He intensified his stare; she was like a
rabbit caught in the glare of oncoming headlights. He
squeezed harder, but the new pain jerked Vivienne out
of her trance and she pulled away with a gasp.

"I'm going to leave now," she said, all pretense
gone. "Move out of my way."

"Of course," he said smoothly, stepping aside.
"Perhaps someday when you have more time . . ."

Vivienne didn't bother to answer. She brushed past
him quickly and almost ran through the waiting room,
out the front door, and past the doorman sorting mail
in the lobby. When she stopped at the corner to catch
her breath, she found she was shaking with indigna-
tion and disgust.

Back in his office, Brian Arnold hesitated before
tackling the erratic screenwriter who was his next patient. He reached for the phone, then recradled it without dialing. Telling Charles would do no good, he
decided. No, he'd have to deal with Vivienne himself.

15

Eric was disappointed. Everything was so normal.

The outer doors of the hospital had opened into a wide, clean reception room, its tile floor mopped and shiny. To one side was a Formica work station which faced the front entrance; from behind it a middle-aged Spanish woman had welcomed him in English. Across from this was a small comfortable-looking seating area.

His request to see Dr. Talmidge had been received as a commonplace event; a phone call was made, and a young man dressed as an orderly had arrived to escort him through an ordinary hospital corridor to this small anteroom where he now sat waiting, a cup of strong black coffee in front of him. He'd placed the string bag of oranges on a low table to one side, wondering what benighted impulse had made him bring them along.

A solid oak door was set in the wall in front of him. Eric studied it. It was closed, probably locked. Unless Talmidge was inside. He got up and tried the door. It was locked. He sat down again, thinking what a stupid move that had been.

There were no pictures or certificates on the walls, no magazines on the coffee table, no windows to look out of. Eric found to his surprise that he was bored. So he did what he'd done in boring situations ever since medical school. He chose a surgical procedure at random and mentally reviewed the steps. Eric's low boredom threshold had been partly responsible for his successful academic career.

He was just starting to close after a rather messy perforation of the duodenum when he became aware of a presence behind him. The presence spoke. "Oranges!" it said.

Eric turned. A friendly round-faced man of about fifty with pale thinning hair and a smattering of freckles was beaming in his direction.

"I love oranges," the man said brightly. "Are they for me?"

When Eric failed to respond, the man smiled apologetically and offered his hand. "Sorry," he said. "Thought you knew. I'm Ben Talmidge."

Eric found himself smiling back. This wasn't at all the way he'd pictured Talmidge. Or the hospital. This was all very nice. Very clean, very friendly. Talmidge even liked oranges. It was all so terrific it made Eric feel extremely nervous.

"Hi," he said. "I'm Eric Rose. I'm a doctor."

I'm also an idiot.

But Talmidge didn't seem to think so. "A doctor? Where did you train?" Then, "Look, let's go into my office." Briefly he fumbled at something to one side of the door, his body shielding it from Eric's view. Then, pushing the door open, he led Eric into a high cool room with a tall window overlooking the side lawns. Seating himself behind the oak trestle table which served as a desk, Talmidge motioned Eric into the high-backed chair across from him, and reached for an orange.

"It's not often I get visitors up here," he said, cutting away the peel with a small pocketknife. He looked over at Eric expectantly.

"I'm not just a visitor," said Eric. "I'm with New York General. That is, I was, until Dr. Harris, John Harris, fired me."

"John Harris."

"Yes. He told me about you, about what you, uh,

might be doing here. He wanted to know if I thought
it was possible. He didn't like the answer.''

''What answer did you give him?''

''I told him it was possible. And exciting. I told him
if I was right, you were revolutionizing a lot more than
transplant techniques. I said I thought it was terrific,
and I wanted to learn more. I guess I told him more
than he wanted to know.''

''How do you mean?''

''Well, we had some . . . uh, disagreements.''

Talmidge ate an orange section. His bright blue eyes
watched Eric intently.

''Harris had a problem with the ethics, the morality
of what I said you were doing here.''

''And you didn't?''

Careful.

''Actually, I did have some doubts at first. But the
more I thought about it, the more ethical it seemed. I
mean, cloning organs from tissue samples lets you heal
people more effectively, and that's what we're here
for.''

''And John didn't see it that way.''

''Well, he might have, I guess, if I hadn't told him
about the other applications of such a technique. That's
when he got angry.''

''Yes?''

''He thought it was immoral. I thought it was great
medicine. I mean, if you can make a heart from a
tissue sample, why not something . . . bigger?''

Talmidge's eyes glittered, but he shook his head and
smiled gently. ''It's not that easy, Eric. I may call you
Eric, yes? We work on a small scale here, nothing big,
nothing dramatic. But we help people, people who
perhaps would not be helped otherwise.'' He paused.
''So Harris fired you? You must have been quite vo-
ciferous.''

''Well, I felt strongly about it. I still do.'' Eric took
a deep breath. ''Dr. Talmidge, throughout the history
of medicine, there have been the dreamers, the dis-
coverers. And there have been the spoilers—people

too stupid or jealous to understand the truly great sci-
entific leaps. Or maybe too scared. I'm not stupid, Dr.
Talmidge. I was top of my class at P&S, and New York
General had offered me an appointment to the surgical
staff before Harris butted in. I'm young but I'm good.
And I'm not scared."

The hell I'm not.

Eric paused. Talmidge finished his orange and
calmly wiped his hands on a white linen handkerchief.
The silence hung in the air between them, palpable
and tense.

Finally Eric spoke again. "Let me work for you.
Let me learn from you."

Talmidge was silent again, and Eric feared he'd laid
it on too thickly. But although Talmidge's mind was
indeed teeming with questions, Eric's worshipful attitude seemed perfectly natural to him. His suspicions
lay elsewhere.

How convenient. Talmidge was thinking, that you
should suddenly arrive, supportive and skilled, just
when I need you. On the other hand, although you
understand better than most people the larger implications of my discovery, you're ready to believe that
only organs are involved. That's convenient. And if
you get too curious, my boy, well, I've handled that
sort of thing before.

He smiled to himself. Hiring Eric Rose would certainly be one in the eye for that sanctimonious bastard
John Harris. And what a joy it would be to deal with
an enthusiastic professional instead of another creep
like the late unlamented Haddad. He decided to probe
further.

"How do you happen to be in Spain?" he asked
pleasantly.

"I came here to see you."

"When did you arrive?"

"Ten days ago. I stayed in Barcelona for a while,
then I drove up and down the coast. I didn't know how
to approach you, or if you'd even talk to me." Rose

smiled. "Besides, I needed some rest. It's been one hell of a year."

"Does John Harris know you're here?"

"Nobody knows I'm here. Oh, friends know I've gone to Spain, but no one knows why."

"Why didn't you tell anyone, your friends perhaps?"

"What if you turn me down? I'd look like a fool."

Again silence descended. Faintly Eric could hear the chirp of birds as the sun dropped toward the hilly landscape beyond the hospital grounds. At last Talmidge spoke.

"Take a room in San Lorenzo. You know the town?"

"I stopped there for lunch. And, uh, shopping."

"Stay the night—the restaurant on the main square rents rooms upstairs. Come back tomorrow at"—he checked his watch—"eight in the evening. I'll give you an answer then."

Eric stood and reached out to shake Talmidge's hand.

"Thank you," he said. "I'll be here."

He turned toward the door, then detoured back for his oranges. "Whatever you decide," he told Talmidge, "it was, well, incredible to meet you."

Ass-kisser.

"Hey, would you like some more oranges for later?" And he swung the bag out toward Talmidge. The webbing gave way and oranges bounced and rolled onto the desk, the floor, Talmidge's lap.

"Shit!"

He scrambled to retrieve the fruit, banging his head on the overhang of the trestle table, dropping oranges and picking them up again, lunging after the ones which threatened to roll out of sight. When at last he got to his feet, arms full of oranges, he saw to his consternation that Ben Talmidge was laughing. Great guffaws rocked him, and his eyes were growing teary.

Come on, it isn't that funny, Eric thought testily. But Talmidge, beyond speech, was waving him toward the door, where the same young man who had brought him here now stood to escort him back to the lobby.

"Uh, see you tomorrow," said Eric weakly, feeling that his exit lacked dignity.

Goddamn stupid oranges.

"Take some," he told the youth as they made their way down the corridor. "Take them all."

"*Gracias,*" the boy said, choosing three oranges with care. "*Me gustan mucho las naranjas.*"

"Yeah," said Eric. "They're real icebreakers."

He threw an orange at a tree beyond the parking lot, dumped the rest onto the back seat of his car, and drove down the mountain to San Lorenzo.

Talmidge would check him out with New York General. He'd even call John Harris and crow a bit. But unbeknownst to Eric, it was the naiveté, the clumsiness, the openness which Talmidge would read into the incident with the oranges, that would convince him to break his rule about not hiring "mainstream" doctors and to welcome Eric to the Reproduction Institute.

Vivienne upended the bottle and watched the last quarter-inch of clear liquid flow into her glass. It's a good thing you're not a drinking woman, she told herself sardonically as she sipped the now-tepid Evian water. Two days had passed since the fateful dinner party she'd given, and although she'd come back from Dr. Arnold's office yesterday to find two dozen roses and a card that said "I love fruitcake!", Charles hadn't telephoned.

Suddenly she went cold: God, I hope Arnold doesn't tell him about my visit; Charles'll kill me! But remembering Arnold fondling her, she felt instinctively that he wouldn't.

She picked up the telephone bill, scanned it, and wrote a check. She sealed the envelope. She stuck on a stamp. She reached for another bill.

Was solving the mystery of the Institute really worth losing Charles over? Maybe I should call him and apologize, she thought remorsefully. Maybe I *am* obsessing. Why not just give it up, promise him I'll forget the whole thing, be a good little fiancée? Then she thought, *Hell no!* I have a right to ask questions if I want to. I have a right to know the truth. Fruitcake, indeed!

But everybody else seems to live with it all quite comfortably, she reflected. Why does it bother me so much?

Maybe because I know more about it . . . or suspect more . . . than most people.

But that was just it; she had nothing but suspicions.

Not true, she argued with herself. I saw Daniel's letter. And Charles won't talk about it. And Brian Arnold lied to me. If there were nothing funny about the Institute, there would have been no reason for Charles to clam up. Or for Arnold to lie.

How do you know he was lying?

Oh, come on!

She wrote another check, sealed another envelope.

I'd love to have a look inside that file cabinet, she thought. But the idea of going anywhere near Arnold made her shiver. Was there anyone else she could talk to? Someone else who might know about the Institute? It couldn't be someone who'd sent a sample there; they'd be as closemouthed as Charles had warned her to be.

So who could have had dealings with it, but not have had a blueprint made? Concentrate.

She leaned back in her chair and reviewed what she knew. One: you send the Institute a blood sample . . . maybe a little flesh, too: her inner elbow was still slightly scabbed. Two: the institute made you a genetic blueprint. Three: if you need a part, you can use it.

How? she wondered. Do you order it and they send it to you? 'Hello, I'd like to order a liver, please. Could you Fedex it by tomorrow?' She smiled at the idea, and took a sip of water, then stopped with the glass in midair. Why not? she thought. That's probably exactly what you do! So a doctor who does transplants might know about the institute. Dr. Mitchell's a cardiologist but maybe he doesn't do heart transplants. That kind of surgery must be highly specialized.

She went and got the heavy Manhattan phone directory and paged through to the M's. Then she reached for the phone.

His secretary didn't recognize her name but Dr. Mitchell did. He was polite but obviously busy. "A referral to a transplant doctor? You still worried about that ghost story your boyfriend told you?"

Vivienne let him humor her; just give me a referral, she thought.

"We don't do much in that line at Park Hill," he told her. "But New York General does. Dr. John Harris is your man."

"Do you know him? Can I use your name?"

There was a brief silence. Mitchell was obviously reluctant to have his name linked with a gullible hysteric, but felt funny refusing her. "Actually, I've never met him," Mitchell said truthfully. "But if you think it will help, tell him I gave you his name, by all means. Afraid I haven't got his phone number. Try information."

Vivienne thanked him, hung up, and turned back to the directory. If this doesn't work, she thought, I'll have to get back into Arnold's office somehow. God, I hope this works!

She called Harris's private office number. A rather severe-sounding woman answered on the second ring: Mrs. Riley, on the job as usual.

"Referred by Dr. Mitchell of Park Hill? I'm afraid the doctor's at the hospital all day. Did you want to make an appointment for a consultation?"

"Uh, yes . . . I guess so."

"Just a moment, please . . ." Mrs. Riley paged through the filled appointment calendar. "I have something two weeks from now . . . Wednesday the fourteenth."

"Nothing before that?"

"Is this an emergency?"

"Well, no, but—"

"Wednesday the fourteenth is the best I can do."

VIvienne sighed. "Okay," she said. "I'll take it."

"Your name?"

"Vivienne La . . . uh, Lester," she said, marveling at her instinctive lie. Charles and Arnold both knew about the institute; maybe they knew Harris too. And if Harris told Arnold and Arnold told Charles . . .

Mrs. Riley carefully wrote down the name. "And your phone number?" she asked.

"It's . . . look, do you ever get cancellations?"

"Rarely. May I take down a little background on the patient?"

"It's, uh, I'm not a patient, exactly. I want to talk to him about the Reproduction Institute."

The what? Oh, that place in Spain?"

Bingo! Vivienne thought triumphantly. "Yes, that's right," she said. "Well, I'll see you on the fourteenth, then."

"And your phone number—?"

But Vivienne had already hung up. She shrugged on a denim jacket and headed out the door. She was scheduled to review the photos for her new composite in an hour, and somehow she suddenly felt like a little fresh air.

Later that day John Harris, excited by this apparently new source of information about the institute, would try to phone Vivienne "Lester" to schedule an immediate appointment. But there was no such person listed in the Manhattan directory. And directory inquiries had never heard of her.

" 'Morning, Luisa."

" 'Morning, Viv. They're in the conference room."

"Thanks."

Vivienne went through the reception room, adorned with framed magazine covers featuring famous faces represented by Lens, her own included, and down the carpeted hallway to the art-deco meeting room. The model agency was housed in what had once been a small loft building, now converted to office space. The decorators had made the most of its high ceilings, exposed pipes, and unusual angles.

"Viv! You look super, sweetie!"

Marcella, Lens's illustrious owner, rose to greet her with a peck on the cheek. Marcella was a legend: sophisticated and chic, with a great sense of style, she had risen above her own spectacular ugliness and achieved a look—and a fortune—completely her own. She was bone-thin and aggressively blond, with bold, strong features and uneven teeth which she refused to have capped. Her instinct was correct: her teeth gave a certain vulnerability to her otherwise unrelenting visage. But then, Marcella's instincts were always correct.

"Bert Maylor says you were a major hit the other day," she told Vivienne. "Well done!"

"Bert makes it easy," Vivienne said. And thank you, Bert, for not mentioning how long it took to make me a hit.

"Well, the clients were ecstatic! Now, have a look at these," Marcella instructed, gesturing toward the large marble table in the center of the room. "Belinda, get Viv some mineral water. I thought we might use this head shot for the front." She tapped on the photograph with a long red lacquered nail.

"Yes," Vivienne agreed. "I love that shot."

"Good. And then"—Marcella pulled five photos from the twenty or so spread out across the table—"three on the reverse. A bathing suit of course; is this one too sexy? And maybe something romantic . . ."

Like most models, Vivienne put together an updated photo composite each year, a printed page with a variety of photos—reproductions of magazine covers and ads she'd appeared in—as well as her name and measurements, and Lens's name, address, and phone number. The agency sent copies of the composite to advertising agencies and photographers when they were casting a commercial or a print ad. And Viv always took five or six to every assignment; clients often asked for one.

Lens insisted on being involved in the choosing of photos for the composite, and that suited Vivienne just fine. They'd done very well by her so far, and she trusted Marcella's taste and business instincts.

Now Marcella began lining up her choices and alternates in order on the table, and she and her assistant, Belinda, discussed the selections dispassionately. Viv felt she looked a little old in this one, Belinda liked her eyes in that. Everyone spoke openly and honestly. It was a business, after all.

Choices made, Marcella studied Vivienne critically. She'd told Viv she looked super when she'd arrived, but close up, Marcella could see the tension and strain.

"You're looking a little tired, sweetie," she said. "Everything OK?" Ever since Angela had taken Marcella into her confidence, Marcella had begun to see symptoms of ill health everywhere.

"Never better," said Vivienne with energy. "Really." She smiled confidently at Marcella, who smiled back and patted her hand.

"Good!" she said. "You working today?"

"No," Vivienne replied. "But I've got a callback for that Revlon thing at four."

"Today? That was fast," Marcella commented. Revlon had begun its search for a "trademark" face for a secret new cosmetic product only a week earlier. "Knock 'em dead, sweetie!" But Marcella had her doubts. Vivienne was looking rather frazzled. She hoped it wasn't drug-related; Viv had always been one of the sane ones. And the agency had enough of that kind of trouble with May-Ann. Poor May-Ann, thought Marcella. Such potential. Such a waste.

The intercom buzzed and a voice spoke. "Marcella, pick up for Lloyd Rogers, Estée Lauder."

Marcella's eyes flicked toward the phone as Vivienne thanked her and Belinda for their help and started out. But Marcella ignored the flashing phone light and followed her to the door. Putting a hand on her shoulder, she looked steadily into Vivienne's eyes. "Just remember," she said. "If I can help, I will."

She held the look for a beat, then turned to Belinda. "Call Viv when the proof comes in, right?" she ordered, then went to the phone.

"Lloyd dearest," she cooed, "who was that gorgeous creature I saw you with at Aureole last night . . . ?"

Vivienne closed the door softly behind her, then stood rooted there. She couldn't believe it—she was shaking, physically shaking. Why? Marcella had been so nice. And the composite was going to be beautiful. The shakes got worse. Her career was going well. She was going to marry a wonderful man. Shake, shake. Charles loved her so much he'd even arranged for the Reproduction Institute to make a . . . Shake, shake, shake, shake!

She breathed deeply, then followed the corridor around to the right until it dead-ended at the bullpen, a circular room with a central console around which sat the agency's bookers. By the time she got there, she felt a little better.

Along the walls were mounted the scheduling sheets, huge plastic-coated blowups of calendar pages divided into weeks, days, and times. Bookers wrote hold dates and bookings on these sheets with erasable colored marking pens, in letters large enough to be read from anywhere in the room. As usual, the phones were ringing and everyone was talking at once, the baffles separating each work station only just tempering the noise.

Angela was at work in the middle of the chaos, a phone in one hand and a sandwich in the other. Vivienne thought she looked thinner. And her hair!

"I like it," she said to Angela's back. "It's different, but it's fun."

Angela turned around, surprised, then waved a hello with her sandwich. "Tuesday the 20th at three," she said. "No makeup, hair in rollers. Two hours firm with a one-hour bump. You got it."

She hung up, and hurried across the room to a

scheduling sheet and wrote down the information boldly in green. "Do you really like it?" she asked, returning to the console where Vivienne was now perched.

"It's cute," said Vivienne.

"Yeah, short and sweet," Angela replied. "I've already lost a lot of my own hair. I figured it was time to stop scaring the children. Hey, don't look so down," she added, seeing Vivienne's expression change. "I'm gonna live, it's gonna grow back eventually. And guess what!"

"What?"

"One of the girls told me about this wigmaker, and he cut my hair short before it started coming out and he saved it to make this. So it's really still my hair."

"You're being disgustingly cheerful about all this," said Vivienne fondly.

"I am, I am." Angela eyed the remains of her sandwich. "And I'm not very hungry these days. Look! Cheekbones!"

Angela really is thinner, Vivienne thought. It looks good on her, but isn't it funny how it took something awful to make her care about her appearance. And it took something a lot of people seem to think is just great to make me screw up my life.

"How about you, chickie?" Angela asked. "Only a friend would tell you, but you look like shit."

"If you think this is shit, you should have seen me yesterday."

"I heard you did great yesterday."

"You didn't hear what I did *after* I did great yesterday."

"What?"

"Well, let's see," said Vivienne. "I got makeup all over a priceless sample blouse, I tried to get a snake named Brian Arnold to tell me about the Institute and ended up letting him pinch my boob, I called Charles to tell him he was an unfeeling monster for making me a genetic-blueprint thingy—fortunately he wasn't home . . . Shall I go on?"

"Christ," said Angela. She looked at her friend with concern. "Look, don't get mad at me for saying this, but . . . do you think maybe you're going a little overboard about this Institute business?"

Vivienne shook her head. "No," she said, "I've thought about it, and I don't think it's just my imagination. I . . . I read some papers in Charles's study . . ."

"You what??"

"Charles's father wrote a letter to Elizabeth. I read only part of it, but . . . Angie, the letter didn't really say anything, but . . . I have a hunch about what they're doing at the institute."

"What?"

"I don't want to say until I'm sure."

"Oh, that's helpful!" said Angela.

"OK, OK! I think they use your blood to make zombies! Zombies, Angela!"

Several of the bookers looked around, curious. "Sounds like a great movie," Angela said loudly. "I must see it! Where did you say it's playing?" And grabbing her handbag and Vivienne's arm, she marched her out of the bullpen and down the corridor to the ladies' room.

"Loose lips sink careers," she told Vivienne. "You want them to think you're drugging or something?" She looked closely at her friend. "Do you know you're shaking?"

Vivienne nodded. "I think it's stress."

Opening the door of a stall, Angela pushed Vivienne inside. "I'll stand guard," she told her through the closed door. "Get yourself together."

Another booker came in and Angela began washing her hands. She washed her hands until the booker left.

For a while after that, all was silence. "You OK in there?" Angela asked.

"Yeah," said Vivienne. "Only there's more. Charles is talking about postponing our wedding."

Angela pulled open the stall door. "He's breaking it off? Bastard!"

"No, no, just putting it off until after the first of the

year, to give me time to . . . uh, get straightened out,
he said. Actually, I'm kind of relieved. Isn't that
funny?''

Behind them the door from the corridor swung open
again.

''Maybe I don't really want to marry him, after all,''
Vivienne continued thoughtfully. ''Especially if he ap-
proves of making zombies. I mean, I'm not *sure* they're
making zombies, but—''

Angela quickly swung the stall door closed and
turned again to the sink. ''Great plot line,'' she said
over her shoulder in the direction of Vivienne's cubicle. ''I must see it. Oh, hi, Belinda!'' She and Belinda
made small talk while Belinda rinsed out the office
coffeepot and refilled it with fresh water. Angela
washed her hands as slowly as she could. At last Belinda left.

Angela pulled open the stall door and looked at Vivienne suspiciously. ''You're sure you're not just saying
you're relieved because he's breaking it off?''

Vivienne shook her head. ''He's not breaking it
off,'' she said. ''He's just giving us both some breathing space.''

''He's breathing; you're hyperventilating. OK, let
me think.'' Angela began pacing the few feet between
the tiny air-shaft window and the sinks. Vivienne went
and leaned against one of the sinks with a bemused
smile.

''Road trip,'' Angela said at last. ''A change of
scene. Don't tell Marcella I suggested it or she'll kill
me. It's not a cover, or much money, so she'd rather
you stayed in town. But—''

Again the door from the corridor swung open, and
both women turned to the sinks, exchanging greetings
with Luisa, who began to wash an apple for lunch.
Vivienne started to repair her makeup, and Angela,
heartily sick of washing, did the same.

''Since when do you wear eye makeup?'' Luisa
asked.

Vivienne looked over, curious. She hadn't noticed

it in the bullpen, but Angie was indeed wearing a soft brown eye shadow, and now she was applying a little liner beneath her lower lashes. She was surprised to see how well Angie was doing it.

"It's good for morale," Angela said.

Luisa looked embarrassed, but Angie winked at her. "It's okay, kid," she said. "Hey, I meant to ask you, what's the name of that lipstick you're wearing? Would it work on me?"

"Cinnamon Soup," said Luisa. "It's in my bag. Come out to reception if you want to try it."

"What do you think, Viv?"

Vivienne smiled; Angie reminded her of herself at fourteen, having just discovered cosmetics. "Sure," she said. "It'll probably look great."

Luisa left with her apple, and Vivienne now studied Angie carefully. Her skirt hung slightly around her waist, but her eyes, now enlarged and emphasized, sparkled. And yes, you could see the beginnings of cheekbones. What surprised her was not that Angela could look good; she'd seen that the night she'd recruited Angie as a date for Charles's political buddy. No, what amazed her was that Angie now cared enough to actually create this transformation herself.

Angela finished fluffing her short curly hairdo and turned back from the mirror, leaning against one of the sinks.

"So. Road trip?"

"I don't know, Angie . . ."

"Do you good to get away. Take your mind off things. Make Charles miss you. Pazula's doing a big promotion for Bloomie's, shooting in Burgundy. Grapes and wine and stuff. Guess what the big color is for fall!"

"Did he ask for me?"

"He hasn't asked for anybody yet. I heard about it from Sean—that's his new assistant—about five minutes ago, when they booked Rachel's hands. Supposed to be a secret. Interested?"

Perhaps it would be good to get away, Vivienne

thought. Location shoots could be a lot of fun. And being away from Charles for a while might be good for both of them.

"I shot with Pazula last year," she said. "We got along fine, and he liked the work. One of the shots is going into my new composite, now I think about it." She was suddenly feeling much better.

"I could tell Sean to tell Pazula that you'd be interested. I'd have to swear you both to secrecy. If Marcella found out . . ."

"France. Yes, I'd like to go to France," said Vivienne. "It might be just what I need to do."

"Let me work on it," said Angela. "Now, let's get out of the john before they start transferring my calls in here."

"Sure," said Vivienne. "And thanks, thanks a lot. Uh, Angie . . ." She hesitated, knowing how Angie hated compliments. "I just want to tell you, you look pretty. Really pretty."

Surprisingly, Angie smiled. "Yeah, I do, don't I? Will wonders never cease!"

16

Eric arrived early for his first day at the Institute, parking in the asphalt lot. The limo was gone, but a black Mercedes with French license plates had taken up residence. Eric walked all around the hospital, soaking his shoes in the dewy grass, but saw nothing unusual.

The receptionist greeted him with respect and took him to a small freshly painted room which served as a staff lounge. Medical magazines were spread on a low table, and a coffeemaker and Styrofoam cups stood ready on a narrow counter along the far wall. The room was empty; as soon as the receptionist left him, he immediately went out into the corridor to explore.

The interior of the building consisted of corridors laid out in the general shape of an elongated H, with the main entrance situated in the crossbar. The lounge was set just beyond the junction of the crossbar and the right-hand upright. Talmidge's office was at the top of the left-hand upright, Rose recalled, so he felt he could explore a little without running into him. He set off down the corridor leading toward the front of the building.

He counted five doors, three on the left and two on the right. Each was numbered. All were closed. At the end was a set of solid-looking double doors, also closed. He retraced his steps, passing the lounge, and came to a small nurses' station. Just behind it he saw gurneys and the entrance to a scrub room. He leaned over the counter. The OR would be just beyond.

"Señor?"

Eric started, banging his hand smartly on the underside of the counter overhang, and swiveled around. A short skinny woman in white glowered at him. *"El paso es prohibido,"* she said sternly. "Eet ees prohibit."

He gave her a dazzling smile. "Delighted to meet you, Nurse . . ."—he looked in vain for a nametag on her starched uniform—"uh, nurse," he finished lamely. He extended his injured hand. "I'm Dr. Rose, Eric Rose. From America. We'll probably be working together."

Maybe, her look seemed to say. And maybe not. She ignored his outstretched hand.

"Well, uh, carry on," he said grandly, flashing her another sparkling smile, and turned back toward the lounge, feeling her eyes on him all the way. As he got to the lounge door, he sneaked a look behind him. She still stood, arms akimbo, watching him distrustfully.

Ah, Eric, you charmer, you.

He crossed to the coffeemaker. Some java, he thought. A magazine. And no moving from this room until they tell you. Got that?

He poured himself a cup of the strong black coffee, looked in vain for milk, and then settled himself in a pale green Naugahyde chair to wait for whatever might happen next.

Ben Talmidge had spent the night in his office, wrestling with unfamiliar emotions. Now he sat hunched over his desk, his chin in his hands, staring inward.

Never, as far back as he could remember, had he questioned his own decisions. He'd known, seemingly from birth, what he wanted and how he was going to get it. His plans had always been quickly made, without undue agonizing. And when they'd gone wrong, which had happened rarely, he'd moved quickly to correct them.

I'm getting old, he thought dispassionately. Though

his boyish countenance belied his age, he was nearing sixty.

No family, he thought; not really. No real friends.

It had never mattered before. In fact he'd consciously rejected such attachments. But the arrival of Eric Rose after such a long period of enforced isolation from his peers had brought to the surface feelings long buried and forgotten.

A professional, Talmidge thought. Someone I can trust; a smart young man who can understand my work. Who can understand me. Or was he seeing Eric through the rosy haze of his own sudden yearnings?

Talmidge rubbed his eyes, then stood up and went to the window. Outside, the air was cool and still. Nothing moved.

"One of our finest," Harris had said despondently when Talmidge had called to gloat. What I could do with such a trained, talented mind, thought Talmidge. What we could do together. What a legacy I could leave him.

Eric was pouring coffee when Talmidge entered.

"Pour me some, will you?" Talmidge said with a smile. Eric noticed that he hadn't changed his shirt since their interview the previous night.

He handed Talmidge a steaming cup and watched in wonder as Talmidge gulped down the painfully hot liquid.

"Come with me," he ordered, so Eric ditched his coffee and followed Talmidge out into the corridor.

Talmidge was crisp, yet affable. "I'll show you around later," he said. "Now I want you to scrub in with me. We have a little procedure."

A test, thought Eric. Good.

The nurse's face lit up when she saw Talmidge, then darkened again at the sight of Eric. *"Prohibido,"* she said, and blocked the way, but Talmidge shook his head. *"El es un médico,"* he explained gently. "A doctor. He will work here with me."

The woman nodded and let them pass, but she didn't smile.

"A talented nurse," Talmidge explained, "but a limited vocabulary." And he swept past her, Eric following in his wake. They scrubbed together in silence; then Talmidge led him into the OR.

The patient, unidentified, lay on the gurney swathed in drapes.

The scrub nurse might have been the twin of the woman in the corridor: sullen but efficient. The anesthetist, introduced simply as Ricardo, was silent. There was no one else.

"Your patient," Talmidge told him. Eric looked at him in surprise. "Go on," said Talmidge testily. "Examine him. Tell me what's wrong."

Eric leaned in and began to pull back the drapes. Talmidge touched his arm. "Not the face, Eric. Leave the face. He's already anesthetized. He can't talk to you anyway."

"What are you using?" Eric asked idly, beginning to undrape the body.

"Cyclopropane," Talmidge said casually.

Instinctively Eric dropped the drape and stepped back. Nobody used Cyclopropane any longer. Nobody sane.

Talmidge chuckled. "Now, don't be a baby, Eric," he said. "Get on with it. We'll talk about the Cyclopropane later."

Feeling trapped, Eric stepped in again, his heart jumping. Cyclopropane. Jesus!

Once the man's body was freed of the drape, the problem became obvious to Eric. He touched the pulsating abdomen gingerly, then turned to Talmidge. "Aneurysm of the aorta," Eric told him. "We need an ultrasound of the area as quickly as possible."

Talmidge nodded to the nurse; the ultrasound unit, already set up, was immediately wheeled over. Talmidge had known exactly what he had here, Eric realized. So how could he simply let the guy wait for me? If that thing had ruptured . . .

Using the ultrasound, he quickly located the site of the aneurysm: the spot was greatly engorged and leaking blood. "We need to open him up immediately," he told Talmidge tensely. He didn't like the look of the thing at all.

"Be my guest, by all means," Talmidge told him graciously.

Like a fucking tea party, Eric thought. Tea with the Mad Hatter. Well, if the guy was already out, he was going in—fast. It occurred to him fleetingly that this was a rather unexpected procedure in a hospital of this kind; presumably they cared for the more affluent villagers on an emergency basis.

Talmidge watched carefully as Eric opened neatly and got to work, rapidly dissecting and cross-clipping the leaking aorta. It was a technically difficult piece of surgery, just the sort of thing Eric loved.

"Dacron graft," said Eric, extending his hand for the piece of plastic which would replace the injured section of aorta. The nurse slapped it into his glove and he cut rapidly through the aorta, stitching the graft into place. A skillfully performed anastomosis, or junction between the graft and the patient's own blood vessels, was crucial to the success of the procedure. Talmidge watched intently as Eric removed the clamps.

"Good 'mose,' " he said. Eric flushed with pleasure and began to close.

When he finally stripped off his bloody scrubs, Eric was surprised to find the operation had taken nearly two hours.

"Well done," Talmidge told him as they stepped out of the surgical changing room and started down the corridor.

I passed, thought Eric with some relief. I wonder who the patient was.

Suddenly Talmidge stood motionless for a moment, as though debating something deep within himself. Then he turned back to Eric, looking at him searchingly, and put out his hand. Somewhat taken aback,

Eric grasped the hand and shook it. To his profound embarrassment, Talmidge did not release it but continued to hold his hand almost tenderly. Then all at once Talmidge shook off the mood.

"How about that tour?" He spoke almost harshly, as if ashamed of some emotion he had just revealed.

Someday, my boy, all this will be yours, Eric thought unsteadily. "I'd like that," he answered.

"Still feeling a little shaky about the Cyclopropane?" Talmidge asked solicitously.

"You bet your . . . er, yeah," Eric told him.

Talmidge smiled. "You'll get used to it," he said. Jauntily he started down the corridor. He found he liked having an assistant who not only was an excellent surgeon but also knew enough to be scared of the Institute's somewhat unusual anesthetic of choice. Then his steps slowed as mentally he pulled himself back. Easy, now, he thought. Don't get sloppy. You acted on impulse. Now study him. Try him. There are too many secrets here. And decisions can be changed.

The hospital tour was uneventful. Eric was shown the private rooms, comfortable and cheery but not luxurious, the small but well-stocked medical library, the supply room, the X-ray lab. Everything had a clean, well-scrubbed look. But they saw few staff members.

At last they came to the large double doors at the end of the corridor Eric had attempted to explore earlier. Talmidge pushed a small button on the wall, looking up at what Rose suddenly realized was a closed-circuit camera. The lock clicked open and they entered a dim, cool chamber, its walls lined with what looked like thin metal drawers. A hum of machinery filled the air. At a table in the center sat a squat ugly little man wearing a lab coat over his jeans. He rose respectfully as Talmidge entered.

"Good morning," Talmidge said pleasantly. "This is Dr. Rose. He'll be working with us now. Eric, meet Jorge."

Despite his Spanish name, the man seemed to understand English, because he nodded to Eric and smiled a shy smile.

"Hi," said Eric. "What happens in here?"

Jorge shrugged apologetically and looked toward Talmidge, who gestured toward the near wall. "Come look at this," he told Eric.

Together they walked to the cabinets, and Talmidge pulled the handle of one of the wide shallow drawers. Slowly, smoothly, the drawer rolled out, releasing a gust of cold which fogged the air above it. Fifty sealed clear plastic boxes were carefully arranged in the drawer. Each was labeled with a name and a date.

Talmidge picked up one of the boxes and handed it to Eric. Inside he could see two oversize covered slides—at least they looked like slides. In the center of one slide was a thick blob of red. In the center of the other was . . . what? He stared, fascinated.

"This is the original sample," Talmidge explained, indicating the first of the two slides. "And here"—he pointed now to the second slide—"is the beginning culture. We develop it only to this point, then we chemically suspend its growth and freeze it until we need it."

He took the box from Eric's hand and placed it back in the drawer, gently rolling it closed. Eric shivered.

Talmidge noticed the shiver and smiled. "I'll show you what happens next," he said, and crossed the room to an identical bank of drawers. Eric started to follow.

"Wait!" Talmidge ordered sharply. Then, "Jorge!"

The little man unlocked a desk drawer. From it he brought out a small metal plate—it looked a bit like a VHS remote control, Eric noticed—and depressing a button, aimed it carefully at a row of drawers. There was a sharp click. Jorge locked the remote control away again, and Talmidge indicated that Eric could now join him at the wall, where he again grasped a drawer handle and pulled.

This time, a four-drawer facade pulled out and hinged down to reveal a cold deep space with a

counter-type base inside. On this were mounted two
large glass containers, each covered and labeled. Suspended in a clear rose-colored liquid inside the containers were organs: a heart in one, a kidney in the
other. Mists of freezing air swirled wraithlike around
the containers and up out of the drawer.

"This is what you came for," Talmidge said dramatically. "The technology I developed and perfected
over the years."

He glanced over at Eric, who was staring down at
the organs. His cheeks were pink, and he was frowning with concentration.

"This is very exciting!" Eric chose his words carefully. "I mean, it's revolutionary, incredible!"

Talmidge allowed himself a superior smile.

"But, well, I don't understand. How does it get from
there"—he indicated the drawers on the opposite
wall—"to this?"

Talmidge gave an avuncular chuckle. "Wouldn't the
world like to know?" he said. "But only Jorge and I
know the, uh, rather complicated process. And we're
not talking!" He smiled as if at some private joke.
"No, we're not talking!"

He looked sharply at Eric. "Someday," he said, "if
you're a good boy, maybe I'll tell you. But it won't be
tomorrow. You'll have to earn it."

Or maybe I could buy Jorge a drink sometime, Eric
thought. He seems to know English. I could get to
know him, make him trust me . . .

Talmidge swung the drawer facade back into place
and pushed it closed, locking away the organs and their
secrets. Then he strode to the double door.

"Jorge! We're going now."

Jorge must have hit a hidden button or switch, for
the door lock clicked open.

Eric went toward the door, then stopped at Jorge's
desk. "Thanks, Jorge," he said. "Nice to meet you.
Uh, see you at lunch, maybe?"

Jorge smiled up at him and nodded.

"Let's go, let's go!" said Talmidge impatiently. He

opened one of the double doors and held it for Eric, who reluctantly passed through into the corridor.

"An interesting case," Talmidge said as they walked toward his office. "A kind of scientific idiot savant. Explain a procedure to him and he grasps it instantly. But strangely enough, he can neither read nor write. He can't calculate the simplest sums. He smiled at you because you spoke to him, but he appears not to experience the most basic human emotions. He's like . . ." Talmidge searched for a simile. "He's like a loyal dog."

"He seems to understand English."

"Oh, yes, he understands French and German too. Peculiar, isn't it?"

"You mean, because he can't learn to read or write?"

"No, Eric. Because he's mute. He was born without vocal cords." Talmidge smiled pleasantly. "He can understand at least five different languages. But he can't speak a word."

Inside the OR, the nurse and the anesthetist had moved the patient onto a gurney, securing him with straps. Now the nurse unlocked a small unobtrusive door half-hidden by a screen, and they wheeled the gurney through, carefully locking the door behind them.

17

Vivienne carefully folded a pink silk blouse and placed it on top of the blue jeans in the open suitcase on her bed. Then she checked her watch: 4:45 P.M. Not much time; she'd have to decide soon. In her handbag was a first-class Air France ticket to Paris for early the following morning, and she still hadn't reached John Harris.

She'd called his office as soon as Angie had confirmed her booking for the Pazula shoot, to try to move up her appointment with him. But still worried that he might be connected in some way with Brian Arnold, she'd left no message with the answering service. Meanwhile, Lens had kept her busy all week with go-sees and last-minute bookings, hoping to dissuade her from spending ten working days out of the country.

She'd called Charles at home twice, and had gotten his answering machine each time. Ah, the wonders of modern communications, she thought. But that wasn't really fair; she could have called him at his office, or late at night. She just wasn't ready to talk to him yet.

Around midday she'd returned from some last-minute shopping and tried Dr. Harris again. This time she'd reached Mrs. Riley.

"The doctor tried to call you," Mrs. Riley had told her reproachfully, "but you're not listed. Give me your number and he'll get to you before five."

Ten minutes to go, Vivienne thought. She folded a red-and-white-striped cotton sweater and placed it in the suitcase. And if he doesn't call? Would she still be able to get into Brian Arnold's office today?

The suitcase was nearly full when the phone rang a few minutes after five. Vivienne lunged across the room and grabbed it on the first ring.

"Vivienne Lester? Dr. John Harris."

"Oh, I'm so glad you called!"

"I tried to reach you, but—"

"I know, I'm not listed. Look, I had an appointment scheduled with you for next week, but I'm flying to Paris tomorrow morning." ("Damn!" said Harris under his breath.) "Would it be possible for me to come talk to you right now?"

"I'm about to go into the OR," he told her. "Emergency. We just got a liver, and when you get it, you have to use it." He paused. "I've got a little time while they're prepping . . ."

"I can be down there in twenty minutes," said Vivienne.

"I'll be scrubbing by then. Why don't we talk a little now? You called me about the Reproduction Institute?"

"That's right. What do you know about them?"

"Not much," Harris said. "I recently had a patient fly to Barcelona for a kidney transplant. Seems his brother would only donate a kidney if the operation were done at the Institute. Please don't think me rude, but what's your interest in the place?"

Careful, Vivienne thought. "I, uh, have a friend who says they offer a program for organ . . . replacement," she said. "You sign up for it and give them a sample of blood and they match you up with an organ if you need one."

"That's interesting," Harris said cautiously. "Did your friend ever use the program?"

"No, not yet. Did your patient, uh, recover?"

"Yes, he did. He's in great shape."

They both fell silent, each not sure how much to trust the other. Is this woman really a new source of information about the Institute, Harris wondered, or could she be spying for Talmidge? Had Eric been found out already? "So you're interested in joining their transplant program," he said at last.

"Not exactly. I'd just like to know more about it."

"So would I. What did your friend tell you?"

"Not very much, I'm afraid. That's why I'm calling you. Dr. Mitchell says you're involved in transplants. I figured you'd know about organ sources."

Harris was silent for a moment, thinking. "Perhaps if you told me what you know already . . ." he suggested.

What the hell, Vivienne thought. Take a chance. "Okay," she said. "My boyfriend arranged a genetic blueprint for me through the Institute. He used the words 'biologically organized.' I asked him what that meant, and he was kind of elusive and that bothered me. So I decided to try to find out for myself. You're part of my . . . investigation, I guess you could call it."

So Eric was right, Harris thought with a frisson of excitement.

"What have you found out so far?" he asked, trying to keep his voice casual.

"Not a great deal," Vivienne told him. Daniel's letter to Elizabeth wasn't something she wanted to talk about, especially if Harris were connected to Brian Arnold. "I was hoping you could help."

"Actually it all sounds rather farfetched," Harris said. "I certainly haven't heard of anything like that."

Vivienne tried again. "Look, I agree I'm working on pure speculation here. But I'm kind of angry that my boyfriend's made certain medical . . . decisions about me without my consent. And frankly, it worries me that it's all so hush-hush."

"Who's being hush-hush?" Harris asked her. "Whom else have you talked to about this?"

"I'm a model," Vivienne continued, ignoring his question. "I'm going to France to do a fashion shoot. If you can't help me, maybe I should just pop over to Barcelona and have a look for myself."

Shit! Harris thought. That's all Eric needs. "It

would be very dangerous for you to do that,'' he said aloud. "Very dangerous indeed.''

"Why?'' Vivienne asked.

"For one thing, the Institute isn't in Barcelona. It's just outside a small mountain town to the north. I understand San Lorenzo is almost . . . medieval, and quite isolated.''

Vivienne was scribbling on her telephone pad.

"Dr. Talmidge is, well, somewhat erratic,'' Harris continued. "He might not be very hospitable.''

He *does* know more than he's telling me, Vivienne thought. He's trying to scare me off. He's probably in on the whole thing, along with Charles and Brian Arnold and Lord knows who else! I was right to use a false name.

"If you'll tell me what you know, I won't have to go and visit,'' she suggested.

"You seem to know more than I do.''

He sounds just like Brian Arnold, she reflected.

I have to convince her to stay away from the institute, thought Harris. "Actually, I'm doing some investigation into this thing myself,'' he said, "along with a colleague of mine. So you really don't need to risk a trip to the Institute. Just give me a call when you get back from Paris and we can all sit down together and share information.''

If he's in league with Arnold, I won't get anything out of him, Vivienne decided. And if he's not, then he doesn't seem to know any more than I do. She glanced at her watch: ten past five. She might just make it.

"That would be fine, Dr. Harris,'' she told him. "I'm afraid I have to go now . . . so many things to do before tomorrow morning. Thanks for your help.''

She disconnected abruptly and quickly dialed Arnold's office, then hung up again. A surprise visit might be more effective. And if she were lucky, he'd have another patient or two on the premises, so she'd have to wait for him. Having to wait was an important part of the plan she'd worked out over the last few days, a plan she'd hoped she wouldn't have to use.

She ripped a piece of plain paper from the telephone pad and scrawled a quick note. Stuffing the note in her handbag, she grabbed a jacket and hurried out.

As he scrubbed, John Harris reviewed the aborted phone call. It troubled him. The Lester woman had confirmed what he and Eric had suspected, but somehow he felt she could have told him even more. He feared he'd mishandled the conversation, but for the life of him, he couldn't figure out how.

"Vivienne Laker," she told the intercom box, and was promptly buzzed in by a surprised Berta.

"Dr. Arnold isn't expecting you, is he?" she said, consulting her appointment diary.

"No . . . it was kind of spur-of-the-moment," Vivienne told her, noticing with satisfaction the thin pale young man paging nervously through a magazine. "Just tell him I wanted to, er, continue our discussion of the other day. The uh, second part." That ought to get him, she thought.

Berta disappeared down the corridor; Vivienne heard a soft buzz of voices, and the nurse returned. "The doctor will see you in just a moment," she said.

Vivienne flushed nervously. She'd assumed Arnold would want to deal with his waiting patient first. Now she was trapped. She perched on the sofa, running through the plan in her head, changing it all to fit this new circumstance. Presently Arnold appeared with a smartly dressed woman of about sixty. They said their good-byes and he held the door open for her as she left. Berta appeared and ushered the pale young man into the corridor, leaving Arnold and Vivienne alone in the waiting room. He turned to her, his eyes cold and bright.

He'd been surprised but delighted when Berta had given him Vivienne's message. He'd been thinking about how best to deal with her; several alternatives had occurred to him. Now she was providing the means of her own destruction, he thought. Sex, augmented by drugs if possible, followed by blackmail: a threat to tell Charles about it if she so much as mentioned the institute again. You don't think Charles will believe me? he could hear himself tell her. Then we'll just have to show him the videotape. You didn't realize you were performing for the camera? No one does, my dear; that's part of the fun.

"I hoped you'd come back," he said. Looking intently into her eyes, he slid a hand between her legs and squeezed. "Come on."

As he'd come down the hall to the waiting room, he'd stepped into his specially equipped private office and hit the innocuous-looking wall switch that turned on the video camera. His last patient would wait. Better yet, he could watch.

Vivienne looked around in panic. "No! I mean, you still have a patient."

"Forget him!" He lowered his head and bit at her breast.

She struggled and finally managed to push him away, hard. He smiled slowly. "You like force? That's always exciting."

"I like privacy," she said. "Get rid of your patient. Berta too."

He stood looking at her for a moment, then wheeled around and walked rapidly up the corridor. Shaking with tension, Vivienne sank onto the sofa, but the sound of a door opening along the corridor jerked her back on her feet again. Berta could come back to the waiting room any minute. Quickly she pulled the scribbled note from her handbag and propped it prominently on the reception desk. Now—where to hide?

She'd mentally reviewed her options at home when she'd first formulated the plan, and settled on the little-used file room. But now she wondered whether the file room was really such a good idea: what if he locked it when he left, and she couldn't get out again? She remembered passing a utility closet on her way to the examining room that first day; could she get to it before the nurse came back?

She pulled the front door open slightly and left it ajar to give the appearance of a hasty exit. Then she hurried back to the desk and peeked around to the corridor in time to see Berta, carrying a pile of crumpled gowns, cross the hallway and disappear into a room at the far end. A laundry room? That seemed a better bet than the tiny utility closet. She'd have to work her way along the hallway toward it. She ran lightly along the corridor and slipped into the utility closet. It held a sink and an assortment of cleaning tools: mop, broom, pail; it was crowded, unlit, and grimy. She looked quickly around to get her bearings, then pulled the door nearly shut and stood still, barely breathing.

Soon she heard Berta return along the corridor; presumably she was heading to her desk and would see Vivienne's note. Now! She pushed open the door and checked the hall: empty. She raced up the corridor and in through the door at the end. She found herself in a small storage room. Though cramped, it was larger than the utility closet and offered more coverage. Several boxes of clean gowns were piled against one wall; a small canvas handcart filled with laundry stood off to one side. A faint light filtered in through one small sooty window. Stifling her repugnance, she climbed carefully into the laundry cart and burrowed down under the contents.

Soon she heard Arnold and his patient exiting from an examination room. Their voices receded down the hallway, and then all at once she heard Arnold, loud and angry. She couldn't make out the words; he'd obviously been given her note: "Sorry, lost my nerve. Maybe next time. V."

Now someone banged the front door shut; someone stomped up the corridor again. How late did Arnold see patients? she wondered. How long before she could get up and look around? People moved about outside the door; she heard Arnold curse. Then all was quiet again. It was warm and airless under the laundry; Vivienne felt herself drifting off. . . .

The sound of the storage-room door banging back against the wall brought her fully awake again; she froze as Berta dumped another load of laundry on top of her. Arnold called out, "Don't forget the security system when you leave!" He sounded furious. The nurse muttered a reply and banged the door shut behind her.

Security system? Vivienne wondered. Well, she was already inside; she'd worry about it when she left.

Slowly she made her way up through the laundry and looked out over the top of the cart. Underneath the door she could see a strip of light. She watched it until it went out. Soon after, she heard the front door slam.

Did Arnold realize he was being tricked? Was he waiting for her out there in the dark? She decided to stay in the laundry cart for a quarter of an hour, just in case. The minutes seemed endless as she stared at the glowing green watch face, but at last it was six o'clock; she climbed out of the laundry cart and opened the door.

The corridor was in shadow, lit only near the waiting room, where light from the street spilled in through the curtained window. Slowly she moved down the hall toward the file room. It was very quiet. She turned the doorknob and felt the door swing slowly inward.

"This is Dr. Brian Arnold!"

Vivienne jumped back, her heart beating wildly.

"Office hours are eleven to five-thirty. Please leave a message at the sound of the beep . . ."

An answering machine. Vivienne listened, fascinated, as a voice begged "Dr. Brian" to call him back immediately. He'd used up his prescription, he said, and was desperate to renew it. She shuddered. How could Charles have sent her to such a man? But of course she understood now. He was the link with the Institute, the only person authorized to send the sam-

ples. And Harris? What was he? Well, Harris wasn't
her problem.

She stepped into the file room. Although the sky
was still light, little of its illumination reached this
room through its small courtyard window. Why hadn't
she thought to bring a flashlight?

She tried the handles on the file cabinet; the drawers
were locked shut, of course. How could she get into
it? Perhaps there were some tools in the utility closet.
Cautiously she made her way across the hall. She felt
sure now that she was alone in the office, but it was
still spooky. Snapping on the light, she looked in vain
for a hammer and screwdriver. Nothing. She turned
off the light again and closed the door and leaned
against it, thinking.

She needed something small and pointy to bang into
the lock and break it. And she needed something heavy
to bang it in with. She went back up the hall, peering
in through the doors she passed. The two examining
rooms didn't suggest anything to her, but then she
opened a third door and found herself looking into a
different sort of room.

She switched on the light. She was in Brian Arnold's
office. Heavy drapes covered the windows; a mahog-
any desk sat in front of built-in bookcases. Set across
from the desk, strangely placed out in the middle of
the room, was a large, wide sofa. Why hadn't he
brought her in here last time she'd visited? she wondered.

She walked over to the desk. There was the usual
desktop clutter: pens and pencils, a yellow lined pad,
a letter opener, several books. In one corner, a large,
heavy crystal paperweight winked in the light. She
hefted it in her hand. All she needed now was something strong and sharp. The letter opener? Too flexi-
ble. Maybe that thin silver ball-point pen.

Back in the file room, she fitted the point of the pen
into the small keyhole in the file lock and banged on
the other end with the paperweight. The lock was
about thigh height and it was hard to put any power

behind her swing. Setting her tools on the desk, she studied the cabinet. Perhaps if she could topple it over on its back . . . The file was heavy, but she maneuvered it into a position where there was clear floor behind it. Then she got behind it and pushed against the base with her foot while tugging at the top of the cabinet. Suddenly it toppled backward and she jumped clear; the cabinet hit the floor with a resounding crash.

The evening doorman, having relieved the day man at five-thirty, was sneaking a quick cigarette around the corner of the lobby when the sound of the crash reached him. It seemed to have come from Dr. Arnold's office, yet he'd seen the doctor and his nurse leave the building some time before. Crushing his smoke underfoot, he went over and tried the door.

Vivienne heard the front door rattle. "Anyone in there?" called a male voice. Vivienne didn't move. Had someone seen the light she'd turned on?

After a long minute the doorman shrugged his shoulders and went back out to his post. Vivienne, having tiptoed out to the waiting room, heard his receding steps. Returning to the file room, she continued her attack on the cabinet, smashing away at the pen in the semidarkness. At last she was rewarded by the sound of the lock clicking out.

Pulling the drawers out from their now-horizontal position was impossible; she managed with difficulty to tumble the cabinet over onto its side.

But instead of the papers she'd been sure had been secreted there, the cabinet was filled with videocassettes. Each cassette was labeled with a series of numbers. Could these be tapes of the Institute? Somehow it seemed unlikely, but she took one at random and jammed it in her handbag.

There wasn't much she could do to tidy the room; she knew she lacked the strength to stand the cabinet up again. So she simply left the cabinet lying on the floor like some disemboweled beast and went back to Arnold's office.

She'd left the light on; no one could see in through

those heavy drapes. Now she dropped her handbag on the sofa and once again approached his desk. She tried each drawer; everything was locked tight.

She went over to the sofa and sat down facing the desk, trying to think where Arnold could have hidden a key. It was simply too depressing, after all this, to believe he carried the only one on his person. She rose and wandered around the room, looking under, in, and behind bric-a-brac carefully placed on shelves, desk, windowsill. Nothing.

She checked the desk drawers again; perhaps she could break into them the way she had the file cabinet. But these locks looked far more solid.

Then she had a thought: perhaps Berta might keep a key somewhere. Berta would have to be privy to Arnold's secrets. She'd be the one to send the samples to Spain, so she'd have to know about the Institute. And she'd also be aware of what kind of practice Arnold ran. Berta would have to be completely trustworthy. And if she were, she could be trusted with the key to his desk. Maybe.

She hurried out to the darkened waiting room and flipped on the light. She had to risk someone seeing it; the search couldn't be done in the dark.

The lock on Berta's fancy desk was more decorative than useful, and Vivienne bashed it in easily. Quickly but thoroughly she rifled through the contents of each drawer, opening every aspirin tin and paper-clip box. At last, way at the back of the bottom drawer, wedged underneath file folders suspended from metal rods, she found a small flattish tin which had once contained English lemon drops. Now it held a small key suspended from a pale silken cord.

She hurried back to Arnold's office and unlocked the desk drawers one by one. Her heart was pounding, and she stood up and took several deep breaths to calm herself before opening the drawers.

The central drawer which nestled under the desktop held the usual clutter of blank stationery, pencils, and prescription pads. Sample boxes of various medications filled the top two side drawers. She shoved all three drawers back in and opened the bottom side drawer.

Inside lay a box of unused file folders. She pulled it out and set it on top of the desk. Underneath was an old red sweater, folded and positioned to make it appear as if it filled the rest of the drawer. Vivienne yanked it out; beneath was an old folder, worn and creased, its contents secured by a thick rubber band. Tossing the sweater onto the desk, she leaned down and took out the folder. The rubber band was old; it split as she pulled it off. Inside were papers. She recognized the letterhead of the Institute.

She carried the folder over to the sofa and began to read.

It was after six-thirty when she replaced the file in Arnold's desk and relocked the drawers. She moved automatically, her mind spinning, wishing she'd never read the papers, never started asking questions. What should she do? What *could* she do?

Turning off the light, she left Arnold's office and headed down the hall and through the waiting room, where she dropped the key back into its candy tin. She hesitated at the front door, remembering the security system, then shrugged. She'd have to take her chances.

She pulled a scarf from her handbag and tied it over her hair. As she pushed the door open, a siren began shrieking loudly just past her ear. Without hesitation, she dashed into the lobby, nearly colliding with the doorman.

"What's happening?" she shouted to him over the din of the alarm. "Is it a fire?"

He looked at her curiously. "Excuse me," he said. "Do you live here?"

"It's coming from over there!" she told him excitedly, pointing toward Arnold's office. "I think I heard someone scream! Call the police!"

The doorman took a few steps in the direction of the office entrance and Vivienne immediately dashed out of the lobby into the street. As she rounded the corner, she heard the doorman shout "Stop!" but he didn't seem to be following her. At Park Avenue she caught a cab and collapsed in the back seat.

Don't worry, she told herself. The evening doorman wasn't on duty when you arrived. Arnold believes you left the office while he was seeing that patient. There's nothing to tie you to the break-in.

Behind the bookcase, the camcorder continued to record, its lens permanently focused on the sofa. It ran out of tape just before the police showed up.

18

Nearly two weeks had gone by, and Eric was comfortably settled in. His room at the top of El Lobo's rickety exterior staircase wasn't fancy, but someone had made a real attempt at homey attractiveness. The walls were freshly whitewashed, the bed was large and covered with a heavy tapestry spread, and the bathroom, though small, was modern and en suite. Blue mountain flowers peeped from a local ceramic vase on the dresser.

Not so surprising, thought Eric; the hotel's few guests were nearly all hospital visitors, people who could well afford to pay dearly for what was in fact the only game in town. Even renting the room by the week, he'd discovered, didn't reduce the cost to what one would reasonably expect to pay in such a backwater.

His days had begun to form a pattern.

Eric arrived at the hospital each morning at eight, having breakfasted on bread, cheese, and fruit in his room. He checked in, made rounds, and assisted or operated as directed by Talmidge, who seemed to enjoy keeping him off-balance with unexpected procedures and schedule changes.

A simple buffet lunch was provided in the hospital staff lounge, but lingering was not encouraged and conversation was stilted and unsatisfying.

Eric rarely finished before eight or nine at night. He'd gotten into the habit of breaking for a walk in the nearby hills if things slowed down. It kept him alert. And it began to establish a practice of random absences at various times during the day; later on, this might prove useful, he thought.

Each evening after a shower and a drink, he ate his dinner alone at El Lobo's outdoor tables, enjoying the sharp tang of the mountain air. Sometimes Vicente and Felipe would join him briefly, and they would have a rather basic conversation in Spanish. Once they introduced him to Vicente's aunt, a heavy, pleasant woman in black. She was friendly but not garrulous, and soon hurried off home to her family.

He'd assumed that, isolated as they were, the hospital staff would get together after hours. But most of the small staff appeared to have been drawn from the local population, and if they socialized, he wasn't included. When he occasionally came upon this one or that in the town square, they exchanged waves or pleasantries, but no one tried to befriend him. They weren't rude, they just kept to themselves.

Eric was beginning to realize how much the town depended on the hospital as a revenue generator. In fact he'd noted with amusement that two days after he'd paid three weeks' rent in advance, the bar's rusting metal tables and chairs had been replaced by modernistic new ones of white plastic. No matter how much they knew or suspected, no San Lorenzian was going to rock Talmidge's boat.

And how did Talmidge spend his evenings? Eric identified an old green Mercedes in the parking lot as belonging Talmidge; It was always parked in the same spot when Eric arrived in the morning and still there when he left in the evening. He sneaked back once just after midnight; there it sat. Was it possible that Talmidge actually lived at the institute? Eric had never spotted the man or the car in town.

It was lonely as hell, but it gave him time to think.

He was thinking now, as he sat outside El Lobo five days later, feeding dinner scraps to the hound at his feet. A bottle of *corriente*—local red wine—and a cloudy glass stood in front of him. The glass was still full. The bottle was empty.

At any hospital in the world, Eric reflected, the work he'd been doing recently would have been considered fairly routine. The setup, on the other hand, was bizarre. In addition to cleaning up that aneurysm on his first day, Eric had assisted Talmidge in several transplants—a kidney, a cornea, the first joint of a finger—specialized operations which anywhere else would have been performed by three different specially trained surgeons. Yet Talmidge confidently performed them all. The man's technical expertise was little short of amazing, and he could operate equally well with both hands.

But the idea of Talmidge blithely cutting and stitching his way from hairline to toenail paled in comparison with the bone-chilling horror of his choice of anesthetic.

Once hailed for the rapidity of its sleep induction and its lack of side effects, Cyclopropane had been banned from operating rooms around the world for at least fifteen years. And rightly so, Eric reflected. There you were, sawing away at somebody's rib cage, and the next thing you knew, your patient was on fire. Along with the curtains, the nurse, and the surgical tray.

"I'm not worried, you understand," he'd told Talmidge the second day they'd scrubbed together. "I'm terrified!"

But Talmidge had been quite serious when he'd explained that despite its tendency to explode into flame, he believed Cyclopropane was the finest anesthetic available. He'd even seemed to take pleasure in its danger, in being the only one daring enough to use it.

"Those fools didn't take proper precautions," he said dismissively. "I've never had any problems with it."

"I didn't even think you could get it anymore," Eric mused.

"I make it myself," Talmidge told him. "My own plant . . . pipe it right in."

"Jesus!"

"Relax, boy. You're working with me now."

The man's a nut case, Eric reflected. Well, of course he is. That's why I'm here.

He fed the dog some bread, then sipped his wine. So Talmidge considers me his protégé. Kinda scary, but also exciting. He might actually warm up to me enough to tell me something important.

Or he might just keep lying to me.

Eric thought again about the operation he'd performed late that afternoon. Did Talmidge really expect me to believe that bullshit about the monitor? he wondered. Do I seem that dumb? I guess I do. And I guess that's good; it's probably the best cover I could have.

The patient, full draped and with his head hidden by a screen, was already on the operating table when Eric entered. As usual, Talmidge hadn't told him what procedure was scheduled, and as usual, Eric was nervous about his ability and experience.

"Can we begin, Ricardo?" Talmidge asked.

Eric glanced over at the monitor; the peaks and valleys were stable and even.

Ricardo gave Talmidge a thumbs-up. "Good," Talmidge said. "Go ahead, Eric. Open."

"Uh, where?"

Talmidge chuckled. "Didn't I tell you?"

No, you damn well didn't, thought Eric.

"Today is a special day, Dr. Rose. This man here is donating his liver. And you are going to remove it."

No wonder you didn't tell me, you bastard, Eric thought. You want me to kill him.

"I can't do that, Dr. Talmidge."

"Of course you can, boy. I'll help you."

"It's not that. He'll die."

Talmidge gave a pleasant little chuckle. "He's already dead."

Eric looked over at the monitor. The line was flat. Oh, shit.

"That can't be, Dr. Talmidge. His screen was healthy just a minute ago. I saw it."

"You're wrong, Eric. This man died of a stroke nearly half an hour ago."

"Then why did you ask Ricardo if we could go in? What's Ricardo giving him?"

It sure as hell wasn't Cyclopropane, Rose thought, his mind whirling. No wonder they'd made sure the guy's head wasn't visible. An IV snaked up under the drapes. They could have given him anything, he thought. Oh, Jesus.

Talmidge flicked his eyes warningly at Ricardo, then turned to Eric. He spoke calmly.

"You're new to our little family. You're not familiar with the methods we use. I've developed a chemical which, when introduced prior to organ removal, reduces the rate of tissue breakdown. Now, get on with it!"

"But I saw the monitor!"

"That monitor is aberrant. Ricardo, get it looked at. Goddammit, Eric, open!"

Suddenly Eric knew what was beneath those drapes, behind that head screen. How could he have been so dense as not to have realized it before? He was about to play a part in the very process he'd outlined to Harris a million years ago, it seemed. He'd been right. But he wished now he'd been wrong.

His head was spinning. His knees were trembling. His hands were steady. He opened.

Eric drained the wine in his glass, then upended the bottle. A few drops trickled out. Think about something else.

He thought of the post-op patients he'd been making rounds on each day: the aging American actress who had just had a face lift—Eric hadn't been asked to assist with that one—and the French politician who was so grateful for the liver transplant he'd just received.

How wonderful, they both said, that no antirejection drugs were needed. You couldn't do that in America. Or France. No, thought Eric. And I know why.

Between duties he'd found reasons to walk the entire floor on his own a number of times, from OR to recovery to patients' rooms to the large locked double doors at the end of the corridor that he knew would not open for him as they had for Talmidge.

He found nothing peculiar, nothing unusual.

It was only on his daily walk, looking down at the hospital from above, that he remembered the small side door he'd noticed the day he'd first arrived to talk Talmidge into letting him stay.

He realized he'd never seen the other, interior, side of that door.

Later he'd managed a short but thorough examination of that part of the building and discovered the side door opened into a utility room. Funny place for a door, he'd thought. And why the paved path up to it?

Now, as he sat over the remnants of his meal thinking about the day's events, another image suddenly came to mind. Like a photograph, he saw the monitor with its peaks and valleys. To one side of it stood Ricardo, large and brawny under his scrubs. And . . . something bothered him, nibbled at his memory. What was it?

The screen. Someone had moved the screen.

The screen had always been in place, he realized, each time he had entered the OR; it seemed to serve no purpose he could think of, but he'd never really thought about it. Today, though, somebody must have repositioned it slightly. Because when Eric studied the scene imprinted on his brain, he saw something just beyond the screen. He saw the edge of a door.

It appeared to be a small door, solid-looking, set flush into the OR wall. Why was it there? Where did it go? It couldn't communicate with the side door; the way the OR was positioned, this door would have to open toward the interior of the building.

* * *

Old Yaller had wandered off into the night, and Eric wiped his nearly empty plate with the last of the bread.

Where are the clones?

Not that mocked-up stuff in the lab with the half-wit guard. Those large refrigerated steel drawers with their slides all neatly labeled might contain the original samples, he conceded, and even the preliminary cultures, held in suspended animation. But surely those museum pieces, those hearts and kidneys in their pink soup, were strictly for the tourists.

He'd been so sure of what he'd find here. Not organs in jars. No, something far larger. Yet despite the evidence of today's operation, the hospital seemed much too small to contain the complex he knew must exist.

Surely Talmidge can't believe I'll accept the crumbs of misinformation he carefully doles out to me, Rose reflected. He must know I'll try to look beyond the metal-drawer room. Especially after today.

But . . . look where?

Eric sighed. You know very well where, he told himself. Behind the door in the OR, of course. The other side.

Okay, he thought, we have two choices. He considered them carefully. One. I can try to figure out a way to get beyond the door without getting caught. Two. I can think up a good excuse for putting it off.

He put some pesetas on the table and stood up slowly. The buildings around the square swayed a little, but he himself, he noticed, was steady as a rock. He picked his way through the little forest of tables and chairs and began climbing the stairs to bed, trying desperately to think of a good excuse.

It was a beautiful summer in France. The weather was kind to the grapes, so the locals were cooperative and relatively pleasant. Of course it didn't hurt that Pazula spoke an unassailable French. People on both sides of the camera were generous and even-tempered. And the fall fashions, though warm to wear, were both pretty and flattering. Days were productive and evenings were fun and nobody ate alone.

Here in her sequestered world of work and friendly colleagues, Vivienne found it easy to banish from her mind the contents of the file folder in Brian Arnold's desk and the repulsive lovemaking on the videocassette she'd taken from his office. This is more like it, Vivienne thought. This is how life should be. When did it change?

Marcella had been furious to lose Vivienne for two weeks, ominously predicting the loss of enormous fees. But Vivienne was glad she'd come, especially after she learned she'd lost the Revlon assignment to a younger model from a different agency. A job is not a life, she thought. I need to get back to that person who used to jump into the river from a tire swing.

For the first time, she began to think about what she would do in five or six years; thirty was old in the modeling business. She was surprised to find that such thoughts didn't scare her, as they did most models. Maybe I really will go to college, she thought. Maybe there I'll find something important to do with my life, something more intellectually stimulating. Dad would like that. Her investigation into the Institute back in New York had made her feel more competent, more confident about her ability to do more than just look beautiful.

She'd finally reached Charles from a phone booth at Kennedy Airport, and they'd both apologized and made up, though the wedding date remained vague. That suited Vivienne; dealing with today was enough right now.

Charles had reluctantly promised to look in on Angela while Vivienne was away. There was something about Angie's cheerfulness, she reflected, which was perhaps a little too hearty. She hoped Angie wouldn't crash. But if she did, Vivienne wanted someone to be there for her. Not that Charles was the ideal choice, she admitted to herself; he himself had been less than enthusiastic about the assignment. Still, she hadn't been able to think of anyone else Angela couldn't get rid of if she tried. One thing you could say for Charles, he was stubborn.

She'd tried to call him several times since her arrival, and had felt not disappointment but relief that she'd gotten through to him only once.

Now she sat in the plain country restaurant, sipping wine and trading war stories. Although stunned by what she'd read in Arnold's office, and repulsed by the video of Dr. Feelgood frolicking in the nude with a famous pop star, she was determined to put it all out of her mind for these few weeks. A little breathing space might help her figure out what to do next.

Damn that woman!

Brian Arnold took a long pull at his Scotch as Vivienne seated herself on the sofa and looked through the Institute file for the fifth time. Damn her! He pushed the search button and Vivienne moved quickly backward, disappearing from the screen; he hit "play" and she entered the frame again, sat down, and began to read.

Arnold was drunk and he felt he had a right to be. If Vivienne went public with what she knew, he'd be destroyed professionally. And if Talmidge found where she'd gotten her information, he'd lose a lot more than those fat fees; Talmidge would destroy *him*.

He had to deal with the woman, now. It was too late for cutesy stuff like sex and videotapes, he decided. Addiction was the only answer. He'd get her back into his office, shoot her up with something. Tell her it's a flu shot or some goddamn thing. One or two follow-up shots and he'd have her for good. But she'd never come back on her own; Charles would have to bring her. Perhaps he should show Charles the videotape, let him know what his girlfriend was up to. But no, he decided; Charles would be furious and break with the girl, and Arnold would lose any access he had.

He punched the pause button, dropped the remote

control on the desk, and dialed Charles's private number in Boston.

"We've got a problem," he said without preamble when Charles answered.

"What? Who is this?"

"It's Brian. We have a problem with Vivienne's sample."

"Brian? You sound funny. You been drinking?"

"Yeah. Look, our friends in Spain screwed up Vivienne's sample. They want another one."

"You're kidding. They're so efficient."

"Right. Well, not this time, apparently. Are you in town tomorrow? Can you, er, bring her in?"

"I've got meetings all day. Anyway, Vivienne's shooting in France. What was that crash?"

Arnold looked sourly at the pale stain where his glass of Scotch had hit the wall before smashing onto the hardwood floor. "Nothing. When's she due back?"

"In about a week. I'll call you."

"OK. Listen, has she . . . said any more about the Institute?"

There was a pause. "No," Charles said shortly. I'll handle my own problems, he thought. "Anything else you wanted, Brian?"

"No."

"Right. Good night, then."

Arnold put down the phone with a bang. France. France was awfully close to Spain, he thought. I wonder . . . He checked the date on his watch, added seven, and made a note on his private desk diary. Then he reached himself a fresh glass from the built-in bar below the bookshelves behind his desk and poured himself another Scotch. Sipping the warm drink, he retrieved the remote control and pressed "rewind" and then "play." Again Vivienne walked to the sofa and began reading through the papers. Arnold tried to picture her naked.

Charles was feeling testy and imposed-upon. The immediate source of his irritation was tomorrow morning's meeting, brought forward in order to include a Merrill Lynch bigwig who was going on vacation. He'd had to hustle his staff to get all the presentation materials ready in time; well, that's what they were there for. But he especially resented having to spend an evening in New York with Vivienne out of town. What on earth had made her suddenly decide to head off to France for two whole weeks? How he hated staying in hotels!

The second reason for his increasingly sour mood was the call he'd received as he was leaving his room that evening: Ingersoll were still undecided. The partners had approved the actual deal, but they needed more time. Time for what? he'd asked. Well, you know, just . . . time, he was told. He scowled. God, they were cautious!

Then, on top of everything, he had to pay this damn duty call. As he balanced unsteadily on the red metal-and-canvas chair and tried to make conversation, his only solace was that Angela seemed as uncomfortable about his being here as he did himself.

"Want some tea?" she asked.

"No thanks."

"Coffee?"

"No."

"Coke? Beer?"

"Nothing, Angela. Really."

"It's not catching, Charles."

"Huh?"

"Cancer. It's not contagious."

Charles looked surprised. "I wasn't even thinking of that," he said honestly. Then, "How do you feel?"

"Crappy," said Angela. "I throw up a lot. But that's okay, it's making me beautiful!" She spoke in self-derision, but Charles saw with a shock that it was true. She had slimmed down considerably, and her features were elegant in their sharpness.

"Look," Angela said. "I know Viv made you come, but you don't have to stay. You've done your duty."

Charles looked at his watch. "Actually, I have a

meeting in an hour not far from here. I'd, uh, planned to stay until then. Frankly, it's too far to go back to the hotel and back downtown again. Do you mind?''

"Nah," Angela said. "If you can stand it, I can stand it.''

"In that case . . .'' Charles reached for his attaché case leaning against the wall behind him. "Do you mind if I do a little work? I'd just like to review these papers . . .''

"Go ahead," Angela told him, and reached for the book she'd put down on the floor when he'd arrived. Then, changing her mind, she uncurled herself and rose from the sofa. "I'll just put on a kettle. Sure you won't have some tea?''

Charles stood too, feeling guilty. "Tea would be nice," he said. "But let me make it.''

"You're kidding!'' The words escaped before she realized it, but Charles laughed. "Oh, I've been known to make a cup of tea in my time," he said. "Where's the kitchen?''

"Just turn around, take three steps, and stick out your left hand!''

The tiny kitchenette was narrow and cramped, but its countertop, small sink, and half-size fridge were spotless. He filled the dented kettle and set it to boil on the two-burner stove, then pawed through the unmatched crockery in the cabinet to locate two mugs. Boxes of tea were jumbled together with ketchup, mustard, and canned tuna fish on the open shelving; he chose Irish Breakfast.

When it was ready, he carried the tea back to the living room and placed one of the mugs on the floor next to Angela's sofa—"Better let it cool," he cautioned—then put his own on a small water-marked side table.

Still standing, he opened his attaché case, removed some papers and a pen, and began to read.

"You gonna stand up for the next hour, Chas? Thanks for the tea.''

"That chair is a menace.''

Angela swept aside the colorful throw rug and swung her feet onto the floor. "Come sit here," she said. "Drag that table over and make yourself at home."

He hesitated, then shrugged and complied. The sofa, though old and spavined, was better than the umbrella chair.

Angela scooped up her book again and began to read. Soon she was chuckling.

Charles looked over. "What is it?"

"*Penguin Island.* Ever read it?"

"Yes indeed," he said. "A great favorite of mine." He studied her with new interest.

"Yes, Chas, even fat ladies have brains," said Angela.

"Now, cut that out!" he said.

"What?"

"That putting-yourself-down crap."

"But I wasn't—"

"The hell you weren't. Anyhow, you're not a fat lady anymore. You're a slim, pretty lady. And a brainy one too . . ." He indicated the book with an angry chop of his hand. "So try to like yourself a little better, OK?"

He turned back to his papers.

Angela looked over at him in fury. Who the hell did he think he was, talking to her like that? Saying those awful things, telling her that she didn't like herself, that she was brainy, that she was pretty.

Telling her that she was pretty.

She turned back to her book, but she couldn't concentrate.

"You really think I'm pretty?" she asked finally, hating herself for it.

"Yes," he said, not looking up from his papers.

There was silence for a moment.

"Well, thanks a lot!" Angela said hotly.

"Well, you're welcome!" Charles answered in kind.

Then they glanced sideways at each other, and the humor of the situation hit them and they broke into smiles and then guffaws and the uncomfortable feeling was gone.

Charles went back to his papers. Angela went back to her book, but again, she couldn't imagine why, her concentration kept slipping. She looked over at Charles. He really is cute, she thought. I never used to like him, but then, I never really talked to him before, not on a personal level. She studied his face. It was sweet of him to make the tea, she reflected. I never would have thought he'd—

"What?" Charles had felt her stare, and was now looking over at her, slightly annoyed. "What is it?"

Angela flushed. "Nothing," she said. "Uh, I was just wondering, er, what big deal you're putting together." As soon as she said it, she felt like a jerk. But Charles seemed pleased.

"Actually, I'd like to talk about it," he said. "Especially now before the presentation. It helps to run through it out loud."

"Go ahead," Angela said, dropping her book on the floor.

Charles stood up and began to pace. "Well, it's a tax-shelter deal in association with a major brokerage firm. We have a plan for five office buildings in three cities, and we're looking for an investment of forty million over a five-year-period . . ."

He outlined the plan, then began to describe the initial tax advantages and potential pay-out. Angela had expected to be bored; she'd asked about his deal because in her embarrassment it had been the first thing that had popped into her head. But now she found herself riveted. Of course she didn't understand everything, but she was surprised to find that when she got up the courage to ask a question, she actually understood the answer. Or most of it.

Charles, too, seemed surprised that she should grasp the concepts so quickly; Vivienne had always found his business deals so hard to follow, he'd stopped attempting to explain them to her. And yet here was

Angela, not only understanding, but getting excited about it.

At last Charles put his papers back in his attaché case and looked at his watch.

"I ought to be going," he said. "You'll be all right?"

"Sure," said Angela. "I'll be fine."

"So long, then." Charles went to the door, then turned back. "I'll, um, I'll try to drop by again sometime," he said.

"Yeah," Angela said. "Anytime."

"Well, g'bye."

Just as the door was closing behind him, Angela called "Good luck!" and his answering "Thanks!" echoed down the narrow stairway.

Angela carried the mugs to the sink and began to wash them. That was fun, she thought. I hope he comes back again. She pushed back her hair with a wet hand, plastering it out of her way. Pretty. He thinks I'm pretty.

Ol' Chas can be awfully nice when he tries, she thought. And his business is fascinating. She grinned to herself. I must tell Vivienne that I'm beginning to understand what she sees in him!

19

"All set, Dr. Harris."

"Thank you."

I didn't really expect to hear from him, John Harris mused as he studied the bloody liver in front of him with distaste.

We both agreed it would be difficult, probably dangerous, for him to contact me. But I'd give a lot to know what he's doing right now.

He prodded the organ experimentally.

I hope I haven't pushed him into anything he can't handle, he thought. And I hope he's learning something.

Although Harris often had second thoughts these days about what he and Eric—mostly Eric, he admitted—were doing, he was sustained, indeed driven, by his need to know.

Gently he pushed the liver to one side.

"Anything wrong, Dr. Harris?"

"I hate liver, Henry," he told the waiter.

"It's very good for you, sir," replied Henry, smiling. He'd noticed that Dr. Harris often ordered liver when he dined here at La Refuge, but he rarely ate it; just paying for it seemed to make him feel healthier. "How about some nice roast chicken instead?"

"No, I'm just being silly," Harris told him, taking up his knife and fork again. The waiter smiled and refilled his wineglass. Harris picked at a brussels sprout. Be careful, Rose, he thought.

* * *

The high sweet piano notes drift across the room, then stop, and the violin takes the melody and creates variations. Now the cello joins in, hesitantly at first, then with greater confidence. The three men are playing together again, and the others are glad. Some time ago, no one remembers exactly when, the blond one and the dark one had argued, unusual as this is for any of them. It had been an argument over music, of course; the only thing that matters enough to either of them to provoke strong emotions.

Now the third member of their trio has returned and made peace between them, and the music is glorious. They don't need to speak; the instruments converse for them.

The room is large and airy, with pale yellow walls touched with white-painted moldings. It is warm and slightly humid, but everyone is lightly dressed.

A blue-uniformed woman enters the room, pushing a serving cart piled with goodies: pink-and-white-frosted cakes, buttered toast, warm biscuits. She begins to dispense tea from a commercial urn.

In contrast to the people now crowding around her, the tea lady is stocky and gray-haired. As usual, she marvels at how they can put away all that food and still keep their figures. Well, they exercise more than she does, she thinks without regret. She'd rather be plump than run around that cinder track and work out on all those machines. Not that they have a choice.

They don't have much to say. So she simply does her job and collects the pay that supports her family. She has no complaints. The work is not hard. The people are cooperative. And they play such beautiful music.

Soon tea is over and she leaves; the people resume their interrupted activities. Along one side of the room where thick dropcloths cover the wall, a dark, intense woman is painting.

The wall drapes are splashed with the magentas, yellows, and purples of her violent palette. Around her, others paint too, but none with her passion, her abandon.

Her canvases are large and strong and faintly troubling. She herself is small and pale and still, as if her emotions have drained away into the paint, onto the canvas.

The painting is finished. She sits on the floor, exhausted, the dripping brush in her lap.

"That is beautiful, Anna," he says.

She smiles shyly at the compliment. "May I name it?" she asks.

He frowns but nods.

"Anger," she says.

"Anger is bad, Anna," he says. "You know that anger is a bad thing."

"Yes." she answers. "But now the anger is here in the painting. Now I will go and tell Miranda I am sorry."

One day she will really harm someone, he thinks. One day the paints will not be enough. I hope we will have sufficient time.

"Go and clean your brushes," he tells her.

She goes to the sink and begins to rinse the brushes. The paint flows into the basin like blood.

Having failed, over the past several days, to come up with a good reason not to, Eric decided to have a look at the door in the OR. He wasn't sure if he'd get past it, but he felt reasonably sure he could get to it.

He figured that the safest time would be when Talmidge had left the hospital for the night, although Eric had not yet determined where he went. Talmidge had still been very much in evidence when Eric left each evening. So for several days now he'd found excuses to stay later than usual. He rechecked patients, wrote chart notes, and made himself generally useful. And he discovered that after about nine, what staff there was tended to thin out, and more important, Talmidge himself was rarely to be seen unless an important procedure had been done that day.

Now it was Friday. The French diplomat had left that morning, and the amazingly restored actress would depart the following day. Two new cases had been admitted for blood work prior to Saturday procedures; by the afternoon they were resting comfortably in their rooms. Nothing dramatic will happen tonight, Eric decided. Talmidge won't have any reason to hang around. And I could be wrong about that car. Tonight it is.

Talmidge ignored him for much of the afternoon, leaving him to do scut: draw bloods, update charts, and the like. Back at New York General, such work would be thrown at the first-year residents; here there were no residents. Eric and the nurses did it all.

By nine-thirty Eric had stretched the work as far as he could. So he went into the tiny on-call room and closed the door. Earlier in the day he'd left two sandwiches and a candy bar in the desk drawer; now he got them out and ate them, a medical book from the library propped up in front of him.

When he finished, he brought his book over to the cot and stretched out. If anyone came in, he'd pretend to be asleep. No one could see anything insidious in his napping in the on-call room. And in fact, he did doze off.

He awoke with a start just before midnight, knocking the book off the cot with his elbow.

He stood and stretched, then opened the door quietly and looked out into the corridor. All was quiet. Turning off the light, he ventured out, walking softly in his sneakers.

There were two entrances to the OR: past the OR nurses' station and through the scrub room, or through the Recovery Room on the opposite side of the operating theater. Across the corridor from Recovery were patient rooms; the nurses' station there would be manned all night. But there were no patients in Critical Care, which was across from the scrub and dressing rooms, and with no scheduled procedures, perhaps the OR nurses' station would be unstaffed.

Eric made his way along the corridor, passing the

lab rooms, the library, the staff lounge, and peeked around the corner of the nurses' station. It was empty.

He went around the desk and into the scrub room, making as little noise as possible. It was dark, but the OR was brighter, lit by a fitful moon which shone its thin light through the curtained windows. The pleated white screen nearly glowed with reflected moonlight. Careful not to move it, Eric stepped behind the screen; there was the door, just as he'd remembered it.

It felt cooly metallic beneath his hand and it fitted smoothly into the wall. Eric took out the only portable light he'd had access to, an illuminated key ring. Holding it close, he examined the door as best he could. There were no hinges on this side of the door, and no doorknob. A smooth metal lock was set into one side at about waist level. On the wall next to it was a digital plate with numbered buttons and a lock light which glowed dull red.

He put his ear to the door, but could hear nothing; the door was too solid. He lay down on the floor in an attempt to discern any source of light beyond the door. Nothing.

OK, he thought, I'm not getting through that door tonight. So what now? Here he was, alone and unobserved in the Institute at night; surely there was something useful he could accomplish.

He left the OR through the doors to the recovery room, moving slowly and silently.

The nurses' station on this corridor had been designed so that the staff could see both the recovery room, which was now dark and empty, and many of the patient rooms. Crouching low, Eric crept along the far side of Recovery, keeping gurneys and equipment between himself and the desk where the night nurse sat drinking coffee and reading a paperback.

In the corridor at last, he stood and stretched his cramped muscles, then turned right. Because of the placement of the nurse's desk, the outer corner of Recovery would screen him as long as he stayed on the

right side of the hallway. But any noise would carry
easily in the quiet night.

The anteroom to Talmidge's office was just up the
corridor; there was no entrance to the inner office except through the anteroom. The door to the anteroom
stood slightly ajar.

Eric entered and stood still, allowing his eyes to
become accustomed to the darkness again. Then he
tried the handle of the oak door. Not surprisingly, the
door was locked. Next to it was the same digital plate
he'd seen in the OR.

Maybe I can figure out the code, he thought. Yeah,
and while I'm at it, I can pick the winning numbers
in the New York State lottery.

He turned to leave, then shrugged and came back to
the digital plate. What the hell, he thought. You've
gotta be in it to win it.

He tried all the obvious combinations: the number
of letters in Talmidge's name, the mathematical equivalents of his initials, various series containing the
number two. He tried emptying his mind and punch-
ing in random numbers. It was nearly one in the morning when he slumped, defeated, in the wing chair. I
just don't know enough about him, he thought, to figure out mathematical equivalents of the significant
events of his life. And I don't know enough about the
way his mind works.

Or do I?

He pictured himself in the stacks, reading about Talmidge for the first time, and at the New York Academy
of Medicine, looking through his membership folder.
He saw himself in the Greek diner, listening to Harris
talk about ego and attitude.

He pondered, and counted on his fingers. After some
time he got up and went back to the plate. By the faint
red glow of the lock light, he carefully punched in four
numbers.

Nothing happened.

It was a long shot, he thought. I didn't really expect
it to work. He was already making his way through

the darkness to the outer door when the click, so faint he almost missed it, made him freeze.

His heart knocked in his chest as he returned to the oak door and pushed. It swung inward, and Talmidge's private office stood open before him.

Pale moonlight spilled faintly through the partly open curtains as Eric made his way around the desk to Talmidge's chair.

7. 2. 6. 21. The year Talmidge had cloned his mouse. And his attitude toward the academic world who had celebrated, then vilified him.

1972. Fuck you.

Talmidge went through the double set of steel doors which led to his private quarters. As in a maximum-security prison, the second door would not open until the first was closed and locked.

Once inside his living space, he threw off his white coat, glancing as he did so at the bold flame-hued painting, a recent acquisition, which covered one wall like a huge open wound. It made him feel restless, uneasy.

Eric stared at the document he'd managed to bring up on the computer monitor. Everything else was code-locked.

First came a list of names. He recognized many of them: celebrities, statesmen, CEO's of major corporations. A former president of the United States. A world-famous tennis player.

He scrolled quickly through the hundreds of names, trying to memorize as many as possible.

The list ended abruptly and Eric scrolled on through several blank pages. That couldn't be all, he thought, and held his finger down firmly.

And suddenly there it was.

"Notes on the Formulation and Care of Human Clones in an Isolated Environment." A philosophical paper, or an owner's manual?

He wondered how loud the printer would sound. Too

loud. He skimmed down the manuscript with the cursor, but found no scientific formulas. He went back to the top of the document and began to read.

Talmidge fixed himself a drink, but couldn't settle anywhere. So much work, he thought as he prowled around the sitting room. I need Eric down here. It's only been a few weeks, but he seems discreet. He hasn't grilled the patients, hasn't pushed to know more than I've told him. He hasn't even called me on what he knows is bullshit. Like the organs I showed him. He knew better, but he kept his mouth shut.

". . . Parents should order a clone for each child when it is born. With accelerated growth hormones, the clone will soon be large enough to grow at the same rate as the child. However, it is advisable to start a second clone for the same child when he or she reaches twenty years of age. This way, when that child is fifty, the second clone will be about twenty-eight years old physically, and therefore the organs, limbs, and so forth will be in better condition for transplant if necessary. For example, a woman of fifty can use her second clone for a face lift, but not her first clone, which will be too old. The original clone can be turned back to laboratory ownership to pay for the upkeep of the second clone. There is always a need for parts . . ."

Is it too soon? Talmidge wondered. He'd waited longer with the others, and every one had disappointed him.

". . . Owners and clones must never meet, partly to keep guilt and sympathy from preventing the owner from using parts if needed, but more important to keep the clone unaware of life outside the cluster . . ."

Pacing with unspent energy, Talmidge gulped the rest of his drink, then went to a closet and pulled on a dark leather coat. Air, he thought, I need to get out for a while.

". . . The legal issue is confusing. The Institute views the clone as property but it could be viewed as a form of slavery. Courts have yet to grapple with the issue since no one except those with a vested interest in the perpetuation of secrecy believes it is possible to clone a human being, or that they can be maintained on the scale we have achieved here. However, should it become public knowledge, so many politicians, judges, and leaders of industry have clones of their own, the legal issues could drag on for years. . . ."

An ornate wooden door was set in the wall across from the painting. Talmidge punched in a combination of numbers and the doorplate clicked and unlocked. He began to climb the steel stairs.

The enormity of what Talmidge had apparently created was nearly overpowering. Eric read avidly, oblivious to everything except the poisonous green glow of the words on the monitor.

The ends of the leather belt flapped at his sides, and the metal buckle pinged against the handrail, echoing in the hollow stairwell. Talmidge pulled at the coat impatiently as he continued rapidly upward.

It was some seconds before Eric realized he'd heard the soft metal ping. He'd carefully closed the inner door when he'd entered the office; had someone unlocked it? Was someone coming in? No, this sound had been different, and somewhat muffled. At once he ejected the disk and punched the off switches on monitor and computer as he looked around, trying to pinpoint the source of the sound.

A sharp crack drew his attention to the wall of books to the right of the desk. As he watched in horror, a vertical section of shelving began to swing out. Eric stood frozen for a beat, then dived for the floor. Still holding the disk, he wiggled himself beneath the trestle table which served as Talmidge's desk. A solid patch of shadow was all the concealment it offered. He hoped it would be enough.

The section of shelving continued to open, folding back upon itself like a page in a book to reveal a door. Next to the door was a digital plate; its glowing lock light was changing from red to green.

Tomorrow, by God! Talmidge shoved at the door with the flat of his hand. I'll start him tomorrow!

He burst into the room like some great prehistoric bird of prey, his leather coat flaring behind him. For a moment he stood silhouetted in the faint light from the stairwell. Then he turned and made straight for the door to the anteroom. In an instant he was gone.

A long minute passed; then Eric got shakily to his feet and approached the bookshelf door. Should he go down the stairs? A few tentative steps took him through and onto the tiny landing beyond. Undecided, he peered down the metal staircase which spiraled away in the dim light.

A tiny whoosh of air made him spin around; the door was closing behind him. Instinctively he leapt back through the closing door and then berated himself for his cowardice. Yet the code for this door lock might be a different, unknown one; he might have been trapped in the airless stairway, where Talmidge would find him when he returned. For it was obvious now where Talmidge spent his nights.

He watched the lock light turn from green to red and the bookshelf section fold back into place. Then he silently retraced his steps through the anteroom, the recovery room, and the OR.

He awoke in the on-call room at six, still clutching the computer disk, surprised that he had slept at all.

20

Charles was bored.

It had taken him most of the evening to realize it, but he was excruciatingly, stupefyingly bored.

Janine was having a wonderful time. Dressed to kill, and flashing her brilliant smile at waiters and celebrities alike, she was making sure everyone noticed that she was dining with *Charles Spencer-Moore*. Janine was violently jealous of Vivienne, which was why Charles had called her. That's what I get for acting out of pique, he thought ruefully as Janine chattered away, holding his hand and scanning the crowd for anyone important she might have missed.

He and Janine had dated off and on for six or seven months, before he'd met Vivienne. He'd been impressed by her four-hundred-year-old family name and dazzled by her beauty: the raven hair, the delicate face, the tiny waist, and the huge bust. But even then, he recalled, she'd had a talent for being immensely irritating.

Still holding tightly to his hand, she winked sexily at the waiter as he placed their expensive dinners in front of them. The good-looking Italian youth colored slightly. The tabletop was at the same level as the plunging neckline of her dress, making her appear pneumatically naked.

Charles attempted to loosen her grip; she resisted. "You used to love holding hands with me," she pouted in that soft baby whisper he had once loved and later come to loathe. "Don't you like me anymore, Charlie?"

She sighed deeply and leaned forward; her breasts rolled above the tablecloth like some antediluvial mountain chain rising from the sea.

"Of course I like you, Janine," said Charles tiredly.

"Then why won't you let me hold your hand, Charlie?"

"Because I'm trying to eat my dinner, Janine," said Charles reasonably. He gave his hand a firm jerk, and it came free. He picked up his fork.

Some celebration, he thought grimly. All she wants from me is a chance to put Viv's nose out of joint. She couldn't care less about me, or the success I've had today. He ordered the raspberry-and-chocolate roll, richest dessert on the menu, but when it came, he couldn't eat it. He felt lonely.

"Let's go dancing!" Janine suggested brightly. "You were always a divine dancer, Charlie! There's a new spot just opened in SoHo. Everything's made of foam rubber, even the tables!"

The thought of Janine, herself resembling nothing so much as foam rubber, bouncing around on foam-rubber furniture made him feel slightly seasick.

"You go, Janine," said Charles. "I've had it." He signed the oversize check without looking at it—something he rarely did—and stood up. Disappointed, Janine stood too, and took possession of his arm, pressing herself against him and gazing soulfully into his eyes.

People will think I'm sleeping with her, Charles thought in alarm, attempting to disengage himself.

People will think he's sleeping with me, Janine thought, and hung on grimly.

Somehow they made their way through the flurry of waiters and out into the street, where Charles managed to push her into a taxi just as a group of people emerged from the restaurant behind them. It was too dark to be sure if she knew them, but Janine played for the crowd, giving Charles a big wet smooch and nearly pulling him down on top of her. When the taxi drove off at last, Charles walked toward Lexington Avenue, wiping saliva from his mouth, chin, and the side of his nose.

It was just after ten; he wandered aimlessly down Lexington feeling sorry for himself. It was only when he noticed the boutiques had given way to Indian groceries that he realized where he was.

She sounded surprised but not angry when he buzzed up from the vestibule, and she was slightly out of breath when she opened the door to him. She smiled, tying the belt of a brightly flowered robe, and it was a nice, genuine smile with no hidden agendas.

"I go to bed early these days," she said without apology.

"Sorry," he said, but he came in anyway and sat down on the sofa. She closed the door and leaned against it, looking over at him. He wondered if she knew she was still smiling.

"It was great," he told her.

"Huh?"

"Ask me how my Merrill Lynch presentation went on Tuesday."

"How did your Merrill Lynch presentation go on Tuesday?"

"It was great. I was brilliant."

"They like the idea of the buy-back after ten years?"

"How did you know about the buy-back?"

"You told me, Chas! Jeez, for a genius, you've got a lousy memory." Angela perched on the edge of the coffee table and grinned at him.

"Oh. Right. Well, yes, they loved the buy-back. Now ask me what incredibly fabulous thing happened *today*."

"What incredibly—"

"Ingersoll Bank! It took me over a year, but they finally signed!"

"Fantastic. Let's celebrate!"

"I've been celebrating."

She studied him critically. "Could have fooled me,"

she said. "How about a cup of tea? Irish Breakfast, right?"

"You make it this time."

"Going macho on me already, huh, Chuck?" She went to fill the kettle.

Charles sprawled out on the sofa. It was the ugliest piece of furniture he had ever seen; no, the second-ugliest. The end table was the ugliest. Yet he felt comfortable here.

Angela brought him his tea and sat down next to him. "Ingersoll's a big deal, huh?" she asked.

"The biggest."

"I'm really glad for you. Uh, if you want to talk about it, I'd love to listen."

"Actually," Charles told her, "I'm all talked out. I just want to sit here and gloat."

"Okay."

He reached for the newspaper, which lay in confusion on the red umbrella chair.

"It's yesterday's," she warned him.

"Oh. Well, d'you have a television?"

"Yeah. And we even have electricity and running water too." She went to a bleached pine cabinet—repro, not antique, he noticed, and disliked himself for it—and opened its doors. A television set was revealed.

"Channel?" she asked.

"Got a *TV Guide?*"

She tossed it over and he studied it. "You like Arsenio?"

"Not much."

"Me neither," he lied. "How about a *Cheers* re-run?"

"Sure," she said, and pushed some buttons.

After *Cheers* they watched *Taxi,* and then an old black-and-white movie. Angela fell asleep partway through it, her head lolling against the sofa cushions.

Around one in the morning, Charles yawned and turned off the set. Angela, awakened by the sudden silence, peeped at him from behind almost-closed eyes as he shrugged on his jacket and left, quietly pulling the door shut behind him.

"You look tired, Eric," Talmidge told him as he entered the OR after his night of near-discovery.

"I'm OK," Eric replied, looking down at the instrument tray. He was finding it extremely difficult to deal with the fierce reality of what had been until last night only an academic suspicion.

"You better be," said Talmidge. "We're working in tandem today." He waved a hand in the direction of the windowed double doors between the OR and the "holding bay," where a draped figure lay on a gurney. "Reynolds there is getting a new lung. I'll be replacing the cancerous one in here. Look at me, Eric!"

Eric turned toward Talmidge. He tried to relax his face muscles, to keep the expression in his eyes neutral, but his stomach was churning.

"And now he's cloning organs," Harris had said months ago as they sat over their Greek pastries.

"There is another possibility," Eric had replied coolly. Well, he'd guessed right.

"You came here because of a theory you had," said Talmidge. "An idea which obsessed you. Today I will make that theory come alive for you. I hope you are worthy of my trust."

Talmidge went to the screen that masked the little door and shoved it aside with his foot. It rattled off on its castors and banged into the far wall. Reaching over to the instrument tray, he picked up a sterile probe and used it to punch out a code on the digital panel. He tossed the now-unsterile probe at the screen as the door swung open. Beyond was a high white room lit by brilliant arc lights. An operating room. "Go in," Talmidge ordered.

This second OR was long and narrow, without doors or windows. A scrub nurse Eric hadn't seen before stood next to an instrument tray.

"In this room, Eric, you will remove the lung. A

scrub nurse will bring it to me for immediate transplant. Do you understand?''

''Where is my patient?''

''He'll be here. But first we have some unfinished business, you and I.'' He motioned Eric back from the door. ''I spoke of trust, of faith. I do not speak of secrecy, because surely you know how vital secrecy is to our work.''

Feeling some response was required, Eric nodded as Talmidge continued.

''You are not the first. The best, but not the first. I'm proud to show you what I've built here, and I hope you are proud to become a part of it. But first, one thing is required.''

Talmidge picked up a scalpel. ''I require this of all who work for me. It binds them close to me, you see. And it gives them an interest in maintaining secrecy. And trust.''

Holding the scalpel ready, he took a step toward Eric, who recoiled. Talmidge smiled grimly. ''If you're as thrilled about my work as you profess to be, you'll consider this an honor.''

The scalpel glittered in the harsh light. Eric scoured his memory for a slip, any mistake he might have made last night which would cause Talmidge to suspect what he'd done. He hadn't moved anything, and surely Talmidge hadn't seen him crouching beneath the table. He'd hidden the disk between the pages of his medical book, which he'd returned to the unsupervised library early that morning; even if Talmidge had missed the disk, he'd hardly suspect Eric. Would he?

Talmidge came closer. ''Marta!'' he called out. The dour scrub nurse appeared at Eric's side. She carried a small three-sided tray; in it were slides, tubing, and other equipment. She put it down on the operating table in front of Talmidge, who nodded approval.

''Our friend is a little nervous,'' he told her. *''Un poco nervoso. Por favor, ayudarle.''*

The nurse made a grab for Eric's arm, but he jerked it back. Help me, my ass!

"Relax, Eric," Talmidge told him. "We take the sample from your arm. Blood from the vein. And a scrape of tissue. It hurts less if you keep your arm still."

Eric took a deep breath, somewhat reassured by the presence of the equipment tray. Besides, he thought, if they were going to kill me, they would have done it by now. He put his left arm down on the table. "Okay," he said. "Go ahead."

"Get him a chair, Marta," Talmidge ordered. "That's a damn uncomfortable position."

Eric sat and watched the procedure. Aside from the tissue scrape, he'd done it himself, many times. When they were finished, Marta left the room with the box— she'll have to scrub all over again, Eric thought—and Talmidge clapped him on the back and smiled. "That was a culture kit," he explained. "You'll be seeing a lot of those."

Eric stood and kicked the chair out of the way. It rolled toward the screen. Getting ourselves a nice little collection over there, he thought inconsequentially.

"You're one of us now, Eric," said Talmidge. "Ready to meet your patient?" And he nodded to the second scrub nurse, who went to the far wall and, using a sterile instrument as Talmidge had done, flipped an unobtrusive metal switch.

Slowly the wall dividing the two operating rooms rose straight up and disappeared into the ceiling.

As Eric watched in fascination, the nurse took several steps to her right. There, set into the floor and protruding slightly above its surface, were two large round buttons, one red, one blue. She stepped on the red button, and immediately a whirring sound echoed from below the floor. Rose started forward but Talmidge grabbed his bandaged arm; Eric gritted his teeth with pain.

A rectangular section of floor slid away, leaving an opening about eight feet by four. Now Talmidge allowed Eric to go forward. The whirring sound continued as slowly a draped form rose up through the hole.

The figure lay on an operating table supported by a long hydraulic steel cylinder which lifted table and patient up into the room. When the table reached a preset height, its upward motion stopped. The mechanics below gave a final whir and a click and then fell silent.

"Your patient," said Talmidge.

21

Charles carefully angled the table through the narrow doorway, then plunked it down unceremoniously, leaning on its polished surface and breathing heavily.

"Good evening, Chas," said Angela. "Who's your friend?"

"Table," Charles gasped.

"Yes," Angela agreed. "But why is it here in my living room?"

A pause while Charles recovered the powers of speech and upright movement; then he went to the ugly side table at the end of Angela's sofa and kicked it.

"Shall we burn this?" he asked. "Or shall I just toss it out the window into the courtyard?"

Together they lifted and positioned the exquisitely carved piece of furniture Charles had brought, then stood back to admire the effect.

"It's very beautiful," said Angela dubiously. "It doesn't go with anything I own."

Then she grinned at him. "Running out of room up at the mansion, Chas?"

"It's a present," he told her. "For me. Because if I have to look at that piece of plywood you call a side table one more time, I'll spit. So don't say 'Oh, Charles, you shouldn't have!' "

"Oh, Charles, you shouldn't have!"

"Now that we've got that straight, let's go out to dinner and celebrate. Go get dressed."

Dinner? Angela was suddenly confused. The casual visits she'd gotten used to over the past week or so—the comfortable banter, the tea and the backhanded sympathy, all enjoyed in the small self-contained world of her apartment—had given her friendship with Charles a definite aura of unreality. And because of that, she hadn't had to think about what the friendship was turning into, what it might mean to both of them. The fact that Charles now wanted to take her, take them, public seemed somehow significant. But of what?

Her response was cut short by the ringing of the phone. She answered and Vivienne's voice said, "Hi, Angie! How're you feeling?"

Angela glanced guiltily at Charles. "Fine," she said, "just fine. And how's life in the fast lane?"

Charles looked at Angela's face. Oops, he thought. I bet that's Vivienne. He wandered into the kitchenette, wondering why he should feel so uncomfortable at the idea of Vivienne knowing he was visiting Angela. After all, he thought, she told me to.

"Life in the fast lane is nice and easy," Vivienne replied. "I'll be sorry to fly home day after tomorrow."

Angela lowered her voice slightly. "Charles won't be," she told Vivienne. "I think he's bored without you."

"How can you tell?"

"Well, for one thing, he's been hanging out a lot at my place." Telling Vivienne made Angela feel less guilty.

For a moment Vivienne felt a stab of . . . what? Jealousy? But that was silly. Angela seemed to pick up her thoughts, because she said quickly, "Don't worry, kid. I'm harmless. Better me than the barracudas out there."

Angie was right of course, Viv thought. Besides, Charles had never liked Angela much. Then why is he spending so much time with her? said a little voice inside her, but she brushed the thought away.

"How's the chemo going?" she asked instead.

"OK, I guess. I mean, it's not nice, but it works. And guess what? I'm getting thin!"

"Are you sure you're supposed to?"

"Who cares? I look great! Even Charles says so!"

Even Charles says so?

"And, Viv," Angela continued, "I hope you won't take this the wrong way or anything, but guess what Charles has arranged as a sort of 'hurray-you've-survived' present for next month?"

"I can't imagine," said Viv quietly. Charles was giving Angela a present?

"Remember how you tried to help when I had to go for surgery? Well, Charles is arranging for me to have one!"

"One what?"

"A blueprint thing. You know, they take your cells and grow them and you can use the parts—"

"Angela, no!"

"Why not? You have one. Besides, even after I'm cured, the cancer can come back somewhere else. I might really need it."

"But when we talked about it before the operation, you told me you thought it sounded kind of scary, remember?"

"I changed my mind."

"Well, change it back! Look, Angie, it's not just cells. Remember those papers I saw at Charles's house?"

"You said you couldn't be sure—"

"I know, I know. But later I broke into Brian Arnold's office and . . . Angie, it's something living, something horrible."

"Look, Charles explained it all to me and I think it's great."

Vivienne gasped. "He explained . . . ?"

"Well, sort of. Listen, Viv, I need it and I'm going to have it!"

"But you can't—"

"Why not? You did!"

"But I didn't know—"

"Well, I don't care! If I get cancer again, in my ovaries, say, I want new ones so I can have a child someday! And I want to have a new breast sometime too, a whole, pretty one! Charles says—" Angela suddenly broke off.

"What did Charles say?" Vivienne asked softly.

"Now, Viv, we were just talking."

"Talking about your breasts."

"It's not like what it sounds like. Listen, Viv, it's different for you. You're whole and healthy. You don't know what it's like to lose a part of you."

"That's true," Viv responded. "But, Angie, think about the other, uh, whatever it is. It'll lose a part of itself to you."

"I don't care. It's made with my cells, so it's really mine. It's a part of me already."

"Angie, it's . . . it's wrong."

"Sure, it's okay for the rich and famous, but for little old Angie, it's a no-no!"

"You know I don't mean that—"

"Don't you?"

"Angie, stop that right now! I'm your friend!"

"Then *be* my friend!"

Vivienne was silent, marshaling her thoughts. "Look, I can understand that it sounds great in theory . . . but you can't know what it's really like. It could be horrible! Please, Angie!"

"Your imagination's working overtime again, Viv," Angela retorted. "*You* don't know what it's like either."

"No, but I'm going to find out!" As the words left her lips, she realized she'd known it all along.

"What do you mean?"

"I'm going to Spain. I'm going to see for myself. It'll only take a day or so. Today's Monday . . . well, almost Tuesday, actually. It's nearly midnight here. So I'll be home Wednesday evening, for sure. Promise me you won't do anything till I get back."

"The hell I will!" Angie shot back. "Why do you

have to try to ruin it all for me? If you were really my friend, you'd be happy for me!''

''I am happy for you,'' said Vivienne tiredly. ''But I'm very sad for the world.'' She hung up.

Angela replaced the receiver with a bang. How dare Vivienne presume to make her decisions for her?

''What's wrong?'' Charles asked.

''Vivienne is!'' said Angela loudly. She felt a sudden sharp pang of disloyalty, but her anger overwhelmed it. ''*She* doesn't think I should have a blueprint! *She's* going on a one-woman crusade to save the world from the Institute!''

''She's what!'' said Charles in alarm.

''She's going to Spain, babycakes! She wants to see it for herself.''

Good God! thought Charles. Good God.

He'd been truthful when he'd told Vivienne he'd never seen the Institute. His father's description had been enough. The Institute had been in its infancy then; by now it would be even worse. No; he could use Talmidge's technology if need be, but he had no desire to see it for himself.

And for Viv to see it was unthinkable.

''Are you sure that's what she said? She's definitely going?''

''Yep. She said she'd be back on Wednesday night, so she must be planning to go tomorrow.''

''Shit!'' Charles reached for the phone.

''She'll be all right, won't she?'' Angela asked him. ''I mean, it's not really so bad, is it?''

Ignoring her, he dialed Brian Arnold at home.

The phone rang and rang. Answer, damn you! Charles urged. At last Arnold picked up, a little out of breath.

''Brian, it's Charles. We have a problem.''

Arnold pulled himself upright among the pillows. ''What's she done now?'' he demanded.

''She's going to Spain,'' Charles said. ''She wants to see for herself.''

"Good going, Charles," Arnold told him sarcastically. "You really calmed her down."

"Screw that. What are we going to do?"

"*You're* not going to do anything," Arnold told him firmly. He paused, thinking furiously. "Listen, Charles, it's not the end of the world. Let her go. Talmidge knows how to handle tourists."

"You really think so?" Charles sounded relieved.

"Of course!" said Arnold reassuringly. The news had caught him off-guard, but now the solution was clear to him. Let Ben handle her, he thought. "There's nothing to worry about," he said soothingly. "I promise."

"But you were so upset the last time we talked about Vivienne's interest in the Institute. You said—"

"Yes, yes, I know. I got a little emotional, but now that I've thought about it, there's really no risk. Talmidge will make sure she doesn't see anything she shouldn't. And if she tried to talk about the place, well, who would believe her?"

"I guess you're right," Charles said. Then a new thought hit him. "You don't think she'll be in any danger, do you?"

"Danger?" Arnold scoffed. "Of course not! Don't be so dramatic, Charles. Anything else? No? Well, I'm rather busy at the moment, so I'll say good-bye." And he did.

Charles sat there for a moment, relief flooding over him. The idea of Vivienne visiting the Institute had badly frightened him, but now that Arnold had assured him it would be all right . . . Why hadn't Vivienne told him how she felt when she'd called from the airport? He sighed in frustration.

He looked over at Angela, half-turned away from him on the sofa, and felt a strange happiness. How comfortable I am here with her, he thought. His feelings had nothing to do with her attitude toward the Institute; she could change her mind about the blueprint and he'd still feel the same. The same what? he wondered.

"How about our dinner date?" he asked her. "I feel like celebrating."

"Celebrating what?" Angela glanced up at him questioningly, and was surprised to see the same sense of puzzlement in his eyes as he walked around the coffee table to her. "Damned if I know!" he said with a little laugh. But something inside him sang: Vivienne's not coming home till the day after tomorrow. I can spend more time with Angela. Guilt nagged at him, but he pushed it away. That damn Institute's more important to Viv than I am, he told himself.

They went to a small neighborhood bistro; Charles ordered a bottle of wine and they sipped it, adjusting slowly to this change in their relationship.

At first Angela's guilty pangs returned; here she was, having dinner with her best friend's fiancé. But as she replayed their phone conversation in her head, guilt was replaced by resentment. How could Vivienne understand what she'd been through? How dare she tell her what was right and wrong? She pushed all thoughts of Vivienne away, determined to enjoy herself.

For Charles, the evening was a revelation. The dinner invitation had sprung to his lips without thought, but as he spoke, the words released a rush of emotions, emotions he now realized had been building in him for weeks.

Why do I feel like this? he wondered as they walked the few blocks back to Angela's apartment. The woman can offer me nothing. She's a glorified secretary, for God's sake; not famous, not rich. No glamour, no connections. And she doesn't seem to mind.

Maybe that was it, he thought, settling himself on the spavined sofa.

Maybe the reason he was so comfortable here was that she was so comfortable with herself. Even his mother wouldn't have been able to shake her, he reflected.

Angela and his mother; it was a bizarre thought, and for some reason it made him grin.

Angela came and sat beside him. ''What's the big joke?''

''I was just thinking about you and my mother. She wouldn't have approved of you at all.''

Angela's first reaction was pain: he'd just been marking time, using her until Vivienne came home. But somehow she didn't really believe that, and the pain quickly turned to resentment: she wasn't good enough for the sainted Elizabeth. Then she realized she didn't give a damn whether Elizabeth would have approved or not.

''Fuck your mother,'' she told him.

Charles looked at her in surprise. He'd been thinking what fun it would have been to watch Angela best his mother, but of course Angela hadn't known that.

''Look,'' said Angela hotly, ''I'm not impressed by your money or your goddamned family. You brought that table. I like that table. Not because it cost more than my old one or because it's been in your family for a million years, or even because it's you that brought it. I like it because it's a terrific table. And I like you because . . . well, I'm not sure why I like you. I didn't used to. But now it seems I do. I mean, a lot. But I will not put up with a bunch of crap about how classy you are and how your mother would have hated me. So maybe you better just get the hell out of here!''

Elizabeth would have been horrified, he thought gleefully.

''And if you're enjoying the idea of a roll in the lower-class muck as a way of thumbing your nose at your mother—''

Lower-class muck? ''Shut up a minute, will you?'' said Charles.

''Why should I?''

''I'm thinking.''

Despite her fury, Angela found herself both moved and amused as his brow furrowed in concentration.

Is that all this is? he wondered. A roll in the muck? But Angela isn't muck. I never really thought she was.

He studied her eyes and the planes of her face. She's strong, he reflected. She's stronger than my mother, yet she needs me in ways no one else has ever needed me.

It made him feel strong and protective. He couldn't ever remember feeling this protective about anyone before.

He continued to stare at her for what seemed like a long time. At last his expression cleared and he leaned forward and took her face in his hands.

It was time to say good-bye to his mother.

Slowly, his eyes never leaving hers, he brought his lips toward hers.

Angela's face betrayed her panic, her confusion. Vivienne, she thought.

"Don't," Angela said. "Please. Don't."

"Shut up," said Charles again. He kissed her.

He could sense his mother's wraith, curling slowly in agony, twisting, bending, dissolving.

Angela's arms went around him, she didn't tell them to, they just did, and he kissed her and kissed her.

I bet I'd look good in a pink shirt, he thought. Angela held him tight. Elizabeth was a faint shadow; now she was gone.

His lips moved against hers, and wandered over her cheek, her ear, her neck . . .

She pulled back, but he held her firmly as his lips moved down her neck to her collarbone. Gently he pulled at her robe as his mouth continued downward.

She recoiled in horror: he couldn't want to kiss her there. She stared at him, frozen with fear and self-loathing. But his expression was gentle and his eyes were kind.

"Relax, Angie," he said softly. "It's just me."

Vivienne, a robe wrapped around her, leaned on the railing of the small balcony outside her hotel room and looked out over the rooftops. She wasn't ready to sleep. She needed to think. Aside from simply visiting the Institute, was there really anything she could do about it?

A cloud drifted across the moon and she shivered in the night air. So Charles was giving Angela gifts . . .

But even if they did listen, who would believe her? Proof. She'd need proof.

She headed back toward the cafe, her steps quickening with her thoughts.

Finding proof shouldn't be so hard. She was Charles's fiancee, after all. And his family had been involved in the Institute from the beginning. Surely they'd give her special treatment. If she asked them to, they'd probably even show her secret things they wouldn't show other people. No one would suspect her of treachery.

Tonight, she thought. I'll fly to Barcelona tonight, check out the Institute tomorrow. As she'd told Angie on the phone, it would only mean an extra day. She pushed open the wrought iron gate and stepped onto the sunlit terrace, a smile on her face. It felt good to decide.

They were laughing at something Pazula had just said when she rejoined her colleagues. They welcomed her back and poured her some wine, and she joined in the general silliness and high spirits. After lunch they played tag along the riverbank until they fell exhausted onto the scrubby grass. Then Pazula sang them a French folk song—probably dirty, they decided with a giggle—and someone sang a Rumanian love song, and then someone else suggested a shopping expedition, and soon it was time for a cool drink. . . . The afternoon was such fun, Vivienne was surprised to notice the shadows lengthening. Four o'clock! she'd never get a flight out tonight.

They arrived back at the hotel around six, and Vivienne filled the bathtub for a long soak before she attacked the packing. But the ringing of the phone soon brought her out again, dripping on the thick carpet. A last-minute addition to the fashion spread had been urgently requested by the magazine, Pazula told her.

Would she and another model stay on for one more day? He promised he'd get them to the airport by tomorrow evening.

Vivienne sighed. Of course, she told him. No problem.

Sliding back into the bath again, she thought vaguely of calling Charles and Angela to alert them to this new delay in her return, but decided against it. She was still very disturbed by Angela's attitude toward Charles's offer of a genetic blueprint. And just how had Charles and Angie suddenly gotten cozy enough for him to make such an offer, she wondered.

She'd told Angie she'd be home in two days—Wednesday evening. Now she wouldn't even get to the Institute until Wednesday. Let them stew for a day, she thought. Let them miss me a little. Do them good.

She reached over and turned on the hot water.

22

"Ben? Brian Arnold."

"Hello, there, Brian." You asshole.

"Sorry to bother you at this hour, but there's something I think you should know." You pomposity.

Brian Arnold and Ben Talmidge had a love-hate relationship which dated back twenty years to the early days of the Institute. Arnold was too poor then to be considered investor material. But he'd known a good thing when he'd heard of it through one of the wealthy young patients who patronized his new "vitamin" practice. He'd flown to Spain in the early days, and been impressed by both the Institute and the concept. But he found Talmidge scientifically overpowering and personally ridiculous.

Over the years, his dealings with Talmidge had been cordial, even friendly, but once the network from his office to the Institute had been established, Brian had never visited again.

It wasn't the place itself; Arnold had no qualms on that score. When Charles once spoke to him of the horrors his father had seen, Arnold only smiled grimly and said that horror was in the eye of the beholder. To him, it had seemed not horrible, but fascinating. In fact, he said, he'd enjoyed it. That seemed to make Charles uncomfortable, which Arnold also enjoyed. Putting people at their ease was not nearly as much fun for him as watching them squirm.

And yet Arnold had always approached Talmidge

with something like awe; he hero-worshiped the scientist, while scorning the man.

Talmidge for his part had little respect for Brian Arnold or for the kind of practice he ran. Brian, he felt, battened off the weaknesses of others in a most unscrupulous way, pandering to their lowest instincts, whereas Talmidge considered himself a savior, a saint.

Still, Arnold was extremely useful "running errands," as Talmidge phrased it to himself. Brian had done a thorough check on Eric Rose, for example. And he often passed on useful gossip.

"What have you got for me, Arnold?" he said. You jerk.

"Charles Spencer-Moore's got himself a girl-friend," said Arnold. You megalomaniac.

"Another one?" Talmidge asked, bored now.

"A curious one," Arnold told him. "Asks too many questions. And Charles gave her too many answers."

"Your problem, surely." I'm not cleaning up your mess.

"Not anymore. She's headed your way." You deal with it, Mr. Big.

"Whatever for?"

"You cultured her recently—Vivienne Laker; remember I sent you the sample?"

"I can't remember all their names. Get to the point."

"Well, she's gone nuts on us. Actually broke into . . . uh, has these crazy ideas about what's going on. Insists on seeing for herself."

"No problem. I'll give her the ten-cent tour and send her home."

"Good, good. Well, I just thought I'd warn you. I mean, unlike most of your visitors, she's not coming to tell you how terrific you are." You crazy old coot. "I mean, she's kind of hysterical about the whole thing. Completely out of proportion."

"Enough said, Brian." You sonofabitch. "I'll look out for her."

"Good. By the way, how are things working out

with that guy you asked me to check out for you—Eric Rose?'' I wonder what that's all about.

"Just fine, fine." *None of your damn business.*

"Well, glad I could help. So long, Ben." *You certifiable old pissant.*

"Good night, Brian." *You sniveling little snake.*

Ben Talmidge, having had the last word, smiled as he replaced the phone on the bedside table. Then he pulled up the quilt and slipped back into a dreamless sleep.

Eric set the razor back on the narrow ledge below the bathroom mirror and inspected his face, running a hand across his chin. His image looked back at him, troubled.

Sleep had been elusive recently as he wrestled with the implications both of the work Talmidge was doing and of his own place in it. He was fascinated and repulsed, excited and horrified. It had seemed so simple when he and Harris had hatched the plot: get in there, look around, grab the secrets, and bring them back for the good of humanity. *Yeah.*

They'd spoken, he recalled, of discovering Talmidge's method of differentiated cell development, of forcing a group of cells to become a liver, a kidney, a heart. But now he knew Talmidge had no such method, because cloning organs was not what Talmidge was doing. Talmidge was cloning people.

Well, surely such a process could be used in other ways, for the good of all.

Cynically he regarded himself in the steamy mirror. *You're only here for humanitarian reasons. Sure.*

For days he'd tried to deny it to himself, but last night he had finally come face-to-face with the fact that he was driven to uncover Talmidge's secrets, not for humanity, but simply for the sake of knowing. His moral outrage, his empathy with both donors and recipients, all paled when compared with his desire for knowledge. He knew he would continue to do what-

ever was required of him here until he had learned all
there was to learn.

Eric wanted to weep at his own weakness. Instead
he splashed some water on his face, toweled off, and
began to dress.

As he walked across to his car, several early risers
waved and smiled. It was the same at the Institute;
colleagues gathered in the staff lounge were friendlier,
more accepting of him. Even Marta seemed less dour.
They all know I'm one of them now, he thought.

But Talmidge remained secretive. While the donor
in their dual procedure of several days before was being carried below by the moving operating table, Talmidge had also disappeared, leaving Eric a list of
duties and minor procedures. The work had taken him
throughout the Institute, but he hadn't run into Talmidge since.

Around midmorning, Eric was just finishing up a
difficult IV insertion when Talmidge suddenly reappeared at his elbow, looking formidable in freshly
pressed whites.

"Let her do that," he ordered, waving at the nurse
who was assisting Eric to tape the Heplock connector
in place. "Put these on." He thrust a pile of whites
into Eric's arms and gestured toward the patients'
bathroom. When he looked surprised, Talmidge became irritated. "Stop mooning about," he said.

Eric changed into the freshly laundered white shirt
and pants, putting on his own white jacket over them.
When he emerged holding his clothes, an impatient
Talmidge was already out in the hall. Eric caught up
with him halfway down the corridor.

They headed up the left-hand upright of the H-shaped
building, bypassing the crossover hallway leading past
reception and around to the OR, and continued past the
recovery-room nurses' station.

"What's up?" Eric asked, but got no answer.

At Recovery, Talmidge stopped, then went to the
door across the corridor. It was marked "Utility" in
Spanish and English. Talmidge pushed the door ajar,

then turned back. "Come on!" he said impatiently. "They're waiting for us!"

Eric had checked out the utility room over a week ago, when he'd sought the interior of that small exterior door which had somehow bothered him. Puzzle solved, he'd thought then, spying a matching door half-masked by two large water heaters and a jumble of floor waxers, mops, and assorted machinery. Now he entered it again, looking around carefully in the shadowy gloom. What had he missed?

"Close the door behind you!" Talmidge ordered. "No, don't switch on the light." Taking a key from his pocket, he approached the water heater, which stood just next to the door, and inserted it into a tiny lock disguised as a manufacturer's label plate. A small panel beneath the label slid open, disclosing a digital plate. Talmidge punched in some numbers, which Rose was too late to see, and the lock clicked open.

I'll be damned, Eric thought. The inside of the door's a fake. It's positioned maybe three feet over; the real door opens . . . into the water heater?

The entire front of the heater was sliding down into the floor; for some reason this struck Eric as very funny. Talmidge was already entering the water heater—Eric really had the giggles now—and gesturing for Eric to follow. He bit his tongue to keep from laughing, tossed the clothes he was carrying onto an old metal chair, and stepped inside. A semicircular landing—yes, there was the real interior side of the outside door just across from him—gave onto a narrow stairway, faintly lit, which led down into the earth.

"Hit that button!" Talmidge ordered, pointing up at a glowing square of yellow plastic, and as Eric did so, the front of the water heater slid back into place.

They descended quickly, Talmidge surefooted, Eric stumbling with nervousness. It got colder as they went deeper. At last they bottomed out at a half-circle of a landing; a curved door was set into the rounded wall. Another of those damned digital panels, Eric thought as Talmidge dialed in four numbers. Then, straining to peer over Talmidge's shoulder, he gasped. Talmidge had used the same combination Eric had used to get inside his office. Did that mean that all the panels were programmed with the same four numbers? Why would Talmidge do such a thing? Or was he so impressed with his own omnipotence, he never imagined his code could be broken?

His speculations were interrupted as Talmidge turned to him, placing his hands on Eric's shoulders.

"What you're about to see," he said solemnly, "has been seen by very few. The workers here on the other side have seen it, of course, but they do not understand. I have told them this is a hospital for the hopelessly deranged. They believe me—or say they do. This is a poor town, and they need the money." He smiled grimly. "The few medically trained people who have worked here knew better. Unfortunately, their knowledge made them greedy. Greed is a terrible thing."

He looked at Eric carefully. "I hope you are not greedy."

"I'm greedy for knowledge," Eric said honestly.

"That will be refreshing," said Talmidge. He turned and gestured toward the doorway; bright light streamed onto the landing. "You know what is in there?" he asked.

"I think so," Eric answered slowly.

Talmidge smiled. "You think so," he repeated. "I don't. Whatever you may have imagined, nothing will have prepared you for what lies beyond this door."

"You mean . . . monsters?" Eric stuttered.

"Judge for yourself," said Talmidge, and together they walked out into the light.

Nearly twenty people, sipping drinks from clear plastic glasses, milled around the high-ceilinged room. A woman—a waitress?—circulated among them with more drinks on a tray. Talmidge took two from her and handed one to Eric, who eyed it suspiciously.

"Apple juice," said Talmidge with an amused smile.

Eric followed Talmidge through the small crowd toward a raised platform at one end of the room, smiling and nodding as Talmidge chatted and introduced him here and there; everyone spoke English and seemed to be on a first-name basis; the staff room, he decided.

He hung back as Talmidge mounted the platform, but Talmidge motioned for Eric to join him. The room was quite warm, especially after the coolness of the stairway. He wished he'd left his jacket in the utility room with his other clothes; nobody else was wearing one. The men and women moved closer to the platform as Talmidge began to speak.

"My friends," he said, "we are here to honor someone newly risen to the rank of the Givers. But first I want to introduce to you a new member of our family, Dr. Eric Rose." He waved toward Eric, who smiled and raised a hand in greeting.

"Dr. Rose is good and kind, and a fine doctor. He will become a familiar face to you all, and you will be happy he has joined us."

The smiling faces pressed closer, welcoming, accepting.

"It is fitting," Talmidge continued, "that he begin his work here by witnessing our most important ceremony."

Eric noticed that everyone was wearing a sort of uniform of loose pastel clothing, ornamented in some cases by small metal pins. Nametags? He couldn't quite see . . .

"First, let us praise the glory of giving, which is the highest state of life."

Strange, thought Eric. The whole staff is so young, not a graybeard among them. You'd think at least one or two would be . . .

"I see before me the decorations of giving. And I see the faces of those who have not yet been called upon to give, but who are ready."

Eric looked around, but saw no one aside from the staff and several powerfully built men in blue orderlies' uniforms, watching attentively from the back of the room. Who could Talmidge be referring to?

"Today we are honoring a man from Cluster Six, a man we love and respect. Yet in honoring him, we honor all."

A ripple of excitement went through the crowd as a man began to make his way slowly toward the platform, a broad smile on his face. Eric thought he looked familiar.

Perhaps this was the staff member in charge of Cluster Six, whatever that was, he thought. He sidled forward to peer closer at the metal pin on the shirt of the woman nearest him. It was shaped like a little . . . holy shit!

"Step forward and receive your Organ Medal!" Talmidge led the applause as the man reached the side of the platform and climbed the three stairs leading up onto it. Talmidge clapped him on the shoulder and shook his hand, beaming. Then he took from his pocket a small white box.

In what was obviously an often-practiced ritual, the man knelt before Talmidge, his hands together, palms up, right hand overlapping. Like taking Communion, thought Eric with a shiver.

"Glory to the Giver!" Talmidge's voice boomed out across the room as he held the box aloft, then placed it in the man's outstretched hands. The man bowed his head to kiss the box. Tears of joy stood in his eyes.

With great reverence Talmidge lifted the cover from the box and withdrew the Organ Medal within: a small bronze-colored pin in the shape of a kidney. And suddenly it all came together for Eric, and he remembered where he'd seen that face before: in the emergency room of New York General. This man was younger, slimmer. But the face was the same.

Talmidge fastened the pin onto the collar of the man's loose-fitting shirt, then lifted his hand in blessing. "Welcome, Jim of Cluster Six, to the rank of Giver!" Slowly Jim rose to his feet as the onlookers applauded.

The brother who doesn't exist, Eric thought. The man willing to donate a kidney only if the operation were performed in Spain; the reason James Abbott didn't need antirejection drugs.

Jim descended the steps to the group below the platform, to be hugged and congratulated by them. Then the blue-clothed guardians came forward and gently herded the group out of the room. Talmidge put an arm around Eric's shoulder and walked him over to the side of the platform where a number of chairs had been pushed to make way for the ceremony he had just witnessed. Eric sank gratefully into one, and Talmidge did the same.

"We usually hold the Giver ceremony sooner—Jim donated in June—but he developed a bad infection as a result of the operation, and he's just now out of the woods." Talmidge's mouth tightened as he thought of Haddad. "I've, uh, made some changes in procedure since then," he said. "It won't happen again."

Eric was experiencing a disorienting sense of unreality. Hang in there, he told himself. He turned to Talmidge. "How many, er, people do you have down here?"

Talmidge looked closely at Eric. He was pale and shaken, yet in control of his emotions. Best of all, he still wanted to learn, not out of greed, but for the pure joy of knowing. You could see it in his eyes, Talmidge thought. This pleased him. The reactions of people like Haddad, insensitive and totally self-involved, were crassly predictable. They were amazed, perhaps frightened, but once past the initial shock, they began to figure the angles, to plan a way to profit from this new information. To Talmidge such people were tools, sometimes useful but ultimately disposable. Eric was different. Good.

"There are fourteen clusters at the moment," he said. "Each cluster contains fifteen to twenty people. More than that and the relationships among them become difficult to control. They know there are other clusters, but only minimal mixing between clusters is allowed. We tell each cluster that it is the finest, the best; we encourage insularity.''

Eric's stomach churned at the thought of nearly three hundred people living out their lives in this sterile underground world. ''But surely they ask questions about life outside,'' he said.

''Outside? They don't know of any world outside. The doctors, nurses, and other attendants come, they think, from a special service cluster, inferior to theirs of course, since the service cluster is not permitted to 'give.' Its sole purpose is to serve the Givers. We encourage them to be kind to the service-cluster members, since service people cannot aspire to the highest state of life.''

''But any book would tell them . . .''

Talmidge looked sternly at Eric. ''Exactly. So we never so much as mention books,'' he said. ''They do not read or write, and neither does anyone else down here, not even the medical personnel. Charts never leave the chart room, in a locked wing.'' He paused reflectively. ''It's difficult,'' he admitted. ''Every now and then a cluster invents symbols of communication—we permit painting, you see. Then we have to punish the inventors harshly. Fortunately, with so little stimulation, lethargy is far more common than inventiveness. Sedatives are administered daily. And stronger drugs are always an option.''

Suddenly Eric had a terrifying thought. He doesn't mean for me to live down here now, does he? As if reading his mind, Talmidge smiled reassuringly. ''Don't worry. You're far too valuable for me to bury you down here. You'll work here when necessary, of course. I'll need you to supervise post-op care, for example. And do simple maintenance procedures in the cluster OR, the one with the hydraulic table. But you'll be invaluable in tandem surgery upstairs, as well as with our, uh, real patients. Monsieur Frayne was quite favorably impressed with you.''

He stood and walked toward the door through which the patients had exited. ''A little tour would be helpful, I think," he said. "Show you the layout, introduce you to some of the staff." He turned back to make sure Eric was following him. "You can be a big help to me, Rose," he said. "And really, our people can be quite pleasant in their way."

Eric thought of the metal-drawer room. "You've never brought any of them into our world?" he asked.

"You're thinking of Jorge, of course. Very observant. Jorge was damaged in some way during the development process. In fact, I'd already decided to destroy him."

Like a burnt cookie, thought Eric.

"But then it hit me: what an opportunity for a fascinating psychological experiment," Talmidge continued. "Of course behavioral psychology is the key to our being able to maintain all this. That and subliminal conditioning during the development phase. Well, I considered how useful his gift could be in a controlled environment. So I put him in a cluster for several years, and then removed him and pointed out the terrible trials of giving. I explained that as long as he did the jobs he was given and followed my orders to the letter, he would never be asked to give. Naturally, I couldn't put him back into a cluster after that. He lives alone in a small cell within the Cold Room. I consider him one of my triumphs."

Talmidge turned to Eric, and taking his open-mouthed horror for awe, he beamed in self-congratulation. "Well, I'll admit that I can't take all the credit," he said. "I was taught by one of the best behavioral psychologists in the country. I met her in graduate school. She was somewhat older than I, but wonderful! Wonderful!" he repeated. "She was fired by my dreams, my vision. She came out here with me, planned the clusters, the medals for giving . . ." He fell silent, remembering.

"What happened to her?" Eric asked cautiously.

"She . . . died," replied Talmidge, his face furrowing with emotion. "Simply wouldn't listen to reason."

He paused, then brightened. "Of course she's still with us, in a sense."

"You mean her work lives on."

"No. Her cells. The first time I reproduced her it was not a success. The spark of brilliance wasn't there. And I had been so sure . . . Someday I'll try again."

Shaking off his reverie, Talmidge opened the door to the cluster corridor; strains of music, haunting and strangely beautiful, curled into the room like smoke.

"Jim's playing again," said Talmidge. "He's celebrating his Organ Medal. Most of our people turn to music or painting for self-expression, but Jim's a sort of genius, really. Quite amazing, considering his hard-headed, er, counterpart."

"Abbott, you mean?" said Eric, reeling.

"Precisely. An interesting argument for environment and conditioning over heredity."

"Just one more question," Eric said. Think of something, he told himself. Talk. Try to sound normal. "You have about three hundred people living here. But surely you've collected many more samples. The staff alone, over the years, must have amounted to . . ."

"Not as many as you'd think," Talmidge replied. "And although we culture each sample, and create and freeze the embryos—that alone takes months; a full-grown young adult takes two years—we don't develop staff embryos."

No need to tell him about Ricardo, Talmidge decided. His moderately successful experiments in doctor-making would no doubt make Eric even more nervous than the Cyclopropane did. Developed from cells taken from one of his early medical assistants, Ricardo had been trained to do the one job Talmidge had chosen for him, but a full medical course was out of the question for many reasons. Still, he served his limited purpose well, and thanks to the constant psychological conditioning, knew his place. Unlike the deceased donor of his cells, thought Talmidge grimly.

Dazed yet exhilarated, Eric followed Talmidge through the doors at the rear of the room and into a narrow hallway painted a dusty blue.

Talmidge led him past a sleeping hall, a dining room, and what he called a recreation room, elegant and airy with a high arched ceiling. Musical instruments lay recently abandoned at one end, paints and easels at the other; it was now bath time, Talmidge explained.

After the events of the morning, the empty clusters seemed anticlimactic. Yet there was still one big question Eric felt no nearer to answering than before. Again Talmidge seemed to sense his thoughts. He turned and smiled.

"You know the ingredients," he said. "But you need the recipe."

"Ingredients?"

"Genes, hormones . . . but how do I do it? That's what you want to know."

Eric nodded.

"I won't tell you," Talmidge said. "But I'll show you something."

Abruptly Talmidge about-faced and led him back through the clusters. Just beyond the meeting room where Jim had received his medal, the corridor curved sharply and ended at a set of steel gates that ran from floor to ceiling. Beyond that the corridor turned sharply right again.

Talmidge punched his ubiquitous code into the lock plate in the central panel of the first gate; it clicked and Talmidge pushed it open, ushering Eric ahead of him.

He waited until the gate had closed behind them, then pushed through the second gate and out into the far corridor.

The light was dimmer here, and as they rounded the corner, the hallway ended at a steel wall.

"I think of this as my garden," said Talmidge. He turned and put a hand on Eric's shoulder. "I can't tell you the recipe. Not yet. But I'll show you the oven."

He spoke his name into the air and a hidden voice-identification mechanism apparently approved, because a panel in the wall began to open. Eric stepped forward but Talmidge stopped him with a gesture.

"First you must understand that what you are seeing is just the beginning," he told Eric proudly. "Yes, this is only the beginning."

He began to pace with excitement. "Despite our incredible achievements, we're still in the early stages. But I have plans, and soon I'll have the financing. Within ten years, more than three thousand people will be living beneath these mountains."

"A secret city," said Eric.

"A secret kingdom," said Talmidge, his eyes gleaming.

III

23

The moon is low in the sky, the shadows long and deep, as a figure moves across the cobblestones. Her face is hidden, but she moves as the young move, lithe and sure. Her body swings freely beneath the longish skirt, the fringed shawl, as she strides forward. Suddenly she glances sideways and the moonlight catches her face; she has the strong beauty of the mountain people.

What has caught her attention? A small sound; a rabbit? A sparkle of reflected light; the moon on a rock? It is late and she has heard the stories. She quickens her pace.

The rabbit moves forward, but it is not a rabbit.

She picks out the path ahead by feel; her feet know it well . . . now under the overhang of crumbly rock festooned with vegetation. The shadows are darker here, but she is almost home.

The rabbit that is not a rabbit also knows the path by foot, by feel. And her name.

She senses it before she sees it, an outline, black on black in the darkness. Strong arms grasp her, hold her, cover her scream. A sparkle of reflected light: the moon, yes, but on metal, not rock. Cloth at her mouth and nose, and the drug races through her and she falls and a figure bends over her, pulling at her clothes.

And now the knife flashes dimly, redly. In her stupor she moans. She will live, and the legend will grow.

And the rabbit disappears back into the mountains.

* * *

"It happened again last night," Vicente told Eric as they sat over their *café negro* outside El Lobo the next day.

"Take the morning off," Talmidge had suggested, and Eric had done just that.

"Elena it was this time," Vicente continued conspiratorially. "They talk of werewolves and vampires." He allowed himself a smug little smile. "They are, I think, very primitive in this village, no?"

Eric wrenched himself away from thoughts of the giant artificial wombs Talmidge called his "ovens," and tried to concentrate on what the boy was saying.

"Werewolves?"

"It is silly, yes? The woman was not hurt on the neck, like a vampire. She will not start to howl at the full moon. None of the others did." He spoke scornfully.

"The others?"

"Ten or twelve, I think. Something comes at night sometimes. No one has seen it. It attacks women, only women. It never kills, just . . ."

Eric looked around him. The day was clear and bright, the square was fresh-scrubbed and innocent-looking. Demonic possession. Sure.

He turned back to Vicente. "So who do you think it is?" he asked. "Who's the town pervert?"

"You mean, what person?"

"It must be someone in the village. Any ideas?"

Vicente looked troubled. "It is no one in the village, of that I am sure," he said slowly.

"Then who . . . ?"

Vicente sighed. "We are a poor village," he said. "But without the hospital we would be poorer still. I think it is better for the people to believe in their demons."

"And you?" Eric asked. "What do you believe?"

Vicente studied his coffee cup. "I have demons of my own," he said at last.

The sound of an approaching car now echoed across

the square, and both men looked up as an old but serviceable taxi with Barcelona plates made its way past the entrance to the square. A blond woman sat in the back seat. Vicente watched as the car disappeared behind the low stone buildings; he followed its unseen progress as it climbed the steep road that led to the hospital.

Abruptly he turned back to the table and drained his cup. Tossing some coins beside the saucer, he stood.

"I leave you now to your work," he said, indicating Eric's notebook. "Perhaps this evening we have a copita, yes? And we talk of something else."

When Vicente was out of sight, Eric opened the book to the notes he had made the previous evening. He'd been determined to keep his journal up to date, but recent events had gotten ahead of him. Last night he'd rectified the situation. There it all was, in black and white. But seeing it written down didn't make it any more believable.

He wondered how to send a copy of his notes to Harris without Talmidge finding out. Obviously he couldn't mail them from here. Perhaps a newly released patient would take them to Barcelona for him. No one could doubt that mail took a lot longer to get anywhere from San Lorenzo. Yes, that's what he'd do.

He ripped some pages from the back of the book and began to write.

Talmidge too was writing, meticulously updating his private records. His head was propped on his hand, his eyes bleary, his face pale. He'd returned from his nocturnal "harvest" and carefully rinsed the blood from his sleeve. So far the villagers were content with supernatural explanations; no need to alarm them with reality.

He'd worked through the night, culturing the new one and checking his stock. And finally, celebrating. Now he was exhausted, but very pleased with himself. The young one, Isabella, was coming along well. Soon he would add her to his revels. And two years from now, the new one. . . .

He picked at some fruit on a tray and drank some coffee. Others might have found his private underground quarters confining, but Talmidge liked the seclusion. The square living-cum-dining room and small but comfortable bedroom were stark yet luxurious, with white stuccoed walls, plush leather furniture, and colorful wall tapestries of local design. Best of all, they were secure. No windows, of course, but so what? Above his steel bunker was his office, with its window looking out to the hills. Sunlight was overrated anyhow.

He grasped the pen again, but the sudden shrill of the intercom phone at his elbow startled him and he dropped it.

"Sorry to bother you, Doctor," said the voice on the other end. "You've got a visitor."

"I'm not expecting anyone," he said.

"She said she was just passing by," Alicia, the day receptionist, told him with more than a hint of sarcasm.

Damn. "Explain to her that I'm quite busy just now. Ask her to make an appointment. Tomorrow, perhaps."

"Of course," the voice told him.

Talmidge went back to his papers, but some minutes later the phone shrilled at him again.

"Yes, what is it, Alicia?" he asked testily.

But it was Bascado who answered him. "She won't take no for an answer," he said.

She must have kicked up quite a fuss for them to have called Bascado, Talmidge reflected. Bascado was "security" with a capital S; he was also not above a bit of well-paid "wet work." Few people had actually seen Bascado, but when they did, one look was enough. For Haddad and his ilk, one look was all they got.

"She said to tell you she's engaged to Charles

Spencer-Moore,'' Bascado continued. ''She seemed to think that would make a difference.''

''It does,'' said Talmidge, remembering his phone conversation with Brian Arnold. Damn. Well, at least Eric was out of the building, that was one good thing. He'd give her the sucker tour and get rid of her before Eric came on duty.

''What's her name again? . . . Vivienne Laker, right. Tell reception to put her in my waiting room,'' he told Bascado. ''I'll be right up.''

He cradled the phone, then stretched and yawned and levered himself out of his chair. Carefully he locked the papers away in the safe set into the wall behind the large bold painting, all violent yellow and magenta slashes. Beautiful but unsettling. Just like Anna.

He checked his watch; after eleven, later than he'd thought. He shrugged on his jacket and dialed the code that unlocked the steel panel which served as his front door. Unhurriedly he began to mount the stairs to his office.

Vivienne stood in the small waiting room trying to psych herself up the way she did before a shoot. The idea of coming here and collecting evidence with which to expose Talmidge's work had seemed such a good idea back in France. Even on the plane, when she'd started to get scared, she'd hung on to her conviction that nobody connected with Charles could possibly hurt her. They wouldn't dare. Now she was here, and she wasn't so sure. She hadn't pictured the institute as being quite so isolated, the surrounding countryside quite so grim.

And Talmidge, what would he be like? Could she convince him to show her around? And if not, how far was she prepared go?

Barcelona suddenly felt a long way away.

From somewhere behind the large oak door in front of her came a low rumble and a click; soft footsteps approached.

What can I say that won't sound stupid? she wondered, then decided that the dumber he thought her, the safer she'd be. That made her feel a little better. And the cheerful, tousled man who opened the door to her made her feel better still.

"Vivienne!" he exclaimed in a genuinely pleased voice. "What a charming surprise!"

He went up to her and grasped her hands in his—strong, capable hands, she noticed—and practically pulled her into his office. He guided her to a seat next to him on the low settee against one wall and studied her brightly.

"So you're Charles's fiancée! And you've come to see us—how delightful!" Vivienne studied him in return. He wasn't at all the way she'd imagined him.

Talmidge kept smiling his most reassuring smile. "Sorry you were delayed at the reception desk," he said, "but it's most unusual to have outside visitors. The staff simply didn't know what to do with you." He laughed lightly.

"Yes, well . . . I was shooting in France—I'm a model, you see—and, well, Barcelona isn't really that far, and . . ."

"And you thought you'd pop in and have a look at us? Splendid!"

Against her will, Vivienne found herself beginning to relax.

"Charles has been telling me so much about you and what you're doing," she said, "that I felt I simply had to see it for myself. I mean, it's so exciting, being able to . . . uh, do what you're doing, er, what Charles says you're doing."

"So you called Charles and said, 'You'll have to do without me for a few more days, darling, I'm off to see your father's old friend Ben Talmidge,' eh?"

"Oh, no," Vivienne said. "Charles doesn't know I'm here. He, uh, wouldn't approve."

"No? Why ever not?"

"Well, uh . . . he thinks I'm, uh, too excited about it all, too enthusiastic." Vivienne put as much energy behind her words as she could. "You see, it was all I could talk about, what you're doing here. I'm just fascinated."

"Well, I for one am delighted with your enthusiasm, Vivienne. Perhaps Charles has become just a little jaded, yes? Don't worry, your visit will stay a secret. Unless," he added, "you've told some talkative friend back home?" He looked at her questioningly.

"No, oh, no," Vivienne said. "I mean, it was just one of those spur-of-the-moment things."

"So. What would you like to see?"

Can it really be this easy? Vivienne wondered. Have I made a mistake about what's going on?

"Everything," she said.

"Okay," Talmidge agreed, noting with satisfaction the sudden confusion this seemed to produce in her.

"You seem surprised," he said easily. "Did you think we were hiding some deep dark secret here?" He smiled avuncularly. "Let me explain something to you, Vivienne. I consider what I do here to be a service to mankind. I'm proud of it. Now, maybe some people wouldn't agree. But then, they're not lucky enough to, uh, participate in our program. No, I find that everyone who's actually a part of what we do here feels as I do. As you do yourself."

"Yes, of course. But . . . if there's nothing to hide, how come we're not supposed to talk about it?"

"Ah, that's for the sake of our, uh, clients. You see, we're still very small. We have a very limited capacity. We can help only a fortunate few. Perhaps someday it will be otherwise. But for now, well, we have to keep it in the family, shall we say?" He sighed theatrically. "Jealousy is a terrible thing."

"And of course there is the legal aspect," Vivienne found herself saying. "I suppose the Institute could be shut down if word got out about what you're doing. I wouldn't want that to happen, of course," she added quickly. "I'm involved now too."

Talmidge patted her hand reassuringly. "Nothing to worry about there," he told her. "We are fortunate to have as clients several Supreme Court justices, major industrialists from many nations, indeed a number of heads of state.''

A faint flush colored his face. "No law exists which can touch us. How could there be, when no one believes it possible to do what I have done?'' The flush deepened and his voice rose. "Even when I told them, all those years ago, they refused to believe.'' He stood and began to pace.

"Believe what?''

"The mouse,'' said Talmidge angrily, turning to face her. "They wouldn't believe I cloned a mouse. They accused me of faking the evidence. They asked me to resign. Me!''

"And did you?'' Vivienne asked, out of her depth now but hanging on.

"I told them, 'Yes, I faked the evidence. I admit it! I know you can never forgive me, so I will leave. I am so ashamed!' And then I took my records, my notes, all the evidence of my discovery, and I came here.''

He turned away from her and went to the window, where he remained, staring out at the hills until, with an effort, he calmed himself.

When he turned to Vivienne, he was all friendliness and charm. "I even took the mouse,'' he said with a smile. "Would you like to see it? No? Never mind, a stuffed mouse is not very interesting to a beautiful young woman.''

"Then it's true . . .''

"Of course it's true, my dear. But it's not very dramatic. I suspect it's not anything like the way you've been picturing it.'' Again he thought of the phone conversation with Brian. "Many people, when faced with the concept of cloning, think of monsters, zombies, things like that.''

Vivienne felt herself blushing under his stare.

"You too?'' he asked kindly. "Don't feel bad, it's very common. But you'll find it's nothing you need lose sleep over. In fact, you'll probably be a little disappointed.''

"But they're alive . . ."

"And so they are. All cells are alive." Talmidge beamed at her.

"I don't mean that kind of alive. Dr. Arnold's papers—" She broke off, terrified that she'd gone too far.

But Talmidge's smile held, though his mind raced. Brian, you fool, he thought. "Dr. Arnold was here in the very early days," he said after a beat. "You'll be relieved to learn we've changed a lot since then. It's all much . . . simpler now."

Can that be true? Vivienne wondered. Can it really all be different?

Sensing her confusion, Talmidge pressed his advantage. "It's not often I get a chance to show off my work to someone bright enough to understand it," he said. "Let's start with the cell-storage facility."

Vivienne rose and followed him to the door. Talmidge had agreed to show her everything. So why did she feel so manipulated?

An hour later, Vivienne was heading back to San Lorenzo, mulling over what she'd seen: the frozen cells in their steel drawers and the sample organs grown from them, two patients calmly awaiting their operations in spare but clean hospital rooms, the operating theater. "Far more than I'd show anyone else," Talmidge had assured her. But although he walked her down every corridor and into nearly every room, it had all seemed a little too simple. And very, very different from what she'd read in Arnold's file.

"I hope you don't think I'm rushing you," Talmidge had said as he led her to the front door of the Institute. "But I'm sure you'll want to be back in Barcelona by evening. Alicia, our receptionist, can drive you into San Lorenzo, and you can get a taxi from there."

Now, seated beside Alicia in the old green Mercedes, Vivienne decided she wasn't at all sure she wanted to be in Barcelona that evening. No, she decided, I think I'll spend the night in San Lorenzo.

Barcelona is too civilized. I want to think about it all right here, where it feels like anything could happen.

Alicia let her off in the main square and Vivienne made her way slowly toward the car the receptionist had assured her was the town taxi. Once she was sure Alicia had driven off, Vivienne turned and looked around her. Was there a hotel of some sort? Across the square a rather good-looking young man was seated at an outside table in front of what looked like a bar. He was sealing an envelope. The remains of breakfast littered the tablecloth. That looks hopeful, she thought.

As she approached, the man looked up; somehow he didn't seem Spanish. Perhaps he was American or British. Perhaps she could ask him about a hotel.

Pretty girl, Eric thought. Another patient for Talmidge, or was she a visitor? The envelope in his hand reminded him that he needed a mail courier; if she was on her way home, perhaps she'd take the letter for him. He smiled and gestured an invitation for her to join him.

"Hi," Vivienne said, dropping her suitcase. "Do you speak English?"

"The Brits would deny it," Eric told her, "but yes, I do. I'm Eric Rose. Uh, won't you join me?"

"Vivienne Laker, and thanks." She sat in the chair opposite him and looked around. "Strange town, isn't it? You get the feeling it hasn't changed in five hundred years."

Eric nodded his agreement. "Part of its elusive charm," he said. "If you'd like some lunch or coffee or something, this is the only game in town."

"Coffee would be nice," said Vivienne.

"Allow me," said Eric, and disappeared into El Lobo. He soon emerged with a heavy white cup of *café con leche* and several blocks of gray sugar.

"Thanks," said Vivienne. "What do I owe you?"

"Nothing . . . no, really. But you could do me a favor."

"Yes?"

Eric toyed with the white envelope addressed to

Harris. "Uh, I think I saw you in a taxi heading toward the Institute this morning," he said. "My favor kind of depends on whether you're staying there or heading back home."

"This *is* a small town." Vivienne smiled. "Actually, I was just visiting. I'm heading back to Barcelona, probably tomorrow. Which reminds me: is there a decent hotel?"

"This is it." Eric gestured behind him. "It's not elegant, but it's clean. I stay here myself."

Vivienne looked at him questioningly.

"I work at the Institute," Eric said. "I'm a doctor. Something wrong?" he nodded, as her expression tightened and her smile died.

"No, of course not. Talmidge is doing wonderful work."

"Yes, isn't he?" Eric agreed.

Vivienne sipped her coffee and Eric toyed with his envelope.

"Uh, who were you visiting?" he asked. Something felt wrong here.

"Dr. Talmidge, actually," Vivienne told him.

Oops, he thought, dropping the envelope into his lap below the table. "So you're a friend of Dr. Talmidge?"

Vivienne laughed. "Oh, no!" she said. "I was just having a look at everything. I mean, I want to know where my money's going! And how did you end up here?"

"Well," said Eric, "I'd heard about what Dr. Talmidge was doing, and it sounded so exciting, I decided to get involved."

Vivienne gave him a radiant smile. She'd suddenly realized that if there were any secrets to be learned, Eric Rose was an excellent source. "I hope you won't think I'm too forward," she said, "but since I'm staying the night, how about dinner? My treat."

"Great," Eric said. "Only be prepared to fight me for the check." She was awfully pretty. He got to his feet, slipping the letter into his pocket. "And now I'm due at the Institute."

"What about that favor?" Vivienne asked.

Eric hesitated. Would she tell Talmidge about the letter? No, she said she was headed home. Besides, what could be more natural than one doctor writing to another? He decided to chance it, and taking the letter from his pocket, handed it to her.

"I, uh, need to mail this to a friend in the States," he explained, "and as you can imagine, the mail service from here is pitiful. If you'd just drop it in a mailbox when you get to Barcelona, I'd appreciate it."

Vivienne took the letter nonchalantly, but her thoughts were racing. "Sure," she said casually. "No problem."

They stood smiling at each other for a moment. "See you this evening," Eric said, and set off across the square toward his car. Vivienne shoved the letter deep into her handbag, then turned and looked after him. When he'd driven off, she went into the bar to arrange about her room.

Dear John,

I'm in! And it's everything we suspected, and a whole lot more. This letter will give the top line; the rest will have to wait until I get back, whenever that may be. Problem is, I know what he's doing but not quite how. He's very secretive—wouldn't you be?—but I think he sees me as the son he never had or a kind of acolyte or something, and if I stick around long enough and keep my nose clean, I think he'll tell me eventually. Only I'm not sure how much longer I can take it, because it's tearing me apart.

On the one hand, I find the work terrifically exciting. Mind-boggling. On the other, it's appalling.

Talmidge is indeed cloning organs. The exciting—and appalling—part is that he's doing it by cloning people. Abbott is here, or rather his clone is. I watched them give him a medal for donating a kidney. Cloning techniques have come a long way since

Talmidge first cloned his mouse (yes, he really did do it, then apparently thought better about sharing his discovery and skulked off to Spain to go it alone), but he's still way ahead.

Basically, he's discovered a technique which not only produces cell cloning but also uses hormones to accelerate growth in the developmental stages. The accelerated-growth technique can be so tightly regulated, he can produce clones of any age. I say "clones" but what we're talking about here is people. People who walk and talk and paint and make music. They're organized in groups called clusters and controlled with highly advanced psychological techniques and selective drugs. At the moment there are about three hundred people, completely isolated, deep underground, and you'd never guess they were there. I bet most people who "have coverage" at the Institute don't suspect that's how it's done.

There are twin operating rooms for removal and implantation of organs, and the techniques here are what you would expect, except that Talmidge insists on using Cyclopropane, which makes surgical procedures even more exciting than usual.

The guy is nuts, absolutely certifiable, but he's also a genius, and I want to hang on and learn from him even though he horrifies me. When I first came, he tried to palm me off with the sucker tour: frozen cell slides and old organs in bottles. But after we'd worked together, he started showing me the real stuff. Now, every few days he reveals a little more.

Yesterday he took me to what he calls his gardens, huge mechanical "wombs" in which he "grows people," as he puts it, using subliminal conditioning and teaching techniques during the incubation period. He's smart; he builds slowly, making sure I'm ready for the next horror and won't writhe on the floor with my eyes rolling back in my head. Not that I haven't come close.

He's a megalomaniac, but that actually helped me. He's so sure of himself and his operation, he actu-

ally appears to use the same computer code to secure all the sensitive areas in the building. In case
something happens to me (I don't mean to sound
dramatic, but the possibility does exist), someone
should know it: 7-2-6-21. Still, he's not as naive as
I'm making him sound; I broke into his office one
night and got into his computer, and although I
found a sort of philosophical treatise on cloning, his
real secrets were locked away with a code word I
couldn't discover before he nearly discovered me.

San Lorenzo is a pretty strange place too. It owes
its continued financial existence to the Institute, so
people are pretty closemouthed about what's going
on there. Many of the townspeople work for Talmidge, so they know about the people ''on the other
side,'' even if they don't know the real story about
how they got there. And last night a woman was
attacked—not the first time, apparently—and although people seem to connect the attacks with the
hospital in some way, they accept them as a sort of
price they have to pay for having the institute support them financially. This is a poor area, and there's
a weird, almost feudal feeling here. We're all at the
mercy of Lord Talmidge.

To sum up, I'm alive and I'm learning, and hopefully I'll be back in the States by mid-September, at
which point you'll clear my name and get me my
job back—*right*???

For the record, I'm staying at the only hotel in
town, the El Lobo Bar. If you're tempted to write
to me, don't.

                                            Eric

Vivienne stared at the letter for a very long time. I
wasn't wrong, she thought. I wasn't.

At last she retrieved the carefully opened envelope
she'd dropped on the floor and fitted the letter back in.
Immediately she pulled it out once again, and taking
a pen from the depths of her handbag, she carefully
copied the computer code into her address book. In a

burst of inspiration, she also wrote it on the skin of her wrist, under her watch strap.

So Eric was a kind of spy too. And Harris was involved too, but not the way she'd thought. Good; he was an ally people would believe. She'd take the letter to Harris personally.

She resealed the envelope and wrapped it in a scarf, then pushed it in among the clothes in her open suitcase.

Now what?

She walked to the small window and stared out. Eric Rose. Now that she knew he was one of the good guys, she admitted to herself that she found him quite attractive. He has a great smile, she thought. And sexy eyes. And that great Belmondo nose. She found herself looking forward to talking to him, and not just because he could tell her about the Reproduction Institute.

Eric drove slowly, thinking about Vivienne. She was very beautiful but there was something that didn't quite compute. He was disturbed by her involvement with the Institute, then reminded himself that most people probably had no idea what really happened there. Meeting her had highlighted the sexual isolation in which he had been living recently. Not surprisingly, he found himself looking forward to the evening with an eagerness he hadn't felt in a long time.

He cut and sutured his way through the morning with a light heart, removing a portion of lower intestine in a tandem procedure which had become routine.

Lunch was exceptionally tasty, he decided.

He was fantasizing about whether he could convince Vivienne to extend her stay ("So many fascinating ruins in the area . . .") when Talmidge joined him at the scrub sink. Perversely, Talmidge continued to brief him on each procedure only minutes before they were due in the OR.

"Got an interesting one for you this afternoon," he told Eric.

Talmidge's smile should have alerted Eric, but his
mood was too ebullient. "Good," he said. "I like a
challenge."

Talmidge noted Eric's mood, wondered at its cause,
and then proceeded to destroy it utterly as he began
to describe in some detail what they were about to do.

Eric stopped scrubbing.

"Remove her what?" he asked Talmidge in disbelief.

"That's right," Talmidge said. "Are you finished
here? Then go get robed. I'll see you inside."

Instinctively Eric gripped the edge of the scrub sink
as a wave of nausea flowed through him. "Goddammit, Rose!" Talmidge exploded. "Now you have to
scrub all over again! You with me or not?" Eric nodded weakly. "Then get a grip on yourself, man!"

Silent and angry, Talmidge watched as Eric re-
scrubbed. "Stay here," he ordered when Eric was
through, as though he thought Eric might disappear if
he turned his back. While he scrubbed, Talmidge began again to describe the procedure, looking up from
time to time to make sure Eric was paying attention.
When both men were sterile, Talmidge walked him
into the main OR, where the scrub nurse robed and
gloved them both. Only then did Talmidge allow Eric
to go through into the tandem OR, and he watched
him carefully.

Throughout the operation, Eric sweated copiously.
Sponging the moisture from his face, the scrub nurse
admired the concentration that could produce so much
sweat. At last the large piece of bloody skin and tissue
was placed in the sterile transfer container and carried
across to the main OR. Eric looked down at the exposed mass of red tissue as a nurse hurried to him
with a second transfer container. Slowly he fitted the
older, wrinkled tissue in place and began to stitch.

The delicate microsurgery required for the procedure was highly specialized, and the procedure itself
was completely unheard-of, in Eric's experience. He
would have said it was impossible, but not, apparently,

for Ben Talmidge. Talmidge's work would be perfect, but Eric knew his own stitches would be far too big. I'm sorry, Anna, he thought, his eyes filling with tears. I know you're only a clone so nobody cares, but I'm truly sorry.

Talmidge got him out of the dressing room afterward, and brought him along to his office for a brandy.

"You didn't do at all badly for a first-timer," he told him.

Eric drank the brandy but said nothing.

"Don't be a baby," Talmidge said. "You've done bigger stuff than this . . . kidneys, lungs. Why make such a big deal over a face lift?"

Evening comes quickly in the mountains. You admire the glow of sunset slanting across the far hills and then you turn around and find the leaves on nearby trees are black shadows and you need a candle to read the menu.

Eric and Vivienne sat across from each other, wine poured, dinner ordered, silent. For Vivienne it was a comfortable silence; she knew, or felt she knew, who Eric was. But he was troubled; still affected by the surgery he had performed, he wondered if Vivienne was the sort of woman who would turn up here twenty years from now, requesting the same procedure.

"More wine?"

"Thank you."

Somewhere a dog barked. Despite his mood, Eric felt warmed by their shared circle of candlelight, which seemed to insulate them from the night, the world.

"It's a long way to come, just to see where your money's going," he said. "Did you like what you saw?"

"Not much," Vivienne said.

"Really?" Eric refilled his own glass. "What did you see?"

"I got the sucker tour," she said. Rose looked up sharply. "I read your letter," she told him.

"Shit!"

"It's okay. We're on the same side."

"The hell we are! Who are you?" Eric's fear showed in his face.

Vivienne reached out and touched his hand. She felt the nerves jump, but he didn't pull away. Softly she told him who she was, how she'd learned about the Institute, how her imagination, then her investigation, and finally the attitude of her friend, had driven her to come here. She told him she'd even spoken to John Harris. Eric listened, wondering if this were some kind of test, or trap. Talmidge would be perfectly capable of it, he knew.

"You don't believe me, do you?" she said at last.

"Why should I?"

"I don't know," Vivienne said. "Maybe because it's true."

"Or maybe you'll go right back to Talmidge and show him the letter and he'll . . ." Just what would Talmidge do in such a case? Eric wondered. He shivered slightly.

"If I were going to do that, I would have done it already," Vivienne said.

"Maybe you did."

"I didn't."

"How do I know that?" Because I'd be dead by now, he thought. That's how I know. Talmidge would never have let me leave the hospital tonight if he'd seen that letter.

"Get the letter," he told her.

"Now?"

"Right now. Where is it?"

"In my suitcase, wrapped in a scarf. Look, I'll be happy to give it back to you. I mean, I only wanted to find out what was really going on there. It's no use to me anymore. But—"

"*Hola,* my friend." Vicente materialized out of the murk. "No, thank you, but I will not interrupt you and your *rubia*—such a beautiful blond color, her hair. You call it honey, do you not? *Miel?*"

Vivienne didn't understand the Spanish, but she

knew he was complimenting her and she managed to smile at him. How long has he been standing there? she wondered. How good is his English?

Eric, who was wondering the same thing, pressed Vicente to join them for a *copita,* but he refused. "Tomorrow," Vicente said, and winked. "Tomorrow you can tell me everything!" He bowed to Vivienne, saluted Eric, and sauntered off across the square.

Eric turned to Vivienne to find her eyes, large with fear, looking at him. And suddenly he was absolutely certain that she was not a Talmidge trap. No, she was on his side, and he could trust her.

Her hand had fled from his at the sudden appearance of Vicente; now he reached for it and held it and something passed between them, a bond was forged, something they were never afterward able to explain, and the fear slowly left her face.

They talked long into the night, mostly about themselves, their dreams, their feelings. By tacit agreement they avoided the subject of the Institute; there would be time for that unpleasantness. But not tonight.

Perhaps it was the isolation they both felt here in this foreign place, coupled with their shared attitude toward Talmidge and his hospital of horrors. For each of them, the other was a refuge of sanity and hope, someone who not only knew what Talmidge was doing but also abhorred it.

The emotional stress each was under certainly played a part, as did some good old-fashioned chemistry. The combination was heady; within the magic circle of candlelight they grew calm and close.

And later when they went up to Vivienne's room, the letter remained hidden in her suitcase.

24

"She didn't go to Barcelona," said Bascado. "She's at the hotel."

"Yes?"

"And she met Eric."

Talmidge's first reaction was annoyance; he hoped Eric wouldn't tell her anything. Then he began to wonder.

"You think it was planned?

"Who can say? Vicente said they were holding hands. His English is not good, he doesn't know what they were saying. But they went to her room afterward."

Talmidge looked relieved. "Just sex," he said. "Good. I thought it might be more serious. Still, you'd better tell Vicente to keep an eye on them.

"Ever hear the story about the famous theatrical producer and the road company? No, of course not. Well, the producer's road manager comes to him, very concerned. 'Have we got problems!' he says. 'All the boys in the chorus are screwing all the girls, the ingenue is screwing the leading man, and the star is screwing the stage manager!'

"The producer is calm. 'Not to worry,' he says. 'That's perfectly normal. But if the screwing leads to kissing, *then* we've got problems!' "

Talmidge was still chuckling to himself as he left his office for morning rounds. He was further amused to catch sight of Eric, tired and slightly hangdog, hurrying to the nurses' station to grab a quick tardy look at the patients' charts. Just sex, he thought. Not to worry.

Eric was preoccupied during rounds, and afterward Talmidge had to remind him to return the charts to the nurses' station. Eric took the charts from Talmidge, then hesitated. He didn't know why he should be so nervous; he hadn't had an afternoon off since he'd started at the Institute. And with no procedures scheduled for the day, Talmidge surely wouldn't object.

Clutching the charts, Eric trailed Talmidge down the hall.

Finally Talmidge stopped and looked back at him. "You wanted something, Rose?" he asked testily.

"Er, yes. That is . . . I haven't had much time off since I got here, I mean like a whole afternoon or anything, and I wondered whether you could, er, spare me today. I mean, just for a little while. I'd come back for evening rounds . . ."

Talmidge studied him. Still just sex? Or was the screwing leading to kissing? Only one way to find out, he thought. He smiled kindly. "Of course, Eric," he said. "You're absolutely right. Why not take off right now? Just be back by seven."

"Sure, absolutely!" Eric promised.

He headed for the main doors, then remembered the charts and retraced his steps, passing Talmidge on his way to the nurses' station. Talmidge's smile had died, and a look of deep suspicion now darkened his face.

For a moment Eric was taken aback; then he told himself not to be foolish. Talmidge had been so nice about allowing him time off. Surely this change of attitude couldn't have anything to do with him.

The old stone exuded a dank, musty smell, the stairs were slanted and worn with age. Pale light flickered through slits and breaks in the thick walls, illuminating the interior of the old church like a patchwork quilt.

They scrambled up the last few yards and, clinging to what handholds they could find, stepped cautiously into the ruined belfry. Vivienne gasped at the view; spread out before them was a landscape which seemingly had not changed in a thousand years.

"Don't let go," Eric cautioned her. "I don't want to lose you now!" The floor through which they'd climbed was rotted and broken. "I guess we really shouldn't be up here."

Vivienne smiled at him. "I'm glad we came," she said. "It's incredible!"

For a moment they stood looking into each other's eyes. Then without embarrassment she turned away and gazed out over the rolling hills again.

When she'd woken that morning, Vivienne had felt distinctly uncomfortable about what had happened the night before. She'd felt disloyal to Charles, yet what had bothered her even more was how deeply she had felt drawn to Eric.

She was faintly embarrassed at the thought of seeing him again. It had all happened too fast. *I should never have agreed to meet him today,* she'd thought then, capturing her tawny hair in a black velvet band.

Yet when she'd looked from her window onto the square below and seen him drinking coffee at the café table where they'd agreed to meet, her feet fairly flew down the stairs. And when she'd looked into his eyes, it was like coming home.

Now, as they stood together in the isolated ruin, she felt at peace for the first time since she'd read the letter in Charles's study. The Institute was still a horror to her, but now she had a partner, someone who knew what she knew and felt what she felt.

"About Talmidge," she said, turning to Eric. "The reason I came here—"

But Eric shook his head. "Please," he said softly. "Not the Institute. Not today. Let's forget all that for just one afternoon."

"But the whole reason I came—" She broke off abruptly. She was being selfish. *These weeks must have been awful for him. We can talk about the Institute tomorrow. Yes, I'll stay till tomorrow.* She felt a vague sense of disquiet; tomorrow is Friday. I said I'd be home last night. But now more than ever, she didn't want to talk to Charles. She had too much to sort out. But not now, she decided. She wouldn't think about it now. She was too happy.

She leaned over and kissed Eric, and the floorboards squeaked in protest. Eric held her against him, inhaling her fragrance, her nearness. A mouse ran across the floor and disappeared into what was left of a wall. "We'd better get down," he said at last.

At the bottom they climbed through a half-rotted door out into the sun-filled churchyard and seated themselves on a low stone wall.

"I love it here," Vivienne told him, breathing in the spicy scent of the wild overgrown grass. "It's so . . . pure."

Eric smiled at her. "Most of my friends back home would find all this a little primitive," he said. "But I know what you mean. I love it too."

Suddenly Vivienne spied some bushes overhanging the wall a little way beyond them. "Blackberries!" she exclaimed. She hopped off the wall and went to investigate.

Eric watched her, amused and charmed.

"Come on!" she soon called to him. "There're hundreds of them!" And she held out a purple-stained handful of fat ripe berries.

They picked and ate their way down the shallow slope of the valley until at last they came to a small clearing. Eric flopped onto the grass and pulled Vivienne down next to him. Their hands and mouths were purple with fruit.

"We'll bring a picnic tomorrow," he promised. "I'll have to work all day, but we can have an early dinner before evening rounds. I know a great spot, if you don't mind a little hike."

Vivienne laughed. "Do I look as if I'd mind a little hike?" One of her shirtsleeves had been torn by brambles, her sneakers were dirty and grass-stained, and a faint sheen of perspiration covered her flushed, smudged, happy face. Eric thought she looked very beautiful.

"You're not like I expected you would be," he said. "I mean, being a model and looking so perfect. You're a lot more fun. More, uh, real."

"You're a fan of reality, are you, Eric?"

"Perfect people are boring," Eric told her. "Besides, I like being able to see the little girl in you." He twirled a wayward tendril of her hair on his finger. "You must have been quite a handful."

"Well, I had spirit!" she laughed. "Still do."

"Good," Eric said. "Otherwise you never would have come here. And I probably would never have met you."

The veiled reference to the Institute caused Vivienne to fall silent, and Eric to consider the time. He was due back for evening rounds in an hour.

"I'm usually finished around nine," he said. "Meet me at El Lobo for dinner?"

But Vivienne shook her head, suddenly overwhelmed by confusion and guilt. She was supposed to be investigating the Institute; was Eric's letter alone enough to justify her trip? And Eric himself—was he just a pleasant interlude? And if that was all he meant to her, wasn't he too good, too trusting, for her to hurt him? She needed time to think about what, exactly, she did or could feel for him. And then of course there was Charles.

"Not tonight," she told him softly. "Not that I wouldn't like to," she added, seeing his disappointment. "It's just . . . a lot has happened, very fast. You, for example." She smiled at him and touched his cheek. "You're a fan of reality, right? Well, I'll be honest with you. I . . . I'm supposed to marry a man back home. I think we're both having second thoughts about it, but I need to sort it out a little more in my mind before I see you again."

She could feel Eric withdraw from her, and she experienced a feeling of loss so deep it rocked her.

"I understand," Eric said neutrally. He began to get up, but she reached for his sleeve.

"No, you don't," she said. "I mean, I don't understand myself." She paused, her brow puckered with the effort of putting her feelings into words. "Look, I know we haven't known each other very long, but I feel . . . close to you. I care about you, a lot. I never believed in love at first sight, so it's kind of weird, but I really want to be with you. I want to be with you today and tomorrow and the next day." She hadn't planned the words, or even thought about them, but as they came out, she realized they were true. "But first I have to . . . make my peace with what came before."

She took his hands between hers and held them tightly as she tried again to explain.

"I don't want to just fall into an affair with you and then go home and marry someone else. You're too good for that, and so am I. I have to make some decisions, hard ones. Let me make them tonight, and tomorrow we can start clean."

Eric was silent for a time. She's right, he thought. We're both better than this. He disentangled his hands from hers and lifted them to her face. He leaned toward her and gently kissed her. "I really do understand," he said tenderly. "You're right. And you're wonderful. And whatever you decide . . . I'll be here for you."

A rush of emotion swept over Vivienne; her mouth sought his as her arms went around him and she pressed her body against him. But Eric gently pushed her away. "Tomorrow," he told her. "Start clean. Your idea, and a good one."

He stood and pulled her to her feet. Slowly they ascended the rise to the old church and the waiting rental car, heady with emotion, their arms around each other.

Talmidge was absent from evening rounds, which Eric decided was fortuitous. His heart was playing volleyball with his stomach, and he doubted Talmidge would miss his confused, excited state, or the reason for it.

He went down the list of chores Talmidge had left for him; it was unusually long. There were even several cluster "bed checks," which Talmidge ordinarily did himself. Funny, Eric thought. It's almost as if he'd planned to keep me here, prevent me from seeing Vivienne tonight. And then he thought bitterly: Well, he needn't have bothered.

When he finally left the Institute around eleven, he was exhausted. He drove slowly down into town, parking as usual against the wall across the square from El Lobo. Vicente and Felipe were seated at a table and waved a bottle of wine at him in invitation.

"No, gracias," Eric told them. "I think tonight I need to sleep."

Vicente smiled lewdly. "Ah, if I had such a *rubia*, I too would need to sleep, eh, Felipe?" And he winked suggestively.

Shit, thought Eric. He glanced up at Vivienne's window; a faint light spilled out through the curtains.

"I wish!" he said truthfully. "But the *rubia* wishes to think about her *novio* in America." He slid into an empty chair. "Maybe I do need a drink."

Above them, Vivienne sat on the narrow bed, surrounded by crumpled paper. Sorting out her feelings was hard, but writing them down was impossible.

Did she love Charles? she asked herself for the hundredth time. Had she ever really loved him?

She pictured him, tousled and wet with spray that evening on the beach when he'd proposed to her. The imported sand, perfectly white and clean . . . the mansion behind them, bright with party lights . . . Charles's dinner jacket slung over his shoulder, her shoes in his hand. Like an ad for some expensive men's cologne, she thought. Our whole relationship was like that. Not real. He dazzled me and maybe I dazzled him too.

She reached for her pen and a clean sheet of paper. It would be easy to say that the Institute came between us. Or his mother. But no, those were symptoms, not causes.

She shivered at the thought of Charles's family pouring money into Talmidge's hands. Still, she refused to believe Charles was as callous as his involvement in the Institute implied. It was hard to defend him, yet she felt sure that if he could only be made to face the reality of it, to experience firsthand what was going on, he too would be appalled. There had to be a way to reach that other, better Charles inside him. But that wasn't her job, not anymore.

Tossing the paper and pen aside, she stood up and walked to the window. Through the filmy curtains she could see three men seated at a table below. One looked up and she drew back: Eric.

A thrill of joy flooded through her, and a feeling of certainty. She turned again to the bed, determined to find the words to tell Charles of her decision, to free herself, and him.

Vicente turned to Eric in surprise. "She has a boyfriend? But when I saw you together last night, I thought . . ."

"Last night was last night," Eric said. He looked up at Vivienne's window again and saw her shadow suddenly withdraw.

Vicente hollered over his shoulder toward the doorway, and a waiter appeared with a cloudy glass which he filled with wine from the bottle on the table and presented to Eric before disappearing back inside again.

"*Salud,*" said Eric, and drained half the glass.

"*Salud,*" they answered. Felipe sniggered, and Vicente looked at him with disapproval. "Don't mind him," he told Eric. "He does not understand about love."

* * *

In the room above, Vivienne gathered up the discarded half-written letters. I can't send him any of these, she thought wretchedly. I owe him more than bare words. I'll tell him myself when I get home.

Tearing them into strips and then into pieces, she dumped them in the small wastebasket under the sink.

"Dear Charles, you were right to postpone our wedding . . ."

"Dear Charles, I realize now how far apart we were in so many ways . . ."

"Dear Charles, please forgive me. I think I have fallen in love with someone else."

Angela sat in her cubicle, doodling on a booking sheet and listening to the rain sheeting down outside the office window. Summer is traditionally a slow time in New York, and although she tired easily these days, Angela disliked having nothing to do. It gave her too much time to think.

The doctors told her she was doing well, but still she worried. What if they were wrong? What if the cancer came back somewhere else? At work she was always happy and positive; nobody likes a drag. But inside, she often felt scared. And the only person she felt comfortable talking to about it was Charles.

Ever since the night of Vivienne's phone call. Charles had been commuting often between New York and Boston, more or less living in her apartment. He'd commandeered several dresser drawers and half her closet space, and threatened to replace the rest of her furniture with family heirlooms. But the joy she felt at seeing his head on her pillow of a morning was matched and sometimes exceeded by the guilt she felt about Vivienne.

She felt even worse whenever she recalled their long-distance argument over Charles's offer of what Angela insisted on thinking of as a genetic blueprint. How could she have said those things to her best friend?

She sipped her tepid coffee and wondered where Vivienne could be. Yesterday evening Angela had gone to her apartment with flowers, but the doorman said she was still away. Since then Angela had called nearly every hour, but she always got the answering machine.

Surprisingly, even Charles hadn't heard from her. He didn't seem to want to talk about it, and managed to look both guilty and annoyed whenever she mentioned Vivienne.

Angela tried not to think about what would happen when Vivienne did return. Despite Charles's protestations, Angela believed that once Vivienne was available again, she would lose his love and Viv's friendship. And wasn't that a fitting retribution for her disloyalty to her friend? Yet she couldn't bring herself to give Charles up before she had to.

The adhesive of the bandage itched terribly, and Angela rubbed the skin around it ineffectually. Another source of guilt: Brian Arnold had taken the cell samples for the Institute yesterday.

The intercom buzzed and Angela reached for the phone, knocking over the half-empty Styrofoam cup. Damn!

"Angie, it's Marcella. Amazingly enough, someone's actually shooting something important this month. What's Vivienne's schedule for early next week? Oh, and they'll want to see her first thing tomorrow."

Blotting furiously, Angela explained that Vivienne's schedule was clear but Viv herself was still out of town.

"That shoot finished two days ago," said Marcella testily. "Where is she?"

"I, uh, I don't know," Angela admitted.

"Well, call that boyfriend of hers, Charles Somebody-Somebody. He'll know. Get a phone number for her."

"He hasn't heard from her either," said Angela.

A pause while Marcella's antennae picked up the vibes.

"You two been comparing notes or something? Never mind. I'll stall them for a few days, see if she turns up. And I thought she was one of the reliable ones," Marcella muttered as she disconnected.

Angela got some paper towels from the bathroom and wiped up her desk, then dialed Charles's number in Boston, something she'd never done before. Having worked her way through a receptionist, a secretary, and a personal assistant, she was at last rewarded by Charles's clipped voice sounding impersonal and peevish.

"Yes, okay, what?" he said.

"Marcella's looking for Vivienne. For a job," Angela said uncomfortably. "I'm worried about her too. Aren't you?"

"Vivienne can take care of herself," said Charles, feeling vaguely guilty.

"Maybe," Angela replied. "But she was due home yesterday and she hasn't even called. Couldn't you . . . ?" She wasn't exactly sure what she expected Charles to do, but somehow she felt he was in a better position to find Vivienne than she was. "I mean, you know the people at the Institute . . ." Angela trailed off.

"She'll be all right," Charles told her. "She's probably doing a little sightseeing, or maybe her flight was canceled or something."

"But wouldn't she have called?" Angela persisted. "You don't think she's. . . . ?"

"She's what?" said Charles, annoyed.

"Well, in trouble or something."

"Look, Viv's a big girl. She's fine. She'll probably get in tonight. I bet she calls in the morning." And then we'll have to tell her about us, he thought.

"Can't you do anything?"

"I don't see what," Charles told her with a mental shrug of his shoulders. It occurred to him that he might call the Institute and check, but he dismissed the idea. Vivienne would resent it, and he didn't relish it much himself.

"I'm sure she's fine," he told Angela. "Now, I'll meet you at the Pierre around eight, don't forget. Oh, and I love you. Don't forget that either." He hung up quickly before she could reply.

Angela cradled the phone with a bittersweet smile, torn between worry for her friend's well-being and a desire for her never to return.

Don't think about it! she told herself fiercely. She got up and prowled around the office, looking for some kind of distraction. In the reception room she found a two-day-old copy of the New York *Post* and carried it back to her desk.

"Coed Raped in College Dormitory . . ." "Guard Dog Killed in Bronx Robbery Attempt . . ." I won't read the bad news, Angela thought, turning pages.

"Hiram Stone's Widow Inherits All."

Wasn't Stone that rich industrialist who'd nearly died a few months back? Angela scanned the story. Stone had had yet another stroke, this one fatal. In the interim between strokes, Stone had apparently made a deal with the children of his first marriage, and tightened up the original will that had left so much to his second wife, Claire. The reporter hinted slyly at a possible romance between Claire and Stone's second in command.

Slow news day, Angela thought, and turned to the comics.

In the conference room beyond Charles's decorator-designed inner office, four powerful and influential men awaited his return. Let them wait, he thought moodily.

Angela's call had unsettled him.

These days, any talk of Vivienne produced in Charles an unpleasant confusion of guilt and resentment. Seeing her through Angela's eyes had made him realize what a special person she was, yet he felt more strongly than ever that they were ill-suited. How right he'd been to postpone the wedding.

Surely she must see that too, he thought. There were so many basic things they disagreed about. All that nonsense about the Institute, for example. The Institute. Charles's flash of anger turned suddenly to guilt again, and worry. Talmidge was used to worshipers at his shrine, not hysterics. Could she be in some sort of trouble? No, he thought. Ben wouldn't dare.

Maybe she's having a fling with a photographer, he told himself hopefully. Maybe she's fallen in love with someone else. That would certainly make things easier for Angela and me.

His feelings for Angela still surprised and overwhelmed him at times. Had she changed so much since he'd first met her—"the fat one at the agency"—or had he? One thing had surely changed: the specter of his mother was gone for good. And Charles had never felt so free.

Angela, he thought. Damaged and imperfect and thoroughly appealing. So brave, and yet so vulnerable. There was so much he wanted to show her, to do for her. That job of hers, for example; might Marcella be receptive to an interesting investment offer in exchange for a promotion for Angela? It would have to be very discreet; Angela would kill him.

The intercom buzzed, startling him out of his reverie. Charles punched the "talk" button before the caller could speak. "Hold your water!" he barked. "I'm on my way!"

He pushed back from the highly polished walnut desk and stood and stretched. Should he call Talmidge? He wavered for a moment, undecided. Give it another day, he thought; see if she turns up. Time enough for phone calls if she doesn't.

25

Vivienne spread the dark blanket over the rough grass, and Eric unpacked the food and wine. Though the early evening air was cool, the sun was still warm, and a secluded picnic seemed both romantic and appropriate.

Eric had slept poorly the night before, suspecting that she too was awake, struggling with her feelings. Today he'd walked through his duties in a kind of haze, waiting for the afternoon to be over, then slipped quietly out of the Institute and returned to San Lorenzo.

He'd knocked on her door around five P.M. with some trepidation, but the moment she opened it he knew what her decision had been. He could see it in her eyes, and feel it in her embrace as she pulled him toward her. The door swung closed behind them as they abandoned themselves to each other, this time with perfect honesty and commitment. A clean start.

Vivienne cut chunks of cheese and tomato with Eric's Swiss army knife as he levered the cork out of the wine bottle. They'd pulled the rental car off the road and climbed for twenty minutes; now they looked out over the mountains as they ate.

"Is that Andorra?" Vivienne asked, pointing.

"Yeah," he said. "Look, we have to talk."

"Now?" Vivienne sighed. It was so peaceful up here.

"Definitely now," he told her. "When are you going home?"

"Tired of me so soon?" She smiled.

Eric shook his head impatiently. "Don't be silly," he said. "You've been here for three days. It isn't safe anymore."

"There's so much I still don't know."

"Leave that to me."

"I can help."

"Not here you can't. Anyhow, it's too dangerous."

"You said that."

"Viv, I'm serious. Talmidge seems to accept me. But if you keep hanging around, he's going to start to wonder about both of us. There's just no reason for you to be here."

Vivienne was silent. Her suspicions had been proven right, her nightmares real. And if Eric could get her the proof she needed . . . What else did she want?

Misunderstanding her silence, he touched her hand. "I love you," he said. "I want to be with you more than anything I can think of. But not here. I'll be back in the States soon, I promise. Nothing will change. But you've got to leave."

Vivienne shook her head. "I don't know if you can understand this," she said at last. "But I've lived with this thing for so long, I just can't walk away from it now. Not without learning more. And then going home and making a big noise about it."

"Ask me what you want to know," Eric said.

"I don't know where to start."

"Just jump in."

"OK." Vivienne thought for a moment. "Who's at the Institute now, and why?"

Eric hesitated, puzzled. This was not the kind of question he had expected. "Let's see," he said. "There's Leona Holland, in for a . . . a face lift." He shuddered as he remembered his part in the operation on the world-famous singer. "And George Benisard, the football player. He's had his knee joint replaced."

"Using parts from their clones?"

"That's right."

Vivienne shivered. "And the clones . . . don't mind?"

"No, they're conditioned to what Talmidge calls 'giving.' It's an honor to donate a part. They even get medals."

"What do the clones do all day? How do they live?"

"Simply," said Eric. "They have good food, pleasant surroundings. They're encouraged to exercise, keep in shape; they have their own gym. They can paint and make music. Some of them are very talented. But they're not taught to read or write. And if they make up letters . . . symbols, really . . . they're punished."

"How horrible," said Vivienne.

"Yes, to us. But they don't know anything different." Eric paused. "There's a calmness about them . . . a humanity, I'd guess you'd call it. They care about each other in a special way. They're prisoners, yes, but they don't realize it."

"It sounds spooky."

"You know what's really spooky?" Eric said. "Seeing people, famous people, walking around, talking, working out . . . only they're not who they seem to be."

He drank some wine from the bottle and broke off a piece of bread.

"That list I got from Talmidge's computer was really something. Wish I could have gotten a printout, but it took so long to break into his office . . ."

Vivienne ate a tomato slice. It wouldn't take me long, she thought. Now that I have the code. Maybe it's true that people listen to "big shots," but no one will believe me without tangible proof.

"Some of those names really got me thinking," Eric continued. "I mean, if a national leader were assassinated, they could just bring in his clone. Only someone else would be running the country."

"Scary," Vivienne agreed.

"Same with the head of a corporation," he mused.

Vivienne had a sudden image of a vague-looking man in a clubroom, surrounded by well-wishers.

"And if a world-famous industrialist's widow is challenged by her stepchildren," she said softly, "she can bring in his clone long enough for him to make a deal with them and tighten up the will. Do you remember whether Hiram Stone was on the list?"

"He was."

"There's a lot more at stake than just organs," she said. "We've got to stop it." She looked at him closely. "That's really why you're here, isn't it?"

Eric had the good grace to look embarrassed. "No," he said. "I don't like it, I'm appalled by it. But I'm here to learn. I know there are medical secrets here that can help people without . . . doing what Talmidge is doing." He sighed. "I'm no crusader, Viv. I'm a doctor, trying to learn something new. I'm sorry if that disappoints you."

The sun had withdrawn from the land and was now bathing the far hills with molten gold. Vivienne rolled bread pills between her fingers and said nothing.

Eric tried again. "I'd like to see the Institute closed. Of course I would. But I don't want to see an outcry against this kind of work if it can be done in a different context. What's going on here is a genetic nightmare. But the underlying techniques are valuable. Publicity about the Institute would not only cause Talmidge to go undercover and take his secrets with him, it would cause a groundswell of public opinion that could set back any kind of genetic research by fifty years."

Vivienne didn't respond, but her mind raced. So much of what he had said was true; the techniques could perhaps be learned, saved, used in ethically acceptable ways. And yet, she'd seen Angela, her dear friend, someone whose humanity and innate goodness she'd have staked her life on, become intoxicated with the idea of a new breast, completely insensitive to what it would mean for her "other." If someone like Angela could be so moved, how could anyone truly believe the technique could be controlled?

And Charles, the man she had been ready to marry;

he too would have been perfectly comfortable maiming, destroying a living creature, flesh of his flesh.

Slowly she reached out and touched Eric's face, drawing her fingers along his cheek and the edge of his mouth as if to memorize his features. I've known him such a short time, she thought, yet with him I feel as if I've found another part of myself.

Such a good person, she thought. And so naive. How he'd hate me thinking that, but it's true. He lives in a world of healing and Hippocratic Oaths; even now he doesn't fully realize man's potential for evil.

Control the applications of Talmidge's techniques? A wonderful dream, but only a dream. She didn't believe mankind was ready for it.

The silence between them became palpable as she weighed her own feelings against his. She'd come here with a mission. Now she had to ask herself whether she was prepared to see it through, even if it meant she might lose Eric because of it.

She studied the far hills, so beautiful and remote. At the end of it all, she thought, the hardest questions to answer are the ones you ask yourself.

At last she leaned over and kissed him. "I understand," she said. "I do. It's all right."

Surprised but pleased, Eric held her tight. "Thank you," he said. "Now promise me that you'll go home. Tomorrow."

"I promise," Vivienne said. "First thing in the morning." Forgive me, Eric, she thought.

"In that case, we have no time to waste," he told her, lifting her sweater.

"Not a minute," she agreed.

Anna lay inert, every fiber of her being in revolt. She'd never imagined she would feel like this. It was supposed to be an honor. Why didn't it feel like an honor?

Her hand was sticky with the syrup, but she was used to that. For many weeks she'd been secretly spitting out the "little drink." And for weeks her anger had grown.

Would the "little drink" make her feel less angry? Did it make them all feel less angry? Was that why they were given it?

She'd asked some of the others, but they'd looked at her strangely. The "little drink" was their special reward. It tasted so delicious. And it made them feel so good. She'd enjoyed it herself, she remembered. Until the day she got mad at the nurse and decided to trick her. Why? She couldn't recall.

Funny, she thought. The "little drink" had always made her feel good. Better even than the sex she and the other clones enjoyed on the sly. But without the "little drink" she felt even better. Well, different. More alert. More herself. And angrier.

The more often she managed to spit out the "little drink," the easier it got to fool the nurses. And the more questions came into her mind. How did we get here, she wondered. Where did we come from? How did the world begin?

Once she had sneaked into the medicine room and looked at the things there. Boxes and papers. Funny squiggles on them. She'd never seen squiggles on anything else. Only in the medicine room. She was curious, so she'd asked the doctor, the new young one. He'd looked so embarrassed, like he wanted to hide. Why? Did he know a secret about the boxes, the squiggles? She was angry that no one would tell her.

The others, they were not curious. They didn't care. The "little drink" made them not care. That made Anna angry too.

So one day she hit one of them, just to see what would happen. And she told about it in her paintings. The big doctor, the old one, he scolded her for the hitting, and made her apologize. She made him think she was sorry, but she wasn't. He liked her paintings, she could tell. He thought they were just paintings. The fool.

Now they had done this thing to her that was supposed to be an honor. And they had given her an extra "little drink." It will help the pain, they told her. Again she had fooled them, though the pain hurt a lot.

But the pain helped the anger grow, and that was good. Because someday she would need the anger. Someday she would use it.

"You're doing fine, Anna," Talmidge told her as he checked the bandages. "Everyone is very proud of you."

He patted her head, but she reached up and pushed his hand away.

Unusual that her erratic behavior pattern should persist even after "giving," he reflected. Well, it was nothing he couldn't handle. In fact, he'd recently started a replacement clone for Anna, in case she proved too obstreperous. Such replacements were necessary from time to time, and the client was never notified, let alone billed. He wondered whether Anna's replacement would have her artistic talent; there was still so much he couldn't control.

He finished his nightly tour of the clusters and headed upstairs, where he was relieved to see Eric in the midst of evening rounds. He'd had a bad moment when Bascado had told him that Eric and Vivienne had disappeared in Eric's car. It wasn't just their collusion he feared. It was losing Eric to someone else.

"Have a nice afternoon yesterday?" he asked now, smiling like a shark.

"Just great, thanks," said Eric.

"And a pleasant picnic this evening?"

Eric looked up sharply from the chart he was studying.

"It's a small town," Talmidge said pleasantly.

"Of course," Eric agreed quickly.

"She's very beautiful, of course," Talmidge continued. "But beauty can be boring without a mind. Does she have a mind too?"

How right he'd been to encourage Vivienne to leave tomorrow, Eric thought. Talmidge was already too curious. Well, we can take care of that right now. "I'll sure miss her," he told Talmidge with a rather theatrical sigh.

"Is she going somewhere?"

"Back home, she says. She leaves tomorrow morning."

Relief flooded through Talmidge at the thought of Vivienne's departure. I'm jealous, he realized with a shock. And then he thought, I have a right to be jealous. Eric is mine.

"Well, finish up and get out of here," he said magnanimously. "Enjoy your last evening together. Unless you're planning to see her again in the States?"

"No," said Eric as casually as he could. "Uh, we decided it was a one-time thing." Unconsciously he fingered the paper in his pocket on which Vivienne's address and phone number were carefully written. "And there's no need for me to quit early," he added lightly. "She's decided to pack tonight." He was disappointed by Vivienne's decision not to see him again before she left, but he was damned if he'd discuss his personal life with Ben Talmidge.

Talmidge was encouraged but not convinced. "Too bad," he said aloud. "I was afraid you might decide to leave together."

What's this? Eric wondered, as little men with danger signs jumped up and down in his head. He breathed deeply, then looked at Talmidge with all the innocence he could muster.

"You mean, leave all this . . . and you? Just for a woman? That would be pretty stupid," he said. Had he overdone it? Surely even Talmidge wouldn't swallow such bilge.

The sudden look of elation in Talmidge's face told Eric that indeed he had. But all Talmidge said was "See you in the morning," and then headed down the corridor to his office, leaving Eric to finish rounds and fill the rest of his evening as best he could.

Talmidge unlocked the oak door to his office and carefully shut it behind him. Then, using his code, he descended the stairs to his apartment. He's mine! he thought joyfully. The beautiful Vivienne couldn't deflect him. He's loyal and he's mine!

As usual at this hour, a modest dinner was laid out on the coffee table. But he was too keyed-up to eat.

He roamed the apartment, restless and excited. And, he was surprised to find, sexually aroused. He stopped to admire one of Anna's newest works, and its violent yet sensual energy seemed to echo his own mood.

He stripped off his shirt and dropped it on the floor, then mixed himself a drink and took it into the small bedroom.

He pictured the scene in his mind's eye: Petra and the others, their filmy clothing clinging and drifting, covering everything, concealing nothing. He liked to go among them sometimes, touching and teasing, making his choice. Would he have Trudi, the beauty who so closely resembled the wife of El Lobo's bartender? Or Clarice, a far more cooperative version of the mayor's haughty daughter? No, tonight he knew that Petra, only Petra would suit his mood. He imagined her languidly uncoiling herself from the satin pillows where she'd been sleeping, pleased to be chosen, eager to be pleasured. The aptly named Petra: strong and lithe, with the angelic face of the famous movie star from whom she'd been made.

He reached for the intercom, then stopped. First he would check his stock. The keen pleasure of walking among the new growths in his wine cellar would be all the greater in his aroused state; soon they too would be ready for the taking. Not for parts, of course. These were for his pleasure alone. The thought of his self-created harem increased his erection to almost painful proportions. Good. He'd check his private clone reproduction section now, and have them send Petra to him in half an hour. The torture of waiting would be exquisite.

He gulped his Scotch and talked into the intercom. Then he punched his code into the plate beneath Anna's painting, pushed impatiently through his slowly opening section of wall, and strode out into the corridor.

26

In her dark sweater and black linen pants she blended into the dusky darkness among the trees at the perimeter of the parking lot. She watched, nervous but determined, ducking back behind the tree line whenever she heard the crunch of gravel. At last the footsteps were his, and she watched Eric climb into the rental car and drive away, headlights raking the driveway. Only then did she emerge, shaking out her balled-up trench coat and pulling it across her shoulders.

The reception hall seemed bright after the darkness, and she blinked as she approached the receptionist. The woman seemed surprised to see a visitor, but Vivienne smiled reassuringly. She'd gambled on a staff change in the evening hours, and she'd been right; this woman had never seen her before.

"I'm Mrs. Benisard," she said. "I came as soon as I could. I mean, I had to find someone to stay with the children . . ."

She hoped the receptionist wouldn't know that back home, George Benisard was a celebrated bachelor.

"Mrs. Benisard?" the woman repeated with a heavy Spanish accent. "But your husband, he sleeps. Better come back in the morning."

"Please." Vivienne begged. "He's expecting me and he'll be so disappointed."

"Tomorrow," the receptionist said firmly.

"Not tomorrow," Vivienne said in her most commanding voice. "Mr. Benisard will be very angry with you if you do not permit me to see him now."

The woman studied her. "I will call a nurse," she said.

"There is no need to disturb anyone," Vivienne said quickly. "Just tell me the room number and point me in the right direction." She smiled reassuringly.

The receptionist seemed uncertain, but she traced down a page in the book which lay open on the desk before her. "Room 103," she said reluctantly. "Down there." She gestured behind her, toward the corridor branching out to the right.

"I hope it's a nice room," Vivienne gushed. "I want him to have the very best care."

"Everyone here has the very best care, Mrs. Benisard," the woman replied stiffly.

"Of course!" enthused Vivienne. "This is a wonderful place. Please excuse me if I sounded . . . well, you know. I'm just so worried about George!"

"I understand," the woman told her. "But your husband is fine. It really would be better to come back in the morning."

She's weakening, thought Vivienne.

"Just a little peek?" she pleaded. "I'll be very quick and we don't have to tell anyone. Please?"

The woman looked at Vivienne, flushed with wifely worry, and relented. "All right. But be quick or I will get in trouble."

"Thank you so much! I'm so grateful to you!" She reached over and squeezed the woman's hand conspiratorially.

The woman smiled. "Hurry up!" she told her.

Vivienne went quickly past the desk to where, well behind the receptionist's desk, the corridor branched left and right. Pausing for just a moment to check her recollection of the tour Talmidge had given her, she turned to the left and disappeared down the hallway.

He couldn't remember when he'd had such intense sexual pleasure. The visions of Eric which had come to him so often during Petra's ministrations he discounted as irrelevant.

Now Talmidge lay on the bed, spent, yet wanting more. Petra was curled at his feet, purring like a cat. How does she do that? he wondered idly.

Then a new thought arose: including Eric in his games. He smiled, imagining Eric's shock and delight at learning of Talmidge's secret harem. He might even allow Eric to choose a few women to be cloned for his own use. What fun they could have together.

Exhausted though he was, he found himself growing hard again at the thought. Levering himself up on an elbow, he reached down for Petra, then stopped. The idea of group sex with Rose was so titillating, he decided to explore the thought for a while, letting his excitement build with the images he drew in his mind. But Petra, feeling him shift on the bed, slid upward to tease his member with her tongue. Talmidge groaned with pleasure. He hoped he could make it last.

She'd forgotten about the nurses' station. She huddled against the wall, just out of sight of the nurse at the desk. The woman was reading a paperback, but Vivienne doubted her concentration was deep enough not to notice someone walking down the corridor. As she waited, uncertain of what her next step should be, Vivienne heard a phone ring nearby. She peeked around the corner in time to see the nurse pick up the instrument and talk. Vivienne quickly retreated to the safety of the corridor and took off her shoes; when she turned back for another look, the nurse was studying papers attached to a clipboard. Similar clipboards hung on pegs behind the desk.

She could see no other way past the nurse; she'd have to run for it when the nurse turned to hang up the clipboard. She waited as the minutes ticked by and the nurse made notes on the chart. As last she hung up the phone and turned to the wall of monitors behind her, and Vivienne took off.

The nurses' station was at a corner of the corridor, and open at two sides. Vivienne had just cleared the first section and was rounding the corner when the nurse looked up, puzzled by the flow of air she suddenly felt. Fortunately, she looked first toward the opening into the first corridor, source of the small eddy of wind caused by Vivienne's passage. Vivienne nearly flew past the opening into the right-angled corridor, and had barely disappeared from view when the nurse turned in her direction, puzzled. She rose as if to investigate, then shrugged her shoulders and settled herself in her chair again. She was back into her book when Vivienne, her heart pounding, reached Talmidge's office. Cautiously she tried the door; it opened and she went into the waiting room.

When she'd waited here for Talmidge three days ago, she hadn't noticed the small metal plate beside the door into the inner office; now she looked for it. The lock light glowed red. She slid her watch strap off the numbers she'd rewritten on her wrist; although she'd memorized them, she wanted no slipups this close to success. Carefully she punched them into the plate. A pause. A click. The red light turned green. She was in!

She closed the heavy oak door softly and blinked in the darkness. Faint moonlight slanting through the curtained windows gave vague outlines to the furniture. Vivienne looked around, waiting for her eyes to accustom themselves to the murk. After several minutes she could see a little better, but not much. Slowly she advanced into the room, holding her hands in front of her to avoid bumping into things. She remembered the general layout, but the darkness made it hard to judge distances between objects.

She wondered if she could get the computer going. Her expertise was minimal, but she didn't think it would be too hard to retrieve and print. As she rounded the desk, her eye was caught by a flash of color. She froze, then looked back toward the bookcases. Yes, there it was again, a faint red light, just like the one on the coded entrance plate outside the office door.

She approached it slowly. The room was too dark for her to see it clearly, so she touched it gently, then ran her fingers over the adjacent area. Another code plate! Eric hadn't mentioned a second plate. Maybe he'd missed it.

She felt around for a door. Nothing. So why the plate? Maybe it's a secret passage, she thought excitedly. Eric doesn't know everything!

She punched in the code by feel, counting the keys. Again the pause, the click. And then suddenly a whirring and the faint creaking of well-oiled machinery. Something hit her cheek and she reached up to find that a section of wall was moving, pushing her out of the way. Quickly she stepped back as a shaft of dim light struck out into the darkness in an ever-widening arc, revealing a narrow stairway.

She hesitated for only a heartbeat, then stepped quickly through the opening and started down the stairs.

Showered and dressed, Talmidge hunkered over the coffee table in front of the sofa on which he sat. His appetite for food had returned, and he ate ravenously, despite the tepidness of the hour-old dinner. Ignored, Petra lay curled in a chair across the room. She didn't mind his lack of interest in her now. It was what she expected. Soon the men would come to take her back to her cluster, and the other women would ask her what they had done together. They would laugh and compare notes, and eat the good food that would surely be provided after the work she had done tonight. She dozed lightly.

The stairs spiraled steeply downward, and Vivienne took her time. She felt as if she were in a frightening fairy tale, descending an elfin staircase that led . . . where? To an ogre's castle deep in the earth, perhaps. Or a treasure cave guarded by tigers with eyes as big as saucers. Who, or what, would greet her at the end of her journey? she wondered fearfully. The air on her face felt cold as she descended deeper into the earth, feeling in the dark for each narrow step.

Then a faint glow of light appeared below her, brightening with each turn of the staircase. Slightly dizzy, she rounded the last bend and stepped down onto the concrete floor. In front of her was a steel door set flush with the wall, a code plate next to it.

She hesitated; what waited beyond the door? Fear coursed through her, and she retreated a few steps. Then, gathering her courage, she walked forward again and punched in the code numbers. For a moment nothing happened. Then the lock plate released with a click. The red light gave way to a green glow.

Slowly the door slid open.

Talmidge looked up, first in puzzlement, then in alarm, at the opening of his private entrance. It couldn't be the men for Petra; they would come through the double doors at the other end of the living room, and they would buzz for admittance first.

He crossed the room in three huge strides and grabbed at the figure in the murky light. His arm grazed her breast—a woman. Without pause, he jerked her into the room and hurled her from him. She stumbled and fell sharply against the coffee table.

A chilling fear washed over her, blotting out the pain in her side, as she realized she'd blundered into Talmidge's apartment.

She heard the sharp intake of breath as he recognized her. He stepped toward her and she thought he would hit her, but then a buzzer rang and he stopped, staring at her. The look in his eyes was terrifying.

The buzzer sounded again, and she could feel him fight to control himself. First he gave the door through which she had come a push, then he went and opened one of a set of double steel doors across the room. Two men in orderlies' blues entered and went toward a woman Vivienne had not noticed. My God, she thought, it's Jane Fawcett!

Petra, who had watched the proceedings with disinterested curiosity, now rose and approached the men.

One of them leered. "How'd it go, Petra?"

Petra? thought Vivienne, now realizing that the woman was all but naked.

"You got a new one, huh?" the other man asked Talmidge, gesturing toward Vivienne, still half-lying between the sofa and coffee table.

"Petra, baby, you're just gonna have to try harder." The first man laughed coarsely as they escorted her from the room. Petra smiled a distant smile. She knew that they were not permitted to touch her. Men had been killed for trying.

"Was that really Jane Fawcett?" Vivienne heard herself asking. Why did I say that? she wondered. Jane Fawcett is the least of my problems.

"Appearances are misleading," Talmidge replied evenly. "She came here to pleasure me. I doubt that you could do better," he added, "but since you have invaded my private quarters, perhaps you would like to try."

Vivienne shrank back in fear and loathing.

"How did you get down here?" Talmidge suddenly shouted. "Why are you here?"

Vivienne started to get up. "Don't move!" he roared. "Answer me!"

"I'm here because I love your work . . ."

"Don't bullshit me!" Talmidge leaned over her menacingly. "I know all about you. Brian Arnold warned me you were coming. You're trouble, he said. He was right."

Brian Arnold? How had he known? "All right," Vivienne said. "It's true. I was very upset when Charles told me about all this. I wanted to see for myself."

"Why?"

"I thought if I saw it I would be better able to . . . accept it." Angela must have told Charles I was coming here, she thought. And Charles told Brian and

Brian told Talmidge. Talmidge was on to me from the beginning.

"Get up," Talmidge told her contemptuously.

Vivienne scrambled up quickly, then looked at Talmidge questioningly. Maybe if she cooperated, she could find a way out.

"Sit there," he told her, gesturing to the sofa. He watched as she seated herself on the sofa's edge, then he settled himself into the chair that Petra had recently vacated and studied her in silence.

At last he spoke. "How did you know the code?"

"I didn't," she said. "The doors were unlocked."

"That's a lie."

"It's the truth. See?" And Vivienne pointed to the door Talmidge had swung closed. The door lock had not engaged and the light glowed green.

Talmidge got up and pushed the door firmly closed. The light turned red. He paced the room, thinking. Of course the doors had not been unlocked. Yet no one knew the code, not even Eric.

Eric. Don't let Eric be behind this, he prayed.

Could Eric have discovered the code and told it to her? No, he thought, not possible. He had shown him so much, there was no need for him to break in. And even if Eric had discovered the code, why should he give it to Vivienne when he himself could use it in greater safety?

The code wasn't the issue now, he decided. It could be instantly changed. The problem was damage containment.

He turned to Vivienne. She looks frightened, he thought. Good.

"So you want to see the clones?" he asked gently.

Vivienne noted the change of tone. He believes me, she thought. "Yes," she replied weakly. "That's why I'm here."

"And after you've learned the truth, you'll go home?"

Vivienne nodded.

"And you won't talk about what you've seen?"

"No, no! I promise!"

Fat chance, Talmidge thought. But a plan was beginning to form in his mind, and it would be easier if she thought he trusted her.

"OK," he said. "I don't know why, but I believe you."

Vivienne let out a long shuddery breath. Thank God, she thought. I'm safe.

"Let me tell you some things, Vivienne," he said. "Would you like a drink? Yes? Scotch all right?" He prepared the drinks and handed one to her as he searched for the right words.

"First of all, there was no need for you to sneak in like this."

"I tried it the other way, but you showed me those organs and things and said that was everything."

"I know, and I'm sorry," Talmidge told her. "But you have to understand that most people don't really want to know what we do here. People want to use their organs, but they'd like to believe we don't remove them from living people. An organ in a jar is much easier to deal with. So we shield them from the truth.

"Look at yourself, Vivienne. Be honest. You were horrified when you realized what we were doing. Isn't it more comfortable to believe the lie?"

"Yes," Vivienne said slowly. "But now I know the truth."

Talmidge nodded. "Yes," he said, "but can you face the truth?"

"I have to."

"Then come." And Talmidge stood.

"Where are we going?" Vivienne asked, fearful again.

"Where you thought you were going when you broke in here," he said. "To the clone clusters."

He disappeared into the bedroom for a moment and returned with two white medical coats. He held one out to her.

"Put this on," he told her. "No, go in there. There's a bathroom too, if you need one."

Vivienne smiled gratefully. Fright had filled her bladder.

As soon as she was out of the room, Talmidge shrugged into his medical coat, then went to the phone and dialed. "Bascado," he said softly, "tell Vicente to take Eric out for a drink, somewhere away from the hotel. Tell him not to take no for an answer. Then you search the rooms, his and the girl's. Hurry." And I hope you don't find anything, he thought fervently.

He was replacing the receiver when Vivienne reentered the room. "Just making sure they're ready for us," he said lightly. "You look very professional in that."

She followed him through the double doors and into a corridor; beyond was a double set of steel-mesh security gates.

"I'll have to make up something for the staff and the clones, to explain why you're here," he told her, taking her arm gently. "So just go along with whatever I say. Oh, and try not to talk too much. We limit the clones' vocabulary, and new words unsettle them."

"I understand," said Vivienne.

"Good."

They approached the first of the security gates. Talmidge pushed it open and gestured for her to precede him. "Here we go," he said.

"I don't feel like a night out!" Eric had protested. But Vicente had insisted. He'd had a severe romantic disappointment, he'd explained, and needed a sympathetic drinking companion.

Now Eric hung on grimly as Vicente threw the heavy motorcycle around the hairpin turns with reckless abandon.

"You will like this place!" Vicente's voice swept past Eric's ear as they hurtled through the night. "Lots of . . . how you say? . . . local color. Except you are with me, they would not welcome you. It will be a rare experience for you, yes?"

Sure, Eric thought. Almost as rare an experience as

the trip back down the mountain with Vicente drunk
as a skunk. I wonder if I can drive this thing.

Bascado prided himself on being thorough. Methodically he went through each room, from ceiling tiles
to floorboards. Aside from the notebook he took from
under Eric's shirts, Bascado found nothing suspicious.
The notebook too might be innocent, but Talmidge
would decide that.

The girl's room was more interesting. Bascado enjoyed the feel of her underwear, so silky and delicate.
He spent much time fondling her bras and panties.
Talmidge must suspect her of something, he thought. Perhaps if she displeases him badly enough, he will give
her to me. Then I could make her put on the underwear and . . .

A sudden noise made him jump. Could she be returning? He froze and waited, but no one came. How
long had he been playing with the underwear? Hurriedly he stuffed it back in the dresser drawer and
moved on to the closet. The few clothes that hung
there were easily searched. On the shelf above was a
suitcase, which he pulled down. Heavy. Must have
more clothes in it.

He carried it to the bed and unzipped it. So many
clothes this woman has, he thought as he sifted through
the sweaters, trousers, T-shirts, and scarves. Then
something made a crinkly noise. He went through the
clothes more carefully and felt something wrapped in
one of the scarves. He pulled it out and, holding the
scarf by a loose end, let the package inside drop onto
the bed.

A letter. He held it up and studied it. It had a stamp,
as though someone meant to mail it. He looked at the
address. USA. The girl was sending a letter home.
Probably not important, but again, Talmidge would
decide.

He put it in his jacket pocket next to the notebook
he'd taken from the other room; time to go.

At the door he hesitated, then returned to the underwear drawer. He decided against a bra; there were only two, and she would surely miss it. But there were many panties, six or seven at least.

He shoved the lacy brief down inside his shirt, enjoying the feel of it against his skin. A minute later he had faded into the darkness of the night.

"This is . . . Vivienne."

Vivienne smiled tentatively at the people in their pastel uniforms. Her mind was spinning. So these were the clones. They seemed like, well, real people. But of course, they were.

"She's come to be with us for a while," Talmidge continued. "I'm sure you will want to welcome her and show her around."

This is wonderful, Vivienne thought. He's actually going to let me talk to them. The clones were smiling at her and she found herself grinning back. Then she remembered where she was and who they were, and her smile died.

Talmidge took her arm and guided her past the group of clones and out into the corridor.

"Let me show you some of the facilities," he said proudly. "This is the gym."

Vivienne looked through the glass door. There were some eight or nine people working out; several of them looked familiar.

"Not quite what you expected, is it?" Talmidge asked her.

"It's worse," Vivienne said. "I mean, it's bright and clean and well-equipped, and yet the . . . people seem so unaware of their . . . fate. It's horrible."

"But their fate, as you call it, is not as horrible for them as it would be for you," he told her. "I have made them unique. I have made them 'Givers.' They do not dread the operating theater. For them it is their greatest glory."

Vivienne shifted uneasily. She was feeling more and more uncomfortable down here, and wondered how, having somehow convinced Talmidge to show her the clones, she could gracefully cut the tour short. But he was on the move again, guiding her along the corridor toward a sound of music.

He flung open the door to a large high-ceilinged room, and the music billowed out at them.

"Our music room," Talmidge told her. "Actually, they also paint in here. Please. Go in."

Tentatively Vivienne stepped into the room. Around the walls, several people were painting on large canvases. Some of the work was quite beautiful. In the center, three young men were producing glorious sounds that touched her soul in a way no music had before.

Drawn by the music, she began to approach the group, then stopped. One of them looked familiar . . .

Eyes wide, she turned suddenly to Talmidge for confirmation. His eyes gleamed as he smiled mirthlessly.

"Would you like to meet him?" he asked. Ignoring her violent shake of the head, he took hold of her arm. "Gentlemen!" he called. "Please come here and meet a new . . . friend."

"No!" Vivienne instinctively drew back.

The music staggered to a stop, and the three musicians approached. Vivienne stared at the cellist, a tall blond good-looking young man. One side of his mouth had a slight upward tilt.

Talmidge thrust her forward. "This is Vivienne," said Talmidge. "Vivienne, say hello to Jim and Larry . . . oh, and Charles, of course. The others call him Chuck, but I always think of him as Charles."

"I can't!"

"Of course you can! She's a little shy," he explained. "Charles, why don't you and Vivienne have a nice chat? I have something I must do."

"You're not leaving?" said Vivienne in sudden panic.

"Only for a few minutes," he reassured her. "Meanwhile, you can find out what these people are like."

"Don't make me stay here!" she implored him, grabbing at his arm.

"But it's what you wanted," he said calmly. "Besides, there are plenty of staff people. They'll take good care of you."

She stood, shocked into immobility, as Talmidge disengaged her hand from his arm, then quickly turned and left, swinging the door shut behind him.

Gently Charles took the hand Talmidge had discarded, and led her into the room.

27

"**S**he still doesn't answer," Angela announced, replacing the receiver. She looked accusingly at Charles, busy fitting a movie cassette into the VCR he'd brought to her apartment that evening.

"What do you want me to do about it?" he asked grumpily.

"There must be something!" Angela told him urgently.

"You're gonna love *The Third Man*," Charles told her. "I can't believe you've never—"

"Goddammit, Chas!" Angela exploded. He looked up, startled. "Vivienne's missing, don't you understand?"

"Don't dramatize," he said. "She's probably—"

"What? She's probably what?" Angela challenged. "Look at me, Chas!"

Charles dropped tiredly onto the sofa.

Angela stood in front of him, hands on her hips. "She said Wednesday evening. Today's Friday. She hasn't called, she hasn't written . . . Don't you wonder what the hell's going on? Don't you *care*?"

"Of course I care," Charles said. "It's just—"

"It's just convenient that she hasn't come back, isn't it? She isn't here so we don't have to tell her about us, so let's not look for her, is that it?"

Charles was silent.

Angela flopped down beside him. "I feel guilty enough about all this as it is," she said sorrowfully.

"But if Vivienne's in trouble and we don't try to help her because of what's happened between us, then I don't like us very much. Do you?"

"Do you really think something's wrong?" Charles asked at last.

"Come on, Chas, think about it. Don't *you*?"

"I don't know what to think," he said at last. Angela rose and began to pace. She'd been tormenting herself the last few days, going over and over her actions of the past week, and her guilt and worry had been growing hourly.

If she hadn't accepted Charles's offer of a blueprint, she and Vivienne wouldn't have fought on the telephone, and then maybe Vivienne wouldn't have felt the need to visit the Institute.

If she hadn't told Charles that Vivienne was going to Spain, he wouldn't have called Brian Arnold.

She'd not only betrayed her best friend, but if Vivienne was now in real trouble, she herself had been the conduit.

She turned back to Charles. "I can't do this anymore," she announced.

"Do what?" Charles looked up sharply, alarmed by her tone.

"I can't . . . be with you anymore. Not like this."

Charles went to her and put an arm around her shoulder, but she pushed him away. "I didn't think it through, not any of it," she told him. "I didn't realize what loving you would mean, how it would tear me apart." Tears started, but she brushed them away impatiently.

"It'll be all right," Charles said soothingly. "I'll look for Vivienne, and we'll tell her about us, and . . ."

"Maybe I didn't think through the genetic blueprint either," Angela continued, not hearing him. "Maybe Vivienne's right. She asked me to wait. Why didn't I?"

Again Charles approached her and again she moved away. "Please. Let me help," he said.

"You want to help? Then go find Vivienne. Make

sure she's okay. Meanwhile, I need some time alone.'' She collapsed on the sofa as tears streaked her face. "I'm confused and I'm angry, Chas! Angry at you and angry at me too. We should never have let this happen, never!''

"Angie, it wasn't our fault . . .''

"Then whose fault was it? Vivienne's?'' said Angela scathingly. She sniffed loudly and Charles reached out his handkerchief and handed it to her. It was soft and white and smelled just like him, which made her start crying again.

"I can't live like this, Chas,'' she told him through her tears. "I think we should stop seeing each other.'' She blew her nose and crumpled the handkerchief in her fist. "I think you should leave.''

"Leave? You mean, that's it?'' Charles stared at her in disbelief. "Just like that? You feel a little guilty and all of a sudden it's over?''

"Not all of a sudden. It's been eating at me for days.'' She looked up at him. "Please understand. My feeling for you . . . that hasn't changed. But I can't live with myself. And I can't live with you, not now. Maybe someday, when you and Vivienne have resolved whatever you have to resolve . . . maybe when you're really free. But for now, yes, it's over.''

She really means it, he thought in amazement. No woman had ever broken up with him before; he'd always been the one to walk out. He shook his head in disbelief. He was hurt and saddened, but he also felt a sneaking respect for her decision. He too had been feeling guilty.

"I'll leave in the morning,'' he told her.

"No, Chas. You'll leave now. Please.''

"Now? You're sure?''

She nodded. "Please.''

Slowly he got to his feet and went to the closet for his coat. They both felt like strangers, suddenly awkward and uncomfortable.

"Keep the VCR,'' he said.

He opened the front door, then turned to see if she'd

changed her mind. She smiled at him and shook her head. "Where will you go?" she asked.

"Oh, you're not the only woman I have in this town!" he told her with an attempt at jocularity. Her expression didn't change. "A hotel," he said with a tiny smile. "I'll go to the Westbury or something."

He crossed the small space between them and kissed her gently on the top of her head. "I'll find her," he said. "I promise."

He turned and walked out of the apartment without closing the door. She listened to his footsteps echoing in the stairwell, leaving her.

Leaving her.

Talmidge strode back to his apartment, his mind churning. Had Bascado returned? So much depended on what he had found.

Bascado answered on the first ring.

"Got anything?" Talmidge demanded without preamble.

"A notebook from the doctor's room. A letter from the girl's. Hey, can I have her afterward?"

"Bring the papers to my office," Talmidge ordered. "Now!" He smashed down the phone and headed upstairs.

Seated at his massive oak desk, Talmidge thought about what Eric's notebook could mean. Spying. He's been spying on me. Yet it was logical for a doctor to take notes. Perhaps the note-taking was innocent. It would have to stop, of course. And he himself would destroy the notebook. Surely Eric would understand. He'd make him understand. God, he didn't want to lose Eric.

The girl's letter was probably nothing. Written before she'd actually seen the clones, it could only contain the same suspicions she'd already voiced to Charles and Brian. If that was all, he had nothing to worry about. And if it wasn't, well, he'd have the letter. And the girl.

A discreet knock told him Bascado had arrived. He

went to the door and pulled it open with some force, reaching for the letter and notebook.

Eric's notes were more or less what he had expected; they could mean anything or nothing. He put the notebook aside and reached for the letter, noticing with a shock that the handwriting on the envelope was the same. It wasn't Vivienne's letter at all; it was Eric's.

As he read it, his face went white with rage. The letter made everything horribly clear. He, Ben Talmidge, had nurtured a serpent in his bosom.

I horrify you, do I? he thought. Just wait, boy. I haven't begun to horrify you.

And little Vivienne is part of the plot, eh? How delightful.

His mind raced, amending the plan he'd formulated for her. I'll catch them both in one net, he decided. And then I'll . . . I'll . . .

A deep sadness overtook him then, at the thought of Eric's destruction. I want to keep him, he thought, but after this, how can I?

Suddenly he pounded the table with his fist, once, twice. "How dare he do this?" he roared. And then more softly he cried out, "How could he do this to me?"

Bascado was embarrassed, but determined. "Can I have the girl?" he asked again.

Talmidge looked over at him. "When I'm through with her, perhaps," he answered. "But I don't think even you will want her then." He waved his hand in the direction of the door. "Thank you for your fine work," he said. "Get out."

When he was alone again, he dialed the number of the cluster-staff supervisor and spoke softly into the phone in rapid Spanish. A wintry smile flitted across his face as he thought of Vivienne down in the cluster. Of course she'd try to tell "Charles" about the outside world. So what? Clone conditioning was far too strong. And besides, she wouldn't be talking for long.

For some moments he sat silent and unmoving. Then he pushed back his chair, swung his feet up onto the desk, and started to plan.

* * *

"Think!"

Once the initial shock of being left in the cluster had worn off a little, Vivienne forced herself to examine her options. Surely Talmidge didn't intend to leave her here permanently; he was just trying to scare her. Well, she could scare him too.

She'd tell Charles's clone what was really going on down here.

"Think!" she urged him again. "There's a whole world outside the cluster."

He shook his head in disbelief. "That is not possible," he told her.

"Where do those people come from?" Vivienne demanded, gesturing at the staff people. "Where do they go at night?"

"They go to a different cluster," Charles told her. "Everyone lives in a cluster."

"But they aren't Giver's, are they? Why not?"

Charles looked down, embarrassed. "They are not worthy," he said sadly. "I do not love them less for that. It is not their fault. But I feel sad for them."

"Sad? Sad for them because they don't get pieces cut out of them to give to other people?"

"Exactly!" Charles's face brightened. "You do understand! At first I thought you were one of them," he said, indicating her medical coat, "but now I understand. You are a Giver too."

Vivienne looked at him in horror. "No," she said. "No one should be a Giver. Not like that."

"But to be chosen as a Giver is the highest honor," Charles told her. "It is hard to tell feelings. I will play music for you to explain."

He positioned himself at the cello and began to play. The music was haunting and beautiful. Tears filled Vivienne's eyes.

How can I make him understand? she thought helplessly. She looked at her watch: she'd been in the cluster for over half an hour. Where was Talmidge?

Jim and Larry were talking softly about the things

Vivienne had told them. They clearly didn't believe her, but they seemed somehow troubled by her ideas.

The door at the far end of the room clanged open and a staff person entered. She smiled brightly at Vivienne as she crossed the room to her.

"The doctor would like you to come with me," she said.

"It's about time!" In her relief Vivienne allowed herself a little irritation, but she followed the woman back across the room. She stepped through the doorway into a small examining room. Talmidge wasn't there, but several blue-uniformed orderlies were.

"Please to sit," said the woman, indicating the examining table.

"Where is Dr. Talmidge?" Vivienne asked.

"Please to sit," the woman repeated, sliding a look at the orderlies, who moved closer.

Vivienne turned toward the door by which she'd entered, but found it blocked by one of the orderlies, who now closed it firmly.

She looked back at the woman and was stunned to see she was now holding a hypodermic needle.

"Relax," the woman said.

"No!" Vivienne went for the door, but the orderlies were too quick. They took hold of her firmly, pulling her back against the examining table.

"Relax," the woman repeated as Vivienne struggled to free herself. "I don't want to hurt you."

The orderlies held her arm tightly. She felt a sharp prick and things started to go misty.

She knew where she was and then she didn't. Her vision blurred, and her arms and legs became powerless. She felt the movement as they carried her back into the music room, but it had no meaning for her. Her face fell into a lax smile and her head lolled to one side.

Charles's face showed real concern as they carried her past him, but the orderlies smiled reassuringly and the woman told him not to worry.

"She has been sick," the woman told him. "Did she say some wrong things?"

Charles nodded. Wrong, yes. The things Vivienne had told him about what she called "outside" were wrong, of course they were. Charles felt relieved.

"We will make her better," the woman said. "We will let her sleep now."

Sleep, Vivienne thought drowsily. I want to sleep.

They placed Vivienne in a chair and strapped her in, head resting on her arm. "Why not play her some music?" the woman asked.

In Talmidge's office, the outside telephone shrilled, startling him out of his almost trancelike state. He took a moment to compose himself, then picked up the receiver.

"Ben Talmidge here," he said with icy calm.

"Ben, this is Charles Spencer-Moore."

How appropriate, Talmidge thought. Aloud he said, "Charles! How nice to hear from you!"

"Yeah," said Charles. "Look, have you heard from a woman named Vivienne Laker?"

Talmidge hesitated. "Laker? No, doesn't ring a bell."

"Screw the bells. She's my fiancée. She was due back from a photographic shoot two days ago and she hasn't turned up. I thought she might have decided to visit you."

"Really? Why would she want to do that, Charles?"

"Well, she had a sample taken for the Institute, and I told her a little of what goes on there, and . . . she got a little upset."

"Upset?"

"Well, it bothered her. A lot, actually. I thought she might have decided to go see for herself."

"Sorry, Charles, but she hasn't turned up here. Naturally, I'll call you if she does."

"Thanks," said Charles. "It was a long shot. Sorry to trouble you."

"No trouble," said Talmidge brightly. "No trouble at all."

28

Eric pushed back the thin white curtains; the morning matched his mood perfectly: dull gray.

As he shaved and breakfasted, he kept glancing out into the courtyard for a glimpse of Vivienne as she drove away. But no taxi appeared. Well, it was still early, he thought. She's probably asleep. His tousled bed was evidence of his own restlessness. He missed Vivienne already.

As he drove to the Institute, he found himself jumpy and distracted. For the first time, neither the danger nor the scientific adventure was enough. He felt tired, strung-out.

I've had it, he thought. I want out.

Impulsively he pulled off the road onto the narrow dirt shoulder. He could turn back right now, pack his suitcase, and head for home. He'd wake Vivienne, offer to drive her to Barcelona Airport, and when they got there, he'd tell her . . . What could he tell her? he wondered. He knew his feelings for her ran deep, and that she, too, cared. Yet they had had so little time together, really. Could he tell her he wanted to go back to the States with her, to marry her? Wouldn't she feel pressured? Presumed upon? Coming on too strong could ruin everything.

Then he mentally shook himself. How could he even think about giving up now, when he was so close? And for such a stupid reason: love.

No, he decided, not just love. Vivienne was the fresh

air of reality blowing through Talmidge's sick, enclosed world. He wanted to breathe that air again. He wanted to go home.

One more week, he vowed. Then I'll take whatever I've got and go.

He put the car into gear and moved out onto the road.

Talmidge was waiting for him in the staff lounge. "We'll start downstairs this morning," he told Eric.

"Someone come in last night?" Eric asked. "The OR wasn't scheduled when I left."

"No surgery today," Talmidge agreed. "But I'd like you to take a look at Cluster Six. There's a new one we should check on."

Talmidge led him down the corridor, talking over his shoulder. "She's a little damaged, I'm afraid. Might have to replace her. Have to keep her sedated. Like you to have a look."

"Sure," said Eric. "Anything you say." Perhaps it was one of the clones he'd seen growing in the giant mechanical wombs Talmidge had shown him. He knew he should be interested in seeing a clone fresh from the "garden," but he couldn't seem to find the energy to get excited about it. One more week, he told himself firmly.

They descended the narrow spiral stairs that had become so familiar, and he followed Talmidge through the now-empty meeting room and out into the corridor. They stopped outside the music room.

"After you," said Talmidge, stepping aside.

Eric pushed through the doors, scanning the people. Anna was back at work, her scars livid, her paintings more violent. The cluster's three favorite musicians were playing their strange, haunting music. Others sat and listened, sketched at the easels around the wall, or spoke softly together.

He moved through the room, smiling and nodding as the clones greeted him. As he approached the musicians, he noticed a female figure slouched in a chair. She was turned away from him, but he saw that her hair was the same color as Vivienne's, only much shorter. He smiled ruefully; he had Vivienne on the brain.

As he got close, he realized there was something wrong with her posture; she seemed propped up.

A nurse materialized at his elbow. "This is the new one," she said. She carried a hypodermic and a vial on a tray.

"Nurse!" Talmidge's voice echoed across the room and the woman turned. "I need you here a moment, please. Eric, just give her the shot, will you?"

The nurse handed Eric the tray with an apologetic smile, and he took it around to the front of the figure.

"Hello there," he said, and the world spun away from him and he felt sick. No wonder he had seen no taxi. How had she gotten here? When? Why?

He looked frantically toward Talmidge, who smiled encouragingly at him from across the room. "Go on," he said. "Give her the shot, Doctor."

Eric looked down at the drugged figure, her head lolling onto one shoulder. He set the tray on a nearby table and slowly filled the hypodermic.

"Surprised?" Talmidge had moved closer and was studying his reaction; he looked very pleased with himself.

"Why did you bring her here?" Eric demanded weakly.

Talmidge permitted himself a small laugh. "I'm surprised at you," he said softly. "After all these weeks we've been together, I thought we trusted each other." He gestured at the figure in the chair. "Don't you know a clone when you see one?"

A clone? Vivienne's clone? Eric leaned closer, studying her. The short hair made her look surprisingly different, and the face itself was puffier.

At last he turned back to Talmidge with a self-deprecating smile. "Of course," he said. "How stupid of me." He raised the hypodermic and squirted it upward to clear it of air. Then he wiped her arm with an alcohol swab and dropped the swab back onto the tray.

He glanced up; Talmidge was close but not that close. With one hand, he steadied her arm against the chair back, shielding the injection site from Talmidge's view. Then he carefully pushed the needle tip through the fake leather and injected the drug into the upholstery.

When he'd replaced the instruments on the tray and looked around, Talmidge was halfway across the room again, heading toward the door into the corridor.

"Come on, Eric!" he called testily.

Eric discovered he'd been holding his breath; now he let it out in a long soft whoosh. When you wake up, he prayed, please, Vivienne, be careful.

Although there was little to do, Talmidge kept Eric with him all day. They even lunched together with the staff, something Talmidge rarely did. Not once did they go back to the clusters. By late afternoon Eric wanted to scream. Surely she's lucid by now, he thought. How will she react when she realizes where she is? Will they sedate her again this evening? How will I get her out of there?

At last Talmidge rose from his desk where he'd been briefing Eric on several upcoming operations—a first, Eric reflected.

"You've been with me for, well, not a long time really, but long enough for me to feel like you belong here," Talmidge told him. "So I have a little celebration planned this evening."

Shit, Eric thought.

"Just the two of us," Talmidge continued. "And I guarantee it'll take your mind off the lovely Vivienne. Now that she's gone back home, I mean."

"Uh, could I have a rain check?" Eric began. "I'm, er, kinda tired . . . ."

"Nonsense," Talmidge insisted. "It's all prepared. Now, why don't you run down to the clusters and see how, uh, Vivienne Mark Two is getting along? I think she's due for another injection.''

Eric's face lit up but he kept his voice slow and quiet. ''Whatever you say,'' he told Talmidge, trying to sound bored. ''Shall I go now?''

''Right now,'' Talmidge agreed, grimly noting Eric's subdued but obvious enthusiasm. ''Be back here in half an hour.''

''Half an hour,'' Eric repeated, heading for the door. Talmidge looked after him bitterly.

Eric took the steep stairs two at a time, arriving at the music room breathless and anxious. From the doorway as he entered he could see her huddled in her chair, an angry Anna bending over her.

He crossed the room in a few strides, grabbing Anna by her shoulder and pulling her back. Both women looked at him, surprised.

'Don't touch her!'' he told Anna fiercely, shuddering at the scars which he himself had created. But Anna stared up at him dumbly.

''You thought I would hurt her?'' she asked slowly. ''But she is my friend, my new friend. She tells me so many things. The men''—here she gestured disdainfully toward Charles and Jim, who were speaking together some way off—''they say it is wrong what she says. But I believe it.'' She put her arm around Vivienne's shoulders protectively. ''The 'little drink' makes us not think. When I stopped drinking it, I had many questions. Now I have answers. They are strange answers. Hard to understand. But I think they are true.''

''Anna.'' Vivienne spoke very softly. ''You are not to tell staff people, remember?'' She smiled up at Eric. ''You were here before? I thought I saw you, but I couldn't be sure. I was . . . drugged, I think.''

''Yes. But I faked the last shot,'' Eric told her. He looked up to see a nurse approaching with a tray. ''I have to do it again now. Be quiet.'' He took the tray from the nurse and waved her away, then turned again to Vivienne. "Don't worry," he told her as he swabbed her arm. "I inject it into the back of the chair. I just have to make it look good." He began to fuss with the needle and vial. "Talk softly. Tell me how you got here."

"I sneaked in," she said. "I used the lock-plate code in the letter to get into Talmidge's office. I wanted proof to take home with me. Please don't be angry, it's too late for that! Anyway, I found a secret door in the bookcase. I thought it led to the clones, but I ended up in his apartment. He had a woman there, nearly naked. A famous actress. Only she wasn't. Then some men came to take her away, and he brought me here . . ."

"Lean your head on your shoulder," Eric hissed suddenly as the nurse approached. "You can go," he told her as he handed her the tray. "I'll stick around a while."

The nurse shook her head. "Dr. Talmidge says I must stay in the room with her," she said, jerking her chin toward Vivienne. She disappeared into the examining room with the tray, but soon came out again and seated herself on a chair against the wall.

"The nurse is watching us," Eric warned her. "I can't stay long."

"Can you forgive me? I lied to you, yes, but I truly believed . . . still believe . . . we're not ready for this kind of knowledge. Look around you, Eric. Look at Talmidge. Are you really sure there won't be more Talmidges, once the techniques are known?"

"Why didn't you tell me how strongly you felt?"

"I tried to, at the picnic."

"But you gave in, at least I thought you did. Why didn't you argue with me, fight harder?"

"You were so in love with the idea of helping people. How could I convince you the world wouldn't let it end there?" She smiled at him sadly. "You think everybody's like you."

"I don't know who's right, Viv, you or me," he told her tiredly. "But I forgive you."

She sagged in relief, then touched her hair tentatively. "They cut my hair, didn't they?"

"It'll grow back."

"Yes."

Suspicious, the nurse half-rose from her chair. "I have to go," he said. "Be careful. I'll find a way to get you out." Jesus, how?

Vivienne looked at him hopefully.

"I love you," he told her.

"I know," she said. "I love you too. It's all happened so fast."

"Is there a problem, Doctor?" The nurse appeared at his side.

"Yes," Eric told her. "Her breathing is too slow. Halve the dosage." He gave Vivienne's arm a squeeze and walked swiftly from the room.

For a moment all was quiet. Then the phone rang in the small examining room. The nurse spoke briefly, then replaced the receiver and began preparing the tray, wondering idly how two doctors could have such different ideas about treatment. Not five minutes ago, she reflected, Dr. Rose had injected the girl and halved the dosage. Yet here was Dr. T. ordering her to administer a second injection, full strength, immediately.

Charles sat in the first-class lounge, fuming. He'd spent a lonely night at the Westbury, utterly miserable about the breakup with Angela and deeply worried after his conversation with Ben Talmidge. Something about that phone call had bothered him enough to book the first flight out in the morning. And now here he was, grounded, thanks to mechanical problems. Damn!

He looked around at the other passengers, sipping drinks, reading, telephoning, resigned to the wait. There were few nonstops to Barcelona on Saturday, and this was the only one until evening.

Charles felt jumpy and anxious. If Talmidge had told him that Vivienne had already been there and had since left, he would have found it perfectly believable. But to say that Vivienne hadn't arrived at all was . . . odd. According to Angela, Vivienne had been very definite about her plans and her timing. The more he thought about it, the more convinced he'd become that Talmidge had been lying.

"May I have your attention, please!" A uniformed airline official was standing by the check-in desk, microphone in hand. "We apologize to our Barcelona-bound passengers for the delay in the departure of Flight 43. We're happy to announce that new equipment is currently en route from Washington, D.C., and should arrive here within the hour. Servicing of the aircraft will be conducted as expeditiously as possible, and we hope to get you on your way in approximately one hour and forty-five minutes."

Halfhearted applause greeted his statement. Everyone was getting logy from the recirculating air and free drinks.

Charles did some quick calculations and sighed in frustration. Even assuming the plane from Washington got them off the ground by two this afternoon, he'd never reach the institute tonight. With the time difference, they'd arrive in Barcelona in the middle of the night. He'd stay at a hotel, he decided, and drive up first thing in the morning.

He sipped his cold coffee disconsolately. Tomorrow was soon enough to make a fool of himself, he thought, beginning to regret his hasty decision. After all, Talmidge had assured him Vivienne wasn't there. She was probably on her way home right now. Maybe she too had had mechanical problems. And he'd look like an idiot, flying halfway around the world to find his fiancée had already left for home.

And yet, it just didn't fit.

Was Angela right? Was Vivienne really in trouble? He still wasn't convinced, but one thing Angela *had* made him see. He'd gotten Vivienne into this thing and he had a responsibility to get her out of it.

* * *

"More wine?" Talmidge filled Eric's glass, then his own.

"No . . . really, I'm fine," Eric protested.

"More pheasant, then?"

"Thank you, no.'

"They shoot it locally."

"So you told me. Delicious. Really." Eric looked with distaste at the small balls of shot lying along the rim of his plate. He'd nearly broken a tooth on the first one, much to Talmidge's amusement.

The marble slab of desk had been cleared off for the occasion and laid with a soft white cloth; real silver and crystal gleamed and sparkled. The old boy does himself very well, Eric thought.

Talmidge had led him down to his private apartment through the secret bookcase door Vivienne had discovered to her sorrow. At first he'd feared a trick, but Talmidge seemed determined to celebrate, eating and drinking with abandon. Eric, though he had little appetite, had forced himself to be convivial, and somehow they'd gotten through the meal and now sat, replete, trying to think of things to talk about.

"Some dessert, perhaps? Oranges? I know how fond you are of oranges!" Talmidge chuckled.

How can I get her out of there? Eric thought desperately. "No, no oranges, thanks. Actually, it's getting late, at least for me," he said. "I, uh, really appreciate this dinner; it was just great!" He smiled a big boyish smile. "But I think I'll head home now." I can sneak back afterward, he thought. I've got the code, and the staff know me . . .

"The night is young!" protested Talmidge. "And I have a surprise for you. Women!" Eric looked surprised. "Ah, you didn't know about my women."

"Your women?"

"They always say yes. And do you know why?"

"They're clones."

Talmidge looked surprised. "Very good," he said. "I didn't think your mind worked that way. Yes, they're my very own clones."

He rose unsteadily; he'd had most of the three bottles of wine. "I can create any woman who's ever sent a sample to the Institute. Sometimes I even take my own samples," he said confidentially. "Wanna see?"

"Er . . ."

"Come on! You can choose whichever one you want. Even Petra. You'll like Petra."

"OK," Eric agreed. "Only let's have another drink first."

"Thought you didn't like to drink," said Talmidge, frowning at Eric's half-filled wineglass.

"Let's have a brandy," said Eric. "You have any brandy?"

"Brandy you shall have."

"You'll have some too."

"I hate brandy."

Uh-oh.

"But for you, my friend, I will drink brandy," Talmidge told him, selecting a bottle from the interior of a cabinet.

It shouldn't take much, Eric calculated as Talmidge poured the brandy into snifters with a shaking hand, then carried the bottle and glasses to the low sofa table.

"After the brandy, women!" Talmidge saluted him and downed his drink, then seated himself heavily. "Go on, boy!" he urged. Swallowing hard, Eric followed suit, then held his glass out for more.

Talmidge looked surprised, but refilled it. "Yours too," said Eric. "It's bad luck to drink brandy alone."

"Bad luck? Then I will drink with you again!" Again Talmidge downed his drink, then rose with difficulty and stood weaving. "Now, the women!" He took a step toward the set of double doors, then stopped. "But first, Eric, my friend," he said. "I must tell you a secret."

"A secret?"

"Yes. Come here."

Eric walked a few steps to where Talmidge was swaying like a tree in a strong breeze. Talmidge put an arm around his shoulder, pulling Eric's face against his own.

"Shhh!" he cautioned loudly. Then he looked thoughtful. "What was I saying?"

"You were telling me a secret," Eric reminded him hopefully.

"Yes, a secret!" Talmidge explained. "The secret is, I'm drunk!"

"Drunk."

"Yes. Can't seem to stand up. Think I'll lie down."

Slowly, like a tree falling to the ax, Talmidge began to crumple. Within seconds he was sprawled full-length on the floor.

Eric was elated. He had the code, and Talmidge was out of the way. Now he'd get Vivienne and . . . He headed for the door.

"Don't leave me!" Talmidge was levering himself up from the floor.

"I have to go," said Eric. "It's almost morning."

"You have to go," Talmidge repeated, struggling to his feet. Again he put an arm around Eric, leaning heavily against him. "You have to work tomorrow. So devoted. So trustworthy. You don't want any women?"

"No. No women."

"No women. So sad. All right, we'll go."

"We?"

"Yes. I will take you home."

"I have my car outside. I'll be fine."

"Then I will walk you to your car. You are drunk, you cannot walk so well. Also"—Talmidge regarded him with a glazed yet gimlet eye—"you do not know the combination to unlock the door."

"Uh, that's right."

"Right. Close your eyes! No, never mind. Tonight, when you leave, I will change all the codes. So you can look if you want to." Still holding on to him, Talmidge staggered over to the door and punched in the code Eric knew so well. Together they stumbled up the stairs, into the office, along the corridor, and out into the reception area.

"My friend Eric Rose is very drunk," Talmidge informed the startled night receptionist. "Very drunk. So we do not let him come back tonight, even if he wants to. He might decide to operate on someone and kill them!" Talmidge threw back his head and laughed heartily, slapping Eric on the back, hard. "If he tries, you call Bascado right away," he told the dazed receptionist. "Now he will go home and sleep."

He pulled Eric along to the front double doors and pushed him outside with some force; one of the doors caught Eric across the shoulder as it banged back. "Good night, Eric Rose," he called after him. "Sleep tight. Don't let the bedbugs bite!"

His howl of laughter echoed across the pitch-black parking lot.

29

Ben Talmidge was feeling very pleased with himself. He'd treated his hangover with an adrenaline shot; now he paced the hall just beyond the reception area, humming with anticipation as he waited for Eric to arrive at the Institute.

Eric was feeling less than optimum. In addition to the lingering effects of the drink he'd consumed the night before, he felt muzzy and slow. Sleep had been elusive as he'd reviewed plan after plan for freeing Vivienne, and rejected them all. Without Talmidge's new lock code, nothing seemed feasible.

He forced his face into a smile as he entered the Institute. There's just time for a cup of good strong coffee, he decided. Make it look like business as usual.

"Eric, glad you're early!" Talmidge greeted him heartily. "Got an unusual one today. One in a million, in fact!"

Eric was unpleasantly surprised. Nothing had been scheduled, and he'd banked on a routine day with time to think.

"It's urgent," Talmidge told him. "Life or death. Happened yesterday." He waved an arm toward the OR. "And I'm giving you the honor of doing it. So scrub up."

Eric didn't move. "What's the procedure?" he asked testily. "If it's that important, don't you think you could break a lifetime's habit and give me a hint?"

"A little hung-over, are we?" Talmidge chided him.

"A little out of sorts?" He peered at Rose owlishly. "Don't worry. I'll be right next to you the whole time. As I said, it's really quite an honor. Now, scat!"

Eric shrugged his shoulders. Business as usual. Better get on with it.

". . . and so one of you is called this very morning!" Talmidge's voice rang out with energy and warmth as he addressed the cluster. "One of you is called for the highest honor possible."

He looked out at the sea of faces. Their reactions appeared normal, yet he sensed a certain disquiet. He noticed that Anna and Charles had placed themselves toward the back of the room alongside the chair in which Vivienne half-sat, half-slumped. Talmidge had not ordered her to be sedated this morning, and she had come round sufficiently to know where she was, though she lacked the strength to do anything about it. Charles looked downcast and Anna scowled. Vivienne had done her work well, thought Talmidge. Not that it mattered.

"Today one of you will join the ranks of the Givers," Talmidge intoned dramatically. "And at the highest level." He'd wanted Vivienne awake this morning so that she would understand what was going to happen. It was no fun if she didn't understand.

Several blue-coated attendants began moving into position.

"Today's Giver is someone who is new to your cluster," he continued, "yet she has proved herself worthy of this honor in so many ways."

He saw Anna take a step toward him, her face dark with rage. Slowly Charles reached out to put a protective arm around Vivienne's shoulders, and only then did the slow shock of realization come into her face. As her eyes grew round with horror and fear, Talmidge felt a rush of pleasure.

"Vivienne," he chanted, "today you will become a Giver."

He saw with satisfaction how Vivienne attempted to

free herself from the restraining strap around her body as Charles kneaded her shoulders in frustrated helplessness, staring at the nurse who now stood by the chair, hypodermic in hand.

Anna was struggling through the crowd toward Talmidge, her eyes blazing. "What will you do to her?" she called out. "What will she give?"

"Hers will be the ultimate honor," Talmidge replied calmly. "She has been called for a heart transplant."

Pleasure flooded through him as he heard Vivienne scream; only then did he nod to the nurse.

As the fast-acting drug coursed through Vivienne's body, the nurse undid the restraining strap and Vivienne slumped forward out of the chair, her head hitting the floor. Now other attendants moved in, pushing everyone away as they lifted the unconscious form onto a gurney.

Suddenly Talmidge felt a sharp pain. Ignored in the confusion, Anna had climbed the low platform and launched herself at him with teeth and nails. He hit her a hard backhand across the face, knocking her down into the crowd, blood from the cut across her mouth spattering those nearby. This sudden violence, the worst sin that could be committed in a cluster, stunned the clones into silent immobility.

In the resulting silence, the gurney rolled slowly toward the door, its wheels creaking softly on the tiled floor. For a moment Talmidge surveyed the cowering men and women before him. Then he turned and followed the gurney out of the room.

Charles threw the rental car into a sharp turn and a scattershot of pebbles rattled against the offside door. After two near-sleepless nights, he was exhausted, yet he felt keyed-up, energized by his tension. He'd been driving up into the hills for over an hour, and the wildness of the scenery, the feeling of isolation and drama, deepened his conviction that there was danger here, that Talmidge had lied.

He recalled his father's descriptions of the Institute in its early days, and his own reluctance to see it for himself. And yet, why should he be so fearful? Wasn't it a scientific miracle?

But Vivienne's actions had caused him to consider for the first time the moral repugnance of something he'd been raised to believe was his birthright. Coming face-to-face with the workings of the Institute would force him into a judgment, a decision he desperately didn't want to make. How he wished none of this had happened.

And how dare Ben Talmidge lie to him! He'd withdraw his financial support, he'd hit Ben where it hurt. It vaguely occurred to him that Talmidge probably had alternate sources of financing by now, but surely there was some way he could strike back at Ben. Anger surged within him.

He drove faster, racing the car around the bends, pushing it up the steep rises. How would he handle Talmidge? What would he say? If he demanded to see Vivienne and Talmidge denied she was there, what then? He hit the steering wheel in frustration. This was Spain, Talmidge's turf. He had no clout here, no resources. What if Talmidge was armed?

No, of course Ben wouldn't shoot him, what was he thinking of? Surely this was just a simple misunderstanding. Vivienne would be quite safe; she'd probably laugh at his concern. In an hour or two they'd be driving back to Barcelona together.

He pulled the car through the next turn and stamped hard on the accelerator. It was so goddamn hard to know what to do.

Eric left the sink, backing through the double doors into the lower-level OR, where the scrub nurse robed and gloved him as usual. Unless Talmidge was scrubbing upstairs, he knew he'd have at least a five-minute wait.

He nodded to Ricardo, who stood robed and ready at the head of the operating table. Eric had often tried to engage the anesthetist in conversation, always without success. While competent, Ricardo worked almost by rote, and chitchat in the OR seemed to distract him. Eric had never run into him outside the institute.

"So what are we doing today?" he asked, not really expecting an answer. He wandered around the room, idly checking the instrument trays in an attempt to guess what would be required of him.

"I cannot say," said Ricardo.

Eric smiled sardonically, and continued his pacing. He noticed that a length of thin transparent tubing as well as a number of sterile containers of various sizes had been placed in readiness on a side counter. Ready for what? he wondered. No good asking Ricardo or the scrub nurse.

He leaned against the operating table and thought about Vivienne. He'd had love affairs before, but never had he felt so strongly about anyone. No, he loved Vivienne not just for the way she looked and felt, but for the person she was. Once he got her out of here, they'd go home together, and stay together. Surely she felt it too. *Once we get this damned procedure out of the way, Talmidge will cut me some slack and I'll figure a way to get her out of here tonight.*

The creak and bang of a gurney coming through the double doors behind him interrupted his reverie. On the gurney lay a figure completely shrouded in sterile drapes. Connected to the gurney was an IV pole holding several bags of transparent liquids; an IV line snaked down and under the drapes.

"I don't understand." Eric turned to Ricardo. "Is he dead?"

"It's all right," Ricardo told him. "The doctor will explain."

The four gurney attendants transferred the draped figure onto the operating table. Then three of them left, rolling the gurney out with them. The fourth, a short, squat, muscular-looking man, took up a position just inside the double doors.

Eric stared at the figure. It must be a clone, he

thought. Real people weren't brought down here to the secret OR. He reached over and fingered the drape over the head of the figure, then felt someone grip his hand hard.

"Drop it," said the gurney attendant.

Startled, he complied, turning to look at the attendant in surprise. Bascado. He'd heard about Bascado; what was he doing here in the OR?

The man smiled an apologetic smile, but his eyes were hard. "Sorry," he said, "Doctor T.'s orders. Uh, why don't we just move back a little?"

The smell of danger was strong. Eric breathed deeply to calm himself. What the hell was under there?

"Good morning, good morning!" Talmidge entered the room, already robed, gloved, and masked. "Is everything ready? Good, good. Let's get started."

"Hang on," Eric protested. "What am I supposed to be doing?"

"Can't you guess?" asked Talmidge gleefully, his voice only slightly muffled by the sterile mask. "The instruments, the containers. . . ?"

Eric sighed in frustration and shrugged.

Above his surgical mask, Talmidge's eyes gleamed. "We've had an urgent call for a living heart. And you will have the honor of removing it."

Eric blanched. "That's murder," he said.

Talmidge ignored him. "The tubing," he explained, "is for the collection of the blood. The containers are for the other major organs. There is always a need for vital parts."

Eric stared at him, speechless.

"Don't worry," said Talmidge. "It's only a clone." He walked to the figure on the table and took hold of the drape. "Or is it?" With a sweep of his arm, he pulled the drape off, dropping it onto the floor. "What do you think, Eric?"

Eric stared in shock at the still form, a bruise blooming on her forehead. Instinctively he stepped forward to touch her. "Vivienne," he said softly. The figure moaned.

"Ah, she's coming round again, I think," said Talmidge brightly. "The drug is strong, but short-lived. She was so anxious to see everything. I didn't want her to miss this part."

"Why have you done this?" Eric demanded, his eyes riveted on the awakening Vivienne.

"Ready to open?" asked Talmidge. "Nurse! Scalpel!" He turned solicitously to Eric. "Or would you prefer she were anesthetized first? It's really a waste of time in this case, but if you insist . . ." He snapped his fingers at Ricardo, who began fiddling with the Cyclopropane controls.

Vivienne stirred and opened her eyes. "Eric!" she said. "I knew you'd come. He's going to . . ." Then she saw Talmidge over Eric's shoulder, and the lights and the machines, the IV line in her arm, and she realized where she was. "Please!" she pleaded. "Don't let him . . . Help me!"

"He can't help you, darling!" Talmidge told her, pushing past Eric and taking Vivienne's hand in his. "No one can. But it might make you feel better to know that he's going to remove your heart. Isn't that nice?"

Vivienne stared at him, frozen with shock and fear. Talmidge leaned over and kissed her gently on the cheek, then pulled off the single drape which covered her body, stepping back to admire her nakedness.

"Very nice," he said. "Bascado will be so disappointed." He glanced briefly at the security man, who was breathing heavily. "No, don't try to get up," he added as Vivienne struggled to rise. "There's no place to run to. Isn't that right, Eric?"

Eric started forward, but Bascado moved faster, pinioning his arms.

"Why?" he asked Talmidge hoarsely. "What's she ever done to you?"

"She's a spy," said Talmidge calmly, his eyes locked on Vivienne's. "Just like you are. As I keep telling you, this is a very small town." He smiled chillingly. "I have your letter. And your notebook."

All at once he turned on Eric and slapped him hard across the face. "You set me up, boy. You and Harris. You're just like the others. No, you're worse! They were greedy, but you—you're a traitor!"

Then as he stared at Eric, Talmidge's anger seemed to subside, and his expression grew sad. "I had such hopes," he said. "We could have shared so much."

Behind him, Vivienne was sobbing and trying to sit upright; the drugs had sapped the strength from her limbs. The scrub nurse stood holding the scalpel Talmidge had called for, unsure of what to do with it.

"But perhaps we still can, my boy," Talmidge continued. "Yes, perhaps we can. The girl must die, of course. She is simply too unstable. But you, you have a chance. Perform the procedure. Kill her. If you kill her, maybe I can trust you again. You can stay here, under tight controls of course. But in time, perhaps I can make you see the value, the virtue of what I do here.

"And the pleasure . . . I can show you pleasures you've never dreamed of. I can create your ideal woman, even that one . . ." and he jerked a thumb toward Vivienne. "I have her tissue sample. I'll make you a new one."

Eric had gone rigid with shock and disgust. Now he forced himself to speak. "Let her go," he said. "Let her go and I'll work for you forever."

"Very dramatic," said Talmidge. "Very gallant. But somewhat impractical. She'll talk, of course. And people will listen. And that will be the end of it all."

"I won't!" Vivienne begged. "I promise I won't tell!" She had managed to sit up.

"Bullshit!" Talmidge dismissed her with an angry wave of his hand. "Now, Eric, choose. Oh, and if you choose badly, I have a very interesting experiment you can play a part in. A passive part, it's true, but an important part nonetheless. You see, I've been making some exciting progress with brain transplants . . ."

Eric gazed at him with loathing, his mind and stomach churning. Vivienne was shaking and sobbing uncontrollably.

"Sedate her," Talmidge ordered, turning to shove her down onto the table as Ricardo took a filled hypodermic from the instrument tray and quickly injected its contents into the intravenous Heplock. Within seconds she lay still. Slowly Talmidge released his hold.

"Pity," he said. "It would have been much more exciting the other way. Scalpel!" The scrub nurse slapped the instrument into his outstretched hand. "Well, Eric? You or me?"

The clones clustered around Anna, dabbing ineffectually at her bleeding mouth. The nurse had tried to intervene, but Anna had reacted so violently, she'd disappeared into the medicine room to prepare a tray of "little drinks." That will calm them down, she thought.

"I tell you again!" Anna exclaimed hoarsely. "It is no honor to give. It is only pain. And now they will pain Vivienne. They will take her heart."

"But isn't that the greatest honor?" Jim asked. "The doctor said it was the greatest honor!"

"It's the greatest murder!" Anna shouted. Murder was one of the strange new ideas Vivienne had taught her. "In murder, you die."

"Die?"

"You don't come back," Anna tried to explain. "You aren't there anymore. You . . . can't see, can't hear. You stop living."

"They will do that to Vivienne?" Charles asked, horrified.

"We must stop them," Anna told him decisively. How will we do it? she wondered. Never mind, I will think of a way. I have not drunk the "little drink."

The nurse emerged from the medicine room with a tray of small paper cups. "Little drinks!" she announced brightly. Several of the clones moved toward the tray but Anna leapt in front of them and punched the tray out of the nurse's hands. The cups flew into the air, their contents falling harmlessly onto the floor.

"No!" she shouted. "The 'little drink' is why you can't understand me. You must never drink it again." The nurse stared at her in fear. Anna smiled dangerously. "Come here," she said.

The nurse backed toward the medicine-room door, but Anna moved fast, faster than the nurse had anticipated, and grabbed her arms. "We must tell the other clusters," she told the clones. "First we must tie her hands so she can't stop us."

The woman tried to pull away, but Anna was fit and muscular, and the nurse was flabby and unprepared. Anna hit her, hard, and the nurse slumped down onto the floor. The clones gasped at this new violence.

"I am doing this for Vivienne," she explained kindly. Poor things, they couldn't understand. They had never felt her anger, or her love. "For Vivienne, and for you."

She motioned them into a circle around her. "I am the doctor now," she said. "I will tell you what to do. But first, I want to tell you about the world. It will be hard for you to understand. It was hard for me. It will make you angry. Let it make you angry. Your anger will help you fight."

"Fighting is wrong," said one of them. Several others nodded.

"*Murder* is wrong," Anna told them. "We must fight to stop them from murdering Vivienne. Then we will stop them from murdering others. No, she is not the first." She smiled at the little group encouragingly. "This is important work. Everyone must help. When I have told you what to do, I will send some of you to tell the other clusters. We are the best, so we will be the leaders. But today all clusters must work together.

"Now, sit down and listen to me. Try to understand."

30

He'd slowed to twenty when he'd turned off at San Lorenzo, and as he followed the unmarked twists and turns of the road, which rapidly grew narrower and more rutted, his foot rarely left the brake pedal. That was fortunate, for the road suddenly became a dirt track, curved sharply left, and ended abruptly at a high stone wall. Charles pounded the steering wheel in sheer frustration. Where were the goddamn signposts?

He reversed up the track for nearly four hundred yards before he found a place wide enough for a U-turn, then retraced his way back to the main road until he came to a crossroads of sorts. Unmarked, of course. Right or left? With a shrug, he turned left. This road, too, twisted and turned, but above the houses and trees Charles could see the spire of a church. It seemed to be getting closer; that was encouraging.

Sure enough, the road took him past a ruined tourist attraction of a church and into a small main square. A more modest stone church, obviously in use, stood at one end. A restaurant of sorts dominated the other side of the square. I could use some coffee, Charles thought.

He parked next to some plastic tables and chairs, pulling the car as close to the building as he could, then got out and stretched. According to the map, San Lorenzo was the closest town to the institute. He looked around: what a dump! Vivienne couldn't be staying here. Still, better check it out.

He seated himself at one of the tables. Although his suspicions of Ben Talmidge were still strong, he'd decided there was just a chance that Vivienne really hadn't yet contacted Talmidge when he, Charles, had called the institute. Perhaps she'd only arrived last night. How embarrassing it would be if he burst in on Ben with all sorts of accusations, and it turned out that Vivienne was tucked up in bed somewhere in the town. Although now that he saw the place, he doubted whether there was a habitable room anywhere in the whole godforsaken place.

Nothing seemed to be happening in the way of waiters, so Charles made his way into the dim interior of El Lobo. A man greeted him in Spanish and he blinked in the murk. "Do you speak English?" he asked the disembodied voice.

"*Momento,*" came the reply. "*Espere usted.*"

There was a rustling from behind what Charles could now identify as a plain wooden bar; the man who had answered him made his way to a small door and banged on it. "*María! Vengas aquí! Un inglés!*" He turned to Charles. "*Café?*"

"Er, *sí,*" Charles replied self-consciously. French had been the language his mother had insisted he learn. "Uh, *gracias.*"

"*De nada.*" The man smiled, revealing several gaps and one gold molar. He began to prepare the coffee. "*Leche?*"

"Er, what?" said Charles. He went toward the bar, tripping over a large yellow dog en route.

"Do you want milk?" A cheery, rather fat woman came through the door behind the bar. "It is from a can."

"Er, no. Thank you."

"I am Señora Torres," the woman said. "You are welcome here." Her husband placed Charles's coffee on the bar. "You are come to see the castle?"

"No." Charles told her. "I'm . . . meeting someone."

"Here?" The woman seemed surprised. "Someone from San Lorenzo?"

"No, from the Institute."

The woman nodded; that made sense. "She is a patient? You go to get her, yes?"

Charles thought for a moment. "No, she had a meeting with Dr. Talmidge. She was to meet me here. She said she might take a room in town. In the hotel There is a hotel?"

"Claro." the woman nodded. "Here is the hotel."

Here? Good God! "Well, is there any other hotel? I don't know which one she went to."

The idea of another hotel seemed to amuse the woman, for she laughed heartily. Imagine, a town with two hotels! "There is only this hotel," she assured him, still chuckling.

"Then perhaps you have seen her," Charles suggested. "Her name is Laker. Miss Laker. She's very pretty . . . blond hair, tall . . ."

The woman gave her husband a knowing look. *"La rubia,"* she told him. "I know her, of course," she said, turning back to Charles. "The blond lady. She stays here. Upstairs."

I was right! Charles thought. She's here and she's fine. Imagine if I'd gone to Talmidge and accused him . . . "Please show me to her room," he said. The woman hesitated. "It's all right," he assured her. "I'm her fiancé . . . er, we're going to be married."

The woman looked surprised and faintly troubled; she shook her head. "She is not here."

"She's left? Checked out?"

"No. I don't think so. Her clothes, her things, they are in her room, but . . ."

"But what?"

Again she looked toward her husband for support, but he only shrugged.

Mrs. Torres assumed a confidential manner. "She went out yesterday evening," she explained. "She

asked me where to find a taxi. Usually it stands there
at the church, but so late at night . . . Guillermo was
having his dinner, so my husband, he drive her . . .''

"Where?" Charles interjected, but she ignored him.

"My husband, he say, do I wait for you? but she
say no. So he come home. This morning the maid goes
to make the bed, but the bed is made already. She not
come."

In truth, Señora Torres was considerably embarrassed. It was bad enough, what Vivienne was doing
with that young doctor. But to do such a thing when
you were engaged to someone else! "So you see, I
cannot take you to her room," she finished. "You no
like the coffee?"

"Screw the coffee!" Charles announced. "Where
did your husband take her?"

"He took her to the the hospital, the *instituto*. And
who will pay for the coffee?" she called after him as
he ran from the bar.

Stupid, stupid, stupid! he berated himself, yanking
open the car door and flinging himself behind the
wheel. He turned the key hard in the ignition and the
car protested, then roared to life. He stomped hard on
the gas, skidding on the damp cobblestones.

Damn Talmidge! I never should have stopped here!

He roared back up the road behind the church to the
crossroads, then turned right toward the far hills, but
the twisty street soon dead-ended at a low wall overlooking some fields. He crushed a fender in his haste
to turn the car around between the narrow walls, then
sped back to the small intersection and set out again
in the opposite direction.

"You or me, Eric?" Talmidge said again. He walked
around to the far side of the operating table and looked
up expectantly. Then with one fluid movement he drew
the razor-sharp scalpel down the middle of Vivienne's
body, opening a shallow incision from her collarbone
to just below her breasts.

Eric lunged forward with a guttural cry, carrying

Bascado with him. Blood was seeping slowly from the cut, and Talmidge was positioning the scalpel again; without thinking, Eric kicked back violently, catching the smaller man in the groin. He pulled his arms free as Bascado went down on his knees in pain, then swiveled and kicked him in the jaw. Bascado fell backward, eyes glazing.

Quickly Eric turned again to the operating table, stunned to see Talmidge calmly deepening the first cut. As the scrub nurse sponged away the blood, Eric lunged at Talmidge, grabbing the scalpel from the unguarded instrument tray.

Talmidge ducked back, shouting to Ricardo, who moved in quickly, grabbing for Eric's shoulder, but Eric surprised him with an upward slash across the wrist. He was feeling rather pleased with himself when a sudden stinging across his back spun him around. Bleeding, he flung himself away from Talmidge, who continued to stab at the empty air, and cannoned into the scrub nurse, throwing her against the instrument tray. She went down in a shower of sharp instruments, sponges, and drapes. Chivalry be damned, thought Eric. He kicked her hard in the stomach.

He swung back as Talmidge lunged at him again, his scalpel thrusts driving Eric across the floor in a flurry of defensive parries. Behind Talmidge, Eric saw Bascado stirring; shit! He thrust hard at Talmidge. Much to his surprise, he felt the scalpel sink into flesh and bounce off bone; Talmidge's scalpel clattered to the floor. Still Talmidge fought on, one hand hanging bleeding and inert by his side, the other grabbing at Eric's throat. Eric sliced at Talmidge's face, removing a portion of ear, then knocked away the restraining hand. Slinging an arm around Talmidge's neck, he held the scalpel tight to his throat.

"Bascado, you fool!" Talmidge shouted, but though he stirred, Bascado didn't wake. "Ricardo! He'll expose us all!" But Ricardo, busy swathing his wrist in bandages and tape, stood irresolute, a frown on his pale face.

"Don't move," Eric told Ricardo. "I'll kill him and then I'll kill you."

"Don't worry about me," Talmidge ordered. "Just stop him!"

A monitor began to flash and beep. "We're losing her," said Ricardo, and moved toward the still figure on the table.

"Fuck her!" Talmidge shouted. "Save the institute!" Ricardo seemed undecided. "I made you!" Talmidge added urgently. "Where else can you go?"

Fear played over Ricardo's face. He took a step toward the two men, then stopped and looked around him for a weapon.

"Scalpels!" Talmidge yelled. "Down on the floor! Quick!"

Ricardo ran for the fallen instrument tray, and Talmidge smiled grimly. "Give it up, Eric!" he said.

Clutching her stomach and moaning, the scrub nurse had crawled painfully from the OR. No one noticed her leave. They were all too busy. Now she pulled herself along the corridor toward the clusters. "Help!" she tried to shout. "They're killing Dr. Talmidge!"

But it wasn't until she'd reached the music room that anyone heard her. And even then, they didn't react with the quick efficiency she'd expected. They had troubles of their own.

She stared in horror at the attendants and nurses tied tightly in chairs along the wall. One of the clones spotted her and came at her: Anna, the violent one. She shrank back, but Anna spoke calmly.

"Don't hurt me and I won't hurt you," she said. "Don't run. Stay here."

The one they called Charles joined her. They seemed to be in charge, the nurse thought. But of what? There were so many of them; other clusters had joined them. Yet a clone revolt was unthinkable. Their conditioning was so strongly against anything like this.

"You have come from the Giving Place," Charles

said, eyeing her scrubs. "Is the woman Vivienne still living?"

"Yes," the nurse said softly. "But Talmidge, they are attacking him. We must help."

Charles turned to the restless, angry group behind him. "We must help!" he cried. Anna's eyes burned at him. "Why help Talmidge?" she demanded fiercely.

Charles shook his head in frustration. "Vivienne," he said. "We will help Vivienne." He took the scrub nurse gently by the arm. "You will lead us to the Giving Place," he said.

I'll lead them, all right, the nurse thought. I'll lead them through the steel gates and lock them in the corridor. . . . But Anna yanked her arm, twisting it back painfully. "I'm strong," she said. "I'll break your bones."

Charles paled, and Anna laughed at his weakness. "You are too good, Charles," she said. "You must be strong like me. Twist her other arm."

Charles raised his hand to the nurse's elbow; it shook and finally dropped back down by his side. "I'm sorry, Anna," he said softly. "I . . . I can't."

"Then I think you will die today," Anna said decisively. "Come!" she called to the shuffling mob behind them. She pushed the scrub nurse hard. "You go," she said. "Faster!"

Charles pulled into the asphalt parking lot and slammed to a halt in front of the Reproduction Institute. Abandoning the car where it stood, he headed for the main entrance. Birdsong cut the empty air, then all was quiet.

He pushed through the double doors into the lobby. Its only inhabitant, a dark-haired woman of middle age, smiled a greeting at him from behind the reception counter.

"Do you speak English?" Charles demanded without preamble.

"Of course," she told him. "How may I help you?"

"I'm Charles Spencer-Moore. I want to see Dr. Talmidge. Now."

The woman consulted an appointment book in front of her. "Dr. Talmidge is in surgery at the moment," she said.

"Well, get him the hell *out* of surgery," said Charles.

"I'm afraid that's impossible," she said.

"Perhaps for you," Charles told her, and started toward the corridor behind the reception area.

The woman rose quickly and stepped in front of him. "I'm sorry, sir, but—"

Charles pushed past her. "Where's the operating theater or whatever you call it around here?"

"Please stop! You can't—"

Charles headed down the corridor, then turned left. Behind him the receptionist's voice rose in protest, but he ignored her. Patients looked up apprehensively as he ran past their rooms. "Talmidge!" he called. "Get out here, you bastard!"

A nurse came out of a patient's room just ahead and stared at him with startled eyes. She was carrying a tray of medications in paper cups. Behind him the receptionist rounded the corner of the hallway, then hesitated, uncertain how far to follow him. "It is not permitted," she called out. "You must stop."

Charles went quickly to the nurse and grabbed her upper arm, hard; the tray tipped and pills rolled across the floor. "Where is he?" he said urgently. "Where's Talmidge?"

"The doctor is not here," the nurse told him nervously. "Who are you? Why you no listen when she tell you stop?" She looked back toward the receptionist, who now retreated back toward the lobby to call for reinforcements.

"My family's money built this place!" Charles told the nurse. "I know Ben Talmidge better than I want to. Now, where's the damn operating room?"

"It is there," she told him, and pointed toward the

end of the corridor toward a nurses' station. "But it is empty."

"Show me!" he told her, tightening his grip as he pulled her along the corridor. They rounded the nurses' station; beyond was a holding area. "Now where?" he asked.

"Ahead, through the doors," the nurse told him. "But no one is there!"

Ignoring the red warning signs posted on doors and walls, he half-dragged her through the large swinging doors into the operating room. It was dark and empty. "Where the hell else do you do surgery around here?" he demanded. But the woman shook her head.

Charles paused, thinking. If he's in surgery and he's not here . . . "He's with the clones, isn't he?" he said. "Where are they?" He took her by the shoulders and shook her in frustration.

The double doors banged open and the receptionist entered in a run. Her hand went to her mouth as she saw them. "I can't find Bascado," she announced tremulously. "I tried to get someone to send up an orderly, but—"

"Stay away!" Charles warned her. He turned again to the nurse. "Where are the clones?" he repeated.

"I do not understand what you want," she said.

"Dammit!" Charles raged. "I want Talmidge! If he's not here, he must be with the clones."

"What are these . . . 'clones'?" the nurse asked.

"Come off it!" Charles said harshly. Then, seeing her genuine confusion, he continued more calmly. "The clones are . . . the ones who give the parts." Still she appeared puzzled. "The others!" he shouted. "The other people, the ones that stay here all the time. Where does he keep them? Where is he?"

Her face brightened and she nodded with understanding. "You mean the *locos*," she said. "The crazy ones. How you know about them?"

"Talmidge told me," said Charles. "You take me there."

"I do not know how to do this," the nurse said.

"The *locos,* they are dangerous. Never do I go down there."

Down there? So the clones were underground. Charles looked at the receptionist. "One of you better find a way to get me down there," he said roughly. "Fast!"

The nurse looked pleadingly at the receptionist, who shrugged. She hadn't been able to locate Bascado, Talmidge was still in surgery, and no one was answering the secret intercom down below. The best thing she could do, she decided, was to get this crazy man off the main floor, away from the patients. Let them deal with him down there.

"Take him down," she told the nurse. "Take him through the kitchen, the way they bring the food. I will get you the key."

The nurse shook her head violently. "Please, no! I don't want to! They say the clusters are very dangerous. *Muy peligroso.* Never go there, they tell me! Never talk about them! They—"

"Go to the staff lounge," the receptionist repeated. "I will bring the key."

Ricardo moved toward them clutching a scalpel; Eric held his weapon firmly against Talmidge's throat. Can I really kill him? he wondered. God, don't let me have to kill him. He cast a frantic eye at the nearby counter. There were the empty containers he'd wondered about before . . . stand-by equipment . . . alcohol . . . Alcohol. Quickly he grabbed for it, and as Ricardo closed with him, he threw it at his face. Gotcha!

Blinded by the alcohol and screaming in pain, Ricardo dropped the scalpel and felt his way toward the sink. Eric dragged Talmidge toward the operating table, his shirt pulling painfully at the drying blood on his back. Quickly he scanned the monitors. Ricardo was still crying with pain as he hunched over the sink, pouring water into his eyes.

"Bring her back!" Eric called out to him. "Bring her back or Talmidge is a dead man!"

"I'm blind!"

"Only temporary," Eric assured him. "But Talmidge will be dead for good. Who will protect you then?"

"Don't listen!" Talmidge told him. "Let the girl die!" Eric drew back and punched him in the face, then grunted with surprise at the pain in his knuckles. It always looked so easy in the movies. Talmidge sagged against him.

Ricardo staggered over, eyes red and streaming. "I can't see!" he moaned, but he managed to stabilize Vivienne and remove her IV. Eric held the scalpel so tightly to Talmidge's throat, a thin rivulet of blood seeped from beneath the blade.

"Do what I tell you," Eric said urgently. "Lidocaine. Inject it into her chest, then close the incision. Use the skin stapler."

"But—"

"Just do it!" Eric ordered firmly.

Ricardo went and got the anesthetic and injected it into Vivienne's chest; it seemed to take forever. At last he reached for the skin stapler.

"I've never used this before," he said.

"It's easy," Eric told him. "Do the best you can." He knew he himself could staple the chest closed in a matter of seconds, but he didn't dare let go of Talmidge.

At last the skin was roughly joined. "Bandage her," he told Ricardo.

The bandages, too, were rough, but they would hold, at least for a while.

"Wake her up now. Fast!"

But Ricardo backed away, his eyes on Talmidge, who was shaking his head very slightly, his neck moving lightly against the scalpel. "It'll wear off soon," Ricardo said.

"Physostigmine," Eric barked at him. "I know you've got it. I've used it myself. Move! And you," he addressed Talmidge out of the corner of his mouth, "I'm just looking for an excuse to kill you!"

Again, long minutes passed before Ricardo found the reversal agent and injected it. Vivienne at last began to stir, and then opened her eyes, and Eric felt the tension ebb from his body. Ricardo went back to the sink to pour more water in his eyes.

Eric frog-marched Talmidge closer to the operating table and leaned over Vivienne. As her eyes focused, her mouth opened to scream, but Eric shook his head. "It's all right," he said. "It's over. It's all over."

Slowly Vivienne sat up. Talmidge, choosing his moment well, jerked free as Bascado, awake and back in the fray, swung Eric around and slugged him in the jaw.

As Eric went down, he spotted the scrub nurse coming through the double doors; she'd brought reinforcements. No. She'd brought . . . clones? Bascado came at him again and he managed to roll away. Bascado kicked him in the side. It hurt a lot.

Anna threw herself at Vivienne. "You live!" she shouted joyfully.

"Yes, yes! Now help Dr. Rose!" But already a group of clones had thrown themselves at Bascado, pulling him away from Eric, who struggled to his feet. Grabbing a heavy instrument tray from the counter, he banged Bascado on the head as hard as he could. Bascado hit the floor and stayed there.

Talmidge ducked behind the operating table, thinking furiously. With the cluster in revolt and Bascado down, he badly needed reinforcements. Staying low, shielded by clones and equipment, he retreated to the door that opened into the corridor.

"Now him!" Anna directed, and the clones turned their attention to Ricardo. "Tie him!" she ordered. "Use the sticky ribbon!" Despite his struggles, they tied his hands to the high arching faucet with bandage adhesive.

In the excitement of Anna's triumph, no one noticed Talmidge crack open the door and squeeze out into the hallway.

31

Talmidge closed the door softly behind him and looked around. Out here in the hallway all was quiet. Apparently the revolt was limited to Anna's cluster; good. Still, he'd increase all sedation this evening. He walked rapidly past several treatment rooms toward the nurses' station which guarded the entrance to the operating-room hallway. Just beyond was a small pantry; further along, a side corridor led to the clusters.

The blue telephone on the nurses' counter was directly connected to an outside line. He reached for it regretfully; there was no choice. He'd have to call in the San Lorenzo police. Fortunately, the chief was both discreet and bribable. Talmidge would explain that some of the mental patients were acting up, and Alfonso would send his men and ask no questions. No one in San Lorenzo was eager to inquire too deeply into the Institute's business.

The nurses' station was deserted; that was unusual. As he dialed, he looked around for the duty nurse, ready with a reprimand. Then two women and a man stepped into the corridor from the pantry. Ah, there she was. But why was Juana with her? And who was that man gripping Juana's arm?

"Talmidge!" Charles shouted, shoving Juana aside as he ran toward the doctor. "Where is she?"

Jesus! Charles Spencer-Moore! "Thank heaven you've come!" he said, cradling the receiver. "I was just telling them to try calling you again. Vivienne's here, and she's been hurt—''

Charles caught Talmidge by the shoulders. "You lying bastard! What have you done to her?"

"I?" said Talmidge mildly. "I'm trying to save her life!" Charles hesitated and he pressed his advantage. "I'm afraid we've had a little security problem," he continued. "I was showing Vivienne around the cluster and some of the clones got loose and attacked her." Behind Charles, the duty nurse was making hand signals.

Charles eyed Talmidge's torn-and-bloody surgical scrubs, his bleeding ear. "Take me to her," he demanded.

"Yes, of course . . . in just a little while," Talmidge said soothingly, his mind churning. He needed to neutralize Charles until he could wrest control of the operating room from the clones and finish off Vivienne and Eric. Charles would then have no choice but to believe him. And if he didn't, Charles's death could also be blamed on the "mental patients."

"Nurse?" he called. "Please prepare the usual sedative." The nurse gave him a knowing look and nodded. She went past them to a treatment room to prepare the injection.

"Why can't I see her now?" Charles asked angrily. Then the implications of Talmidge's instructions to the nurse hit him. "What are you giving her?" he roared, shoving Talmidge hard in the chest.

"Are you mad, Charles?" Talmidge gasped. "I'm the good guy!"

"The hell you are!" Charles shoved him again and Talmidge stumbled. He swung at Talmidge but missed as the doctor recovered and backed off, his eyes widening in surprise as he glanced behind Charles. A group of some ten or more clones had entered the hallway from the side corridor leading to the clusters. As he watched, another group emerged.

Talmidge ducked and ran past Charles. If he could get to the pantry, he could get upstairs. Lock himself

in his office. Call the police. The clones were still
down near the end of the corridor. "Go back!" he
shouted to them as he ran. "Go back to your cluster!"
They hesitated, but their leader—a clone leader, he
noted apprehensively—got them moving again. Talmidge bulled past a terrified Juana cowering in the
doorway and disappeared into the pantry.

But Charles was younger and faster, and he was right
behind him. As Talmidge reached for the steel door,
Charles spun him around. "Where is she?" he
shouted. Talmidge doubled him over with a sudden jab
to the stomach and ran past him, back into the corridor. Where could he go now? he thought frantically.
He was tired and hurt; he'd never get past Charles and
up the pantry stairs. And with the clones on the loose
and heading his way, he wouldn't get past them to his
apartment either. Then he remembered the nurse and
the sedative. Was Charles still following? He was.
Good. Talmidge headed back up the corridor toward
the treatment rooms.

Charles skidded into the corridor, which was rapidly
filling. Who were all these people? Where had they
come from? What had Talmidge yelled to them just
now—something about a cluster? Suddenly it hit him:
these were clones. He stopped and looked at them.
Why, they looked just like . . . people. Normal, real
people.

The realization was staggering; I never pictured
them this way, he thought. A tall, intelligent-looking
man, propelled by the growing crowd behind him,
cannoned into Charles, then turned to him apologetically. "I am sorry," he said kindly. "I did not mean
to hurt you. Are you all right?"

Charles stared at the man. These people would never
harm Vivienne. They wouldn't harm anyone. He noticed a small pin on the man's shirt collar. It was
shaped like a kidney. "Did I hurt you?" the man
asked, concern wrinkling his forehead.

"No," Charles said softly. "I hurt you."

"No, not at all," the man said, and continued his jog down the hallway.

Charles gazed after him, distraught. I never realized what it would be like, he thought. Clones streamed past him; God, so many of them!

Two women passed him; one was very pretty. "Come with us!" she said.

"Where are you going?"

"I'm not sure," the woman said. "We are trying to stop the murder. Do you know what that means?"

"I'm beginning to," Charles said.

"Well, we must stop it!"

Up ahead, Talmidge had paused just beyond a half-open door and was looking back at him. Charles took a few steps toward him. The clone—the woman—was right. The killing must stop. Charles began to run. My father helped put this together, he thought. It's up to me to pull it apart.

Talmidge smiled. That's right, boy. Follow me. "She's in here!" he called to Charles. "Vivienne's here!"

Inside, the nurse held the hypodermic syringe ready.

Talmidge nodded brightly as Charles approached, expecting that Charles's run would take him straight into the room in search of Vivienne. Instead, Charles drew even with him and grabbed Talmidge by the shoulders.

"It must stop!" he said. "All this. It's finished."

Talmidge looked surprised. "I thought you were our biggest fan," he said sardonically. Behind Charles he saw the nurse moving closer.

"Not anymore, Ben. It's over."

"If you say so," Talmidge agreed easily, and nodded to the nurse. "Sedate the clone," he ordered, and she plunged the needle through Charles's trousers. Charles roared and swung around, shoving the woman with one hand while batting at the syringe dangling from his leg until it fell onto the floor.

How much did he get? Talmidge wondered as he moved quickly away. No time to find out; he had to get back down the corridor to the pantry and up the stairs to safety. But from the nurses' station back, the hallway was a mass of clones pouring from the cluster hallway. Escape was impossible. Charles was shouting at him, trying to push through the gathering crowd, his eyes already starting to glaze. The mass of clones had moved quickly and now surged around Talmidge, driving him back up the corridor in the direction of the operating room and separating him from Charles's anger.

He had no choice now, no escape except through the OR. He had to go back. He had to finish it.

In the operating room Eric was attempting to push through the shifting crowd of confused and excited clones toward Vivienne. Where had Talmidge got to? He moved cautiously, fearful that Talmidge would rise in ambush from wherever he was hiding. Outside the OR, the noise increased; something was happening out there. He wondered what it was.

He looked over his shoulder; Anna was at the sink, filling a beaker to give Vivienne a drink. Water poured over Ricardo, still bandaged securely to the faucet, and he blinked at her balefully. Suddenly she looked down and screamed, and a shot rang out.

"Get down!" Eric yelled to Anna as Bascado, conscious once more, rose from the floor and fired again over the heads of the crowd. Panicked and disoriented, the clones ran here and there.

"Don't shoot!" Eric shouted. "There's oxygen here!" Could gunfire ignite oxygen? he wondered. Then he thought, shit, the Cyclopropane!

Bascado took a step or two through the milling clones. He had one hell of a headache. Steadying his gun at Eric's chest, he looked around for Talmidge. Better not kill either of them without permission, he decided, still hoping Talmidge would give him the girl for a while before he killed her.

Eric eyed the gun nervously. The clones stared; what was this new thing? Behind them, the sounds from the

corridor swelled, then receded: Eric turned in time to
see Talmidge jam the door closed behind him and disappear among the thirty or so new clones who had
pushed into the OR with him. People began hammer-
ing on the door from outside. Eric moved toward where
he'd last seen Talmidge, then changed his mind and
headed for Vivienne.

Bascado fired into the wall just above him. "Stop!"

Fuck you, thought Eric, and kept moving, staying
low.

Vivienne looked unsteady but determined as she
reached out to him. Then an arm snaked around her
waist, and another around her neck. Unseen, Talmidge
had come up on the far side of the table. Now he
dragged her off the operating table, holding her naked
body in front of his. Blood began to seep from her ill-
made bandages. Bending her down with him, Talmidge retrieved a bloody scalpel from the floor.

"Sacrilege!" he shouted. "Violence is forbidden!
Stop now and listen!"

Slowly the clones turned toward Talmidge, doubt
showing in their faces. Eric tried to push forward, but
the crowd of clones hemmed him in tightly.

"Look what you have done!" Talmidge told them.
"You have disobeyed me. You have injured others. You
have injured yourselves. All this is forbidden."

Some of the clones nodded, all looked uncomfortable.

"Go back to your clusters. Go back now and I will
forgive you."

A general movement started in the clone ranks, and
many moved toward the door. But Anna's voice rang
out, stopping them. "Vivienne!" she shouted. "Give
us Vivienne!"

"When you are back in the clusters, I will bring
her," Talmidge said.

"No! Give her now!" And Anna threw herself at
Talmidge, who slashed at her violently as Vivienne
twisted away. Tossing aside the bleeding Anna, Tal-

midge moved toward Vivienne, who edged into the crowd.

Shouting, Eric again tried to push through the confusion of clones separating him from Vivienne. "Stop Talmidge!" he yelled.

"Anna is wrong!" Talmidge shouted. "Listen to me, all of you! Vivienne is sick. See how she is bandaged. I came here to help her. That man"—he pointed at Eric dramatically—"Dr. Rose, is the one who hurt her. Look how he moved to her, to hurt her again! You must stop *him*!"

Several of the clones made tentative grabs at Eric, who pushed them away. "He's lying!" Anna called weakly from where she had fallen, blood pooling around her. "Don't believe him!" But many of the clones were once again under Talmidge's sway, and blocked Eric's progress.

"That's good . . . very good," Talmidge told the clones soothingly. "Just keep him there, that's right. First I will take care of Vivienne, because she is sick. Then I will deal with Dr. Rose."

Vivienne continued to limp away, moving slowly in her pain, her frightened eyes on Talmidge as he came inexorably toward her through the clones who moved aside to let him pass.

Meanwhile the noise from the corridor had been increasing; now the doors burst open and a flood of people surged into the room.

Talmidge spun around in panic: Was Charles there? No, thank heaven. The sedative had been effective. "Bascado!" he ordered. "Get out there! Stop them! Shoot if necessary!" Bascado hesitated. "Others will help you," Talmidge assured him. "I have called them. The girl will still be here when you get back. Now, go! Go!"

Bascado rushed to the doors and fired out into the hallway. The crowd surged back, and he pushed out into it, firing as he went. It was impossible to reclose the doors.

Talmidge turned his attention to Eric, struggling but

immobilized by a group of clones. "Their conditioning is too strong, Eric," he said smugly. "They belong to me. And now for the lovely Vivienne."

Eric lashed out—an elbow to the stomach of the man beside him, a kick to the rear—but the clones absorbed the blows and hung on dutifully.

Vivienne was growing weak; Eric watched, helpless, as she staggered and fell. A small circle opened around her.

Talmidge walked forward, smiling. The scalpel glittered in his hand. "It's time, my dear," he said.

Suddenly two strong hands grabbed his and pried the knife from his grasp. He looked up in disbelief at the clone called Charles.

"You cut our bodies," the clone told him calmly. "Sometimes you killed us. Now I will kill you. Then it will stop."

Talmidge's face softened. "Give me the knife, Charles," he said kindly. "Clones do not kill." From the corridor came shouts and screams and occasional gunfire.

"Yes. I will kill you," said Charles, but he began to look doubtful.

"You will not kill me, Charles," said Talmidge soothingly. "Clones cannot kill. Clones hate violence. It is a sin to hurt anyone. It is a sin to kill." His eyes held Charles's as he inched his right hand toward the knife. Just a little farther . . . now!

"Look out!" Vivienne gasped. Too late. Talmidge had the knife . . . or did he? With a cry, Charles grappled with Talmidge, using fists, feet, even teeth. There was a large red place in his mind, a heat in his chest. What was happening? Never had he felt so strong, so angry. The scalpel rose and fell in his hand. Again. Again. Talmidge fell to the floor but Charles didn't notice. His hands became slippery and red, his feet hurt from kicking. He felt elated, transformed. And then the knife was wrenched from him. Talmidge sat up for a moment, the scalpel flashed, and there was a deep ripping pain in Charles's belly.

Everything slowed down. He felt a new wetness on his hands and on his shirt. He stumbled backward as the pain hit him, and then he was sitting on the floor as blood and soft, squishy things were coming out of his stomach. He felt very tired . . .

He looked over at the doctor lying next to him, his green clothes covered with blood. He also seemed tired. His mouth hung open and he didn't seem to see Charles . . .

Now the room was getting dark and the shops were blurring. He lay down too . . .

Slowly, cautiously, the clones began to gather around Charles's body. The floor was slippery with blood. They stared at it wonderingly. So that was what was inside a man.

"There's nothing I can do," Eric whispered, rocking Vivienne in his arms as she sobbed softly. "He's gone. They both are."

"Talmidge too? You're sure?"

"I'm sure."

"Thank God!"

A shot rang out and a clone fell to the floor; Bascado, on his knees, was firing into the crowd in the OR.

"He's nuts!" Eric said. "It's too late!" he called out to Bascado. "Talmidge is dead!"

But Bascado continued to fire wildly. Now the clones were screaming and shouting; several more had fallen. A monitor exploded in a shower of glass. A bullet bounced off the metal cylinder of Cyclopropane.

Cyclopropane.

Running toward the operating table, Eric stamped hard on the floor button and the table began to rise. He grabbed Vivienne's arm and pulled her to the table, shoving her on as it ascended. Almost too late, he leapt for a handhold on its edge and pulled himself up, opening the cut on his back. Blood trickled down inside his shirt as he grappled with Vivienne, who was trying to jump off the table to join the clones below.

"Run! Get out!" he shouted to them.

"They don't understand! They'll die!"

* * *

Charles blinked and looked around him. He must have blacked out, he thought. Then he remembered the nurse with the needle. How long had he been lying here? He got to his feet, swaying, and stepped out into the hallway. Immediately he was caught up in the scream of clones, flailing and nearly falling, then finding his feet again.

Eric held her tightly. The ceiling panel had begun to open. Below them, more clones pushed into the small room and were caught up in the panic and confusion. Bascado continued to fire. Eric stripped off his surgical gown and wrapped it around Vivienne.

"Charles! It's Charles!" she cried suddenly, pointing to someone in the crowd below.

"Charles is dead," he told her gently. "Remember? Talmidge killed him."

"No, the other Charles," she insisted. "There!"

She's been through so much, Eric thought. She's seeing things, and no wonder. He held her close and wished they were moving faster.

"Look, over by the sink . . . no, I've lost him." She turned to Eric. "But it was Charles, I'm sure of it!"

Below them, Charles fought his way through the crowd. "Vivienne!" he yelled. "Vivienne! Here!" Who was that man? Where were they taking her? He thought for a moment she'd seen him, but then he tripped over a body and the crowd swallowed him up.

Eric held her face between his hands. "I love you," he said. "It's all right." He kissed her softly.

When Charles looked up again, the ceiling panel was fully open and the operating table was still rising; they were nearly halfway up. The man was kissing Vivienne; against her will or with it? He couldn't tell. A long restraining strap dangled down from the operating table; could he reach it?

Pushing frantically through the crowd, he leapt, arms straining upward, and caught hold of the strap, which immediately began slipping through his hand. With great effort he held on, feet scrabbling on the smooth steel column which was lifting the table above him, and managed to get his other hand around the rough, strong webbing. Several people grabbed at him as he was carried aloft beneath the operating table, but he kicked them away.

The table carrying Eric and Vivienne was rising into the upper operating theater now, and the hole below it was closing. The wall between the tandem OR's was open; so Talmidge had intended to take Vivienne's body out through the Institute itself, Eric thought. He remembered Vivienne talking to Anna; even before he'd learned of the clone revolt, Talmidge hadn't wanted to risk the wrath of the cluster by taking her out the usual way: through the meeting room, up the utility-room stairs, and out the insignificant side door.

Beneath them but unnoticed, Charles was frantically pulling himself up through the closing ceiling panel. His upper body was through the diminishing hole . . . now his right leg . . . God, he was tired! His limbs shook with muscle fatigue. He was slowly dragging himself out from under the operating table when the ceiling panel closed firmly around his left foot. He tugged and kicked in panic.

Eric pulled Vivienne across the double room, then hurled a stool through the window. It shattered, leaving a jagged hole. He smashed out the glass with an instrument stand, then pushed Vivienne, still struggling, through the opening and leapt out himself, landing hard on one shoulder.

Scratched and bleeding, Eric half-dragged, half-carried Vivienne across the lawn toward the car park, moving fast. He was nearly at the car when the explosion came, knocking them both to the ground and showering the lawn with shards of glass.

"He's hit the Cyclopropane!"

In the lobby, the receptionist felt the blast before she heard it, a shock wave which hurled her out of her

chair and over the top of her work station. She hit the
opposite wall and crumpled in pain. In the patient
rooms and along the corridors, chaos reigned. Chunks
of floor were blown out in several places, and people
plummeted through bent metal and broken plaster into
the maelstrom below. Everywhere, people were
screaming.

In the upper operating room, the ceiling panel below the table suddenly exploded upward: Charles was
lifted into the air in a trail of blood and thrust through
the window onto the grass.

Dimly through the smoke and pain Eric saw a fireball rising up through the operating room, and he
imagined the roil of flame, the searing heat and smoke
racing along the corridors and into the open rooms
below.

There it goes, he thought. The secrets, the madness,
and the brilliance, everything Talmidge knew and I
didn't. Gone.

And now a second fireball bloomed in the upper
theater as the fire snaked through the Cyclopropane
lines from below. Eric began to move again, hoisting
Vivienne up in an awkward fireman's carry. He
wrenched the car door open and dumped her into the
back seat. She'd fainted: her color was bad and her
breathing shallow. Blood was again seeping from beneath the bandages. Straddling her, he laid her head
back and put his hands behind her jaw, pulling it forward to keep the airway open. She gulped once or
twice and her color improved a little. Live, dammit!

He slid into the driver's seat, his blood staining the
upholstery. Then he stomped on the accelerator and
drove down the mountain.

32

In San Lorenzo, confusion reigned. The volunteer fire brigade was attempting to marshal its members for a rescue effort, and the main square was filled with confused and frightened townspeople. Eric drove through the crowd, his horn blaring, and braked hard in front of El Lobo. Tend Vivienne as best I can, he thought. Get her things. Get mine. Expunge any evidence that we were here.

He wrenched the door open and got out. Already people were crowding around him, gazing with curiosity through the car window at Vivienne's immobile, nearly naked form. He feared to leave her unguarded.

As he hesitated, Vicente materialized out of the crowd. *"Vaya!"* he shouted at the gathering throng. "Get away!" His expression was angry, and people looked at him and moved back. He peered in at the window. "Go and get your medical things," he told Eric. "I will stay with her."

Still Eric hesitated, but Vicente draped an arm around his shoulder. "It is over, friend," he said. "Am I right?" Smoke from the explosion was already drifting across the square.

Eric nodded.

"Good," Vicente said. "I am sorry for those inside—on both sides—but it is good that it is ended." He clapped his hands and glared at several young boys who were attempting to approach the car, and they scampered off into the crowd. "He paid me, of course.

He paid me to be your friend, to spy on you. But I liked you all the same.''

Vivienne stirred and moaned, but didn't wake. ''Hurry and get your bag,'' said Vicente. ''I promise she will not come to harm.'' He removed his arm from Eric's shoulder. ''I give you my word.''

Eric nodded. Talmidge was dead. There was no reason for Vicente to lie anymore.

He took the stairs three at a time and headed first for his own room. Quickly he grabbed his medical bag from the closet floor where he'd stashed it ever since he'd started at the Institute, hauled down his battered suitcase, stuffed his clothes inside, and sat on it to make it flat enough to zip. He dumped the suitcase and medical bag out on the landing and headed to Vivienne's room, where he pulled the drawers from the dresser and dumped their contents on the bed. He chose some clothing and a makeup bag, then filled her suitcase and carryall with the rest and lugged everything out onto the landing too. Below, Vicente had seated himself on the car hood, arms akimbo, as though daring anyone to come close. Eric struggled the baggage down the stairs and over to the car; Vicente jumped off to help him load the trunk.

''Better we leave now,'' Vicente said. He stared at Eric's shoulder; the wound had again re-opened and his shirt was soaked in blood. ''I will drive.''

''All the way to Barcelona? How will you get home?''

''My father is dead. From today, Barcelona is my home.''

''Your father?''

''So many times I said to him, 'Let me go to Barcelona. Let me live my life away from here.' '' Vicente sighed and fell silent as he drove carefully through the crowd and out onto the south road. Eric tended Vivienne's incision and she half-woke while he was attempting to dress her. She was muzzy and confused, but her color had returned.

''Dr. Talmidge was my father,'' Vicente said at last.

"When he first came here, he had not yet his . . . harem, you say in English? And my mother was very beautiful. A small town like this, a baby out of marriage . . . it was never easy for her, but he made sure she was protected. When I got older, he told me she would be safe so long as I . . . obeyed. For her sake, I had to stay. Now I am free."

"He never taught you medicine? He didn't even teach you English?"

"He did not love me enough," said Vicente without rancor. "He did not love me at all. I was just . . . useful."

"Can I help you?" Eric offered. "I have money, pesetas . . ."

"Thank you, no," Vicente said with dignity. "I have friends in Barcelona, people who have left San Lorenzo. Soon everyone will leave, I think. I will find a job, send for my mother . . ." He turned around and smiled at Eric and Vivienne, holding each other close. "Something bad ends," he said. "Something good begins."

As the plane lifted into the air, Eric discovered he was ravenous. While Vivienne picked at her salad, he cleaned both their trays, then sat back, replete. Vicente's bandaging had been inexpert, but at least he wouldn't soil the upholstery.

Vivienne huddled in her first-class seat, exhausted and weak. Eric had gotten her some pills at the airport pharmacy. But though the incision in her chest was no longer painful, her thoughts were. Talmidge was gone, but so was everything else. And Eric . . .

"Can you really forgive me?" she asked him softly. "You were so close . . . if I hadn't come, you'd be flying home with the secrets in your pocket."

He smiled sadly. "He would never have told me," he said bitterly. "He'd have kept me hanging on, year after year. Sure, he saw me as his . . . heir, maybe. But would he really have just handed over my legacy without years of loyalty and reassurance from me? Never!''

He took her hand between his. ''Don't blame yourself,'' he said. Then he brightened. ''There are a few things I did learn,'' he told her. ''And other things I can guess at. I can't do what he did—God knows I wouldn't want to—but . . .'' He thought of the computer disk he'd rescued from its hiding place in the library several nights before, currently nestling innocuously among his shirts and shorts. Someday someone would figure out how to unlock the data on it. But thanks to Vivienne, he now knew how important it would be to guard that data carefully.

He touched her cheek. ''I found something far more valuable than Talmidge's secrets,'' he said, and was only a little surprised to find that he meant it.

33

From the *International Herald Tribune:*

An explosion of unknown origin destroyed a small
private clinic outside Barcelona yesterday. The in-
tensity of the heat and smoke greatly hampered rescue operations, and aside from an American,
Charles Spencer-Moore, who was apparently blown
through a window by the force of the blast, it is
believed that there are no survivors. Mr. Spencer-
Moore was evacuated to Sisters of Mercy Hospital
in Barcelona, where he is in critical condition.

Founded by Dr. Benjamin Talmidge some twenty
years ago, the Reproduction Institute catered primarily to the very wealthy, and was known chiefly
for its cosmetic surgery. . . .

Gently Vivienne took the straw from Charles's lips
and set the glass of apple juice back on the hospital
tray. He smiled at her. At least she thought he did.
With all those bandages, it was hard to tell. Again a
wave of guilt washed over her. If not for her . . .

As though reading her thoughts, he shook his head
very slightly. "Not your fault," he whispered. He
closed his eyes briefly, then opened them again. "Is
Angela still here?"

"She's outside," Vivienne told him. "I'll send her
in."

Charles caught at her arm with a bandaged paw. "I'm sorry, Viv," he said.

She stood and smiled sadly down at him. "Me too," she said. She bent and kissed him lightly on the forehead. "We've all hurt each other. Now it's time to heal."

Angela had been hovering as near to Charles's door as the duty nurse would let her, but as Vivienne emerged, she turned quickly away. They'd been playing this game for days, ever since Charles had been flown back from Spain to New York General Hospital. But today Vivienne followed Angela down the hallway and put a hand on her shoulder. Angela stopped, but didn't turn around.

"Please, Angie," said Vivienne. "I know it's hard. But for Charles's sake, we have to talk."

Angela was silent.

"You were my best friend," Vivienne said. "You slept with my fiancé, and yes, that stinks. But I slept with Eric while I was still engaged to Charles. And Charles was unfaithful to me, with you. It all stinks."

She paused, searching for words. "What I mean is, we're none of us perfect. But, Angie, these past few weeks I've seen so much worse. . . .

"We all need to be forgiven. And we all need to forgive. At least you had the strength to give Charles up. And you sent him to look for me—yes, he told me about all that—even though you knew that finding me might mean losing him. And I love you for it."

Slowly Angela turned to face Vivienne; tears stood in her eyes. "I love you too, Viv," she said. "I've been so miserable . . . ."

The two women embraced. "Clean start?" Vivienne asked.

"Clean start."

Vivienne put her arm around her friend and walked Angela back up the hallway toward Charles's room. "Clean up that face before you go in," she ordered. "He'll think you're crying about him."

"He *will* be all right, won't he?" Angela asked anxiously.

"Yes, Eric says he's doing very well." Neither mentioned the mangled foot.

Suddenly Angela stopped. "I have an idea," she said tentatively. "Now, if you don't like it, say so, OK?"

Vivienne smiled and nodded.

"Charles wants us to get married. Soon. It'll be a real simple ceremony, probably right here in the hospital. But—if this is awkward for you, just say so—it would really be great if you and Eric could be there for us."

Vivienne examined her feelings. First, a rush of joy; Angela had forgiven both Vivienne and herself. Then, a pang of jealousy—good God, could she still be in love with Charles?

But the appearance of Eric at that moment, striding along the corridor toward them, immediately put that fear to rest. The swell of love she felt for Eric made her realize that what she'd mistaken for jealousy had been no more than a conditioned reflex; Charles had been hers for so long.

"We'd love to," she told Angela sincerely. "Now, fix your face and go tell Charles."

Angela waved a greeting to Eric and scurried toward the ladies' room. Eric looked after her, surprised.

"We've made up," Vivienne explained. "Everything's fine again. In fact, you and I are going to stand up for them at their wedding."

"They're getting married?"

"Yes, and quite soon."

He studied her face carefully. How did she really feel about it? But apparently what he saw in her eyes reassured him, because he kissed her deeply.

"Your patient stop breathing, Dr. Rose?"

Startled, they moved apart. Dr. Harris stood in the corridor, trying to look stern. He and Vivienne had had a long talk when she and Eric had returned to the States, and she now considered him a family friend.

Still, they were both embarrassed to be caught embracing in the middle of the corridor.

"The transplant conference starts in about ten minutes," Harris told them, "and I wanted a word with our new staff surgeon here beforehand."

"Of course, John," Eric assured him. "No problem. I just came down for a quick look at Charles. Not that his own doctors aren't doing a great job," he added hurriedly. Vivienne had explained that Charles found his occasional visits reassuring, but Eric had made certain the specialists in charge understood he was there only as a friend.

"I'll come with you," Harris offered.

"And I'll see you tonight," Vivienne said.

"He'll be late. And tired," Harris assured her.

"So what else is new?" She smiled.

"And hungry," Eric added. "What do you say we try out the new barbecue grill? I could fix us a couple of steaks, maybe some hash-browns."

"I've gained four pounds since this guy moved in," she complained, laughing. "I'll never work again!"

They parted, she toward the bank of elevators, the two doctors toward Charles's door. A fourth-year medical student came out of the room, freshly filled blood tubes in her hand.

She watched as Eric knocked softly and both doctors disappeared inside. She'd discussed this patient during rounds, and studied the treatments for his various injuries. He seemed so nice; she hoped they'd be able to save his foot, although it didn't look likely.

She turned and headed toward the nurses' station with the blood tubes. Of course Mr. Spencer-Moore's doctors were doing everything they could. Still, in this age of transplants, shouldn't there be a better technique? For example, there were any number of cases in which doctors had reattached patients' own extremeties; why not use a donor foot, the way they did with livers and kidneys? The surgical techniques existed. But of course the chances of matching a donor limb physically, let alone genetically, were extremely unlikely. Besides, who ever donated their feet to science?

She was placing the blood tubes in the laboratory pickup cart when another thought came to her. Why couldn't you use a person's own cells to grow a new part for him? That way you wouldn't have to worry about rejection. And attachment would be so easy! You'd make a razor-sharp cut across the top of the new foot, just where you wanted to join it, hook everything up perfectly . . . There were so many advantages, she thought excitedly. You could maintain the length of the blood vessels because you'd have all that new genetically matched material to work with. And the bone ends would knit together easily and heal just like a fracture, nice and clean.

For a fleeting moment she considered asking Dr. Harris about it, see what he thought. But Harris could be so formidable. And she was embarrassingly aware of how much she had yet to learn. She'd look like a dork, telling him what she was thinking. There were probably a hundred reasons against it.

But what if there weren't? She leaned against the pickup cart, lost in speculation. What if you *could* grow someone a new hand or foot, even a new organ? Better still, what if you could grow a whole body! Then you'd have it all: heart and liver and limbs and eyes. They were making such progress in cloning techniques. Sure, it was a little science-fiction-y, but so was the idea of a moon landing once, and that had happened.

"Andi, you finished with those charts?"

Startled, she blinked, then smiled at the waiting nurse. "Five minutes," she promised, and turned toward the nearby console table with its pile of waiting paperwork. Someday, she thought, someone would discover how to do such things. Maybe she would herself! Wouldn't it be wonderful?